THE GIFT

THE GIFT

KIM PRITEKEL

SAPPHIRE BOOKS

SALINAS, CALIFORNIA

Editor - Heather Flournoy
Book Design - LJ Reynolds
Cover Design - Treehouse Studio

Sapphire Books Publishing, LLC
P.O. Box 8142
Salinas, CA 93912
www.sapphirebooks.com

Printed in the United States of America
First Edition – September 2018

This and other Sapphire Books titles can be found at
www.sapphirebooks.com

Dedication

For *Her*

Acknowledgments

For the women and men in blue who do what most of us would never have the courage to do.

Chapter One

The images on the Super 8mm film were fuzzy and jumpy with flat colors and the pop and sizzle from inferior technology. The patches of grass the kids ran around on were an olive green, their clothing vivid to the human eye but dull and grainy on film. The lake beyond was a muddy blue, the waves lapping gently at the wooden dock.

Suddenly a little girl with long dark hair in braids popped up in front of the camera, her five-year-old self making funny faces, her little brother waddling up beside her, trying to copy whatever she did.

Out of nowhere, an older boy ran across the yard, tube socks pulled up to his knees, shaggy black hair hanging in equally black eyes. A Beagle yapped at his heels. The black, brown, and white tail wagging like crazy. The young teenager disappeared out of the shot followed by both the dog and a young girl of similar age with short dark hair, denim-covered knees pumping as she ran after him.

The little girl turned to her brother, and with a gentle touch helped him waggle his fingers on either side of his head like she was, as the toddler was struggling with the finger coordination.

"You're such a good big sister, Kitty Cat," a disembodied voice praised from behind the camera. "You two look at me now! Matteo!"

The siblings turned back to the camera, the little

guy slowly waggling his fingers. Like a flash, the older boy ran into the frame again, the toddler swept up into his arms, a blood-curdling scream following behind.

"Damn it, Jason! You know he doesn't like to be touched!" the same disembodied voice yelled out, the picture turning into a wedge shot of a sideways close up of the grass and sneaker-covered feet running past and out of frame.

❧❧❧❧

Catania d'Giovanni glanced over at the bedside clock and groaned. "You've got to be kidding me," she muttered. "Okay!" she yelled at the second round of knocks at her apartment door.

Pulling herself out of the soft comfort of her bed, she tugged on a T-shirt and mesh shorts before padding down the hall past the empty second bedroom and bathroom, through the nearly equally empty living room where the clothing from her prior shift was still strewn across the hardwood floor, and finally the narrow hallway which led to the back door of the eleven-hundred-square-foot apartment. She passed what was touted as a laundry room when she'd first been shown the place, but it was actually not much more than a closet with a washer and dryer inside.

Disengaging the locks, she pulled open the oversized metal door that led out to the parking lot behind the old brick textiles factory. She was not remotely surprised to see her mother standing on the other side.

"Why you not answer my knock?" the older woman asked. Catania certain her hands would be on rounded hips had they not been filled with an overloaded paper sack.

"Obviously I did answer your knock, Mamma. You're looking at me."

"Take this," Antonia d'Giovanni said, waiting for her only daughter to grab the bundle from her hands before delivering a light tap to the younger woman's cheek. "Don't talk to your Madre that way. Now, let me in, too cold out."

Catania rolled her eyes once her mother passed, then cradled the heavy bag in one arm as she used her other hand to shut out the cold early November afternoon.

"Catania!"

"Crap," she muttered, engaging the locks before turning to hurry inside to see what her mother was going to start with first. She mentally counted to five as she headed toward the kitchen. Right on cue, the barrage began.

"Why clothes thrown everywhere? Why your hair sticking up all over your head? I did *not* raise my daughter to look like a rooster!"

Taking a deep, cleansing breath, Catania rested the paper bag on the butcher block island in her kitchen. "Mamma, I got home from work about forty-five minutes ago. I was far more interested in sleep than hanging up my pants."

"So I see," Antonia muttered, using forefinger and thumb to pick up Catania's service pistol from the counter like it was the tail end of a mouse.

"Okay. Give me that." The detective sighed, snatching the weapon from an inexperienced hand. "Be careful with that." Though the 9mm was secured, she went ahead and placed it inside a nearby cabinet to keep it out of grabby hands. "Mamma, can we do this later?" she asked, fatigue gripping her in an iron fist.

"Do what?" Antonia had the fridge door open and half-empty milk carton in hand. She sniffed the contents before wincing and dumping the souring milk and carton into the sink.

"Whatever *this* is," Catania said, watching as item after item was tossed from her fridge. "I just bought that sour cream Tuesday!"

"Of what year?" Antonia asked dryly. "Besides," she added, tossing the plastic tub into the sink. "You have nothing to put it on. It is a condiment, not a meal."

Keeping her patience in check as well as she could, Catania decided to distract herself by removing the contents from the paper bag. "What's all this?" she asked, peeking into the Tupperware dish with the pink lid.

"Well, since you missed Sunday dinner *again*," she said with a pointed look to her daughter. "I brought you leftovers, *again*."

Though her mouth was watering with thoughts of her mother's famous spaghetti sauce and her father's meatballs, she wasn't about to give her mother the satisfaction of showing it. So, she responded with the incredibly witty, "Oh?"

"You should be there with your family and not running around playing cops and robbers, Catania," Antonia admonished, pointing a banana at her that was a bit too browned as it had been lounging forgotten in the fruit basket on the counter.

"Mamma," Catania said. Though irritated and tired, she kept her voice calm and understanding as she knew her parents, immigrants from a different country and a different time with a very different mindset, did not understand a woman wanting a career. "I'm sorry I missed Sunday dinner," she began, handing her mother the covered dishes of food so she could load them into the fridge. "What I do is important. It gives families closure and peace for their loved ones." As soon as the words were out of her mouth, she knew they had been chosen poorly.

"And, what about your family, hmm?" Antonia asked, hurt and accusation evident in her voice and dark brown eyes.

"Mamma, I know, but—"

"You should be home with your brothers and your father and me," she continued. "You're unmarried, no business, living..." Antonia looked around the messy apartment with dismay. "Alone." With the angry crunch of the emptied paper bag, Antonia glared at her daughter, tossing the paper bag into the trash can. "You need a husband! You are nearly forty years old. I give up on grandchildren from you, but not a husband!" She waggled her finger at her. "You play games long enough."

"I know, Mamma," Catania said with a conciliatory nod of her head to the weekly indictment. "I promise I'll do all that I can to be there for Sunday dinner this week, okay?"

"And your time with Matteo?"

"Yes, and my time with Matteo. I've got his towel and juice boxes all ready to go." Catania lied with what she hoped was a convincing smile.

The older woman met her daughter's eyes for a long moment before turning away, nodding. Catania knew her mother felt she'd won the battle but would never stop fighting the war. "I go now and let you rest."

Catania accepted a kiss and hug from the shorter woman and, with a promise to clean her apartment after some sleep, walked her unwanted guest to the door. Left alone, she considered making herself a small plate before going back to bed, but when she nearly fell asleep leaning against the open fridge door, she decided bed first, food second.

ᔈᔈᔈᔈ

The bathroom filled with steam, Catania stepped out, using a fluffy green towel to dry off her body as she padded to her bedroom. She'd ironed her blouse for her shift before her shower, so now she focused on moisturizing. As much as she loved her home state of Colorado, fall and winter could be murder on the skin.

Smoothing the fragrant goop onto her arms after she'd finished with her freshly shaved legs, she walked over to her dresser and pulled open the top two drawers. She eyed her options before snagging green silk panties and a pair of socks.

Carrying those and her bra to the bed, she tossed the garments down and grabbed the comb she'd left there before heading to the shower and after making her bed. She hadn't bothered making the antique four-poster in weeks; she'd been so busy and tired with work. But, her mother's earlier scolding made her feel guilty so she'd made it nice and pretty, just as she'd been taught.

Looking around the room, she took in the furniture. The bedroom set had been the only things she'd taken with her after her last relationship, four years before. They'd been willed to her by her beloved grandmother, and as much as Lydia had tried to get at least the stand-alone mirror from her, Catania had stood her ground.

The comb glided through the wet strands of her dark hair, snagging on a small tangle at the back of her head which made her wince slightly. She'd had long hair her entire life, but the first time she'd had to spend hours washing blood and brain matter out of the long strands after a domestic call that had gone terribly wrong during her days as a beat cop, she'd cut it off. She wondered if part of that had also been to forget about the horrific events of that night.

By nature, she was a quiet person. She was introspective and had turned self-analysis into an art form. The problem was, once she had the answers, she didn't often talk it out, get feedback, or make a post on social media. She filed the information away to make a different choice the next time, then would do something physical to mark the inner change, such as chopping her hair.

She supposed that ability to analyze, recognize, then file it away for when it was needed was what made her so good at her job.

Padding over to the mirror, she took in her naked body as she absently continued to comb her hair back away from her face. Once all the tangles were out, she'd do a quick finger comb and the drying strands would fall into place.

She definitely held the Italian features of the blood that ran through her veins, but she had the stone-gray eyes of her father. Out of her immediate family of two parents and five brothers, she and her father alone shared the unique eye color. Her fifth-grade teacher had called her Stormy all throughout that school year, and to this day if Catania ran into her in town.

She was happy enough with her physique, though her mother constantly told her she was too thin. Part of that was she'd gone on a dieting and exercise mission with her partner at work. Afraid he'd drop dead of a heart attack, she'd made him a deal: they'd both give up caffeine, give up sugar, and had to walk at least two miles a day. She'd lost weight she hadn't needed to, but it had helped him to drop seventy-five of the one hundred and ten pounds he needed to, so it had been worth it. Truth be told, she was pleased that she could once again drink fully-leaded coffee and have the occasional sweet treat.

Tossing her comb to the dresser top, Catania dressed, applied light makeup, and headed out of the bathroom, nearly walking out with the light still on. She stopped long enough to hit the light switch, then hurried down the hall to the living room.

She stopped, looking around at the mess that still met her. In truth, she didn't like it, either, but they were working on a tough case and home was an afterthought most days.

"Tomorrow," she said with a nod of commitment. "I'll clean tomorrow."

Walking to the coat closet, she grabbed her long black coat and shrugged into it, reaching into the pockets to make sure her black leather gloves were in the pockets. Gathering her gear and everything else she'd need for a long shift, Catania made her way to the door and out, the frigid evening air taking her breath away.

She pulled the heavy metal door shut and locked it before scurrying down the short staircase from the small perch that led from the handful of cement stairs up to the door. Hers was the only apartment in the old building that had two entrances, one outside, the other inside, though it led down to an inner, treacherous staircase that was narrow and nearly vertical to climb, so it was the rare event that she used it.

"Detective!"

Catania smiled when she saw Mr. Horvat near her 1976 army-green Jeep. "Hey, Mr. Horvat." She greeted him warmly, walking up to him. "What are you doing out in this cold? You should be up with Mrs. Horvat," she added, pointing up to the top floor where the retired school bus driver and his wife lived.

"Not before I make sure you get out okay," he said, reaching up and adjusting his flat cap. "S'posed to snow again later. But," he said with a grizzly smile. "All's clear."

Catania smiled, noting he'd already scraped her windows for her and had cleared a path for the large tires of her vehicle. "Thank you, Mr. Horvat." She gave a peck to his chilled cheek, amused at the little blush that colored his cheeks every time. "I'll bring you and the missus potica. Randy's just started making it for the holidays."

"Oh, yes!" the older man crowed, clapping gloved hands together. "I'll tell Esther."

Catania smiled and climbed behind the wheel of her Jeep. She raised a hand to wave at the older man who stood on the sidewalk, snow shovel in hand. In her mind's eye, it was easy to switch the original farmer out of the famous Grant Wood painting *American Gothic* and place Josef Horvat in the frozen tundra version.

The streets of Pueblo were quiet, the cold pushing people inside far more than the evening hours. Pueblo was a town of a hundred thousand people, give or take, a steel town at one time. When the mill had gone under in the early 1980s, the town had pretty much gone under with it.

The d'Giovanni family had barely hung on. Catania's father's plumbing business was not even bringing in enough to feed the large family. As the two oldest that lived at home, Catania and her older brother Paul watched the younger three as their parents disappeared into the night cleaning office buildings for extra income, though the siblings were barely out of the stroller themselves.

Now, she drove through the streets of her hometown, taking the turn slowly so as not to spin out on potential ice beneath the packed snow as she pulled into the small parking lot of the small diner called Randy's. It was a dive, and most of the food sucked, but their waffles were crazy good, and Catania and her partner couldn't get enough of them.

Walking into the greasy spoon, Catania looked around, noting a few of the dozen tables or so were occupied, but overall it was quiet. The diner was something out of the past, though it wasn't trying to be trendy. There was lots of chrome, as well as a long breakfast bar with a scarred Formica top, light blue with little sparkles in it. The waitresses wore the uniforms of their predecessors, replete with knee-length light gray button-up dresses with white piping around the collar, sleeves, and single breast pocket.

"Be with ya in just a sec, hon," Lizzie called from the kitchen, glancing at the newcomer through the order-up window that passed between it and the dining room.

"No worries, Lizzie," Catania said, taking a seat on the chrome and vinyl stool, third from the end at the bar. She glanced at her watch, happy when the older waitress made her way in front of her, two stacked Styrofoam cups with plastic lids in one hand and a full coffee carafe in the other. "Are they ready?" Catania asked, glancing over Lizzie's shoulder to see if she'd see Louis's familiar form scurrying around the kitchen. Her gaze returned to the redhead standing in front of her staring at her with apologetic brown eyes. "What?"

"How about two lemon bars?" she asked, pulling one cup from where it was tucked inside the other and placing it on the counter next to its twin.

"Wait, what? Why?" Catania's heart fell. "Oh no. Is the waffle maker broken again?"

"Not exactly," Lizzie hedged, screwing her mouth into a sardonic smile.

Catania raised an eyebrow in question, reaching for the first cup Lizzie had filled with steaming coffee, which she knew had been brewed freshly for her. She carefully placed the plastic lid on the cheap cup, the small burn scar on her thumb proof of lesson learned.

"Louis is. He quit today."

"I'm torn on whether to sit here and throw an all-out fit, or just arrest you," Catania said dryly.

Lizzie chuckled. "I'm sorry, hon. We're supposed to get a new cook in tomorrow or the next day for the fancy stuff. So, how 'bout those lemon bars?"

Catania let out a heavy sigh and sent her bottom lip out into a playful pout. "Fine."

Ten minutes later, she carried the Randy's branded paper bag in hand by the handles as she balanced the two Styrofoam cups in her other hand into the large room she shared with the other detectives. She weaved her way through the maze of desks, conversations, debates, and the occasional—and sadly, expected—cat whistles and hissing sounds to her desk toward the back.

"Finally, my dinner!"

"Yes, because we know it's all about the 'O.'" Catania smirked.

"Hell yeah," her partner, Oscar exclaimed, accepting one of the cups of coffee and a moment later, a Styrofoam takeout container.

"That's right," Catania added.

"Yup," Oscar Riley responded with a nod, peeling the plastic lid off his coffee. He tugged open one of the drawers in his desk before heavy strawberry blond eyebrows fell. "Shit. You got any of that sweetener stuff you'll let me use, Nia?"

Catania plopped down in her desk chair after placing her food and coffee down on the square of desk space she cleared off with a shove of her hand. Opening her own drawer, she tossed a few packets Oscar's way. "Forgot to get some from Lizzie," she explained. "I'll load up tomorrow." She picked herself out a couple packets and one of powdered creamer. Glancing at her partner of six years, she asked, "How did court go today?"

He nodded, what was left of his double chin making an appearance with each bob of his head. "Son of a bitch looked as smug as ever," he said, pulling the meal box toward him. "So glad our part of that case is done. Real piece of shit, that guy."

Catania eyed him, waiting for what she knew would be disappointed surprise. She broke into laughter at the look on his very expressive face. "*That*," she said, responding to his whined *What's this?* "Is a lemon bar."

Oscar glared over at her, holding the yellow treat in sausage-like fingers. "No shit, Sherlock. This isn't what I ordered, nor was it part of my weight-losing gig to give up Louis's waffles."

"It was not, nor what I ordered," Catania admitted, bringing her own lemon bar out of the box and raising it for inspection. "But, it's what we got. Louis quit."

"Damn," he said, taking a healthy bite of the tart dessert. "Did you threaten to shoot Lizzie if she didn't give us waffles?" he asked, mouth full.

Catania grinned. "Something like that. Though these are pretty good, I have to say. Should have given them a chance before." She reached over and grabbed her coffee, which now seemed super sweet from the tartness of the lemon. Setting the cup down, she glanced across the narrow aisle between her desk and Oscar's. "I think we should go by Frank Costner's house tonight," she suggested, referring to the elusive witness to their current case difficult to nail down for some questions.

Oscar nodded, finishing his "dinner." "I'm game with that."

"Awesome." Catania took another swig of her coffee after finishing her own lemon bar and glanced over at her partner, noting the wrinkled dirt-brown suit with a dark brown and tan tie that looked like it had been snatched from 1978. "Can you possibly be any more of a cliché if you tried?" she asked, closing the Styrofoam carry-out box and tucking it back into the paper bag.

"What?" Oscar asked, looking down at himself. "Shit," he muttered, sweeping a few crumbs off his tie. He sipped from his coffee before reaching inside the suit jacket to remove what the clinging waxy paper claimed was a grape-flavored Dum Dum from within. He peeled off the wrapper and stuck the sucker into his mouth, white stick hanging out. "What?" he asked again.

Catania shook her head. "Friggin' Kojak."

"Hey," he said, the sucker removed from his mouth with a sickening wet pop. "If you hadn't convinced Linda that I needed to stop smoking, I wouldn't need this."

"Yes, yes, bring your binky," Catania muttered with a tired sigh. "Come on, let's get to Costner's place."

❧ ❧ ❧ ❧

It had been a long day, made longer because of the slow nature of their shift. Though this was a good thing in that everyone in the city went home that night, it made for a lot of continuous paperwork that caused Catania to rub her tired, red eyes as she pulled her Jeep up to a slow stop at the red traffic light. Letting out a sigh, she glanced over to the passenger seat next to her to the box of coffee she'd picked up at Starbucks the minute they'd opened, a stack of plastic-wrapped cups next to it. She continued when the light turned green, headed toward the river walk in downtown, not but a mile from her apartment.

Downtown Pueblo had been a real pit for years. A town that had begun in the late nineteenth century with the steel mill, it had fallen on hard times after the mill went down in the early 1980s, causing a great deal of poverty and the rise of Hispanic gangs.

In the 1990s, the town was coming back and work had been done to revitalize the downtown area. Now, it was littered with trendy antique shops, eateries, museums, and the river walk, a mile-long meandering cement path around a man-made canal where folks could bring their kayaks or take one of the leisurely boat rides. During the day it was full of walkers and runners. In the cold night, a different clientele tended to stroll around the icy water.

As Catania turned her Jeep onto Main Street, she saw the small group of women standing near the Main Street entrance of the river walk near the pagoda where public restrooms were. As she neared, she could see Maria and Trish, two young Hispanic women, both of which she'd had in her patrol car more than once during her time on the beat, and a young African American woman that she hadn't seen before.

She slowed as she pulled to the curb, coming to a stop next to the threesome. Leaving the engine idling, she reached down and took hold of the knob to crank down the squeaky window.

"'Mornin' ladies," she said to the group that made their way over to her. "Cold one, huh?"

"Bet your tits," Maria muttered, arms hugging herself over a light jacket that was no match for the early morning temperatures. "What's up, G?"

"Not much," Catania said, tearing the thin plastic wrap around the cups before she filled one with steaming brew. She handed it to the shivering woman. "Any luck, ladies?" she asked, eyeing the trio.

"What, you a cop?" the unfamiliar woman asked, a cocky lift to her left eyebrow.

"Yeah, she is," Trish said, reaching for her own coffee, which she wrapped cold-reddened hands around. "She cool, Liv."

"What I don't get," Maria added after a sip of her own coffee. "Is how them pigs keep their things up in this cold."

Catania smirked. "I wouldn't know."

Trish glanced over at Liv, who looked confused. "She like Miranda."

"Oh," Liv said with a nod, taking the third offered cup. "What the hell is in this shit?" she asked, looking into the light brown depths.

"Cream and sugar," Catania said simply. "Things been quiet?" she asked conversationally, meeting Maria and Trish's dark gazes.

The twenty-eight-year-old shrugged. "Eh, I guess." She took another sip of the hot coffee, the layer of dark red lipstick she left on the edge of the cup in stark contrast to the white wax-coated paper

"Where's Chantal?" Catania asked, noting Liv had pulled a cigarette out of her jacket pocket. Without thinking, the detective reached over to her glove compartment and snatched a book of matches, simple white with her name and work phone printed on it, noting the number eighteen was scrawled across it in black Sharpie. She made a mental note of that before handing over the matches. "She been around?" she continued, curious about the young woman she often saw with Maria and Trish.

"She ain't been around for a few days," Maria said, bumming a cigarette off Liv, as well as one of her matches. She glanced at the handwritten number then grinned over at Catania. "Feel like you're cheatin' on me or something," she quipped. "Mine was number twelve."

Catania returned the grin for a moment. "Want some more?" she asked Trish, who was finishing her coffee.

"Yeah." The young woman handed Catania her empty cup. "I seen that dude you was asking about last week," she said conversationally.

Catania spared a glance at her before returning her gaze back to the box of hot coffee as it poured into the cup. "Yeah? He say anything to you?"

"He asked for directions to Bingo Burger." Trish smirked, taking her refilled cup back. "Told him to go suck himself."

"Did he comply?" Catania asked, an arched eyebrow raised.

"Nah. He took off."

"Alright, ladies. Well," Catania said, glancing at each of the three women one last time. "I better get going. Anyone want more before I go?" she asked, holding up the box. Two cups thrust at her followed by Maria's half-filled one. She poured out the rest of the coffee then wished the women a safe journey home before she rolled her window back up and headed home herself.

A few blocks down, she saw a lone figure walking along the street. It was a young woman, maybe a teenager. She had short dark hair, one side tucked behind an ear. Her shoulders were hunched slightly in the light blue and gray jacket she wore, as though she was trying to block out the cold. Her hands were tucked into the front pockets of her jeans.

Catania slowed her Jeep and pulled up alongside her. "Hey," she called from the partially opened window which she was slowly rolling down. The figure stopped and turned to face her. Catania watched as the young woman walked over to her. "How's it goin'?"

The young woman shrugged then brought a hand up to wipe at her cold-reddened nose. "S'okay, I guess."

"Where are you headed?" Catania asked, both as a suspicious law enforcement officer but also as a concerned adult. It wasn't safe for a young woman to be walking the streets alone.

"The place I'm staying at right now," she said noncommittally.

Catania smirked. "So I would assume. What's your name?"

Another shrug. "Squirrel."

"Squirrel? Your parents not like you?"

The girl chuckled. "Yeah, something like that. So look, I'm cold, can I go?"

"Sure. Hey," Catania said, reaching to her glove compartment and snagging matchbook number nineteen. "Give me a call if you need anything," she said, tossing the small item which was easily caught in one hand. Catania knew a street-smart kid when she saw one. "Get somewhere warm and safe," she added as she cranked her window closed and drove on.

Chapter Two

Catania shifted her weight to her other leg as she fully opened the tri-fold brochure, eyes scanning the glossy pages. "You think this is a good idea, Papa?" she asked softly.

"I don't know," Alberto d'Giovanni said, shaking his head. The self-made business owner let out a heavy sigh and rested large, calloused hands atop the counter. "I know he seems to connect with you more than anyone. I thought maybe you could talk to him." He shrugged a shoulder. "See what he wants."

Catania was about to respond when she stopped, glancing past her father toward the hallway that led to the bathroom. "Do you hear the shower?"

"Nope," he said, turning to follow her gaze with his own.

"Hang on, Papa." She reached out and squeezed her father's arm as she passed him, padding toward the bathroom in her baggy cotton shorts and T-shirt. "Matty?"

She could hear her father following her down the hall stopping when she did at the bathroom doorway. Her gaze went first to the shelf above the toilet, which was empty. She silently cursed her forgetfulness before her gaze dropped to her brother who sat on the floor. He had gotten into the box of Q-tips that she now remembered she'd left on the vanity. His pattern and number-oriented brain was directing him to slowly and carefully place the cotton swabs along the thin lines of dark gray grout, parallel little lines of Q-tips like soldiers marching off to battle.

"Papa," she said quietly, glancing over her shoulder at him. "Open the closet door to the washer and dryer. On the dryer is a laundry basket with folded clean clothes. There should be a colorful beach towel on top. Would you bring that over here, please?"

Left alone, Catania didn't make a big deal out of it as she reached into Matteo's packed overnight bag, which he'd placed on the closed toilet lid and removed his bottle of shampoo and conditioner as well as body wash. Though Catania had all those things already in the shower stall, she knew her brother would never use them. They had to be the only brand he trusted, which he'd used since the day Catania had brought them home for him—picked randomly—twenty years before. The family always worried what would happen should they no longer sell it.

"Alright, come on, Matty," she said cheerfully, stepping past him to put the toiletries into the large shower stall. "Time for your shower."

Matteo glanced up at her from his creation and, without a word stood, turning away from the Q-tips as though they weren't even there. "You have an uneven number of tiles on the west side of the bathroom," he said, tugging his sweater off over his head, revealing a thin, pale chest sprinkled with dark hair.

"Here you go," Alberto said, bracing himself with a hand on the doorframe as he leaned in to hand his daughter the asked-for towel.

"Thanks, Papa." She grabbed it and put it on the shelf where she knew Matteo had expected it to be. When it wasn't there and the bathroom wasn't set up as he expected it to be, he'd become distracted. "Okay, all set?" she asked, clapping her hands together. She surreptitiously glanced around to make sure she hadn't forgotten anything else.

"You can leave," he said, continuing to disrobe regardless of who else was in the room.

Catania quickly gathered all the cotton swabs from the floor as well as the nearly empty box and hurried from the room, closing the door behind her.

"Sorry, Papa," she said with a tired sigh as she joined him back in the kitchen. "I'm sorry, I'm being rude. Do you want some coffee or something?"

"No, no," he said, waving her offer away. "I have to go back to the shop." He tapped the glossy brochure where it was left on the counter. "Give it some thought and let me know what you think." He grinned at her, revealing the gap where one of his teeth was missing, a story she'd never been told. "I figure maybe I'll get some space to myself."

"Matteo's bedroom?" she asked, amused though surprised to hear him say such a thing.

"You betcha. With six kids and a wife, I haven't had my own space since the womb."

Catania chuckled. "I told Mama to clean out my room long ago. I don't know why she won't."

"In hopes you'll come back home," he said simply, reaching for his jacket which he'd tossed over the breakfast bar counter. He shrugged into it. "She's convinced you'll come to your senses some day and come home to tell us you're staying until the wedding day."

"Yeah, well," she said with a snort. "Hell will freeze over first."

"Don't say such a thing," he said, reaching up to

lightly touch the crucifix that rested around his neck hidden by his shirt. He leaned over and placed a kiss on his daughter's cheek. "See you tomorrow, *amati*."

"Goodnight, Papa," she said, following him to the door and holding it open as he exited. "I love you."

Alberto raised a hand in acknowledgment as he disappeared into the cold night.

 ❧ ❧ ❧ ❧

Catania glanced up from time to time where she was curled up in the recliner in the living room. A fire snapped and popped in the fireplace, sending a dancing orange glow into the room. Matteo sat in the gamer chair Catania kept in the corner for his weekly visits, and he played whatever game he was into on the gaming station she kept for him and the flat screen that was mounted to the wall.

Gray eyes fell back to the notebook resting on Catania's lap. She read through a few of the notes she'd taken on her current case before turning the page, which opened up to her "Matchbook Girls" list. She flicked her pen against her leg as she scanned the list, noting with sadness some of the numbers and descriptions that had been crossed out, either the matchbook owner found dead or the matchbook found ownerless.

She tapped the end of the pen against her knee to click the business end into place and began to record the numbered matchbooks she'd given to Liv and Squirrel a few nights before. Oscar used to give her crap about them until three deaths had been solved directly because of the matchbooks, one murdered and the other two from drug overdoses. He never said another word.

"Do you think they were killed in a car accident?"

Catania glanced up again at her brother's unexpected voice. "What?"

"The pizza delivery guy. Do you think he was killed in a fiery crash while on the way to deliver our dinner?"

She smirked and grabbed her cell phone, which lay on the small table next to her recliner. She glanced at the progress bar of their ordered pizza to see the driver should be there any time. "Soon, buddy," she said, setting the phone down. "I know it's taking longer than usual."

"So far three hundred and sixty-eight seconds longer than last time," he complained, never once tearing his attention away from his game.

"Do you want a juice box to curb your appetite until they get here?" she asked, setting her notebook aside in preparation to get up and head to the kitchen. At the sound of a loud buzzing, Catania realized there must be a new delivery person because they hadn't gone around back as requested on her online order, but instead the front door. "Be right back, Matty. Pizza's here."

Grabbing the cash she'd taken from her wallet earlier, Catania padded to the front door of the apartment that led to the narrow staircase and trotted down, unlocking it and opening it to the cold evening air.

"Hello. Large pepperoni and two-liter of Coke?" the older driver asked, his branded baseball cap slightly askew atop snow-white hair.

"Yup." Catania handed over the cash and took the hot pizza box and cold bottle of soda, then hurried back up the stairs, passing the archway that opened into a narrow hallway to another flight of stairs that headed up to the other two apartments on the third floor. Before she entered the apartment, she removed the single-page menu with coupons and shoved it into her pocket as she needed Matteo's attention for her planned discussion during dinner and knew he'd get immediately distracted.

Glancing to the living room, she saw that Matteo was still engrossed in his game, so she headed to the kitchen and left the food and drink on the island before gathering plates and glasses, setting two places at the table after she cleared off the unopened mail.

"Dinner, Matty."

Catania slapped two pieces onto her plate and poured a glass of Coke, leaving the box open and cap off for her brother to do the same. Once they were seated and eating, she studied the man, younger by three years. He was a very handsome man with dark, naturally wavy hair and dark, penetrating eyes. No matter how often he shaved, he always had a shadow of stubble on his strong jaw and upper lip.

She'd always thought it sad and a waste, as his family and doctors felt that likely he'd never be able to participate in the formalities of life as a romantic partner or father. His intelligence was off the charts, and though he could do your taxes in five minutes no matter how complicated, he couldn't remember to shower or even change his clothing without daily reminders.

"So," she began, taking a quick sip from her drink. "Papa tells me you're interested in having some space. Of your own, that is."

He eyed her for a moment. "Do you have any idea how annoying it gets when Mamma continually goes through your things?"

Catania smirked and nodded. "Yes, yes I do. Why do you think I live here?" She took a bite of her pizza and chewed thoughtfully, trying to decide what tack to take. "So," she began, grabbing the paper towel she'd placed beside her plate and wiping her mouth as she swallowed. "What exactly are you looking to do? What's the goal?"

Matteo took his time chewing on the bite of pizza he'd taken, opening his mouth to pop in a piece of pepperoni. "Well," he finally said. "I want all my things to be where I want them to be. I want them all to be where I left them when I return."

Catania chuckled at that one. It drove her absolutely insane when she came home from school or work only to find her bedroom rearranged. She never understood how her mother couldn't understand her anger or irritation at the total lack of privacy in the d'Giovanni home.

"I want to eat dinner if I want to or eat a donut instead if I want."

"Makes sense." She wiped her fingers on her paper towel and cleared her throat. "Matteo, Jason—"

"I don't like Jason."

"I know, but you *do* like Miss Karen, right?" she prodded, knowing full well that the wife of their older half-brother had always been good to them.

"Yes. She makes good chocolate cake."

"That's no lie. Well listen, Miss Karen runs a place called Aberdeen House—"

"No!" He began to retreat, terror in his dark eyes.

"Hey," she said softly, reaching out and covering his hand with one of hers. "It's okay, Matty. It's not the bad hospital place. It's a house, a big house divided up into a bunch of apartments." She waited for her words to sink in. When she saw him begin to relax, she continued. "You'd have a place for your bed, a little living area, like this," she said, indicating her own living room where his video game was paused on the mounted TV. "We could get you a little fridge and microwave so you could keep all your juice boxes in there and heat up your mac 'n cheese cups you like for lunch. And, you'll have your own bathroom."

He mulled over what she'd told him, chewing on his bottom lip before sipping from his Coke. "And, I'd be left alone? I could work?"

"Absolutely. You can still do your job on the computer, and yes, you'd be left alone. I think she'll come and make sure everything is okay once a week or so, but other than that...You and the other tenants would eat breakfast and dinner downstairs." She grinned and added, "If you want to."

He screwed his face up in consternation. "When they 'make sure everything is okay once a week or so,'" he said using finger quotes. "What all does that entail?"

Catania shrugged, picking up her second slice. "Probably just making sure you're keeping the place clean."

He raised an eyebrow. "Like your place?" he drawled.

"Hey, mister," she said, pointing a finger at him. "Unopened mail and a couple magazines lying on a table isn't exactly not changing my sheets for six months, now is it?"

He sat back in his chair, arms crossed over his chest as he stared off into thoughts Catania couldn't join him in. Finally, he gave her a side glance. "Can we still do our visits here?"

⚘⚘⚘⚘

Catania stood at the center of the bedroom portion of the apartment with hands on hips and looked around. She reached up and adjusted the baseball cap she wore, tired and hungry after a long day of moving her brother into his new apartment. She and the two youngest d'Giovanni boys, twenty-four-year-old Dino and high school junior Leonardo, had essentially moved everything from Matteo's bedroom at the family home into his new digs.

"What do you think, boys?" she asked, satisfied with this new chapter in her favorite brother's life.

The house they'd moved him into had been built in the thirties and still held a lot of the era's charm, even as it had been renovated and turned into various residences and businesses over the years. It had been bought a handful of years back by a group that owned nursing homes and assisted living situations—much like this one—that was extremely reputable and in good standing with the state. Having Karen d'Giovanni run the place certainly helped.

The six apartments were just under five hundred square feet each, plenty of space for a single person with only their most important possessions, like Matteo, to stretch out their legs and make a home for themselves while still having discreet supervision

The apartment was set up nicely, including the gifts the family had come together to purchase for Matteo: dorm-sized fridge with a microwave sitting atop it; a small, intimate table for two in the corner; and, the cherry on that sundae, a brand new forty-two-inch flat screen that the electronically gifted of the brothers, Leonardo, had hooked up to cable as well as Matteo's beloved gaming system.

"Well, what do you think, Matty?" Not entirely surprised, she turned to see Matteo already seated on the love seat positioned back from the entertainment center where the TV sat, playing one of his video games. She glanced at the screen to see zombie-like creatures ambling toward the point-of-view character only to have their heads or some other body part blown off in a bloody gore-fest. "Ew," she muttered. She turned to her youngest brothers. "Come on, guys. I believe our work is done here."

"Finally," Dino said, running a hand over his ever-perfect hair.

"Stop whining," Leonardo said, giving Matteo a fist bump before pushing his older brother toward the door.

"Matty," Catania said, getting no response. "Matty, I need you to listen to me."

The young man paused his game and looked up at her, splattered zombie brains frozen on the large screen.

"Okay," she began. "You have more than enough mac 'n cheese in the fridge to get you through the next few days, as well as juice boxes. I showed you how to use the microwave earlier. You remember where I showed you all the dishes and things are stored, right?" At his nod, she continued. "I'll be back on my day off and we can go grab some groceries, okay?" Another nod.

Catania walked over to the door where she'd mounted a three-hook hat rack to the wall. Hanging on the middle hook was a black carabiner with a silver key dangling from it.

"Matty, this is your key and you will always hang it here when you're at home, okay? Just like you had the fish bowl at Mamma and Papa's house in your old bedroom. Always clip this to your belt, okay?" she advised, knowing her brother's fondness for always wearing a leather belt.

"Alright," he said with a firm nod, letting Catania know he'd etched it into his incredible memory, which was a steel trap when he chose to use it.

"Okay, good. And," she said, walking over to him. "This is your address, Matty." She handed him a note card with the address written in clear, bold letters and numbers. "Put it in your wallet."

"Done," he said, retrieving the brown leather billfold from the back pocket of his khakis.

"Alright," she said, releasing a long breath. She felt like she was leaving her little boy to ride the bus to school by himself for the first time. She knew they'd left her mother to cry all afternoon as she cleaned the empty bedroom that her second son had occupied for his entire thirty-five years on the planet. "Are you going to be okay?"

He nodded, grabbing the control for his game system, quite obviously not as emotionally moved by Catania's exit as she was.

She leaned down and placed a kiss on his cheek and hugged his shoulders from behind. She was the only person in his life who could hug him freely without sending him into one of his "episodes." "I love you, bud. Get some sleep and I'll call you tomorrow."

Without another sound from Matteo except the screams and music from the game he unpaused, Catania left the apartment, making sure the door was locked behind her. She had the second of the two keys he'd been given after signing his lease.

❧❧❧❧

"And, uh, can I have a side of hash browns to go with that?" Leonardo asked, looking up at Lizzie with a charming smile.

"You got it, cutie," she said through smacked gum. "Regular for you?"

"Yup," Catania said, handing the waitress her menu. "Let's go with American instead of cheddar this time."

"Med-well, USA, side of mayo," Lizzie murmured as she scratched out Catania's order on her pad. "Okay. Be back in a sec with your drinks."

Just the two of them, Catania looked across the table at her baby brother. "I'm glad Dino went home to get ready for his date with Gina." The second-youngest was constantly in heat with his carousel of "dates." "Last time we were together you mentioned you wanted to talk to me about something." She eyed him, Leonardo the spitting image of Matteo, though taller and with deep dimples. They'd always been his ticket out of trouble with their mother. "Remember?"

He let out a heavy breath, taking a moment to shrug out of his high school letterman jacket before responding. "Yes, I do." He reached out and began to play with the chrome-and-glass straw dispenser, his dark gaze focused on it. "I think I've made a decision... finally."

"Okay," she said, sitting back in the booth. She studied him, feeling she knew what he was going to tell her. It was the same thing she hadn't been able to tell her very Catholic parents nor any of her brothers. Only the few women that had been close to her heart or in her bed knew. "Hit me."

He took a deep, steadying breath then blurted, "I faked an injury to get out of wrestling and am going to try out for the school play."

She blinked several times, her brain trying to parse out what she'd just heard. "Wait, what?"

"Okay, here we go," Lizzie said, placing Catania's Coke in front of her and Sprite in front of her companion.

Catania glanced up at the sudden interruption and someone caught her eye. Looking past the older waitress, she noticed someone scurrying around in the kitchen that she'd never seen before. It was a woman who looked to be in her thirties somewhere. Her blond hair was pulled back into a ponytail. She stopped at the order window where waitresses could pick up their orders.

"Order up!" she called, tapping the bell that sat there before she disappeared farther back into the kitchen.

"Who's that?"

Lizzie glanced over her shoulder to look before returning her attention to her table. "Ally."

"She replacing Louis?" Catania asked, casting one last glance to the kitchen before grabbing a straw and tearing off the paper.

"Nah." Lizzie smirked, hands on apron-clad hips. "Randy is too much of a sexist for that. He thinks women in the kitchen is bad luck."

Leonardo smirked. "What, was he a sailor in a past life or something?"

Lizzie grinned, blowing a small bubble with her gum. "Yeah, right. Women are bad luck or something."

She rolled her eyes, two of the fake lashes attached above her left eye fluttering slightly with the cold breeze as a patron entered the diner. "Nah, she was hired as a waitress, but we saw she was a short order cook at her last job, so we needed her to help out today." She shrugged. "Folks seem to like her food, so…" She gave them both a smile and walked away to greet the new customers.

Catania dropped the straw into her drink only to watch it bob up slightly in the bubbles. "Okay, so can I have that again, this time in English?"

He sighed, ripping the paper off his own straw. "I told the coach I had a pulled hamstring and I couldn't wrestle," he said, sparing her a glance.

Catania's eyebrows lifted. "What did Dino say?" she asked, knowing full well that their brother had been Wrestling State Champion all four years at Pueblo County High School.

"He doesn't know. Nobody does." He glanced over at his letterman jacket, heavy with pins and medals of his achievements in sports. "I want to do something different."

"And, I believe I heard the words 'school play' in there," Catania said. Though it hadn't been what she'd thought he was going to say, there was a part of her that wasn't entirely surprised. She met his gaze with a raised eyebrow.

"I knew I shouldn't have told you," he muttered, looking down at his folded hands resting on the table before him.

"Hey, Leo, I didn't say anything bad about it, bud. Don't you remember my friend Clarice? The ultimate drama queen in school?" At his nod she continued. "Well, now she teaches musical theater at DU."

He grinned. "That's cool."

"And hey," Catania added with a smirk. "It makes perfect sense. You're the ultimate drama queen yourself."

"Oh, aren't you cute!" He laughed, throwing his balled-up straw wrapper at her.

"Okay, who gets the omelet?"

Catania turned at the sound of the unfamiliar female voice. The blond cook stood next to their table, three plates stacked awkwardly up one arm while a bottle of ketchup and mustard were balanced in the opposite hand.

"Here," Leonardo said, pushing his drink away to make room for his plates.

It was as though time slowed down and Catania saw the plate that her cheeseburger and fries were on begin to wobble horribly as the plate with the omelet was removed. As if in slow motion, on instinct her hand reached out in perfect timing as the cheeseburger slid from the teetering plate, landing top-bun-side down onto her palm, a sea of French fries falling onto her wrist and the floor.

"Oh god!" The waitress gasped, the plate clanging loudly to the floor along with the small plate that held Leonardo's hash browns.

Time was back at its normal level as Catania caught up to what had happened. She brought her hand up and looked in awed curiosity at the upside-down burger in her palm. The sleeve of her hoodie was splattered with goops of mayonnaise and juices from the sliced pickles and tomatoes that had garnished the plate.

"I'm so sorry. Here, let me take that."

"No, no it's okay. This was saved," Catania said

with a chuckle, snagging a napkin from the chrome dispenser and placing the cheeseburger right side up on it.

"God." Ally gasped again, sounding like she was about to cry. "I'm so sorry."

Catania met her gaze and for a moment couldn't breathe. She found herself looking into the bluest eyes she'd ever seen, dark blue, like the sky before it turned fully black. She shook herself out of it. "It's okay, really," she said as the blond waitress began to wipe at the mess on her arm. "In my line of work, dinner spilled on me is the least of my worries."

For just a moment Ally's gaze met Catania's again, the tiniest of a smile brushing her lips before she returned to cleaning.

"Damn it, Ally." Lizzie let out a growl as she appeared next to the kneeling waitress. "Just go. I'll clean this up. Your sausages are beginning to burn."

"Okay," Ally whispered, giving Catania and Leonardo an apologetic smile before hurrying off.

"Don't be so hard on her, Lizzie," Catania said, watching as the older waitress slowly lowered herself to the floor with popping knees and a loud groan of discomfort. "She didn't mean to do it, and besides, not everyone has been a waitress since God was a boy."

Lizzie glanced up at her from halfway under the table where she'd followed two runaway fries. "Just for that," she said, pointing at her with said fries. "I'm gonna dig your 'new' fries out of the trash."

A couple hours later, Catania stood next to her Jeep as Leonardo leaned back against the passenger's side door of the white Sentra that had been passed down from Dino.

"Thanks again for dinner, Nia," he said, shoving

his hands into the pockets of his jacket. "And, thanks for listening."

"Hey, it's okay. With work, I may be busy as hell, but you know I'm here for you, bud." She reached across the distance between them and lightly punched him in the shoulder.

"Yeah. So, uh," he said, bringing a hand up and rubbing the back of his neck. "Do you know that little blond waitress? The one who made a mess?"

Catania looked at him with drawn eyebrows, confused. "No, why?"

His grin made her nervous. "Nothing. Just noticed you looking over at her a lot."

Catania rolled her eyes, suddenly feeling nervous. "Shut up."

His grin widened and his eyes bore into hers. "She's cute."

As she met his gaze, she felt he was almost sending out an olive branch to her, saying, *Hey, I sort of let you in on a little secret of mine...Your turn.* She let out a heavy sigh then dug her keys out of her pocket. "Yeah, yeah she is."

He stepped forward and wrapped her in a firm but quick hug. "See you later, Sis."

"I'll try and be by Sunday," she said, releasing him. "I think Mamma will have my hide if I don't."

"Probably." He smirked, making his way around his car to the driver's side.

"Hey, when is your tryout?"

"Thursday, after school."

"Break a leg, mister."

With a beaming smile, he climbed into his car and was gone.

"Damn kid," she muttered, turning to her Jeep

and inserting the key into the lock. She stopped short when she felt she was being watched. Hand paused at the lock, she turned and scanned the near-empty parking lot. Evening had fallen and the few street lamps scattered around weren't enough to fully illuminate the area.

Leaving the keys dangling from the door, she brought her hand to the general area where her sidearm could be reached should she need it. Her attention was drawn to the darkened corner where the diner's trash dumpsters were kept.

Taking a couple steps toward noises she was hearing, she tried to strain to see into the shadows.

"Hello?"

She froze when she saw a humanoid shadow step out from behind the dumpster, blacker than the darkest shadow. The form moved, and she could swear it was looking right at her.

"Hello?" she said again. Though through her training and years of experience she knew how to quiet the natural reactions in her body, still her pulse began to race as her heart began to thud in her chest.

Catania gasped and took several steps back as the shadow seemed to launch itself toward her, vanishing before her eyes but not before a wave of energy crashed over her in a soul-searing wave.

It took several minutes for her world to right itself, her heart rate slowing down as she gradually became aware of the cold air and sounds of distant traffic.

Chapter Three

*O*kay, so, on this sixth day of May, nineteen
hundred and ninety, we are...Wait, where
the hell is the picture? Dude. Mike, how do you use this
thing?" an unseen male voice asked, the screen black.

The muffled sounds of two men talking ensued
until finally the darkness was thrust into a bright
sunny day. The large backyard was decorated with
cream and maroon streamers and bells. The grass was
emerald green. The festive view was suddenly blocked
by the extreme close-up of a laughing man, his maroon
bowtie pulled loose, the ends hanging out from beneath
the undone collar. His brown eyes were glassy and
unfocused, his reddish-brown hair mussed.

"You had to take the lens cap off, dumbass!"

"Whoops!" There was laughter from behind the
camera, the same voice as the first speaker. "Anywhoo,
get the hell outta the way, Mike."

Once the drunken man moved out of frame, the
picture moved in a dizzying track to the opposite side
of the yard. A covered patio housed a dozen people in
various states of their Sunday best—obviously members
of the wedding party. At the center of all the chatter
was a man with thinning strawberry-blond hair and
a beard. His white tuxedo shirt was still buttoned up
with bow tie in place as well as a maroon vest. He wore
no jacket. Standing next to him was a brunette wearing
her long, satin wedding gown. Her hands rested on a

bulging belly.

The sound of footsteps on a thick carpet of grass rent the air as the camera got closer to the group. "And, there they are," the voice behind the camera said. As he neared, a hand reached into frame and rested upon the bride's beach-ball belly. "Damn, Oscar. Couldn't you even wait until after the wedding?" The image bobbed as the man behind the camera laughed, his hand falling out of frame. "But then, I guess you wanted my niece or nephew to see their dad before he lost what was left of his hair."

Oscar's head fell back as laughter erupted from his throat. "You're an asshole, Max."

"Yeah, well welcome to the family, jerkoff."

Both men laughed, the disembodied hand coming back into view as Oscar reached out to shake the hand in the secret way that only men seem to know how to do.

"Hey, let's make a toast to Oscar and my sister, Linda," the man behind the camera shouted, someone reaching over to hand him a glass of champagne.

"Oscar?" the bride said quietly, looking at her new husband who was turned away from her to listen to a woman on the other side of him.

"Everyone! Come over here. Let's—" The image slid quickly down the length of the bride's body until it settled on green grass and shined men's dress shoes. "Linda?" could be heard distantly. "Are you okay?" The feet began to move, the shot tracking their progress to the edge of the cement patio. "Hey."

"My water just broke!"

"Oh god! Oh shit. Oscar, man, someone call an ambulance!"

༄ ༄ ༄ ༄

"Can you believe that little shit can already play Christmas songs?"

Catania glanced over at her partner from behind the wheel of their assigned car, a dirt-brown Crown Vic, a retired and repainted police cruiser. "Wait, whose daughter is Hunter?"

"Greg's," Oscar said, beaming with pride as he spoke of his son's and his daughter-in-law Tammy's first born.

"Oh yeah. The adorable little one who likes to wear the angel wings right?" she asked, slowing as she eased up to a red traffic light.

"Yeah." His smile was huge, face tinted pink from the emotion he always showed when it came to his only granddaughter. Both his daughters had given them grandsons. "She's six this year, can you believe it?"

Catania blew out a soft whistle. "Damn, time flies." She got the car going again.

They pulled up to the house, the night aglow with flashing blue and red. Her heart sank when she saw an ambulance sitting at the curb, dark. No lights meant no life. As she watched, it started up and headed out, the coroner's van easing into its place. Police cars were everywhere, a few uniformed men standing around, which told Catania the threat was over or had been contained.

"Jesus," Oscar muttered, followed by a soft whistle through his teeth.

She followed his gaze to see a black-and-white parked in the driveway of the small house, someone in the backseat going berserk. His arms were pulled behind his back—obviously cuffed—and he was thrashing his body in every direction. The words and sounds he yelled were muffled through the bulletproof glass, but the entire car was moving from his violent jerks.

One thing Catania did notice was that he was covered in blood.

"That guy is strung the hell out," Oscar muttered.

"Yeah." Catania turned when she saw a uniformed officer walking toward the car. She unbuckled her seat belt and killed the engine before opening the door and stepping out. "What do we have?" she asked.

The young officer was pale as he shook a blond head. "It's pretty bad."

"Alright, thanks." She pushed the door closed and let out a heavy breath as she glanced over the top of the car to see Oscar also stepping out of the vehicle. They met at the front, he handing her a pair of latex gloves that he'd grabbed from their stash in the glove compartment.

Together they walked up the cracked pathway, autumn-deadened grass in patches on either side. The hard, square heel of Catania's loafer clicked dully on the similarly cracked cement stairs leading up to the small covered porch. The front door to the home was open, the quick flash of the police photographer's camera welcoming them. Steeling herself as she always did at this point of a case, Catania tugged on the light blue gloves, wiggling her fingers to get a snug fit.

She let out a quiet breath as she looked around. The front door opened to a smallish living room, appointed as a typical home: couch along the far wall, mismatched love seat on the wall under the window. An oval coffee table was situated so those seated on the two pieces of furniture placed perpendicular to each other could have access to it.

She noted a couple Matchbox cars resting on the table next to a yellow plastic sippy cup. She also noted there was an ashtray with cold butts in it and five bottles of beer—Peroni—two empty, the contents in the other three in various stages of consumption, never to be finished.

"Expensive taste in beer," Oscar muttered.

Catania nodded. "I remember my dad drinking that brand when I was a kid."

The room looked lived in, if a bit messy and cluttered. A young child definitely lived there. She scanned everything one more time, filing it away for what she wanted to come back for after they'd taken in the entire house. Glancing over her shoulder, she met Oscar's gaze then moved on into the small L-shaped kitchen.

A big pot sat on a cold burner filled halfway with water, intact spaghetti noodles nestled at the bottom. Catania walked over and waved her hand over it, finding it to be totally cool. It didn't look like the noodles had been boiled at all.

"You put an open jar of sauce in the fridge, right?" Oscar asked, pointing at the jar of Prego sitting on the counter, a fourth of the marinara missing from the jar.

"Yeah, why?"

He reached out and touched the very top of the metal lid. "Room temperature."

"Okay. We'll have to find out how long it would take to warm from fridge tempts. Could help determine when things began to happen."

Oscar nodded, already scribbling a note on the pad he'd been carrying.

As Catania glanced at the small, round kitchen

table, she saw an open box of Crayola crayons and an unfinished child's drawing. It looked as though it would be a house, maybe the very house she stood in.

"Oh boy," she whispered, letting out a heavy breath.

They passed the back door—locked—and traveled down a dim hallway, bathroom to the left, nothing special, nothing seemingly out of place. Catania peeked in, then continued on. She noticed the coppery, nauseating scent of blood was present and growing very strong.

"Jesus," Oscar murmured just behind Catania as they stepped the few feet farther to the open doorway of one of the two bedrooms in the small house.

Catania said nothing as she stared at the scene before her.

The bedroom was basic, appointed as most others save for an overflowing laundry basket sitting on the stained carpet under the one window. The queen-sized bed wasn't made, the faded yellow blanket halfway hanging off one side.

Near the foot of the bed lay a man. He lay on his back, legs straight out and slightly spread. He wore dark blue jeans and a long-sleeved, light gray T-shirt, though it was only from the long tail of the shirt the color could be ascertained. A large part of it was scarlet, though in places where the blood was drying, it was much darker maroon.

Catania walked over to him, looking down at his face, which looked back up at her. His lips were slightly parted, eyes heavily hooded, no life in their dark brown depths. She shook her head slowly, sad for a man who looked to be no more than his early or mid-twenties.

"Such a waste," she said softly. One thing both

she and Oscar honored was the fact that at a homicide scene, the person was once a daughter or son, once a sibling or parent. They both tried to give the victims the quiet reverence they felt they deserved.

"Looks like he was stabbed right in the heart," Oscar noted, knees cracking louder than either of their words. "Hey, David?" he called, looking toward the bedroom door.

"Yeah?" came a distant response.

"You shot the bodies, right?"

"Yup. All yours."

Oscar brought up a hand and fingered the long, single tear in the shirt. "One stab, right into the heart."

Catania took in the information she'd just been given as she turned her attention to the woman. She lay on her stomach, arms down at her sides. Her long, dark hair draped around her head, which was lying facedown.

"Where are her pants or lower garments?" Catania wondered aloud, noting the woman wore only a green sweatshirt. She was naked from the waist down, though it looked as though she wore red panties there was so much blood. She squatted down and reached out to push her hair back and away from what could be seen of her face.

"I think her throat's been slit. Oscar, help me turn her over."

On three, they turned the woman's body over, a gasp escaping both their lips. Not only was her throat slip from ear to ear, whoever had done this to her had stabbed her in the lower belly so many times the entire region of her ovaries, uterus, and genitals were mutilated, gore smashed into the carpeting beneath the weight of her body where it had lain.

"Jesus Christ," Oscar whispered.

Catania couldn't take her eyes off the animalistic damage that had been done to the young woman. She couldn't help but feel like they'd stumbled into White Chapel, England in 1888. "That is some rage," she finally managed.

"Do you think her genitals were removed?" Oscar asked, glancing over at her.

Catania shook her head slowly. "I don't know." She blew out a breath as she pushed to her feet. "Let's check the other bedroom." She needed a break from the unbelievable sight before her, needed to catch her breath.

They made their way back down the hall toward the second bedroom, walls painted light blue and decorated for a little boy. Catania glanced into the room, her gaze immediately drawn upward. She gasped as her hand went to her mouth.

"Oh, my god."

❧❧❧❧

Catania glanced over at Oscar, who sat next to her, forearms resting on the bar top in front of them, his left hand wrapped around his Heineken. He hadn't said anything since they'd arrived at Deuces, a local neighborhood bar they only went to after particularly difficult cases.

"How are you doing over there, partner?" she asked before sipping from her whiskey and Coke.

He let out a sigh and tipped the green bottle to his lips before responding. Finally, he met her concerned gaze. "I don't think I'll ever get that image out of my head."

Catania nodded, no need for him to elaborate on just which image he was talking about after a bloody, horrible night. "I know. I hope like hell they get good fingerprints off that electrical cord that was used."

"Why? They got the guy, Nia."

"We don't know that, Oscar," she reminded, taking a sip of her drink. "We'll find out when prints and DNA come back."

"That guy was so fucking out of his mind on god only knows what, he's got a rap sheet as long as my arm, including," he added, pointing his bottle at her to emphasize his point. "Domestic violence, fighting, rampant drug charges—"

"Yeah, I read the reports, but slaughtering his girlfriend, her child, and the child's father is a huge leap from assault and battery, Oscar. You've got to admit that."

"I do, but Nia, he was covered in blood!" He nearly roared, face reddening with his rising emotions and volume.

She turned on her stool and placed a hand on his shoulder. "Bud," she said softly. "I know you're upset. We both want to get the fucker who would hang a four-year-old from a ceiling fan. But," she added with a squeeze before her hand dropped to her own knee, "we've got a job to do."

He let out an angry breath, running his hand over what was left of his hair. "I know. I'm just so goddamn angry. Fucking monster."

"Yeah. Look, I'm heading back to the station to work on some of my notes."

"I'll go with you."

"No. You go home. Spend some time with Linda, go see Hunter. I know that's who you were seeing when you saw that little guy tonight."

He nodded. "Yup." He downed what was left of the beer he'd been nursing for an hour. "Okay." He slid off the stool and slapped her on the back. "See you tomorrow."

"Tell Linda I said hi."

"Will do."

Sitting alone at the bar, Catania looked at her reflection in the mirror that ran along the wall behind the bar. She looked tired, her face pale. She was exhausted and knew she needed to try to get sleep, but after a case like they'd had that day, it wasn't likely to happen anytime soon.

☙ ☙ ❧ ❧

It was nearly two in the morning as Catania made her way toward her apartment. She had gone through her second, third, and fourth winds more than an hour before as she'd sat at her desk going over notes, filling out reports, and trying to put a few puzzle pieces together on this new case.

There wasn't a lot that could be done until the lab work came back, including that of the man who had been arrested at the scene—Jerry DeHererra, boyfriend of the female victim Anastasia Luhan. Family members had told Catania that Jerry hated Aaron Gomez, the father of Anastasia's four-year-old son Eric.

So, for the time being, she decided to head home, hoping her long day would be sufficient to knock her out. She turned down the street that would take her past Randy's. She glanced over at the diner, which was essentially a ghost town. She was about to turn away when she saw a familiar figure trot her way across the parking lot headed to the sidewalk. She was in the diner's uniform and bundled up in a less-than-appropriate jacket for the freezing temperatures.

Making a U-turn at the stop sign, Catania headed the way she'd come, pulling her Jeep up alongside the woman who was quickly making her way.

"Hey!" The blonde hurried her pace, her ponytail swishing back and forth in her haste. Catania tried again, pulling up a bit to match her speed. "Hey! From the diner, remember me?"

The woman slowed than halted, turning to look at Catania before she walked the few feet over to the window that was being cranked down.

"Hey," Catania said with a smile. "Remember? The cheeseburger?"

The waitress bowed her head, her small smile barely seen. "Yes. Again, sorry about that."

"No worries. Listen, it's seriously cold out there and not real safe for you to be walking alone."

"Oh, thanks for your concern." Again a smile. "I don't want to inconvenience you. Again."

"Are you sure? It's honestly no trouble."

"No—" Her words were interrupted by the squealing of tires and roar of a distant engine followed by the scream of a siren. "Okay."

Catania pulled the lock pin on the passenger door so it could be opened. "Uh, just crank the window there to close it. Yeah, you'll need a little elbow grease." She observed her unexpected passenger, noting the woman's teeth were chattering. "You look frozen."

"I am," she admitted, rolling up the window.

"I'll turn up the heat." Catania cranked it then met the other woman's questioning gaze. "Where am I going?"

"Oh! Right. Um, just go on straight on this road until you hit Anderson Avenue. Take a right."

"Okay, I can do that."

Catania got the Jeep going and they drove in silence for a few minutes until the waitress's voice broke the silence.

"I really appreciate this," she said softly, hands held up to the closest heater vent, wiggling and bending her fingers.

"Absolutely. They call me Nia, by the way. I don't remember catching your name that night at Randy's."

"Alexandra. Well, Ally. Why do they call you that? Is it not your name?"

"Catania," she responded. She took her eyes off the road just long enough to meet dark blue eyes, black in the dimness of the Jeep other than the quick flash of pinkish-orange light when they drove under a streetlight.

"I've never heard that. It's really beautiful."

Catania grinned. "Thanks. So, how did the rest of your shift go the other night?"

Ally smiled. "Eh, it was okay. Lizzie didn't fire me, so I guess I managed to do something right."

"You know, people don't realize, but waiting tables is tough work." She chuckled. "I did it once, in high school."

"Yeah? How long did you work wherever for?"

"Village Inn. An hour."

Ally burst into laughter. "I guess you really did do it once."

"Yes, ma'am. I broke down and did what I promised myself I'd never do—work for my father."

"What does he do?"

"Uh, he's a plumber," Catania said, flicking her

turn signal as she changed lanes to get ready to turn on Anderson. "He owns Big Daddy's Plumbing and Heating."

"Ah." Ally grinned. "I've seen the commercials."

Catania turned right on the requested street. "How far down?"

"Just past the ballpark."

"Okay." She rolled up to a red traffic light. "You know, this is really far to walk, Ally. Well, so late at night, anyway. I mean, the ballpark is at least a couple miles from the diner." She met Ally's gaze, the blonde's hands now in her lap, apparently warmed enough.

"I know." She shrugged. "The busses don't run this early. Or late, whatever it is."

Catania nodded, the Jeep in motion again at the quick change to green. "Well." She smirked. "If you end up being as good a waitress as you are a cook, maybe you can get some wheels with your tips." She grinned, Ally giving her a small smile in return but said nothing.

Minutes later, Ally pointed Catania in the direction of a small stucco house with a one-car garage. The Jeep eased to the curb, the engine idling.

"Here you are, madam."

"Thanks again," Ally said, her fingers wrapping around the pull to open the door. "I really appreciate it."

"You're more than welcome. I'll wait until you get in."

"No, it's okay," Ally said quickly, for a moment almost looking panicked. "My...my boyfriend leaves the door unlocked for me, so I'll just run in." She gave Catania a quick smile, eased the door shut, then backed away from the Jeep, raising her hand in a small wave.

Catania returned the wave and drove on.

Chapter Four

Catania pulled her Jeep to a stop in her parents' driveway and parked behind a shiny black Silverado. She knew the large truck belonged to their half-brother, Jason. She and Matty didn't see him often, and she was surprised her mother had invited him to Sunday dinner to join a family Catania knew he never felt he belonged to.

She turned to her brother, who was deeply invested in a handheld electronic poker game. "Matty," she said softly. She waited until she had his attention. "Jason is here."

Instantly his jaw began to clench, jaw muscles bulging. "I want to go home.'

"I know, bud. I know you don't like him, but hey, Mamma misses you so much. She's been telling me all week how much she can't wait to see you," she lied, only briefly speaking to her mother two days before on the way to the morgue to speak to the M.E. But she knew he adored their mother and, though the words may not have come from their mother's mouth, she knew they came from her heart.

He let out an irritated sigh, hugging the game to his chest like a shield to protect him from what Catania knew he viewed as the antagonist of his personal story. It wasn't wise to cross Matteo d'Giovanni. Chances of him *ever* forgetting was akin to asking an elephant to forget her herd.

"Miss Karen is here, too," she added, trying to sweeten the deal. "I know you said you were bummed you didn't get to thank her for the extra piece of chocolate cake last night. Well," she said, indicating the truck in front of them. "Here's your chance."

He glared over at her, looking more like a petulant child than a grown man in his mid-thirties. "Fine."

"Come on, bud." She patted him affectionately on his khaki-clad thigh before opening her door and climbing out of her Jeep.

"About time you showed up," Leonardo exclaimed dramatically, hurrying from the two-story house.

"I don't even want to hear it," she said, glaring good-naturedly at him. "Be useful and carry in that tray of strudel, will ya?"

"Sure." He grabbed the heavy pan in both hands. "Mamma knows you've only got an hour so she's running around like crazy to get dinner ready. She's already cursing in Italian."

Catania rolled her eyes. "Great." She slammed the back door of the Jeep. "Dino's helping her, right?" When she heard nothing forthcoming behind her, she glanced over her shoulder. "Right?"

Catania stalked into the house, only one mission in mind when she saw Rico Suave sitting on the couch giggling with a brunette. Catania couldn't decide if her hair or her tits were bigger.

"Hello, Papa," she said, giving her seated father a quick one-armed hug and a kiss to his grizzled cheek before continuing toward her target. She reached down and grabbed the hand that rested on the woman's knee and yanked Dino to his feet. "Mamma needs your help in the kitchen."

As if on cue, shrill railings erupted in Italian from the kitchen, Catania's name the star.

Turning back to her brother, she yanked again on his hand. "Let's go."

"Hey, hey, hey!" Dino ripped his hand out of her grasp. "Excuse me, but you're here now and can go help. I'm busy with Melanie," he said through clenched teeth, eyes on fire.

"Melanie?" Catania looked the woman up and down. "Where's Gina?"

"Gina?" the woman gasp, glaring from brother to sister.

"Okay, yeah, yeah, let's go help Mamma," Dino said, a forced smile aimed down at the woman whose arms were now crossed over her large chest. "Be back in a jiffy, baby doll." Dino grabbed Catania by the wrist and nearly tugged her off her feet as he dragged her toward the short hallway that led to the swinging door and kitchen beyond. "What the fuck is the matter with you?" He glanced over his shoulder toward the living room to make sure they hadn't been followed.

"What's the matter with me?" she asked, hand to her chest and eyebrows raised. "Are you seriously asking me that?"

"You embarrassed the shit out of me back there. That ain't cool, Nia!"

"Are you serious right now?" she asked, voice low and deadly. "What's not cool is the fact that your mother has been on her feet in there for hours to feed your lazy ass, to feed some bimbo who has to endure Mr. Three Pump Chump later at *her* place because you're a twenty-five-year-old man who still lives with his mother who does his laundry, cooks his meals, and puts up with your ass!" She jabbed him hard in the chest with a finger at every word. "Now, you get in there and you act like you give two shits about anything but yourself." She turned away, intending to head into the kitchen when she was stopped.

"Yeah, well if you're such a great fuckin' person, where the hell have you been all day?"

Catania felt her anger build up so fast and so hot she was worried she was going to hit him. Instead, she moved into his personal space, their faces mere inches apart. "Trying to find justice for a goddamn baby killer." She took satisfaction in the pallor that fell over her brother's handsome face, but still felt the burning anger festering inside her, not all of it due to his selfish actions. "Now, get in there and help your mother."

❧ ❧ ❧ ❧

Catania smiled slightly as she studied the small plastic and brass trophy in her hand: *Nia d'Giovanni Spelling Bee Champion – 1989, Jefferson Elementary School.*

"You were always my little genius."

Catania turned to see her mother enter her old bedroom. "Well, I was good at spelling anyway," she said with a grin, raising the trophy to emphasize her point before returning it to the dresser top, the long, heavy mahogany behemoth with a mirror mounted against the wall. All of her knickknacks and anything once beloved still resided in its place, dusted weekly by a mother who wasn't ready to let her daughter grow up.

Antonia walked to her and reached up, cupping the side of Catania's face for a moment. "Such a beautiful young woman," she murmured, pride in her smile. "You are deeply troubled, I can see it in your eyes."

Catania gave her a tired smile. "They say the eyes are the window to the soul."

"Especially you, *mio bella*. What is bothering you? You barely ate." She waggled a finger playfully at her. "I cook all day for you."

Catania smiled, looking down at her hands, which fidgeted together. "Just a tough case, Mamma. I'll be okay." She almost held her breath, waiting for her mother to go into her familiar battle cry of marriage, marriage, marriage.

Instead, Antonia said, "You were always a fighter for justice, *bella*. Whether you were protecting Matteo or that little girl down the street who used to get picked on by that nasty Richard boy across the way." She looked at her with so much love that it nearly brought tears to Catania's eyes. "This," Antonia continued, tapping two fingers to the spot where Catania's heart was. "Always so big. I worry about you, but I'm proud of you."

"Thanks, Mamma," Catania whispered. Her eyes fell closed when her head was clasped between gentle hands and guided down so her shorter mother could leave a kiss on one cheek and then the other.

"I packed a nice bag of leftovers for you," Antonia said, the quiet, intimate moment between mother and daughter over, the bossy Italian matriarch firmly back in place.

"Thanks. I'll get Leonardo to help load the Jeep. He can carry the pan of what's left of the strudel." She paused at the look on her mother's face. "What?"

"You no taking that strudel anywhere! I'm glad you had that German friend to teach you how to make it. It'll save me making breakfast for your father for at least three days."

Catania smirked. She couldn't help but wonder what her mother would think of that "German friend" if she knew she'd shared Catania's bed for two years. "Okay." She took her mother in a tight hug. "I have to get back to work, Mamma. Is Matteo coming with me or is he going to stay?"

"He's with your Papa in the basement. We'll get him back to that place later."

Catania laughed, a bit annoyed. "Mamma, he's happy in his new apartment. Isn't that what matters? And," she said with a shrug. "He's really proud of himself."

Antonia gasped. "Proud he left his mother's house?"

"Mamma." Catania sighed, running a hand through her hair. "That's unfair and you know it. This can't be about you. Don't you want your children to be happy? To figure out who they are? Without you and Papa?" she added.

Antonia looked away and crossed her arms stubbornly over a large bosom. "This house will be empty soon."

Catania snorted. "Oh, come on. You know our family's favorite bloviate Dino will live here forever and eventually bring whoever he manages to capture here with him." She met her mother's hard gaze with an amused one of her own. "They'll take over the house, but they'll be here."

Finally, and Catania had no doubt reluctantly, Antonia gave her a ghost of a smile. "You get some rest tonight."

Catania accepted her mother's second hug. "And

besides, Paul will always be back when his newest wife leaves him. This one is what, number four?" She flinched at the smack to her behind.

❧ ❧ ❦ ❦

Catania could hear the boys downstairs hooting and hollering over one video game or other so she decided not to bother them and carry everything out herself. She gathered the extra loaf of garlic bread her mother had made for her as per usual and set it on the counter from the sheet pan on the stove. She reached for the box of foil when suddenly it was in front of her face.

Following the box up to the person presenting it to her, she met the small smile on Jason's face. "Thanks."

"Didn't get to talk to you much at dinner," he said, leaning against the counter. "How are things going? Still with the department?"

She nodded, tearing off a sheet of foil large enough to wrap the bread in. "Yeah. Things are good. It just gets a little frustrating," she added, grinning up at the tall man who was essentially a Caucasian version of their very Italian-featured father.

Jason had the dark hair and brown eyes, which were shaped like their father's, as well as his d'Giovanni jawline, but his skin tone was more pinkish. She'd been told his mother had light features—dirty blond hair and hazel eyes.

Alberto d'Giovanni had met Lisa Ross in high school, she a fifteen-year-old freshman, he a sixteen-year-old sophomore. They'd begun to date and, one unexpected night—the way her father told it—he learned about the birds and the bees. Excited about this new knowledge, a handful of weeks later he learned that Lisa's family had suddenly moved away and Alberto was left confused and hurt, his first girlfriend vanishing in an instant.

Time marched on, and eventually Alberto met and married Antonia, started a family and his business. When Paul was six and Catania was four, their parents received a phone call that nearly ended the d'Giovanni's seven-year marriage. Over time, Antonia had forgiven him and believed he had no idea he'd fathered a child, and together they'd tried to bring Jason into their lives as much as he'd allow them to.

Now, there they stood in Catania's mother's kitchen. "It gets frustrating because we get stuff cleaned up only for it to get messy again before the case is even filed."

He smiled with a nod, bringing up his left hand and wiggling his fingers. "I get it. I had to rewire a bakery four times because the owner's kid kept popping breakers. Lost the tips of my fingers in the process."

Catania winced. "Ow, damn! Guess that'll wake you up in the morning, huh?"

He gave her a crooked grin. "Definitely. Want some help carrying that stuff out?"

"Thanks."

Together the siblings carried out the massive amount of food Antonia had packed away for her. She balanced the heavy bag on a hip to free up a hand to pull open the driver's side back door.

"I wanted to thank you and Karen for helping Matteo get into the apartment. He's pretty happy there."

"Sure, no biggie," Jason said, handing her the bag

of food he'd been carrying after she got the first one placed safely so it wouldn't fall over in transit. "Paul had mentioned to me that he was wanting to get out on his own, so Karen had the perfect solution."

"It really has been, thanks. Truly thoughtful of you." Second bag secure, Catania closed the door and rested her hand on the top ridge of the Jeep.

"Well, I have to get going." He gave her a quick, one-armed hug before turning to head to his truck. "Oh," he said, facing her again as he pulled his keys from the pocket of his jeans. "If you happen to know a good cook, Karen is looking for someone for Matteo's building. It's getting to be too much for her to run back and forth between three different places. I think it's a live-in position, but not sure."

"Will do. Take it easy, Jason."

ﬂﬁﬀﬃﬂ

Dressed casually in jeans and a heavy wool sweater, Catania ducked under the yellow crime tape and walked up to the locked front door. Extracting the house key she'd checked out from Evidence from her pocket, she inserted it into the lock and entered the deathly quiet house.

Though everything had been inventoried, photographed, and swept by the crime scene unit, she pulled on a pair of latex gloves anyway. In a case that didn't sit well with her, she often liked to return to the scene of the crime, whether it was an alleyway, a car, or a single-family home like this one. Now that everything was quiet, the bodies had been removed, and the various departments had done their work, it was her time to listen to the scene around her, listen for the soft whispers of the ghosts left behind.

A few things were moved, some removed and put into evidence since Catania had been in the house last. Hands on hips, she stood at the center of the living room and made a slow scan of it, taking it in as it was, but also bringing up the clear mental image of what things had looked like the day of the murder. As it had the first day she'd been there, her gaze was drawn to where the five bottles of beer had been on the coffee table, since removed. She walked over to the table, able to smell the fingerprint powder used during the dusting done by crime scene techs.

Walking over to the table, she closed her eyes and brought up the image of that first day, the placement of all the bottles, and considered one of the bottles, the slight waxy discoloration of lipstick visible at the mouth. Glancing at the couch, she tried to imagine where Anastasia would have been sitting. Sinking down into the worn couch, she glanced at the bottle in her mind, reached out with her right hand as the victim had been right-handed, and adjusted herself a couple inches to the left where her reach was more comfortable and natural. She'd only consumed just under half of her beer. Fingerprints on the closest set of three—the two empty and the third nearly finished—belonged to Aaron Gomez.

Doing the same thing with Aaron's bottles, she tried to gauge how closely he and Anastasia were sitting together. Yes, they had a child together, but from what friends and family had said, though fairly friendly before their deaths their relationship had been volatile while romantically involved. In other words, while they weren't enemies in their co-parenting duties, they weren't besties, either.

"So," she murmured, glancing again at the spot where she'd just been sitting. "Why were they sitting so close together?"

Her gaze drifted over to the love seat where the third person likely sat. She remembered the beer inside that bottle had barely been touched and no prints had been found on it.

She tapped her fingers on her knees as she considered what she was seeing. "You were uncomfortable around this third person, weren't you, Anastasia?" she said softly. "Did you know him? Or her," she added, though reluctantly. Unless the perp was Special Ops-trained, she just couldn't see a woman being strong enough to accomplish the carnage that was done here, as well as overpower three people, one an average-sized man.

Something else she decided she wanted to check for was the sixth bottle. It wasn't listed in evidence as anything taken or found, but she wanted to make sure it was looked for as she'd found in research that this brand was only sold in six-packs in the area.

She pushed up from the couch and was startled when her cell phone rang. She pulled it out of her back pocket and answered the call. "D'Giovanni here."

"Hey, Nia, we have DNA results," the woman on the other end of the line said.

"Great, Tammy. What'cha got for me?"

"Not much. Unfortunately, the damage was just too expansive to get any sort of conclusive DNA sampling from the female to point at a suspect or anyone else that may have been there when she was killed. However, she was pregnant. Her hCG levels point at about eight weeks. The baby is not related to either Gomez or DeHererra. But, the two hairs found on the female's body belonged to DeHererra."

"Ah, jeez. You just threw a big ol' grenade into my case." Catania sighed, leaning against the coat closet door. "Anything else?"

"There was what looks to be an arm hair attached to the electric cord used with Eric, but the profile does not appear in CODIS."

"Damn," she said. "Okay, thanks, Tammy." Ending the call with the woman who ran the lab they used, she tapped the side of her phone against her chin. "Well, shit. That is one seriously big ol' fly in the ointment."

Chapter Five

*T*he timestamp at the bottom of the frame claimed it to be 05/13/1995. Music thumped in the distant background, heavily muffled. The shot included the shiny, reflective hood of a red car, the night beyond, and a well-lit parking lot, though where the red car was parked was more dim and full of shadows.

Two teenage boys appeared, one dressed in a dark gray tuxedo, the other in classic black. One was smoking a cigarette, the other holding a bottle of whiskey, letting out a dramatic hoot after he took a fiery sip.

"Shit tastes like fucking gasoline." He coughed, handing over the bottle to his companion. "You gonna go to After Prom?"

"Fuck, Laurie's mom threw a shit fit when she brought it up. 'You have to be home by midnight or else!'," he said, imitating a nagging woman's voice. "You?"

"Yup." He grinned, taking the bottle back after his friend took a long drink. "Me and Jennifer got all night." He indicated the camera. "Why the hell you think I brought this thing?

"Lucky fuck." The two teens stopped and turned when a tan sedan pulled into the parking lot, settling into a space halfway between the red car and the larger grouping of cars under the lot lights. "Oh, hey. It's Alexandra. She's hot as fuck."

"Who?" the boy in gray asked, trying to get a better view into the car.

"*Alexandra Findley. Had her in Langly's class last year.*"

His buddy laughed. "*Yeah, you wish you had her.*"

The two boys giggled conspiratorially, smacking each other.

The passenger door of the sedan opened and a stunningly beautiful blond young woman stepped out. Her silvery blue gown was fitted, showing off a womanly figure.

"*Hey, Johnny,*" she called out with a small wave, her voice soft and distant.

"*Hey, Alexandra,*" he replied.

"*Who's the dude?*"

"*Older guy. People say she's dating her half-brother or foster brother. I don't know. Something weird.*"

The two teens moved off to the side, their voices muffled away from the camera's direction-limited microphone. The blonde named Alexandra pushed her door closed as the driver of the car joined her on the passenger side. He wore a black tuxedo, though his bowtie matched the color of her dress.

He grabbed her by the arms, obvious indentions in the skin from the firm grip. He indicated the two teenage boys with the nod of his head, his voice too low for the camera to pick up. Alexandra looked as though she was desperately trying to explain something to him, pleading her case with quick gestures and raised eyebrows.

SLAP!

Stunned, her hand came up to her cheek, her companion who looked to be around twenty grabbing her other hand in a vice-like grip, tugging her away from the car and out of frame.

☙ ☙ ❧ ❧

Oscar remained silent as he chewed on the bite of chicken fried steak he'd just put into his mouth, his expression thoughtful. Catania sat across from him, her ever-present cheeseburger and fries before her. She'd shared everything she'd learned regarding the Luhan/Gomez murders.

"So, that sixth bottle wasn't anywhere, huh?" he asked after washing down the food with a drink of coffee.

"Nope. I went through the trash, garage, crawl space, wherever I could think of," she said, dragging two fries through her mayo and ketchup mixture before popping them into her mouth.

"Why are you so hung up on beer?" He smirked, stabbing some carrots with his next bite of meat. "Ain't even that good a beer anyway."

"Because," she said, ignoring his comment. She wasn't a fan; to her just about every beer smelled like wet dog. "Because my gut tells me if we find that sixth beer, we'll find our guy."

"But, Nia," he said, sitting back against the booth which creaked under his weight. "We have Jerry DeHererra's DNA on Anastasia Luhan's body, he was covered in blood when first responders arrived, he admitted it was possible he did it when you and I interrogated him, and," he said, holding up a beefy finger to emphasize his point. "He failed the polygraph."

"Which, as you know, is not admissible in court," she reminded. "But even so, Oscar, consider this. You saw the toxicology report on that guy. He was higher than a damn kite on more things than the alphabet has letters for. There is no possible way he could remember the events of that day clearly to be remotely useful on either the polygraph or our little chat with him." She shook her head as she sipped her Coke. "That dog don't hunt."

"Okay, so back to the beer. That beer could have been from a case from a month ago, who knows?"

"I do," Catania said with a shit-eating grin. She grabbed her phone from the table and swiped and tapped until she was in her email. She found the right one and handed the phone to her partner.

He grabbed it and glanced up at her. "You contacted the maker?"

"Yup, who then sent me on to the bottling company."

"I hate it when you get clever," he groused, using his finger to scroll down. "So, this serial number series was sent to stores here in Pueblo, liquor stores, grocery stores, convenience stores, stuff like that, huh?" he asked.

"Yep. I called around this morning to see who carries the brand and came up with the two King Soopers grocery stores here, a couple of the Loaf 'N Jug convenience stores in town, and the Big Bear liquor store. They're going to get back to me when they find when that series was sold and, if we're lucky, to whom."

He let out a sigh with a nod. "Alright, sounds like a plan. Be right back, gotta pee."

Catania watched as Oscar scooted out of the booth, then turned back to her lunch.

"Here's your check. Do you guys need anything else? Dessert, maybe?"

Catania glanced up as she chewed a bit of her burger, giving Ally a quick smile before grabbing a napkin to wipe at her mouth as she quickly chewed and swallowed. "Hey. Nothing for me, but maybe Oscar."

"Okay. I can come back," Ally said, tucking her order pad into the pocket of her uniform dress. Today her hair was down and pulled back from her face. Catania thought it looked so soft and silky. She gave her a smile and turned to leave only to stop and turn back to Catania. "I really wanted to thank you again for the ride home the other night. It was sweet of you and definitely helpful to get home faster since I already wasn't going to get much sleep before I had to head to my other job."

"Oh, absolutely. Hey, anytime you see me puttin' around town or around here, I'll help you out." Catania leaned back in the booth, an arm draped casually along the back ledge. "What's your other job?"

"I have a small business of cleaning houses."

"Yeah?" Catania asked, ears perking up as she sat up straighter in the booth. "You got room on your roster for one more?" She grabbed the pen and pad she'd been scribbling on during her and Oscar's brain-scratching session. She looked up at Ally expectantly, pen poised over a blank page. "Name of company? Phone number? Availability?"

Ally threw her head back as she let out what Catania thought was an adorable giggle. "I said 'small' for a reason. I have two houses."

"Want a third?"

Ally tucked her bottom lip in and glanced away, looking as though she were trying not to break out into laughter. After a moment, she gave her a side glance. "Yeah. Sure."

❧ ❧ ❧ ❧

"Well," Catania said, hands on hips as she looked

at the gathered supplies. "I hope I got everything you should need."

Ally stood next to her, taking in the veritable sea of cleaning supplies that surrounded them. "Uh, yeah. Do you always keep four different brands of floor cleaner around?"

Catania grinned at her, bringing a hand up to rub at the back of her neck. "Yeah, uh, wasn't sure what you prefer."

Ally nodded, seeming to take it all in. She glanced around the sparsely furnished room. "Lived here long?"

"Four years."

"Oh."

Catania looked around, seeing things through the eyes of a newcomer. "Well, uh...want the tour?"

Ally followed her from the living room into the kitchen. "I love these old buildings," she commented, trailing her fingers over the exposed brick of one of the walls. "Do you know the history of it?"

"Uh," Catania said, stopping and resting her hands on the butcher block island. "I know it used to be a textiles factory or something. You can still even see a bit of the original sign painted on the brick outside, *Samson Bros. Textile,* I think it says. Something like that."

"So cool," Ally said with a bright smile, meeting Catania's gaze. "So much history in this building. Is it haunted?"

Taken aback by the question, Catania just blinked at her for a moment. "Uh, not to my knowledge, no."

"I love that kind of stuff," the waitress said with reverence as she reached out to touch some of the original woodwork around one of the windows. "Okay, sorry. I'm done geeking out. What exactly do you need?"

"Well, basically, I'm just not home that much," Catania explained. "I grew up with a cleaning Nazi and I'm sick of hearing my mother bitch when she's here." She grinned. "Don't get me wrong, I like my place clean and picked up, but with my job, that's not exactly what I choose to do to unwind and decompress."

Ally chuckled. "That's funny because cleaning is exactly what I love to do to decompress."

"See?" Catania said with exaggerated cheer in her voice. "I am so generous to give that to you plus a few bucks in your pocket."

༄ ༄ ༄ ༄

Catania glanced over her shoulder when she heard the shuffling of papers. "Hey. Be done in a sec."

"Good, I gotta pee." The bank robbery division detective's voice bordered on a grumble, though a lopsided grin cut through the tone.

"Yeah, and what's new?" she asked, chuckling at his glare as she retuned her attention back to the copier she was using. Their lieutenant preferred to have his own copy of each of their cases to go over during their brainstorming sessions where they'd also get him caught up. "How's it going, big guy?" she asked the thirty-two-year department veteran.

"Eh, got some shoplifter," he said, raising the few pages in his hands, which she assumed was his report to file on the issue.

"Oh, good times." Catania gathered her copies and her originals and moved away from the copy machine. "Trade ya."

"Not on your friggin' life, Big D!"

She burst into laughter as she squeezed past him out of the small cubby to head back to her own desk. She was about to pass Rodney's desk when she noticed someone sitting in the chair next to his desk, the so-called "perp chair." She recognized the light blue and gray jacket.

"Hey, don't I know you?" she asked the young girl who was sitting there, picking at her thumbnail. When dark eyes glanced up at her from shaggy dark bangs, she knew she had the right girl. "Rat. No, ferret? Crap, no. Some sort of rodent."

"Squirrel."

"Squirrel!" She hugged the hefty stack of pages she'd just copied with their originals to her chest. "You been a bad girl this year?"

The teen smirked. "Yes, Santa."

Catania grinned. "Take care, kid," she said, playfully smacking the girl's shoulder with her papers. "Stay out of trouble." She was about to walk on when something caught her eye.

She turned back to the teen, eyebrows drawing. Reaching a hand out, she gently took Squirrel's chin between thumb and forefinger, turning her head so the girl was in profile. The beginnings of what looked like would be a decent shiner decorated her left eye.

"Are you okay?" she asked quietly, concerned but not wanting to make a big deal out of it. Her hand dropped away. "Anything you want to tell me, or Rodney when he gets back to his desk?"

Squirrel looked away and let out a sigh. She looked as though she was about to say something when she glanced past Catania and closed her lips.

Following the teen's line of sight, Catania saw Rodney headed their way, copies in hand. Most detectives weren't keen on someone else talking to their perp, so she squeezed Squirrel's shoulder and moved on.

"Hey, you ready for this?" she asked Oscar as she walked up to their desks, flapping down the original pages of her report on the corner of hers and keeping the copied pages in hand.

He glanced up at her, an eyebrow raised. "Do you really want an answer to that question?"

She grinned, fishing out a large paper clip from a container on Oscar's desk. "Come on, big guy. Let's get this over with."

Oscar rose, grabbing his suit jacket off the back of his chair. "Yup," he said, shoving his arms into the sleeves.

"You betcha."

"Oh yeah."

"Yes, siree," Catania added as they headed toward their supervisor's office.

"Definitely," he said with a nod.

"Absolutely."

"Let's get 'er done."

"Asshole," she muttered when they hit the open doorway, her partner getting the last word this time. "Next time, Riley."

He chuckled and stepped inside.

Fifteen minutes later, Sergeant Price's deep baritone boomed over the large room.

"What do you mean you haven't arrested DeHererra yet?"

Catania reached a hand up and rubbed at the back of her neck, giving a side glance to Oscar, whose eyes were already on her before they shifted back to their supervisor. "Sir, I think it's a mistake. We don't have grounds to arrest him."

"What are you talking about?" the African American man bellowed, staring her down, his thick black beard almost hiding his frown. Almost. He stabbed a finger at the pile of pages on his desk blotter. "Did you read this report, d'Giovanni?"

"I should hope so, sir, I compiled it.

He pointed a long finger at her. "Don't get cute. Listen, you two. A four-year-old boy is dead and I want to know why. The community wants to know why, and most importantly, my lieutenant wants to know why. Got it?" At Catania and Oscar's nod, he shoved the report toward them. "Go find me a suspect!"

"That guy is such an asshole," Catania growled quietly as they walked back to their desks.

"Total Trump voter," Oscar muttered in response.

ॐ ॐ ॐ ॐ

Standing next to Oscar, Catania watched the large crowd from behind her sunglasses where they stood back near a tree. The tent for the family was set up over the double gravesite. This funeral was more difficult than usual to case, as it seemed half the town had shown up to it. Anastasia and Eric were being buried today, Aaron the following day. Mother and son were to be buried in the same grave. The four-year-old's tiny casket had left not one eye dry—including Catania's—but it was her and Oscar's job to seek out those who were possibly responsible for this, and sick enough to show up at the funeral. Sadly, a sociopath who could do that to a child would certainly relish the effect of his or her work as their victims were laid to rest.

"This is crazy," Oscar said softly next to her. "Not one goddamn person has caught my eye. Nobody looks out of place."

Catania sighed and nodded. "I know. I'm thinking the same thing."

Suddenly, a loud wail rent the air.

"They must be lowering the caskets," Oscar mumbled. "Jesus, I can't even imagine."

Catania felt the sting of fresh tears trying to come and brought up the wadded tissue she'd been holding, reaching up under the left lens of her sunglasses to dab at her eye. "So messed up," she whispered.

"Wanna get out of here?" Oscar asked gently, a hand briefly touching her back.

Catania took a deep, cleansing breath, then nodded. "Yeah. I don't think we're going to get anything more here." She turned and was about to follow Oscar back to the car when she stopped, movement catching her eye.

About thirty yards away sat a stand of trees, and the space between them was dark, pitch-black dark. She turned to face that direction, trying to make out what she was seeing. The harder she looked the deeper the darkness seemed to get, and as the world seemed to fade around her, she felt the pull of that darkness. She could feel a pulsing chill from it, as though a heartbeat of ice beckoned.

Not of her own accord, Catania took a step toward it, only for the beating pulse to get faster, so fast she could feel it in her stomach, like the low bass of a powerful music system. She felt as though she were losing her will, drawn in to the abyss...

"You comin'?"

"What?" She whirled around at the touch on her

arm.

Oscar looked at her with wide eyes, his hand pulled back as though burned. "Sorry. Are you okay?"

Her forehead pounding, Catania dropped her head as her hand rose to meet it. "Whoa," she murmured, for a moment no idea where she was or what had just happened. She removed her sunglasses and rubbed her eyes before glancing at her partner again. "Sorry. I uh…" She glanced back over at the trees only to see the sunny day and tombstones beyond. "Let's go."

Chapter Six

Catania felt like she was in a daze as she
locked her Jeep and made her way up the
short flight of stairs that would take her to the back
door of her apartment. She glanced down at the keys
she held in her hand and sorted through them until
she found the house key and unlocked the door, letting
herself inside.

Yes, she'd been emotionally affected—deeply
so—by this recent case, but after the funeral she felt
physically drained, emotionally spent, and absolutely
mentally foggy. She entered her kitchen and, though
she considered getting a bite to eat, she walked on
through, headed for her bedroom.

Standing next to her bed, she shrugged out of
her long black coat and tossed it across the comforter
before reaching up to unbutton her blouse. Her energy
left her and suddenly all she wanted to do was sit down.

Plopping down backward across the bed, Catania
stared up at the ceiling fan, studying the five unmoving
blades. She felt a combination of tired, sad, a touch of
depression, and absolute loneliness swell inside her.
She had her moments of feeling lonely, wishing she
had someone in her life, but then she'd just turn to her
work to quell that notion. The irony this time was that
it was her job making her wish she'd had someone to
lean on.

Her thoughts stopped with a screech when she

heard something. The door opened and then closed, followed by footfalls on the wood floor. Lifting her upper body, Catania braced herself on her elbows and listened.

The footsteps grew more faint, as though headed away from the hallway where the bedrooms were and toward the kitchen. Soft humming began as water was turned on.

"Ally." Catania exhaled the breath she had been holding in. "Right, it's Wednesday." They'd made the deal that Ally's day to clean the apartment was best smack-dab in the middle of the week for her schedule at the diner.

"Ow! Damn, that's hot."

Catania smiled at the words that drifted through the otherwise quiet apartment.

The humming continued, joined by the sound of the pantry door squeaking open. The humming stopped only for soft murmuring to begin.

"Okay, I used you last week, so let's try you. Let's see if you're as zesty orange as you claim...Whoa! Orange cough syrup. Maybe not."

Catania sat up, a full grin on her face as she listened to Ally talk to the cleaning products she'd bought for her.

"Roses, huh? Well, what girl doesn't like roses. Let's see...Uh, not horrible, but I've never exactly smelled a bouquet like you before. I think you'll make the bathroom smell awesome. Roses it is."

The humming started again in earnest as the sounds of sweeping commenced. Moments later, a full-on a cappella concert began. Curious, Catania pushed up from the bed and headed down the hall, slowly approaching the living room. She saw Ally over by the wall where the TV was, her hair pulled up into a messy bun. She had earbuds in and her very shapely behind was moving in time to whatever song she was listening to. Unfortunately, her very off-key singing wasn't helping Catania's identification attempts.

Ally picked up the broom, using it as a de facto microphone. She whipped around, belting out the song at the top of her lungs. Catania realized she was going to scare the living hell out of the poor woman, and stopped advancing so she wouldn't be a victim of death by broom. Too late.

Ally screamed as her eyes went round, the broom coming up as the waitress took a defensive pose. Catania's hands instantly went up in surrender.

Letting out a relieved breath, Ally lowered the broom and tugged the earbuds out of her ears. "My god, you scared the crap out of me!"

"I'm really sorry," Catania said, lowering her hands and walking toward her.

Ally sent a glare her way, hand covering her heart. Finally, she met Catania's steady gaze. "Am I here on the wrong day?"

"No, I'm sorry," Catania said, tucking her hands into the front pockets of her slacks. "I decided to come home for lunch and forgot. I'll leave and get out of your way."

Ally gave her a sweet smile. "No need. It's your place, Nia." She studied her for a moment then stepped up to her, hugging the broom to her chest. "Are you okay? You look like you're about to cry."

Catania felt ashamed and childish as she sucked her bottom lip under her top teeth in an attempt to keep her emotions at bay. The gentle, caring look in those dark blue eyes was her undoing.

"Come here," Ally murmured, leaning the broom against the wall as she opened her arms to Catania, holding her close. "It's okay."

To Catania's eternal embarrassment, the tears came. She allowed herself to be held and wrapped her own arms around Ally's slender frame. The upset came hard and fast but seemed to wind down just as quickly. Within moments the tears abated and she let out a heavy sigh, relieved to get some of the pent-up emotion out. She smiled slightly when Ally ran her hand over Catania's back in small circles before giving her a tight squeeze.

Ally pulled back and looked into Nia's eyes. "Are you okay?" She reached up and lightly wiped away a small tear trail left after Catania used her sleeve to wipe at her face.

Catania took a couple deep breaths and let them out slowly with a nod. "Yes. I'm really sorry about that. Just seeing a friendly face…You know how it is." She gave her an awkward smile.

"I do," she said, returning the smile with the sunshine that was uniquely her. "Come on," she added, tugging lightly on Catania's hand. "Let's sit down." She looked around them, the recliner their only option. "You really need to get a couch or something," she said playfully, lowering herself to the floor, followed by Catania.

Feeling like a real idiot—random emotional bursts, no furniture—she figured Ally thought as much about her as well. She sat cross-legged, as opposed to Ally who sat with legs stretched out, crossed at the ankle. Her upper body reclined back slightly as she rested her weight on her hands, which were placed against the floor behind her.

"What happened?" Ally asked softly, head slightly cocked to the side, full attention on Catania.

"Oh," Catania said, running a hand through her hair. "Just a tough case I'm working on. Kinda got to me." She spared a glance and small smile Ally's way before studying her hands as they poked at a knot in the wood flooring.

"Case? Are you an attorney?"

She shook her head. "Nope. Homicide detective."

Ally's eyes grew wide for a moment. "Really? Wow. I've never met one in real life before. I can't imagine how difficult that must be. I'm sure you've heard of that horrible murder that happened recently...a family, I think it was." She shook her head. "A little boy."

"Yeah," Catania said softly. "I know the case well." She reached over and lightly tapped Ally's shin. "You wanna get something to eat?"

ᔑᔑᔑᔑ

By mutual agreement they avoided Randy's, instead choosing a pizza joint.

"Wait, you guys actually had a second house?" Ally asked, straw halfway to her mouth to sip from her Pepsi.

"Sure did. We all referred to it as the Lake House." Catania tossed the last bit of crust into her mouth from the piece she'd had and finished on her plate. The medium pepperoni pizza they'd ordered to share had been just the right size. "God, we had so much fun there when I was a kid. Even Jason would come up and spend a weekend with us."

"Okay, wait," Ally said, setting her soda back

to the checkered-cloth-covered table. "Which one is Jason again?"

"The oldest," Catania said, sitting back casually in the booth as she wadded up her napkin and tossed it on her empty plate, sated and full.

"Wait. I thought Paul was the oldest."

"He is."

Ally stared at her. "You just said Jason is."

"He is."

"Okay!" Ally reached over and snatched a napkin from the dispenser and slapped it on the table in front of her after she shoved her plate away. "Miss, can I borrow your pen, please?" she called out to the waitress, who wasn't paying a lick of attention to them. She grinned at Catania "How many brothers do you have?"

"Five. Okay, you have Jason that is my father's son from a high school girlfriend. He came into our lives when I was a little kid. Then—"

"What does he do?

"He's an electrician. Used to work with our dad, but they just couldn't get along. So, he started his own business, fixing TVs and stuff." She shrugged. "Pretty successful, now. Works with contractors. He has this huge workshop behind his house, always tinkering, fixing stuff, and making stuff."

"Are you guys close?" Ally asked, raising her cup when their waitress glanced their way, the clear plastic cup filled with only what was left of her ice. "Want a refill?" She took the cup Catania offered and handed them both to the waitress when she stopped by their table. "Okay, and Paul?"

"Paul is the oldest of my parents' kids. He's a mess, to be honest. He's battled the bottle for years.

Gets sober and gets married. Falls off the wagon and begins drinking, and she leaves him. Gets sober, gets married." She rolled her eyes and waved off the subject of her brother. "It's sad. I lose track of how many kids he has. Most want nothing to do with him." She smirked. "The irony is, he's the only one out of all us kids who has any kids, but I think he's reproduced enough for all of us."

"Is he married now?"

"Last time I heard. A lady named Pam. I only met her a couple times, hair stylist or something. I think she has like three or four kids herself."

"Good lord! Productive couple." Ally laughed, smiling up at the waitress when she brought their refilled drinks back. She handed Catania's to her. "Okay, next?"

"Well, there's me, of course. Then, Matteo. He's...interesting." She chuckled, removing the paper at the top of the new straw put into her Pepsi before taking a sip. "He's the closest brother to me, not just our age, but he's my bud. He's an absolute math genius and does all the accounting for my dad's company. He just got his own place recently. I'm super proud of him."

"Why? And, why 'interesting?'" Ally asked, sitting back in the booth, her hand resting on the table next to her drink.

"He's on the spectrum. When he was little my parents didn't understand him. I think they thought he was crazy or mentally ill." She shook her head. "To understand Matty is to understand he's illogically logical. If you can get that into your head, expect it, and not question it where he's concerned, you'll do fine."

"Not to be disrespectful or anything, but is this kind of a *Rain Man* thing?"

"Kinda. Maybe not quite as severe as the Dustin Hoffman character, but yeah, you got it." Catania took a sip of her Pepsi before switching gears. "Next is God's gift to women—so he thinks—my brother Dino, who is a millennial poster child."

Ally groaned and rolled her eyes. "One of those."

"One of those. He works for my dad, lives at home, and believes everyone should wait on him hand and foot. I love Dino, but not always a fan. And finally, the baby, Leonardo. Sweet kid. He graduates high school next year."

Ally shook her head. "Wow. Your poor mother, and poor you. That can't have been easy growing up with so many men and so much testosterone in the house."

Catania chuckled. "You have no idea. What about you?"

"What about me?" Ally asked, her tone slightly defensive.

"Where did you grow up? Siblings? Are you close to your folks?

"Ladies, here's the check whenever you're ready," the waitress said, leaving the ticket in a shallow black plastic tray before walking away.

Catania snagged it before Ally could even react. "I've got this."

"What? Why? I've got money, Nia."

"I know, but I also know I interrupted your afternoon and took it over. So, let me treat, okay?"

Ally studied her for a moment, arms crossed over her chest, and finally nodded. "Okay. Can I leave the tip?"

"Sure." She grabbed her jacket, which lay in the booth beside her, and dug her wallet out of the pocket. "So?" she said, eyeing her companion. "Your family?"

"Oh. Well." Ally cleared her throat and looked down. "It's pretty complicated. And honestly, nowhere near as exciting as your situation."

"Ah, come on! Now I'm intrigued." Catania glanced at her phone on the table when Oscar's unique ring began to play. She met Ally's gaze. "Saved by the bell."

⁂⁂⁂⁂

Catania drove back to her apartment and dropped Ally off so she could finish her housekeeping work, then went on to the crime scene where she met Oscar. She found herself in the middle of nowhere off Hwy 50 West, a long stretch of prairie that led to a handful of smaller towns northwest of Pueblo.

She spotted the sedan that she and Oscar typically used for work, though it was empty. Her partner and three uniformed police were all standing around a site about fifty yards off the road.

Pulling the Jeep to a stop behind the old Crown Victoria, she grabbed her phone and notepad before climbing out. The mild November day had turned colder, the wind picking up in the wild, open space along the highway. Pulling her long coat tighter around her, she headed to the quartet, her booted footfalls crunching on the dead vegetation.

"Hey, guys. What we got?" she asked, steeling herself for what she may see.

"Dead woman," Oscar said unnecessarily as he indicated the body at their feet.

Catania squatted down next to her, pushing her personal thoughts and feelings aside as she allowed her professional indifference to take over. The woman was dressed in what looked to be a summer dress, the kind that slips on over the head with a flowing skirt and spaghetti straps over the shoulders. She was obviously missing undergarments, no bra or panties, and her feet were bare.

Her gaze turned to the woman's face, the expression relaxed. She saw no outward sign of damage or wound—no bullet wound, no stabbing wounds, or rips to the dress. There was no blood, and a closer look at her neck showed discoloration. She also noticed the unusual spider web tattoo that spread over half of her neck and down to her back, though it was impossible to see how far because of how she was lying. Catania returned her attention to the bruising.

"Definitely looks like she was strangled," she noted. "We'll have to see if the M.E. finds petechiae or that her hyoid bone is broken. Any identification on her?"

"Nothing," Oscar said. "She was just like this when we arrived, and the guy who found her said he didn't touch her or anything on the scene."

Catania stood. "Who found her?"

"A guy who works at one of the prisons up near Canon City," one of the uniformed officers said, hitching his thumb up Hwy 50 toward the small town where nine prisons were clustered in a large complex. "He's a corrections officer. Drives this route every single day, so he noticed her."

Catania nodded. "Where's he at now?"

"He went on down to the station," Oscar explained. "Borger is talking to him, getting his statement."

"Okay."

Looking back at their victim, Catania noticed something about the woman who looked to be in her late forties or older. Her red hair looked to be a bottle job. But what caught her eye as odd, aside from the woman wearing a summer dress, were the soles of her feet.

"Oscar?" she said, bringing her finger up to run the pad over rough skin. "What would you say would cause calluses on the bottom of your feet?"

"Calluses?" Oscar asked, stepping up next to her.

"Yeah." She met his confused gaze. "What would make you get calluses on your feet?"

He shrugged, shoving his hands into the pockets of his trousers to jiggle his keys and change. "Going around barefoot. Sandals, maybe."

"Agreed." She indicated the autumn-dead ground around them. "In autumn in Colorado?" She reached over and tugged at the overcoat he wore over the wrinkled suit jacket. "And, a little cold for a summer dress, don't you think?"

Oscar looked down at the woman as he chewed on his bottom lip. Seeming to come to some sort of conclusion in his mind, he nodded. "The summer dress can be explained. She could have it on for a million reasons, or someone else could have put it on her. But the calluses..."

"The calluses."

"You're wanting to look outside of Colorado, aren't you?"

She ran her hands through her hair, studying the woman's feet to make sure Oscar's conclusion was in fact what her gut was telling her. "Yup. Gut feeling. Missing persons maybe in Florida, down south somewhere. Mexico." She shrugged and let out a heavy sigh. "Who knows."

"Nia," Oscar warned. "It's entirely possible that this lady just enjoys being barefoot, even in cold weather. Maybe she has warm, comfy carpeting in her house."

Catania made a noise of contemplation, then something else caught her eye. She reached into the pocket of her jacket and tugged out the latex gloves she'd snagged before leaving her Jeep. Wiggling her fingers into them, she squatted again and lightly touched the woman's big toe. Taking a closer look, she saw what she was looking for.

"Look," she said, looking up to see Oscar leaning over her. "Pretty deep indention where the toe piece would be on flip-flops or the type of sandal that either wraps around the big toe or goes between your toes."

"You're right. Yeah, I see it." The two detectives stood erect, the officers looking back at them. "This woman is definitely not from around here."

Chapter Seven

Catania stood in front of the mirror in the women's room and looked into the eyes of the reflection that stared back at her. She puffed her cheeks out before blowing out a loud breath, preparing herself for the interview she was about to do. She took in her women's cut suit, light gray with tiny black pinstripes. Reaching up, she straightened the jacket a bit before turning and walking out of the room, the chunky heels of her shoes clicking on the tile floor.

Walking up to Interview Room 2, Catania put a smile on her face to acknowledge the man who sat on one side of the small, rectangular table, two plastic chairs on either side.

"Good morning, Mr. Tanner." She took the chair across from the slender blond man with large, green eyes. She slapped her notebook down onto the table and set a small recorder next to it. "I'm Detective Catania d'Giovanni. My partner, Oscar Riley, whom you spoke to on the phone, won't be joining us today." She eyed him, curious of his reaction to that news. She and Oscar had decided to send her in alone, a woman, considering that he'd mentioned to Oscar what he wanted to talk about and what Catania intended to try and get out of him.

"Uh, okay," he said, nodding. He was dressed in jeans and a V-neck sweater. The Denver Broncos baseball cap he wore was perched atop his head, revealing some of his bangs and giving him a boyish innocence even as his unshaven face and tired eyes belied a man in his late thirties.

"Can I call you Kevin?" she asked conversationally, opening up her notebook to a clean page and jotting down across the top the date, time, and the name, *Kevin Tanner – Luhan/Gomez case.*

"Sure. That's fine."

"Do you mind if I record this, Kevin?" she asked, tapping the recorder.

"Uh, no. Go ahead. I've got nothing to hide," he said, clasping his hands on the table in front of him.

Catania glanced at his hands, noting his thumbs were fidgeting nervously. She also noticed they were big hands, rough, a working man's hands. She reached over and hit the Record button on the recorder and turned her focus to her companion.

"Okay, I'm sitting here with Kevin Tanner. Kevin, you're here of your own volition and can leave at any time. You are not under arrest and you've agreed to tell your story and answer any questions, correct?"

"Yes."

"Okay, great. Tell me why you're here."

"Well, I'm here to talk about Ana."

"Ana?" Catania asked, cocking her head slightly. Though she knew exactly why he was there, she didn't want him to know that. She wanted to see how similar the facts were compared to the bit he'd told Oscar.

"Anastasia, sorry. Anastasia Luhan, the woman who was murdered." He cleared his throat, bringing up a hand to rub the back of his neck before adjusting his baseball cap only to return that hand to its mate on the table. "I, uh, I'm the father of the baby she was carrying."

Catania didn't react even as her jaw was dropping inside.

"After I heard about what happened to her..." He looked away and swallowed, rubbing at his chin before returning his attention to her. "I felt I should come in."

"Okay. Why don't you start at the beginning, Kevin. How did you know Anastasia?"

"I met her where she worked. You probably know she was the manager at Loaf 'N Jug over on Fourth Street. I work for Grumble & Co., so we met because of that."

"What is Grumble & Co.?" Catania asked, pen poised over her notepad.

"Uh, a distributor to various places in Pueblo. Foods, beer, that kind of stuff. I dealt with the imported beers for a handful of stores here in town."

Her eyes flicked up to him for a moment before jotting down the new information. "Alright."

"Anyway, so it started out as just chatting, that kind of thing. Maybe a little flirting. I was having problems in my marriage, she was having issues with Jerry." He shrugged. "You know, just kind of commiserating together, I guess."

Catania sat back in her chair. "Were you dating?"

"No. No, nothing like that. I mean, we got close, obviously," he explained, letting out an exasperated sigh. "But it was never anything like that. We were together twice, maybe three times, that was it."

She could hear the earnest tone of his voice but was still skeptical. "'Together.' As in, the two of you had sex two, maybe three times?" At his nod she continued. "Okay, so then what happened?"

"Ana got pregnant. She told me right away. See, we'd already decided by that point to not see each other like that anymore. I was trying to work on my marriage and she said she was afraid of Jerry finding out. She said she was afraid of Jerry, period." He studied his hands and added softly. "She said he'd kill us if he found out."

"Did Jerry know about the pregnancy?

"No. At least, that's what she told me. I don't know if he found out somehow. But, one night I met with Ana and Aaron to decide—"

"Aaron Gomez?" Catania asked, surprised.

He met her gaze. "Yeah. Eric's father."

"Aaron knew about you and Anastasia? And the baby?"

"He was helping us find someone to take it."

Catania stared at him, stunned at this tidbit that Oscar hadn't told her. She had to assume his conversation with Kevin hadn't gotten this far. "Okay. So, Anastasia was going to continue with the pregnancy, then? What about Jerry?"

"She was planning to break it off with him, she told me. Before the pregnancy was obvious. Or," he added. "He thought it was his."

Catania nodded. "I see. So, the plan was to give it up for adoption?"

"Well, Aaron said he knew of some guy who was willing to take it. I guess him and his wife weren't able to have kids or something."

Interest definitely piqued, Catania was ready to write again. "Do you know who this man is?"

Kevin shook his head. "No. I know they were supposed to meet with him at some point, but I don't know if it happened before…well, before." Again he cleared his throat. He shook his head. "I never saw this coming, Detective. I just can't believe this happened to her. Ana was a good person." He brought a hand up and swiped roughly at his left eye.

"I know," Catania said softly. "It's a horrible thing." She grew silent as he pulled himself together, his emotions clearly threatening to break. "Can I get you anything, Kevin? Coffee? A Coke from the machine?"

"A Coke, please," he muttered, covering his face with his hands.

Without a word, Catania pushed her chair back from the table and excused herself, taking his unspoken plea for what it was: he was about to break down and didn't want an audience. She'd seen it a million times in situations like this, and wanted to give him the respect and space he deserved.

Closing the door softly behind her, she reached into her hip pocket as she headed for the break room where the vending machines were. Bringing out some change, she nodded at a couple of officers who were eating their lunch and playing on their phones. That made her reach for her own phone and jet off a text to Oscar, who moments later appeared in the break room in response.

"Hey," he said. "So?"

"This goes so deep, Oscar," she said, eyeing him as she stepped up to the Coke machine. She sorted through the coins in her palm. "Shit. Do you have a dime?"

The older man reached into his pocket and pulled out a few singles, handing her one. "What do you mean?

"Thanks. Well, not only is Kevin Tanner the father of Anastasia's baby, but according to him, she was planning to go full term, dump DeHererra, and she, Tanner, and Aaron Gomez were in cahoots to find someone to take the baby."

Oscar stared at her before handing her another dollar. "Get me one too, will ya?"

Smiling at her partner's antics, she did as asked. He took the cold twenty-ounce plastic bottle from her. "Jesus Christ. Do you buy it?"

Catania tapped her fingernails on the red cap of the bottle she held as she contemplated his question, one she'd asked herself over the past half an hour. "I don't know. I think so. He seems very genuine and pretty upset by the murders, but I don't know."

"You should get a sample," Oscar suggested, twisting off the cap of his soda and taking a drink.

Catania raised the bottle to eye level and grinned at him. "Already plan to." She clapped him on the shoulder before heading back to Kevin Tanner.

ᘓ ᘓ ᘗ ᘗ

Catania waited a moment before raising her fist and knocking again. This time she heard movement on the other side of the door before locks were disengaged and the door was pulled open. She put a smile on her face and held up the packaged carrot cake she'd bought at the bakery on her way over.

Matteo appeared in the opened doorway and glanced at her then down at the cake. "Can you come back in twenty minutes?"

She stared at him, blinking a few times. "Uh, okay. Sure."

"Thanks." Grabbing the cake out of her hands, the door was slammed in her face and locks reengaged.

"Alrighty, then."

Glancing at her phone to get the time, she sighed and turned away from the second-floor door and headed down the hall, deciding to find Karen and see how things were going from her perspective.

Trotting down the long staircase, Catania smiled and nodded at another resident who gave her a small wave as they passed on the third stair. Reaching the main floor, Catania trailed her fingers over the large, round finial as she took the turn off the stairs and made her way down the main hall past the etched glass front doors.

She passed the doors of two apartments, hearing the muffled sounds of what seemed to be a TV behind one. Knowing the kitchen was at the back of the large house, she headed in that direction but stopped when she heard Karen's voice, followed by Jason's.

Following the voices, she ended up at an open doorway, smaller than the average with a rounded top. She ducked her head under the doorframe and slipped into the small room beyond. It was the door tucked underneath the staircase that typically would lead to a coat closet or the basement stairs, but in this case it opened up to a room about the size of a large walk-in closet. Half of it was a small nook with limited headroom and an octagonal stained glass window bathing the space in blue and green light. Catania was surprised to find the seemingly subterranean room was actually high enough to accommodate a window to let in the natural light.

"Higher, Karen. I can't do this if you don't hold it up higher."

"I'm trying, damn it! My arms are only so long."

Chuckling to herself, Catania turned to the right, surprised to see a short, narrow hallway that took a sharp turn to the left and ended at the top of a staircase. She headed down, the rubber soles of her tennis shoes thudding on the wood.

"Hey, you got some issues down here?" she called as she went.

"Hello?" Karen said.

"Hey there." Catania left the stairwell to find herself in a single room that was the size of a large bedroom. A small kitchenette was tucked against the wall to the left, a curtained-off area with a toilet and bath tub straight ahead, and the lion's share of the room was empty to the right.

"Nia! Thank god. Help!"

Her focus back to the kitchenette area, she saw Karen on her tiptoes holding up a large ceiling fan as Jason worked to wire it into the ceiling. Hurrying over there, she reached up and took the burden from the shorter woman, easily hoisting it up closer to where Jason was trying to finish his task.

"Whew," the older woman said, brushing her hands together before wiping them on the thighs of her jeans. "Great timing."

"For who?" Catania teased, grinning down at her sister-in-law.

"Can you move it a little to the left, Nia?" Jason asked from where he stood on the stepladder.

Doing his bidding, Catania looked back at Karen. "What is this place? Got a new resident moving in?"

"No, this is for either the groundskeeper or cook," Karen explained, watching Jason's fingers work with the wires.

"It's adorable as heck," she said, looking around the area even as she continued to hold up the fan. "Like a little Hobbit home or something."

"Isn't it?" Karen agreed, hands on wide hips. "I think it's just cute as a button. We're trying to get it ready so I can bring in someone as an on-site cook. I just can't do all this by myself anymore, Nia."

"Yeah, that's what Jason was saying at dinner the other day."

"Okay, you can let it go. I think," Jason said, slowly moving his hands away.

Catania removed her hands, noting it was wobbly. "Or not." She quickly grabbed it again.

"Damn it. This old wiring is going to be the death of me."

She grinned up at him. "You are an electrician, ya know."

"Cute," he said, returning her grin. "No time to do this whole place."

"So, what's in it for the cook or groundskeeper?"

"Room and board and a small wage," Karen said, walking over to the long counter in the kitchenette that ran the span of the wall, an apartment-sized fridge on one end, stove on the other, with a sink positioned in the middle leaving counter space on either side. Bottles of cleaning products were gathered there, as well as a roll of paper towels and package of sponges.

"Okay, it's good now, Nia," Jason said, stepping down from the stepladder.

Lowering her arms, Catania nodded. "Definitely cute." She turned to Karen. "So, how's Matteo been? Terrorizing the other tenants yet?"

Karen smiled as she sprayed down the outside of the avocado-green fridge door with one of the cleaning products. "Not yet. He's actually pretty quiet, to be honest."

Both women turned when the bar light above the sink was no longer the only light source in the room. All three bulbs were alight and the fan blades were slowly beginning to spin. Jason, who stood over by the entrance to the room, had his finger on the light switch, looking up at his handiwork.

"Okay, Karen," he said, walking over to the fan and reaching up to tug three times on the chain which controlled the fan, the blades lazily coming to a stop. He left the light on and walked over to Catania, giving her a quick one-armed hug and his wife a kiss to the cheek. "I have to get back to work."

"Okay. Thanks, Jay," Karen said, accepting the kiss. "Are you going to be home for dinner?"

Jason halted halfway to the doorway which led to the stairwell. "Uh," he said, sparing a glance back at her. "Possibly. Not sure."

"Okay. See you later."

"Bye, Jason." Catania watched him go and turned to Karen, noting the troubled look on her face as she turned back to her cleaning. She wasn't exactly close to Karen, but she did like her. "Everything okay?" she asked lightly, not wanting to make anything too heavy if Karen didn't want or need to talk.

Karen glanced back toward the vacant stairwell before briefly meeting Catania's concerned gaze. She gave a one-shoulder shrug. "It's okay, I guess. Some days he's so moody." She set the spray cleaner down on the counter which she leaned back against, arms crossed over a full bosom. "I know we've been married for a long time and things certainly can cool. But..." She shook her head. "I even bought some of that sexy lingerie he loves so much."

Catania felt sorry for the woman by the sad and disappointed expression on her face. "Nothing, huh?"

"Nope. Didn't help a lick. Tried to get him to talk to his doctor about those pills men can take." She snorted. "Huge mistake. I tried to tell him it was no big deal and he got absolutely furious with me." Karen burst into laughter, giving Catania a quick hug. "I'm so sorry. I seriously doubt you want to know this about your brother."

She returned the hug and joined in the laughter. "Hey, I'd rather hear this than about Dino, self-proclaimed Italian Stallion."

Twenty minutes later Catania was once again standing in front of Matteo's closed door. He responded to her knock, opening the door and staring out at her.

"I said twenty minutes, not twenty minutes times two."

࿊ ࿊ ࿊ ࿊

Catania had begun to change her route home from work when she left late, prowling the way she knew Ally would be walking home from the diner. She had come to understand the proud woman, and knew she'd never ask her for a ride, though Catania wished she would. She worried about her, and if she was honest with herself, enjoyed her company. She'd caught her a few times on her way out the door or after a quick dinner stop, and she'd run Ally home when she got off work.

The guy at the diner had told her that Ally had left about twenty minutes before, and admittedly Catania felt like a stalker as she prowled the streets to see if she could catch up to Ally before she reached her house. She had to laugh at her ridiculousness, but in truth, she felt protective of Ally. Something about her was so strong yet so incredibly vulnerable.

She was just past the ballpark when she saw a

figure hurrying along the sidewalk, a blond ponytail spotlighted as the person passed beneath a streetlight before disappearing into the shadows again.

Knowing the brick house with the green garage door was just a little way down, Catania slowed her Jeep so as not to scare the waitress, but she did want to make sure she made it into the house okay. She pulled up to the curb in front of a gray two-story building with a houseful of lights on and waited. To her surprise and confusion, Ally walked right past the brick house and hurried to an alleyway a few houses down.

"Where the hell is she going?" She tried to think where that alley would lead to.

Pulling away from the curb, she drove past the brick house and took a right at the next street, finding herself at the intersection of another residential street. She spotted Ally hurrying across the street only to vanish into the continuing alley, so she pressed on.

At the next corner, she could go straight or right, a huge apartment complex to her left. She turned right and found herself in a small business area. A gas station and small shopping center were to her right, and on the left a little way down was a two-story whitewashed brick building. There was a large, blacked-out front window, and the glass panes in the door were covered by posters. But what caught her attention was the sign above the door: *Haven House*.

Movement catching her eye, she saw Ally scurry out of the alley that connected this street to the residential one. Catania pulled into the parking lot of the shopping center and watched as her friend nearly ran across the street, straight to the two-story building. An African American woman pushed open the glass door, the two women sharing a brief hug before Ally disappeared inside, the black woman disappearing behind her.

Confused, Catania pulled her phone out and quickly searched to see exactly what Haven House was. She gasped when she read that it was a women's shelter that promised to protect victims of domestic violence until the women could get themselves back on their feet again.

"Oh, Ally," she whispered.

Chapter Eight

*T*he lens took in the small, generic motel room, showing the chained door with instruction placard attached just under the peephole. *The large window was covered by faded, drab curtains, a bit of pink light from the neon motel sign beyond creeping around one edge.*

An old-model television sat on a rolling stand in front of the window, the sound turned low. On the screen was Dick Clark holding court over Times Square for his New Year's Rockin' Eve, *the numbers 2004 scrolling across the banner at the bottom of the screen.*

In the foreground was the bed, sheets and blankets in a tangled mess. Lying on the rumpled bottom sheet, which still covered the mattress nearest the camera, was a redheaded woman, naked and lying on her back. Her right leg lay straight out, her left bent at the knee. Her right hand was lightly trailing fingernails over her stomach while the other reached out to the man who sat on the edge of the bed, his back to the camera. He was also naked, shoulders broad. His hair was dark and long, reaching well past his upper back.

"That was awesome, baby," she said, her tone seductive but not entirely genuine.

"Yeah, all two minutes of it," the man said, a hand appearing as it ran through his hair before dropping out of sight in front of him again.

"Aw, come on, stud." The woman sat up, turning

her back to the camera as she pressed her breasts against his back. An expansive tattoo could be seen, a spider web extending from the side of her neck to trail down over her shoulder to the center of her back, ending in a teardrop. "I know just what to do to get my baby excited."

She placed a trail of kisses along his shoulder, reaching up to brush the long strands of his hair aside. He roughly pushed her hand aside. "Stop."

"Baby, don't be that way." She reached around him, her hand having an obvious destination in mind. "I know exactly how to blow your mind. And..." She let out a sexy chuckle deep in her throat as she seemed to have found her target.

Abruptly the man stood, the redhead woman falling forward and off the bed as the man walked out of frame. A disembodied grunt and growl sounded before the woman reappeared, her pretty face twisted with rage.

"What the fuck? What did you do that for?" She got to her feet and brought a hand up to touch her eye, looking at the fingertips as she pulled them away. "I could have really gotten hurt. If you give me a black eye, I'll fucking kill you."

Snickering could be heard near the microphone on the camera. "Yeah, I'd like to see you try. I told you to stop. It's not my fault if you don't listen."

The image wobbled for a moment before it sailed downward, showing the floor and a man's bare feet as well as two of the three legs of a tripod.

"Why are you leaving?" the woman asked, her voice close the camera, sadness replacing the anger in her tone. "You said we were going to spend New Year's together."

"Yeah, well I gotta go."
Darkness.

ꔮ ꔮ ꔮ ꔮ

Catania felt Ally's gaze on her. She took her attention off the road just long enough to look at her. "What?"

"Are you sure your family won't mind? I know you guys are close and I really don't want to intrude, Nia."

"Nah, you won't intrude, I promise." Catania grinned. "Besides, it'll give me a break from my mother's incessant chatter."

"Great," Ally muttered.

"Just joking. No, trust me, even though she raised five and a half kids, my mother feels her only real talent and accomplishment is her cooking." She shrugged. "I figure you two will actually have something to talk about." She spared a glance at her passenger. "I know you cook and are pretty darn good at it."

"I really enjoy it," Ally said, a bit of happiness in her voice. "I don't know, I guess it speaks to my nurturing nature."

"I think that's really great. I enjoy some baking, but I'm just not real into it. I do love to eat, though."

"What is your last name, Nia?"

Eyebrows drawn, Catania maneuvered her Jeep skillfully along the mountain road with all its twists and turns. "Why?"

"So I know what to call your mother and father."

"Oh, no, no. See, you don't understand. My mother sees it in the way that, if we've brought someone home, no matter if it's a friend or a romantic entanglement, that person means enough to us to let her cook for them. So," she said, holding up a finger for emphasis. "'Mamma' it is."

"Wait, I'm supposed to call your mother Mamma?" Ally asked, shock in her voice. At Catania's nod she said, "Huh. Come to think of it, I haven't called anyone Mamma in…ever."

"Ever? Okay, what about Mom? Mother?" Catania's eyebrows shot up at the three separate shakes of Ally's head. "Wow." They drove in silence for a moment as she contemplated this. "What did you call your mother?"

"Aunt Kathy," Ally responded, her voice flat. "She raised me until I was thirteen."

Catania was surprised by the information but said nothing, allowing Ally to tell her what she would as she got them closer and closer to the lake house where the family would be spending Thanksgiving.

"Then," Ally continued quietly as her focus seemed to be on the passing scenery through the passenger-side window. "She died."

"I'm sorry, Ally," Catania said softly, meeting Ally's gaze.

"Thanks," Ally said with a small, tight smile before she turned away again.

Catania was filled with questions, but decided to simply ask, "Where did you go?"

"The System," she responded after a moment. "Bounced around to various foster homes, that kind of thing. The problem is, people want babies, not thirteen-year-old orphans."

"Like I hear people say about adopting puppies and kittens," Catania said absently.

"Exactly. Well, I ended up with the Porter family.

I remember it well. It was a month before my fourteenth birthday." She let out a heavy sigh.

"Was it a good family?"

Ally shrugged, looking briefly at Catania. "They weren't looking for any sort of daughter. Well, let me say, I suppose they were. They were looking for a daughter-in-law. Their son, Ian, essentially looked me over like I was a mare on a selling block. With the approval of the Crown Prince, I was theirs."

"Wait, what?" Catania asked, baffled. The narrow, two-lane road they were on ended and they pulled into a small, picturesque mountain town. "What do you mean?"

"Ian was twenty and ready to settle down. I was what he was looking for, I guess. By the time I was pushing fifteen, we'd been dating for almost a year. It was awful," she said, shaking her head. "I had to take him to school dances, any football games or whatever I wanted to go to, he was there." She chuckled ruefully. "I honestly don't think he cared for a second about my world, just wanted to make sure I wasn't talking to any other boys."

Catania had no idea what to say for a long moment, this newest bit of information stunning as it somersaulted around in her brain. She drove through the mile-long town and turned off on a dirt road that would lead to the family land. "Wait," she finally managed. "How much older was this guy than you?"

"Um, six, seven years."

"That is a ton at that age."

"A lifetime." Ally blew out a breath. "Anyway, at sixteen his parents signed off on the marriage license."

Yet again, Catania was taken by surprise. She slowed her Jeep as the road hadn't been plowed and she had to be careful to follow the deep tire tracks in the snow from those who had arrived at the lake house the night before.

"You married him? This Ian guy?" At Ally's nod, she asked, "Did you want that?"

"No," was all Ally said, her tone making it clear the conversation had ended. "All this snow is so beautiful."

Catania took Ally's cue and followed her friend's new train of thought. "It's absolutely gorgeous. Look at those mountains surrounding us. So blue."

"Wait, did that street sign say, *Bubble Butt Way*?" Ally laughed, turning in her seat to see the homemade street sign they'd just passed.

Catania grinned. "It did. This is all our land," she explained, indicating the seemingly endless snowy wonderland around them with a wave of her hand. "Two hundred acres all told. When we were younger, my dad made us wooden street signs to map out all the trails and paths on the property. We used to try and outdo each other."

"How fun!" Ally cackled. "*Snot Pot Road*. Whoa, okay, that's unsettling. *Decapitation Circle*."

"That would be Matteo. What can I say? The boy loves his horror movies and violent video games."

Five minutes later, the Jeep turned down the quarter-mile-long driveway of the large cabin, which had been added onto over the years. The partially frozen lake lay beyond. The large, snow-covered driveway looked like a small used car lot, Catania the last family member to show due to work. Even Oscar and Linda had already arrived.

She pulled off to the side so she wasn't blocking anyone, nor could she be blocked. Ally had agreed to accompany Catania as long as she was able to return to town for her late shift at the diner. Catania was more than fine with that as it gave her a reason to duck out when she'd had enough family time.

"Okay, here we are." Catania killed the engine and pulled the key out of the ignition, looking over at Ally who looked up at the cabin before them. "You okay?"

Ally nodded. "Nervous. Looks like a lot of people."

"I know. It's a problem with being from a large family. But, it will only be my parents and brothers and whomever they may have brought. Oh, and my partner, Oscar, is here, too, with his wife Linda. You've met him at Randy's."

"Oh yeah. Really nice guy."

"He is. Their kids are spread around the country for Thanksgiving this year, all to come back for Christmas, so they're spending the day with us."

The cabin was abuzz with noise, the men in the living room talking, and drinking beer and spiked eggnog. Paul and Dino were arguing over how to get the fire bigger in the massive stone fireplace, which was the great room's centerpiece.

Catania glanced at Ally, only to see her looking around like a deer caught in headlights. She smiled and nudged her with her shoulder. "Come on, let's head to the kitchen."

She led the way through the huge dining room into the kitchen where her mother and Karen and, to her shock, Dino's woman-of-the-hour from a few weeks ago, Melanie, were cooking and chatting.

"Well, finally!" Antonia exclaimed from her spot at the stove. She held the spoon straight up in the pan she'd been stirring in. "Karen," she said, no other instruction.

The blond woman took over the stirring. "Hey, Nia."

"Hi, Karen." Catania accepted the tight hug and loud cheek kiss she received. "Mamma, I want you to meet my friend, Ally. I told you about her on the phone."

"Hello, Ally!" Antonia grabbed Ally in a firm hug and left a kiss on each cheek. "Welcome. Such a beautiful young woman. Look at this," she continued, lightly running her fingers through Ally's long blond hair, which lay loose around her shoulders. "See, Catania?" she said, giving her daughter the evil eye. "You should never have cut that beautiful hair of yours."

"And," Catania said, louder than her mother's continued protestations as she grabbed Ally by the hand and tugged her away from her mother's octopus hands. "This is my sister-in-law, Karen. She's married to Jason who was standing over by the piano in the other room, and this is my brother, Dino's..." She eyed Melanie, no idea where the two sat in their relationship, or better to say, where Melanie *felt* they sat in their relationship.

"I'm Dino's girlfriend. Nice to meet you, Ally." The younger woman extended a welcoming hand to Ally, who took it.

"Do you like to cook?" Antonia asked, returning to Ally's side like a shooed fly to a crumb on the counter.

"Uh, yes. I do."

"Excellent." The older woman reached up to put her arm around Ally's shoulders, leading her toward the stove. She looked over her shoulder at Catania.

"You go. Go play with your brothers."

Left staring and feeling utterly rejected, Catania did as told.

☙ ☙ ❧ ❧

Once everyone was seated around the massive dining room table, two leaves added, Alberto spoke. Surrounded by family and friends and tons of food on the table, he stood from his seat at the head.

"Everyone, grab your wine." He waited for everyone to comply, looking like the proud papa he was. "On this Thanksgiving Day, I want to say I am a happy man. All my children are here. Paul, I am not pleased that none of your children decided to honor their father or grandmother today. Even Matteo left his video games and Leonardo left his studies to be with us. Yes, son, I know about that huge paper due when you return after the holiday," Alberto said with a warning look to his youngest. The smile returned to his face as he continued. "But, instead, we have good friends." He smiled and raised his glass in the direction of Oscar and Linda and Ally. "Our dear friends Oscar and his beautiful wife Linda. Linda, my greatest apologies that your husband has to cover my daughter's behind every single day."

Laughter erupted, including the wife of Catania's partner. "She's the only woman I'd allow it for," Linda exclaimed, raising her own glass.

"A good woman, Oscar. Hold on to that one. But," Alberto continued. "We also have a new friend today. Ally, it is a pleasure to have you in my home."

Ally, who was seated next to Catania, gave him a shy smile. "Thank you. I'm very happy to be here."

"Excellent. *Mangiare!*"

᪥ ᪥ ᪥ ᪥

"Okay, so you have to be able to picture Joe Friday over here," Oscar explained, a whiskey and Coke in his hand as he rose from the couch where he'd been sitting with Linda and Paul. He put his hands together as though the tumbler he held was the grip of a pistol. "'Be quiet,'" he said, imitating Catania's voice. She laughed from where she and Ally sat on the massive stone hearth. "'I hear the guy in the bedroom. He sounds like he's stuck or something.'" He handed his drink to Linda and resumed the position of his hands. "So, with the force of friggin' Jean-Claude Van Damme, she kicks the door open." He raised his foot and kicked through a pretend door. "'Freeze!'"

"Oh god," Catania groaned, covering her face.

"'Oh shit,'" Oscar said, voice flat, still pantomiming his partner's actions. "'Uh, I'm real sorry, guys,'" he said, backing away from the imaginary scene. "'Uh, carry on.'"

The room erupted into laughter, totally at Catania's expense. Face red, she emerged from behind her hands to see Ally looking at her, amusement dancing in her deep blue eyes.

Clearing her throat to try to get Ally's beautiful face out of her mind, she returned her attention to Oscar. "Yeah, shall we talk about the time you mistook gum for a used condom?"

"You wouldn't," Oscar drawled, reaching for his drink again.

Catania gave him a shit-eating grin. "Oh, I would."

With massive amounts of hugs, goodbyes, and leftovers to last for days, Catania and Ally were headed back toward town. Ally had to arrive for her shift in two hours, but Catania wanted to make sure they had plenty of time for the little stop she had planned. She'd pulled Karen aside and they'd spoken about her idea. Catania was thrilled that she was on board.

"So, did you have fun?" Catania asked, taking a left on *Training Bra Blvd.*

"I did." Ally gave her an incredibly serene smile. "Your mom is great. She really loves you guys. I'm just stunned at how much your family just kind of gathered us non-family right in." She grinned. "Linda is great, too. I really liked her. We swapped numbers."

"Oh, Linda scored your digits, huh?" Catania asked.

"Oh yeah, totally," Ally replied, the same teasing tone in her voice. "We're going to work out a way to sneak her out next Friday night, get past this week of Black Friday and all the madness, you know."

"Sweet. Hey, speaking of sweets, where on earth did you pull that cream bread recipe from? I honestly think my mother is ready to kick me out of the tree and stick you on the branch in my stead."

Ally let out a full-on laugh that Catania found adorable. She sounded so happy and carefree, something she hadn't seen in the usually quiet woman in the entirety of the time she'd known her. "I came up with that recipe during my first year in school."

"School?"

"Yeah. I...I'm a graduate of culinary school."

Catania's eyebrows shot up as she looked over at

her. "Seriously?" At Ally's nod, she added, "Why are you a waitress and part-time cook at the diner? You should be in a restaurant somewhere."

Ally sighed. "My degree is under my married name. I'm too afraid to use it. I pretty much stay working at places that will…" She gave Catania a side glance. "Help me out."

Finally reaching the highway that would lead back into town from the mountains, Catania slowed at the first traffic light they'd hit on the return trip. She studied Ally's profile for a moment. "He's looking for you, isn't he?"

"I think so, yes," Ally admitted softly.

Catania was quiet for a long moment, so many thoughts and emotions going through her mind. She'd already made her decision before she spoke with Karen, but now she was even more determined.

After a thirty-minute drive filled with idle chatter, Catania turned off the road she was on and onto a tree-lined side street, their skeletal branches frosted with the light snow they'd received the day before.

"Uh, Nia, the diner is back that way." Ally hitched her thumb in the correct direction.

"I know. I want to show you something first."

The Jeep pulled up in front of Aberdeen House. It was quiet; no cars or foot traffic out in the chilly early evening. Cutting the engine, Catania gave Ally a quick smile of encouragement before climbing out, her boots crunching on the packed snow.

"This is quite the house," Ally exclaimed, her words a puff of steam. "Is this a single residence?"

"Sadly, no. It's been broken up into so many different things over the years. Now, it's apartments." They reached the front door and Catania turned the knob and pushed one side of the large double doors open, indicating Ally should enter before her.

Door closed behind her, Catania retook the lead and led Ally down the long hallway to the kitchen. She glanced at her, curious what her reaction would be to such a wonderfully modern commercial kitchen.

"Nice, huh?"

"Beautiful. You could do some serious cooking in here," Ally said, trailing her fingertips over the five-burner gas stove and along polished countertops.

Catania headed to the pantry, where Karen had told her to go. There, just as she'd been directed, she found a ring of keys hanging on a hook behind the huge container of flour.

"Bingo. Okay, let's go back this way." Leading the way back toward the under-the-stairs apartment, she picked through the keys. "How are we doing on time?"

"My shift starts in about forty-five minutes," Ally said from behind her.

"Okay." Catania stopped in front of the rounded top door. "She said third silver key from the left... or not. Let's try the other left." The key inserted and turned and she was able to open the door. "Come on," she said, holding the door open for Ally.

"What is this? Oh, wow. I figured it would be a closet."

"Yeah, me too the first time. Isn't it wild?"

"This is so cool. It's like a fun little hideaway," Ally said, walking around the small space, immediately going to the stained glass window. "I bet this is stunning in the sunlight," she said, grinning at Catania. With the sun already down, the artificial overhead light was all they had.

"Come on, there's more."

The two headed down the narrow hallway and stairway to the lower level, which had been completely repainted since Catania had been there last, drywall hung to create a tiny but private bathroom. The worn carpeting had been ripped out, replaced with engineered, medium-stained wood flooring.

"What is this place?" Ally asked, walking over to the kitchenette before checking out the small bathroom. The bathtub had been replaced by a stand-up shower to save space.

"Well, that's up to you," Catania said, leaning back against the counter. "See, I told you this was split into apartments. The residents here have some minor issues and need a little extra eyeball on them now and then. Part of their rent is breakfast and dinner, if they want it." She shoved her hands nervously into the pockets of her jeans and shrugged. "Karen needs a cook."

Ally nodded, seeming to understand what she'd just been told. "Okay," she drawled quietly. "So, what does this place have to do with that?"

"Well, see, along with a small monthly salary, room and board is also part of the compensation for whomever he or *she* happens to be that takes the job."

"Wait, are you telling me that for working here as a cook for two meals a day in that crazy cool kitchen, you get to live here?" she asked, indicating the room around them.

Catania nodded. "That I am."

Ally looked around, seeming to disappear inside her own head and emotions for a moment. At length, she met Catania's understanding gaze. "It would be all mine?" Her voice was barely above a whisper.

"Yes."

"And, would I have to put it under my name?"

Catania smiled, shaking her head. "Hell, I bet if I spoke to Karen you could even put it under *my* name if you want. Ally, I'm going to protect you." She reached inside her flannel button-up and pulled out the badge she always wore on a chain around her neck, even when off duty. "That's what I do, right?"

Catania was taken aback when she suddenly had an armful of Ally. She smiled, holding the trembling woman to her. "You know," she added softly. "Just in case you want to change your digs."

Ally laughed through her tears. "You're a good investigator."

"Eh, it pays the bills."

Chapter Nine

*C*atania *found herself sitting on a couch in a dark room, only the light from a massive screen on the wall lighting the indefinable space. She looked at the pair on the screen and realized it was a scene from the 1980s' romantic comedy* Can't Buy Me Love. *The two stars, the still-gangly Patrick Dempsey and the pretty Amanda Peterson, portraying Ronald and Cindy, were in the scene.*

Sensing she wasn't alone, she glanced to her left to see Squirrel sitting next to her, a bucket of popcorn on her lap. The teen smiled at her.

"Love this movie," she said, tossing a handful of popcorn into her mouth.

Confused, Catania looked back to the movie, startled to see the blond actress on screen looking directly at her, even as her male counterpart continued to remain in character and deliver his lines.

"You should go find her," the actress said.

Catania pointed at herself. "Are you talking to me?"

"Of course. You better hurry. Time will run out soon." With those cryptic words, the actress returned her focus to the scene on the screen.

Confused, she looked to her left and saw Squirrel's bucket of popcorn lying on the couch, but the teen had vanished. Standing, she looked around the dim space, now noting there seemed to be an opening to a dark alleyway.

"Find her," she heard whispered.

Turning back to where the movie screen was, she now saw it was the other side of the rain-slicked street she stood on. Disoriented, she tried to get her bearings when she realized she was on a street in Pueblo, on the East side. Not a good part of town.

Her attention was caught by the sound of light giggling in the air. This returned her focus to the alleyway. Her natural defense was to reach for her service pistol, but she was unarmed. Deciding to continue on, she hurried to the mouth of the alleyway, parts awash with reflected moonlight in what seemed to be puddles of rain water.

"Squirrel?"

She saw movement farther into the alley so she started forward, eyes wide to see as much as possible. Entering the alley, she surreptitiously took in all her surroundings, left and right, just as she'd been taught as a rookie. She'd also been taught to listen to her instincts. Her first sergeant had told her that ability was known as The Gift. Every good cop had it.

She froze, a soft sound coming from the left. She studied the deep shadows that painted the brick wall of a building, the rust-orange ladder of the fire escape catching her eye, as well as a tattered poster for the 1997 movie Titanic *taped to the brick. Confused by the randomness of it, she moved her focus back from the poster to the area where she'd heard the noise, which she heard again, though this time it was farther away down the alley.*

She stopped, realizing what she was hearing was a name, whispered, almost hummed. Initially she thought perhaps it was her name, but she was hearing "Nene."

Nobody called her Nene. It was always her full name or Nia.

"Hello? Are you talking to me?" she called out, wondering if perhaps there was someone else out there.

She heard a short but sharp scream that sent her running. Her tennis shoes slapped on the wet, pitted pavement, water splashing up the legs of her jeans as she passed more puddles. She came to a sudden stop as the alley ended in a brick wall. She could turn left or she could turn right. More humming caught her attention, humming that was closer and sounded like a familiar voice.

"Best not go this way, honey," a woman's voice said to her right.

Catania would have found it funny if she didn't have such a feeling of dire panic in her heart. Natalie Cole leaned against the side of the building, filing her nails.

"What?"

Without another word, the talented woman pointed a well-filed nail in the opposite direction.

Catania barely had time to consider the absurdity of what was happening before she heard the scream again, sending her off at a sprint. She stopped short once again, horrified as she saw Squirrel pinned against the wall of yet another building in the alleyway maze. A large hand held her off the ground by her throat, the teen flailing uselessly at her attacker.

To her horror, the humanoid shadow leveled a brutal punch to the teen's stomach, causing her to cry out even as her body jerked against the hand that pinned her. She received several more punches and slaps to the face before, in a move so quick Catani didn't see it coming, the figure yanked Squirrel away from the wall and held her back against it, now facing the detective.

Again, she reached for her gun, but again was disappointed to find it missing. She stood not more than fifteen feet away from the duo and, no matter how hard she tried, could move no closer, her feet refusing to lift off the pavement. Unable to do anything physically, she decided to study the perp. It was the strangest thing she'd ever seen. She assumed it was male by its size, but it was literally like a shadow figure, solid black, yet only humanoid in shape. There were no discernable features, no details, just moving smoke.

"You helped kill me," it said, a muddy voice that sounded male, but absolutely no way to determine who it belonged to. It almost sounded like several men speaking in unison.

More creeped out than she'd ever been, Catania held her ground even though she didn't physically have a choice. "Who are you?"

"I am all this little whore will never be," he said with a growl. "I am what she made me."

"Who?" Catania asked, desperately trying to understand what he was trying to tell her. "Who are you talking about, because I don't think it's Squirrel."

"Squirrel," he mocked, a hand coming up in what almost looked to be a gentle, loving caress of the side of her face, beaten and bloody. The shadowy fingers grazed along the jawline before, in the blink of an eye, the other hand came up and cupped Squirrel's chin, jerking so hard sideways that the teen had no chance to react as her neck snapped with a sickening crunch.

"No!" Catania yelled, her eyes bulging in shock and distress as she watched Squirrel's lifeless body slump to the ground at her killer's feet. "You son of a bitch!" She could feel the figure's eyes on her and she swore he *was smiling.*

"*Indeed.*" *He stepped over his victim's body and headed down the alley before he stopped, glancing over his amorphous shoulder. "Good luck, Catania."*

Catania wrestled with the blankets and shot up as her scream echoed throughout her bedroom. She gasped for air, eyes huge as the darkness of that alley dissipated, revealing the early morning beginning to come in through the blinds.

Realizing she was safe in her own bed and that Squirrel wasn't dead—she hoped—she flopped back down on the mattress, a hand flopping down on her heaving chest.

"Jesus, what a fucked-up dream," she gasped. "Fuck!" she yelled, startled as her phone's ring tone sounded again. Figuring that's probably what had woken her, she reached over to the bedside table and brought the phone to her ear after tapping the button to answer. "D'Giovanni...Hey, Gwen, how's it going?" she asked once the Deputy Medical Examiner identified herself. "Okay...Yeah, right. No I.D. yet, no...Okay, be there in twenty minutes, bye."

Blowing out a breath, she ended the call and scrubbed her face with her hands to pull herself fully out of that dream that stayed with her.

❦❦❦❦

Catania chewed nervously on a fingernail, the heels of her boots echoing in the cement tunnel she was walking in. She hated going down there, but in her line of work, there were times when it just was unavoidable. Gwen hadn't told her on the phone what she had for her, so the mystery continued.

"Hey, Tracy," she said, and accompanied her verbal acknowledgement of the morgue intern with a small wave. "Thanks," she said, walking through the door to the main office that the young pre-med student held open for her.

She made her way to the back where, as Gwen put it, the magic happened. Gwen Sweeney was a beautiful black woman who looked far more like she should have been backing Tina Turner as an Ikette in 1968 rather than a pathologist in the Pueblo County morgue.

"Is Nia here yet?" Gwen called from her office, tucked next to the M.E.'s office. "If she ain't, you call her and tell her white ass to get here! I ain't got all damn day!"

Catania chuckled as she rounded the corner to look into the small office, neat as a pin, just like the lovely woman sitting behind the desk. "I told you give me twenty minutes," she said, glancing at her watch. "Eighteen. Jeesh."

Dr. Sweeney looked at her, looking startled behind her stylish glasses, which she yanked off and tossed to her desk. "Come on," she said, hurrying around her desk, high heels clicking on the tile. "I have something to show you."

Catania followed the fashionable woman into the room where examinations were conducted, and on the stainless steel table was the Jane Doe that had been discovered in the field a few days before. She was naked, only covered by a sheet to her neck. Catania knew the autopsy had already been performed, the victim essentially sewn back together just enough to keep her intact.

"Okay," Gwen said, grabbing a report that rested

on the dead woman's covered chest. "We got all the samples back, toxicology, all the fun stuff. She had nothing in her system at all, no alcohol, drugs, clean as a whistle."

Catania nodded, taking the report she was handed, flipping through the pages and data that would be added to the woman's Murder Book. "Okay. I'm going to guess she was strangled?" she asked, nodding at the woman on the table.

"Yup. Look here." Gwen walked over to the victim and pulled the sheet back just enough to reveal her throat. "See all the bruising here? Pretty consistent with manual strangulation. Someone used their hand." She met Catania's gaze. "Pretty strong fella, too. I'd wager no ropes or garrote." She reached her hand out and, just shy of actually touching the pale, grayish flesh, spread her fingers out, the tips lined up with the bruising. "One hand." She shook her head, removing her hand. "He meant business. And, from the amount of petechiae in her eyes, I think this was a long, slow process." She crossed her arms over her ample chest. "As sick of a dude as this was, it gets worse."

"How can it possibly get worse?" Catania asked, disturbed by what she was being told about her victim.

"Well, when we got her tissue results back, there was a substantial amount cellular decay."

Catania eyed her. "Meaning?"

"Meaning, she was frozen, postmortem. Whoever did this to her had her on ice for a prolonged period of time."

All Catania could do for a moment before she regained her composure was stare. "Wow. Any idea how long?"

Gwen nodded, pulling the sheet back up to just

under the victim's chin. That was one thing Catania greatly admired about the doctor: she always tried to maintain the dignity and grace of the people who appeared on her table.

"I don't have that information for you today, we need to run a few more tests. But, as soon as we have it, I'll drop you a ring. I figured I'd at least give you this information so you have something to nibble on in your investigation."

Catania nodded, chewing her bottom lip. She studied the dead woman's face for a long moment. "Yeah. I appreciate it. And, the sketch artist came in and did a rendering for the media, right?"

"Yep. I emailed it to you just before you finally showed up."

Catania glared at her colleague and friend's good-natured smile. "Alright. Anything else?"

"Nope. Good luck."

Good luck, Catania.

She shook her head mentally to get the voice of her dream tormentor out of her mind. She smiled at Gwen and reached out to lightly squeeze her arm. "Thanks, lady. I appreciate everything."

❧❧❧❧

Catania perched on the edge of the small desk that rested against the wall where the long whiteboard was in the conference room. She'd made copies of the coroner's report, her and Oscar's reports, and the sketch artist's rendering, and stapled them into packets that were scattered across the large table at the center of the room. She waited as those called to the meeting trickled in, chatting amongst themselves.

"Hey," Oscar said, squeezing in between two detectives who thought catching up in the doorway was an excellent idea. He walked up to her and handed her a cup of coffee, a matching one in his other hand.

"Thanks. Did Sarah call you?"

"Yeah, she's on her way."

"Great." Catania sipped from her coffee, a smile coming to her face when she saw the logo for Randy's on the side of the cup. The image of Ally instantly came to mind. Pushing that and the cup aside, she clapped her hands. "Alright, gang. Let's get settled and listen up." She waited for the seven detectives to find a seat, some grabbing a packet and flipping through it. "Price asked Oscar and I to get a bit of a task force going here. Thus, your fancy invitations to join us." She grinned. "Here's what we're dealing with. You can see from your packets there that we've got us a Jane Doe, found just under a week ago. No identification at all, no vehicle, nothing."

"Sorry," a woman said in a harried voice from the doorway.

Catania was glad to see Detective Sergeant Sarah Sanchez of the Missing Persons unit scurry into the room, grabbing an empty chair and plopping down into it. She gave her a small nod and smile. Sarah had been instrumental in helping her find her way and her wings in the department when she'd joined.

"Here's the problem, guys. We don't know when she was killed," Catania said, glancing around the room, receiving several confused looks in return.

"Wait, what?" one of the detectives said. "She was found what, five, six days ago?"

"Yes, but she was frozen postmortem." She wasn't surprised by the shocked gasps and mumbled words of shock she heard.

"Jesus," someone said.

"Yeah, pretty awful. Gwen said they can give us a pretty close approximation to the time of freezing, but we don't have that today. So, what I'm thinking is this. If you look at the picture there of the soles of her feet, I believe she was killed or perhaps taken in either a warmer climate or during the summer or early fall. Our Jane Doe was warm enough to walk around barefoot or in sandals. If it's the calendar we're battling, then we need to be scouring records from bare minimum six months ago up to eighteen, thirty-six months ago. The media has been given the sketch of our lady, also. So," she said, reaching around to grab an erasable marker from the tray that ran along the bottom of the whiteboard. "Let's throw around some ideas."

She looked out over the crowd of fellow investigators, noting only one or two were looking at her, the others messing with their phones or giving each other side glances.

"John?" she said, calling to one of the men on their phone who had been friendly to her at times. "Thoughts?" When he said nothing, Catania felt her anger and frustration begin to build. Before she could open her mouth, she felt Oscar step up beside her.

"Guys, wake up! We got us a lady here who is dead. Okay? She's been murdered and stuck in a fucking freezer somewhere and likely she's got family who has no idea what the hell happened to her." He walked over to the table and picked up one of the packets, slapping it on the table. "Let's get some fucking ideas on this!"

Catania cleared her throat in order not to laugh at the startled reaction from the room. Hands on hips, she raised an eyebrow. "So, John, care to try again?"

❦❦❦❦

Catania slammed her notebook and extra packets onto her desk before she whirled on Oscar, who walked over to his desk. "What the fuck?" she demanded. "Forgive my language, but What. The. Fuck? Was it really necessary for you to step up and add to what I had already said? Was it?"

Oscar looked at her, wide-eyed. "I'm sorry, Nia. God, I'm really sorry. I was honestly just trying to get those assholes to stop being assholes because they were absolutely *being* assholes."

As she looked at his reddening face, she couldn't stop the smile that teased her lips. She understood her mistake. "No, no, I'm sorry. I said that wrong. You were amazing and I thank you for saying what you did. I just meant, why was it necessary for a guy to have to prod them in the ass to do their job when a woman asked them to do it?"

"Whew!" He let out a bark of laughter as he leaned back against his desk, the wood creaking beneath his weight. "Damn, for a minute there I thought I'd really pissed you off." He studied her, the look in his eyes pure affection and respect. "Listen, kiddo, there are a million and one reasons I could give you why they acted like that." He gave her a shit-eating grin as he raised his hand, thumb, and forefinger a couple inches apart. "Some pretty *small* reasons."

Catania laughed, a small snort escaping in her mirth.

He chuckled in response. "But at the end of the day, there really is only one simple answer to an age-old and complicated question. Men are idiots, and why are we idiots? Because we're missing the fourth leg of our second 'X.'"

Catania shook her head as she continued to laugh, accepting a quick, one-armed hug from her partner and dear friend.

"You did good today, kid. Don't let a bunch of insecure assholes get to you."

"Thanks. Oh, are you still going to help me hang that cabinet in Matteo's apartment?"

"Yup. Brought my screwdrivers," Oscar said, reaching into his desk to produce the battery-powered tool. He gave the trigger a few tugs, zzzzz, zzzzz.

Catania stared at the screwdriver before meeting his gaze. "You always bring your tools to work with you?"

"Well, I figure if I had to see it in my drawer every time I opened it, I wouldn't forget and just take off after work."

"Chicken fried steak night at the Riley house, is it?" She chuckled and rolled her eyes at his boyish grin. "Get to work, you pain in the ass."

Smiling at her partner's antics, she grabbed the notebook she'd dropped onto her desk and opened the cover. Glancing up, she saw the front desk officer weaving her way through the maze of desks toward her, a woman following with what looked to be a teenage boy, assumedly her son since he looked just like her.

"This is Detective d'Giovanni," the desk officer introduced. "Nia, this young man here has some information he wants to share with you." Duty done, she left the way she'd come, leaving the woman and teen behind.

Catania smiled at the woman who looked to be around her age, if not a little older. "Hello. I'm Nia," she said, extending her hand out to the woman, who shook it.

"Hi, Detective. I'm Toni and this is my son, Jackson. He wanted to talk to you for a minute."

"Jackson," she said extending her hand to the young man who took it in a clammy, limp shake. The poor boy looked scared out of his mind. He had a short, stocky build with slightly oversized glasses and short, light brown hair. "Toni," she said, addressing the woman "Mind if Jackson has a seat here so he can chat with me?" she asked, only one chair available in the tight space by her and Oscar's desks.

"Absolutely. Go ahead and sit, son," Toni said softly, nudging him forward and moving in to stand behind his chair, her hands on his shoulders for support.

Jackson got seated as Catania sat in her chair on the other side of the desk. She flipped through her notebook until she was on a fresh page, clicking her pen into readiness with a flourish and a smile.

"Well," he began, clearing his throat when his voice broke slightly. "Um, I was driving today back to town on the highway, and I saw something."

"Okay. Which highway, Jackson?"

"Um, Highway Fifty."

Catania nodded, scribbling down the information. "Okay. What did you see?"

"Well," he said before glancing back and up at his mother.

"It's okay, honey. Go ahead and tell her."

"Well, I saw on the news today, that lady you guys found. Um, the one in the field."

Catania nodded to let him know she was following what he was saying. She wanted to shake the information out of him to move this along, but knew with a skittish potential witness, that was the worst thing to do.

"I saw a car parked there, along that stretch of road."

Catania's ears perked up. "You did?" At the boy's nod, she asked, "And, it was the same day?"

Jackson reached into one of the side pockets in his cargo pants and pulled out his phone. He tapped and swiped for a moment before he presented the screen of text messages to Catania. "This is a text from my friend Moe."

Catania took the phone from him and read until she found what was pertinent.

Hey, dude. Be at my place Sunday by 1:30. That's when I told Sheila to be here.

She handed the phone back and met the boy's eyes. "And you were coming from Canon City into Pueblo?"

"Yes, ma'am."

"Okay," she said, sitting back in her chair, doing a little mental math in her head. It took about forty-five minutes to drive from Canon City to Pueblo, so he would have left around twenty to quarter till, likely. She estimated he would have passed this mystery car around 1:10 or so. She was curious what he would say. Not that she was concerned Jackson was lying, but in her line of work, everyone was lying until they were proven not to be. "So," she continued. "What time do you think you saw the car?"

"It was right at one twelve. I know because I thought I was going to be late so I looked at the clock in the car. When I looked at the road again, I saw it."

"Okay," she said, quickly jotting down what he

said. "And, what did the car look like?"

"It was white. Like, old school, you know, the kind of car with the door thing you can open in the back?" he said, using his hands to pantomime the upward opening and closing.

"Like a hatchback?" Catania offered, meeting his gaze.

"Yeah! But, it was a longer car. Um..." He turned to look up at his mother. "What's that car Dad used to have? The really ugly one."

"The orange station wagon?" she asked, sparing Catania an apologetic glance.

"Yeah! Station wagon. It was a white station wagon," Jackson exclaimed.

"Okay, and by 'old school,' what do you mean?" Catania asked. She knew to a sixteen- or seventeen-year-old kid, old school could mean 1995.

"Is it like Dad's?" the mom asked, seeming to understand Catania's potential problem with nailing down just exactly what "old school" meant to her son.

"Yeah, but not as old."

"Well," Toni said, meeting Catania's gaze. "His father has a 1977. Maybe an eighties' model?"

"Let's try this, Jackson." Catania dropped her pen on her pad and turned her focus to her computer. "I'm going to look up eighties' models of white station wagons and let's see if anything jumps out at you, okay?" She gave him a friendly smile.

"Yeah, great, okay," he said, excitement in his voice.

She felt this teen was entirely credible, and going to the trouble of finding out exactly what he saw was key. She typed in her search and hit Images, dozens of thumbnails of white station wagons popping up.

Turning her computer monitor so Jackson could peruse the offerings, she patiently scrolled through the lines of pictures, waiting for the light bulb to go off for him.

Finally, Jackson jumped out of his seat, partially leaning over the desk. "That one! Yeah, exactly like that."

Catania clicked on the thumbnail of a 1983 Subaru GL wagon he pointed at, enlarging the image. She met his gaze. "You're sure?"

"Positive. The one I saw had a little rust spot on the driver's side fender, though."

Catania saved the picture of the car to her computer before scribbling down the new information she'd been given. "Excellent work, Jackson. Did you see the driver? License plate?"

"I didn't really get a good look at the person, but it wasn't a chick, I mean, a woman. Unless it was a really big woman. I think it was a guy. And, all I saw on the plates was they weren't Colorado plates. They were a dark color with light writing." He shrugged sheepishly. "Really sorry. That's all."

"I'm impressed as all get-out, there, partner."

Catania was surprised to hear Oscar's voice so close. She'd been so interested in what Jackson had to say that she hadn't noticed him perched on his own desk listening.

Jackson glanced up at him and beamed. "Thank you, sir."

Chapter Ten

She held the cabinet steady as Oscar used his handy screwdriver to screw it into place. She looked around the piece of furniture to read his face. "Did you hear me?"

"Yeah," he answered at length. "Okay, let go. She's in there good." The two of them stepped back from the mounted cabinet, the doors to be attached next. "I'm just trying to figure out what the hell all that crazy dream meant. I mean," he said, strawberry blond eyebrows drawn. "It's like some weird riddle. I get you'd be out on the street, I even get that teenager you seem fond of being in some sort of trouble. That's what we do. But, what do the movie *Titanic*, Natalie Cole, and a cheesy romantic comedy from the eighties have in common? It's not like you're some nut ball fan of any of them."

"You two are terrifically blind."

Catania and Oscar both looked over to where Matteo sat at his computer, never missing a beat as he typed away with one hand on the ten-key portion of his keyboard as he jotted something down on a pad of paper on the table next to it.

"Care to illuminate us?" Catania asked, helping Oscar clean up the mess that they'd made after unpacking the cabinet from its packaging to get it out of the way so they could get the doors installed.

"It's a numbers game, and your common

denominator is two zero one five," he said, never once taking his eyes off the screen of his computer.

"What?" Catania asked, her hand stilling mid-motion of handing one of the hinges to Oscar.

"Your equation is as follows: six twenty-two, twelve thirty-one and finally, seven three." He turned in his seat and faced the two people who were staring at him, baffled looks on their faces. "You take all those numbers and put them under the numbers two zero one five. What do you get?" When there were only cricket chirps in response, Matteo slammed his palm against his thigh. "Jesus, people! They all croaked in 2015!"

"Natalie Cole died?" Oscar asked, an eyebrow raised in surprise.

"Wait," Catania said, ignoring her friend's question. "What are all the numbers you gave us?" At the sound of Oscar's voice again, she turned to look at him. He held his phone, a pudgy finger tapping and scrolling.

"Amanda Peterson, actress, died July third. Apparently an accidental drug overdose. Um, composer James Horner died June twenty-second in a plane crash. Damn, that sucks," he muttered. "And, finally Natalie Cole died December thirty-first." He tucked his phone into his pocket. "Congestive heart failure. All died the same year, 2015."

"In 2015," Catania added. At Oscar's nod, she turned back to her brother, who had gone back to his work. "How did you know all that, Matty?"

"How did you *not*?" he asked, hands raised in consternation.

Catania and Oscar shared a glance, both shrugging their shoulders as they got back to work.

❧❧❧❧

After paroling Oscar from Matteo's odd, quirky little world after they finished the cabinet, Catania spent some time with her brother before she decided to head home. She stood at the front door to Aberdeen House, shrugging her jacket onto her shoulders, when she looked down the hall, the soft sounds of pans bumping together beckoning.

"Damn it," she murmured, knowing full well she'd never be able to leave. "I'll say hi. That's all. I'm here anyway to see Matty, I'll just say hi and head home."

Pep talk complete, Catania headed down the long hall, the kitchen sounds getting louder, as well as the incredible smells of dinner being prepared. The closer she got, the wider her smile grew, no matter how hard she tried to bring it in. She reached the archway and stopped, leaning her shoulder against it as she watched.

It was one of a handful of times she'd seen Ally out of her diner uniform. She wore jeans that fit her petite form beautifully, showing off a shapely behind that Catania's eyes fell to. Guiltily she looked away before she was busted, clearing her throat to announce her presence.

Ally turned from where she stood at the counter carefully slicing open a long loaf of French bread. "Hi!" She dropped the knife on the cutting board and hurried over to Catania, taking her in a quick but tight hug.

She accepted the hug, surprised by it. She squeezed the small woman, noting she very much liked her perfume, before releasing her. "How's it going?"

"Great." Ally gave her the warmest smile Catania

had ever seen from her. "You're actually just in time. I need a taster."

"Oh yeah?" she followed the perky younger woman over to the stove where a massive pot was simmering. It smelled absolutely divine. "What's for dinner?" she asked, though it was completely unnecessary as she knew the smells of her childhood well.

"Spaghetti and meatballs," Ally said, reaching into a nearby drawer and pulling out a spoon. She dipped it into the pot of fragrant red sauce and brought it out, using her own cupped hand to catch any drips.

"And, with who my mother is, you expect me to give you an opinion on your sauce, huh?"

Ally gave her a side glance that sent delicious little chills down Catania's spine. "Who do you think gave me the recipe?"

"Uh," she managed, bringing up a hand to rub the back of her neck. "Got it." She leaned her head in to shorten the distance Ally would have to lift the spoon. She blew over the hot offering before slurping the thick sauce into her mouth. She closed her eyes at the warm, familiar notes of her mother's homemade sauce.

"Good?" Ally asked softly, her tone hopeful.

All Catania could do was nod as she relished the tastes and spices coating her tongue. "Mmm hmm." Giving another nod and thumbs-up, she smiled. "Excellent."

Ally clapped her hands like a small child after putting the used spoon into a pan that had other dishes to be washed later. "I'm so glad. Yay!"

Catania chuckled, enjoying the happy energy that Ally exuded. In the time she'd known her, she'd never seen her look so happy, so playful, so...free.

"What?" Ally asked, looking down at the deep green sweater she wore. "Did I get something on myself?"

Catania shook her head, wiping the soft, relieved expression she had on her face off. "You're going to spoil these folks, you know. From what I gather from my brother, your food is way better than Karen's was."

Ally's smile was sweet. "I'm so glad. I enjoy it. Do you have a minute?"

"Yeah, sure. What's up?"

Without a word, Ally quickly turned down the burner and grabbed Catania's hand, tugging her out of the kitchen and a short way down the hall to the rounded door. She unlocked it and turned to her before entering. "I want you to see what I've done."

Catania hadn't seen the apartment since Thanksgiving night when she'd initially showed it to Ally and proposed the idea for the job. Now, she was in awe. She'd turned the tiny space upstairs into a cozy little living room. A small love seat was a perfect fit in the nook beneath the stained glass window, a scarred entertainment center on the opposite wall with a nineteen-inch flat screen tucked into it. A warm, welcoming rug was placed on the center of the wood floor, all the colors from the window represented.

"This is adorable," Catania said, grinning at her. "Where did the furniture come from?" she asked. She knew it was possible it belonged to Ally and she'd had it stored somewhere, but had the feeling Ally moved into this place with not much more than a few trash bags of clothing.

"Lizzie and Marla from the diner," Ally said softly, looking around with pride in her eyes. "They surprised me with all this." She indicated the living room furnishings. "And then," she continued, moving on toward the stairs, Catania following. "Lizzie's son gave me his old bed and some dishes. I guess he and his girlfriend moved into a larger place, so...."

They headed into the lower area, equally as adorable as above. The bed was black wrought iron, a double. It had a colorful quilt on it and a handful of throw pillows. More throw rugs adorned the floor and decorative pictures hung on the walls. But, what caught Catania's attention were the two shelves mounted on one of the walls created to close off the bathroom. On one shelf, near the bed, were three snow globes.

Walking over to them, she glanced over at Ally, who stood near the small table for two butted against the wall near the stove. "May I?"

"Go ahead."

Catania reached out and took one in hand. It had a plain white porcelain base with a few faded butterflies painted on it. Inside the glass globe was a park bench with a little girl sitting on it, her blond hair blowing back from her face and a small, orange kitten on the bench next to her, batting at a butterfly that was fluttering by, the two ever-frozen in the age-old game of prey and predator.

"I got that one when I was twelve," Ally explained softly, suddenly standing beside Catania. "It was the last thing my aunt gave me before she died."

"It must mean a lot to you." Catania wanted to take a slight step away, feeling suddenly very uncomfortable with the closeness of Ally's presence. She felt her heart pounding and breathing hitch. She tried to push it all down and focus on the object in her hands.

"It does, but it has nothing to do with my aunt.

You see, I used to stare at the little girl and pretend she was me. I always wanted a cat, too." She gave Catania a small smile. "Never got one. Anyway, I would pretend I was sitting on that park bench. When I was little, I used to pretend that I was waiting for my mom to come get me. Then, as I got older, some knight in shining armor to come save me."

"And now?" Catania asked, meeting Ally's gaze.

"Now." Ally let out a relieved-sounding breath. "Now, I just see her sitting on that bench enjoying the day, watching the butterflies and smelling the flowers."

"Free."

"Free."

Catania handled the snow globe as though it were a priceless piece of china as she placed it back on the shelf.

"I'm sorry I lied to you."

She looked back to Ally at her soft words. "Lied to me?"

Ally nodded, seemingly nervous as she tucked her hands into the back pockets of her jeans. "Yeah. About living in that house with a boyfriend." She gave her a shy smile. "I really hate lying, and really wanted to tell you the truth."

Catania shook her head. "Don't apologize, Ally. I'm just glad it worked out and you're okay. That's all that matters."

Catania could feel the air in the room growing heavy, so much so that she could barely take a breath. She could feel Ally's body heat so close, almost burning her with its intensity. She felt so lightheaded she worried she'd pass out. In the moment she focused on Ally's eyes, she saw so much vulnerability there and wanted to kiss the softest looking lips she'd ever seen.

She couldn't.

Stumbling backward a few steps, she found herself banging into the wall, which startled her. Pushing away from it, she cleared her throat and moved past a confused-looking Ally so she was closer to the stairs and escape.

"Um, I better get going," she stuttered. "Dinner soon. I'm sure the natives are hungry." With those lame words and an even lamer smile, she bolted.

🖎🖎🖎🖎🖎

Catania sat in her Jeep outside of the Aberdeen House, staring off into space even as she froze in the cold evening. Shaking her head yet again, she ran her hand through her hair.

"A fourteen-year-old boy," she blew out. "I ran like a goddamn fourteen-year-old boy from a woman who is five foot three or four, maybe one hundred and twenty pounds." She hung her head and let out a pitiful chuckle, that very body she described passing in front of her mind's eye. "Pathetic."

She raised her head and looked at the house again. For a moment she considered going back in and, if nothing else, offering to help serve dinner. Deciding against it as she wasn't ready to see Ally so soon after her intense reaction to her, she reached down and inserted the key into the ignition and got the large Jeep started.

Deciding she didn't want to go home right away and definitely had no desire to cook, she put in a quick order for a pizza to be delivered, then pulled away from the curb. She drove around, wasting time until her dinner arrived. She knew if she were at the apartment, all she'd be able to think about was Ally, as she knew when she stepped inside it would smell clean and fresh from the blonde's amazing cleaning chops.

She drove down the street where Randy's was located, and even though she knew she wouldn't be seeing Ally heading out, all bundled and fighting against the early December weather, she still looked for her anyway.

"Stop it, Catania!" she yelled, startling herself at how loud her frustration erupted. She let out an equally loud growl as she stopped at the stop sign, flipping the turn signal to take a left. Something stopped her.

Jeep idled, the turn signal clicking lightly with each outside blink, Catania looked across the street out her side window. She saw a huddled figure slumped in the recessed doorway of a closed antique store.

Waiting for a red Ford Focus to pass, Catania whipped a U-turn and parked at the curb in front of the brick building. She reached across the cab and rolled down the passenger side window.

"Hey! Squirrel?" The huddled figure barely moved. "Squirrel, you okay?" When the small body curled farther in on itself, Catania rolled the window back up and turned off the Jeep.

Climbing out, she trotted around the front, headlight beams spotlighting her as she passed in front of them. She slowed when she reached the teen, squatting down. Squirrel was huddled in the doorway in her ever-present light blue and gray windbreaker. She was shivering violently.

"Hey," she said softly, reaching out a hand to touch the teen's arm. "Jesus, you're cold. Squirrel, look at me."

It took a moment, but finally the teen raised her

head and met Catania's gaze.

"Oh my god. Come on." Catania stood, reaching down for Squirrel's hand, which was eventually offered to her. She pulled the girl to her feet. "Can you stand? Are you okay?"

Squirrel nodded, though her movements were slow, almost as though she were in a daze. "Just great."

Catania gave her a ghost of a smile. As they made it toward the Jeep, Squirrel's face became more visible. "Jesus, Squirrel," she whispered, lifting a hand and leaving a featherlight touch to the darker bruising of a shiner, and cuts on her full bottom lip and her left nostril. "Come on," she said, looking around to see if anyone was around, watching. "You're coming home with me for the night. Get you out of this cold, anyway."

Both loaded into the Jeep, Catania felt nervous as she drove them to her apartment. She knew she should be taking Squirrel to the police station or to the protection of CPS, as it seemed obvious she didn't exactly have a good or permanent home situation. But, as cold as it was and after the incredibly disturbing dream that Squirrel had starred in, she felt her protective instincts kick in.

Catania pulled into her parking spot at her building, glad that it looked like she'd beat the pizza delivery person. She helped Squirrel out of the Jeep. "Come on, kid. Let's get you warm and fed."

Nearly ten minutes later, Squirrel sat on the hearth of the fireplace after Catania had gotten a fire going. Her clothing was humming in the washing machine as she drowned in a borrowed pair of flannel pants and a sweatshirt.

"Alright, kiddo," Catania said, opening the box

of pizza on the kitchen table. She'd only ordered a small, not expecting a dinner guest. "Food."

Squirrel joined her, taking a slice and plopping it on the plate Catania provided, her own pizza on her plate as she sat across from her. She looked at the girl, who picked at her pizza.

"How are you feeling?"

Squirrel glanced up at her and shrugged a shoulder as she blew her cheeks out, looking for a moment like her namesake. "Okay, I guess. Why did you bring me in here?"

"Why do you think?" Catania asked, tearing off a bite of pizza with her teeth. She chewed thoughtfully as she studied Squirrel's new injuries. "We should clean those," she said after swallowing and taking a sip from her Coke. "You've got some answering to do, kiddo."

Dark eyebrows drew as Squirrel sat back in her chair. "What? Why?"

"What is your situation? Hmm? Where are your parents? Why are you on the street, and who hurt you?"

"It doesn't matter," Squirrel said, tossing a piece of pepperoni that she'd picked off to the plate. She eyed Catania for a long moment before very sage words left her lips. "Have you ever wondered what life is really about? Why we're here and just how we're supposed to change things?"

Catania studied her for a long moment before she nodded. "Actually yes. I have wondered that." She smiled. "My hope is, I'm supposed to change everything." She grinned. "Pretty deep words for a... how old are you?"

"Sixteen. And yes, I am deep." Squirrel returned the grin. "Real deep."

"You're not going to tell me anything, are you?"

Catania asked, grabbing a second slice from the box.

"All you need to know about me is I won't steal from you."

"Oh, nice," Catania said with a bark of laughter, considering the last time they'd seen each other. "Why should I not run you in right now as a runaway, huh?"

"How do you know I'm a runaway?" Squirrel challenged. "Hmm? How do you know I didn't get kicked out?"

"That's it, isn't it?"

"Or, how do you know that I'm not a vampire and wander the streets at night?"

"Because I've seen you during the day."

"Good point. Okay, how do you know this isn't by mutual agreement with my folks? I'm gone, they know that, so give me my space."

Catania shook her head and waved her off. "Alright, smart-ass. Eat your dinner so I can get you a bed made on the blow-up mattress."

❧ ❧ ❧ ❧

A soft sigh escaped Catania's lips as she readjusted her head on the pillow. Her body began to settle into a slightly new position when her eyes popped open. Looking around, she was surprised to see the sun was already up and she actually felt rested.

She sat up in bed when she remembered she had company. Glancing toward the closed door to her bedroom, she listened. The apartment was very quiet. Pushing the blankets off of her legs, she slid them over the side until her feet hit the floor, then she stood. Stretching her arms high overhead, she let out a little squeak before heading to the door.

Turning the knob, she slowly pulled the door open, listening closely for anything out of place. Nothing. Stepping out into the hall, she glanced into the bathroom, which was empty.

"Squirrel?"

She made her way to the second bedroom and spied Matteo's blow-up mattress that he used on his "visits." It was empty, the comforter, blanket, and sheets she'd provided for her guest the night before neatly folded and placed atop it next to her equally neatly folded flannel pants and sweatshirt.

"Squirrel?" she called out again, heading farther into the apartment.

The TV was off, everything left as it had been the night before. The dryer proved to be empty, as well.

Hands on hips as she stood in the center of the living room, Catania let out a breath. "Okay. Guess that's that."

Chapter Eleven

Catania stroked her chin, eyebrows drawn as she scanned the images on the screen before her. Where there wasn't an image she read through the details of the case. She'd seen a couple pictures that she'd stopped on after doing a double take, but no, the woman's face was burned into her brain.

Still, nothing.

"Damn," she whispered, sitting back in her chair. She reached absently for her coffee, sipping from the warm brew, never taking her eyes from the screen of her computer.

What's the common denominator?

Catania jumped, startled. She glanced around the near-empty room, looking for Matteo. His voice had been so clear, so loud in her ear. All she saw was a fellow detective sitting at his desk across the room talking quietly on the phone. It was early on a Sunday morning and the place was quiet, desk lamps off, computer screens dark, and empty mugs sitting on desks waiting to be filled with bad coffee.

Hand to her chest, she shook off the weirdness she felt and returned her focus to her search. She did, however, take to heart the words.

"What's the common denominator," she repeated, chewing on her bottom lip as she tapped the edge of the desk with two fingertips.

As though of their own accord, both hands raised

and went to the keyboard. She quickly typed in her search criteria. Instantly, the numbers of results went from the thousands to thirty-two.

"Okay," she murmured, again scanning images and reading case details.

The fourth profile down, she stopped, a chill heading straight down her spine. Staring back at her was forty-six-year-old Megan Murphy. She was a resident of Tucson, Arizona since 2005. She'd been declared a missing person August 3, 2015.

The woman she was studying was definitely the woman that had been found in the field on Hwy 50. Her hair was longer in the picture, her eyes a grayish-green. They were full of life.

Glancing at the contact information for that police department, she grabbed her desk phone and quickly typed in the number before sitting back in her chair, waiting for the call to be picked up.

ৠৣৣ

Catania sat quietly, waiting for her news to sink in and those who received it to react. This was a part of her job that she hated, but it came with the badge. The tears of the woman sitting across from her cleared, but Catania offered another tissue from the box sitting on the coffee table between them.

"I'm sorry," Megan's niece Lara said with a heavy sigh as she wiped at her nose with the fresh tissue.

"No need. I'm truly sorry my news isn't better."

"No, I'm glad to know, to be honest, Detective. It's been more than two years." The young brunette dropped her hands into her lap where she watched as she fiddled with the tissue she held. "How do you guys know for sure it's her?"

"Fingerprints. Your aunt was arrested for a DUI back in 2012. They were able to compare them." She grabbed the notebook she'd set on the coffee table, pen attached, and set it on her lap. "Can you tell me anything about her? Did she have any enemies, any issues with anyone?"

Lara shook her head. "No. Aunt Meg was a really amazing woman. Very generous, fun. Everybody loved her."

All except for one, Catania thought to herself. "Can you give me a road map of her life? How did she end up in Arizona since she'd lived her entire life here, right?"

Lara nodded. "Yes. She was born up in Denver, but my grandparents moved with Aunt Meg and my mom here when they were little. But, yeah, she'd never lived anywhere else."

Lara's husband re-entered the room, a cup of coffee in both hands. He handed one to Catania and set one in front of his wife before sitting on the couch next to her.

"Thanks, Mike," Catania said, carefully sipping the hot brew.

"What about that dude she was dating?" he asked, looking to Lara.

"What dude?"

"The one when you and me first got together. She thought he was following her and stuff. Remember?"

"Oh! Yeah. Damn, what was his name?" Lara whispered, snapping her fingers as though the motion would revive her memory.

"What can you tell me about him?" Catania asked Mike. "Why did you bring him up?"

"Well," Mike explained, resting his elbows on spread knees as he used his hands to gesticulate as he explained. "She started seeing this guy back in 2002 or around there. I remember that because me and her had just gotten together," he said, indicating his wife. "So, this dude was really secretive. Meg used to talk about it a lot. It made her really mad. Like, they'd meet at hotels and stuff to hook up, rather than going to her place or his place."

"Was he married?" Catania asked, notating what she was being told.

Mike shook his head, running a hand over the shaved scalp. "Not that he told her or that she knew of. I mean, it's possible, but she never said nothing about that."

"Do you know this guy's name? How long did they date? What did he look like?"

"I don't remember his name at all. We never even met him or saw a picture of him. I think she said once he had long hair. He used to braid it or something. She didn't bring him around us, just talked about him. Like, she'd invite him to family stuff all the time and he'd not show. Just a real jerk. Finally she had enough." He turned to his wife again. "What was it, baby? Something happened over Christmas or something, wasn't it?"

"No, it was New Year's," Lara said, hands cupped around the warmth of her coffee mug. "He got angry or something. I'm not real sure what happened. But it got violent and she had enough. Broke it off."

"That's right, that's what it was. She was pretty sure he was following her after that," Mike added.

Catania glanced at him, meeting a troubled hazel gaze. "Tell me more about that."

"Well, when she'd go to work or home or our

place, whatever, she was being followed. She'd get weird notes left on her car, stuff like that. I honestly don't think she told us everything. But," he added with a heavy sigh, "she was pretty damn spooked."

"Did she ever go to the police?" Catania asked, looking from Mike to Lara.

Lara shook her head. "No. She said she knew they wouldn't do anything, so finally she decided to leave."

"To Tucson?"

"She started in Gilbert, but yeah, she ended up in Tucson. Loved it there."

"Did she come back here that much?" Catania asked, making a few notes before looking back to the couple sitting across from her.

"Not really. We usually went down to see her when the kids were on summer break, or during the holidays once in a while."

Catania sat back in her chair, studying Lara for a moment. "Did she not come back up here because she didn't want to? Couldn't afford it?"

The couple exchanged a quick glance before Mike responded. "She was afraid."

"She only came back once, and that was for our son's birthday," Lara said softly.

After a moment, Lara pushed up from the couch and disappeared for a moment to another room before returning with a photo album. She reclaimed her seat next to Mike and opened it up. With tears in her eyes she flipped through a few of the stiff pages before settling on one. Carefully she pulled the clear plastic up and worked to dislodge one of the snapshots.

"This is the last time we saw her," she explained softly, handing the picture over. "She was headed back home."

Catania took the picture and was struck by what she saw. The woman's face was one she'd come to know, but this one was smiling, alive and full of energy. It came across through in the image, frozen forever. But what stopped her cold was the summer dress she was wearing and the car she was standing next to, her arm resting along the top of the open driver's side door.

"Lara," she said softly. "Can I please take this with me? I promise I'll return it."

Lara nodded. "Whatever you need to do, Detective."

❧❧❧❧

Oscar studied the photograph even as he absently reached for a French fry. Munching quietly, he nodded, seeming to come to some conclusion in his mind. Setting the picture on the table—a copy, as Catania wanted to get the original safely back to the family—he met her gaze.

"And, the kid identified this as the car he'd seen?" he asked.

She nodded. "Yup. Dropped by his high school yesterday and it took him about three seconds. Same car. I got a BOLO sent out for it."

"Damn, you're good at this cop thing."

"I know," she said with a grin. "We've got to find this old boyfriend. But, every person I've spoken to who knew Megan Murphy either didn't know about him then, doesn't remember his name, or doesn't remember enough to be helpful."

"Agreed. We need to find this guy."

"I heard from Gwen today," Catania said, pushing her empty plate away, only the pickle and tomato brought to top her cheeseburger left on the plate. "Tests came back on Megan's tissues. They're dating it between September or October when she was frozen."

Oscar nodded, pushing his own plate away as he finished the last of his French fries. "What year?"

"Two zero one five," she said, holding his gaze.

"Kind of creepy, isn't it?" He wiped his mouth with his napkin before tossing it onto the empty plate. "Like your dream, if your brother was right."

"Yep, Exactly. Total coincidence, but still weird. Anyway, what a sick bastard. She was reported missing in early August, but Gwen said they feel she was frozen late fall."

"You think he was keeping her alive somewhere?"

"Makes me wonder."

"Stomach contents?"

Catania chewed on her bottom lip, noting out of the corner of her eye that Ally had just strolled in, still wrapped in her heavy winter jacket. Her heart swelled before it nearly imploded, remembering her childish reaction to her last time they'd seen each other. She cleared her throat and forced herself to focus on Oscar and their discussion.

"That's my thought, too. We've got to retrace her steps from the moment she left her niece's house to her home in Tucson. We haven't found a single soul who seems to have seen her in between."

"Alright," Oscar said, leaning to the side so he could pull his wallet out from the back pocket of his trousers. He pulled some money out and grabbed the check their waitress had left for their individual meals several minutes before. "I gotta get to Hunter's piano recital. I'll be back at the station later."

"Okay. Tell Linda I said hi." Catania grabbed her own ticket to see the amount, which was the same as it always was, of course, considering she always ordered the same thing.

Left alone, she pulled out her wallet and some money, tossing a few bills on the table for a tip. Sliding out of the booth, she saw that Ally was at a table full of men, all three of them seemed to be slightly—if not a lot—intoxicated. But one specifically caught Catania's eye.

"Come on, sugar," he said, his mouth nearly hidden behind the massive lumberjack beard he sported. "When do you get off work?"

"Sorry, I just got here," she said in a singsong voice and flashed a polite smile. "What can I get for you fellas?"

"What you can get me ain't on the menu," the Paul Bunyan of the trio said, the other two laughing.

"Well, how about I give you some help," Ally said, her voice becoming a bit less firm and all business. "Our specials today are—"

"Honey, until you're on the menu, I don't give two shits about specials."

Somehow stopping herself from flying across the distance between her and that asshole and murdering him where he sat, Catania got to her feet and made her way over, making sure her badge was visible.

"Good evening, gentlemen," she said, her "cop face" fully on display. "How are things going tonight?"

The two men who had remained silent glanced at her badge, then buried their noses in the single-page menu in their hands. The loudmouth, however, obviously wasn't so inclined to back off.

"What do you want?" he asked, getting to his

feet. He easily had eight or nine inches of height on Catania and was using it to try and intimidate her.

"Sir, I'm Detective d'Giovanni and I recommend you sit back down and find your manners with this lady."

He smirked down at her. "And I don't recall asking for the help or advice from some pussy with a badge."

"John, man, cut it out," one of the big man's companions said. "Knock it off."

"Shut the fuck up, Frank," John said, never taking his eyes off Catania.

"Sir, I'm going to ask you again to sit down," she said, her voice remaining calm even as she was already making a decision of how to handle this guy, who she could tell wasn't about to back down. His tiny ego was being fueled by his insecurity and two buddies watching.

"You can ask all you want, bitch." He grinned, looking back at his mates at the table, neither of which was even looking at him.

Catania put her hands on her hips, her finger just barely touching the cold canister of PAVA spray that was clipped to her belt should she need it. "I'm going to ask you for a third and final time, sir," she said, voice low and filled with warning. "Sit down and be quiet or I will assist you out of this diner."

"And again, ask all you want, you stupid cunt." His whiskey-scented breath wafted down into Catania's face.

He reached out a large hand and went to flip her badge when, before he could get out his startled yelp, the man found himself whirled around and flat on his face on the floor with his arms yanked behind him and the solid click of handcuffs holding his wrists tight.

"Jesus, bitch!" he yelled, struggling to turn over, but Catania's hand at the center of his back held him.

"You have the right to remain silent. Anything you say can and will be used against you in a court of law. Understand?" She lessened the pressure of her hand just slightly as she felt the fight going out of him. "You have the right to speak to an attorney, and to have an attorney present during any questioning." She saw movement out of the corner of her eye and glanced up to see a uniformed cop enter the diner, the lights of his cruiser seen flashing in the parking lot. Apparently, someone thought she needed backup. "Nice to see you," she told the officer. "Do you understand your rights as I've explained them to you?" she asked, returning her attention to the large man on the floor.

"Yes," he muttered. "Why are you doing this?"

"You're under arrest for disorderly conduct as well as refusing to obey a direct order from an officer."

"Fuck," the man growled.

"Officer," she called out, waving the young rookie over. "Help me get our friend here to his feet before you take him away."

The drama contained, Catania turned to Ally, who was huddled in a nearby booth. She looked like a frightened little girl, nearly curled up in on herself. She walked over to her and slid into the booth across from her friend.

"Hey, sweetie," she said softly, bending her head down a bit to try and catch Ally's downcast eyes with her own. When she did, she gave her an encouraging smile. "You okay?" When all she got was the vigorous shake of Ally's head in the negative, Catania slid back out of the booth and reached down to grab Ally's hand, gently tugging her to her feet. "Come on."

Holding firm to Ally's hand, Catania led her down the narrow hallway of the diner where the pay phone and bathrooms were, the old pay phone a relic of the aging diner that remarkably still carried a dial tone. Once they arrived there, she took her into her arms and held her, Ally's smaller body trembling.

She ran her hand in small circles over her back as the other cupped the back of her neck, Ally's hair up in a tight bun. She expected tears to come, but they never did. Instead, Ally took several deep breaths then seemed to sink into Catania, who tightened her arms around her.

"You okay?" she asked into the hug.

After a moment, Ally nodded, but didn't retreat. "Yeah. Just brought back some really bad memories for me."

"I'm sorry." Catania pulled back and looked at Ally's beautiful face. "I have to get to the office to deal with that jackass, but I'll be back. Okay? What time are you off tonight?"

"Midnight. It's only a six-hour shift."

"Okay. I'll be back before then." She smiled at her, feeling a surge of affection and protectiveness over the lovely woman standing before her. She had to stop herself from bringing up a hand and running her fingers down the softness of Ally's face. "See you soon," she said instead, giving Ally's hand a squeeze before turning and returning to the main part of the diner to pay her bill and head out.

❧❧❧❧

Catania stood back, hands on hips and head

slightly cocked to the side as she studied the timeline she and Oscar had created. Red dry-erase marker in hand, she stepped up and underlined where Oscar had written "Burger King" in green.

"Here," she said, tapping the words with the re-capped marker. "According to the financial records you got from her bank, this was the last time she made any sort of purchase. And that was, what?" She looked at the date scribbled next to it. "August first. She wasn't reported as missing until two days later." Eyebrows falling, she turned and looked at Oscar, who was perched on the edge of the conference room table, arms crossed over his large belly. "How long does it take to get to Tucson, Arizona?"

He shrugged. "It's about a ten, eleven-hour drive, give or take. She could have easily gotten home by the second. And it was the neighbor who reported her missing."

"An eleven-hour road trip. She would have had to stop to get food, gas, possibly a hotel. But, nothing," Catania, again tapping the fast-food chain name. "This meal isn't going to suffice." She placed the marker into the metal tray. "I don't think she ever made it out of Pueblo."

"Well, she was found here, Nia," Oscar said, pushing up from the table with a grunt of exertion. He reached into his pocket and pulled out a wrapped sucker, pulling off the paper before popping the blueberry-blue candy into his mouth, white stick bobbing as he spoke. "Obviously she was at least dumped here."

"I know, but I think she's been kept here. The whole time. Somewhere in this town of a hundred thousand people, she was on ice. And, here's the thing, Oscar," she continued. "Whoever did this kept her car, doesn't appear to have used any of her credit cards, or accessed her bank account. Why? I mean, if you had done something like this, would you hold on to not only major evidence like your victim's body, but also her car?"

Oscar shook his head. "No way. Unless it was revenge. If it was simply opportunity for rape or a thrill kill, her car would have been found in the Pueblo Reservoir by now."

Catania smirked. "Yeah, likely with her in it. Yet he kept everything, and I mean, *everything*." She met his gaze, troubled. "That says to me he was punishing her. 'I own you, now.'"

Oscar nodded as a jaw-splitting yawn took over his face. "It's late," he said after.

"What time is it?" Catania asked, suddenly panicked.

"Uh…" Oscar checked his wristwatch. "Almost midnight."

"Shit!" She quickly began to gather her reports and papers. "I told Ally I'd be back to the diner before she got off work." When she heard nothing forthcoming from her partner, she spared a glance at him over her shoulder. "What? Why are you looking at me like that?"

"You like this girl, don't you?" he said, removing the sucker from his mouth. "You really like her," he added, pointing the half-dissolved candy head at her.

"Why do you say that?" she said, scoffing his words aside as she finished her task. "I just made a promise and I like to keep them." She met his gaze again. "Damn it, would you stop?"

"Nia," Oscar said calmly, gathering his own notes and papers. "You took the woman home to meet your mamma during a major holiday."

Catania turned away. "Yeah, well whatever. I have to go." She glared at him as she passed, his belly jiggling with the intensity of his laughter. "Laugh it up, fuzz ball," she muttered.

Hurrying back to her desk to stow everything she didn't plan to take home and study, she nearly sprinted outside to her Jeep. Roaring through town, she finally pulled into the empty parking lot of Randy's, cursing when she saw the lights inside turn off, section by section.

"Damn it."

But then, Ally appeared in the large single-pane glass window. The waitress leaned across a booth and reached for the pull on the metal blinds. Stopping mid-tug, she spotted Catania sitting in the Jeep. Waggling a finger at her good-naturedly, she brought a smile to Catania's face, which seemed to spread to Ally's lips. She waved Catania inside.

Putting the Jeep in Park, she cut the engine and climbed out of the tall vehicle and made her way across the parking lot to the back door by the dumpster where Ally was waiting for her.

"Hey, you. Didn't think you were coming."

"I know. I'm so sorry." Catania made sure the heavy steel door was closed securely behind her before following Ally into the dimly-lit restaurant. "Oscar and I got into a brainstorming session about the case we're dealing with."

"Gee, you'd think you guys were like saving lives or something..." Ally turned once they reached the table she'd been at when Catania had spotted her, and gave her a sweet smile. "It's truly okay. I'm glad you made it."

"Anything I can do to help?" Catania asked, feeling like a complete pervert as she found particular interest in Ally's uniform-clad behind as the waitress leaned across the booth to tug the blinds into place. Yet again, she was mesmerized, and yet again, she felt guilty about it.

"Well," Ally said, looking over her shoulder at Catania, who hoped she had looked away quickly enough. "See that mop and bucket over there by the jukebox? Do me a favor and wheel it back to the maintenance closet over by the bathrooms, will you?"

"Yes, ma'am."

Together they finished closing the diner and Catania offered Ally a ride home, which was quickly accepted. Parked outside the Aberdeen House, Ally looked at her companion as they sat in the idling Jeep.

"I know it's late, Nia," she said softly. "But would you be willing to come in and make sure everything is okay?"

"Yeah, absolutely." Catania turned off the engine and removed the key from the ignition. She gave Ally a quick smile before climbing out of her Jeep and locking it up. "It is so cold tonight," she commented as they hurried toward the large house. "Smells like snow, too."

"It does." She pulled out her own keys and let them into the locked house. "What are you doing for Christmas?" she asked quietly, the house still, no noise coming from any of the apartments they passed on their way to Ally's door. "Your mom's?"

Catania shook her head. "No. Jason and Karen are actually hosting this year. First time in many years." She waited patiently behind Ally as the smaller woman unlocked her door. "I have to work, so won't be there for long. You should come."

"I can't," Ally said, stepping aside to let Catania enter first. "Please?" she asked sweetly, nodding toward the dark apartment beyond.

Charmed and sad for Ally's fear, Catania reached in and felt around for the light switch, which she flicked on. Everything was exactly as it had been last time she was there, save for a throw that had been tossed to the love seat. Continuing on, she switched on the light at the top of the stairs, her mind mentally weighing exactly where her hand would have to go should she need to pull a weapon, the instincts of a trained officer kicking in.

As she figured, the downstairs was clear as well, though she still checked the bathroom and closet. Glancing up at the ceiling fan, she noticed a small loop of wire that peeked through the drywall. "I'll have to get Jason to look at that," she said, pointing up. "Looks like some of the wiring from the fan and light has poked down through the hole."

Ally looked up and nodded. "Okay. I hadn't noticed that. He's usually in a couple times a week, so I can snag him next time I see him."

"Well," Catania said, looking around a final time with hands on hips before she smiled at her. "I think you're all good here. No boogie men tonight." Her smile fell at the look in Ally's eyes. "Are you okay? Has something happened, Ally?" she asked gently, reaching out to rest a hand on Ally's arm. "Is someone here giving you trouble?" She tried to lighten the mood slightly with a small smile. "If it's my brother, Oscar and I will take turns kicking his ass."

Ally smiled shyly and looked down. "No, nothing like that. I guess after today, I just...I just feel a bit uneasy."

"Ally, do you want me to stay?" Catania asked softly. When her friend didn't even look up as she nodded, Catania melted. "Hey, come here." She took her into her arms just like she had seven hours before. "It's okay. It's no problem. We can just cut off my legs at the knee so I can crash on the love seat." She smiled when she heard a soft chuckle against her neck. Catania's eyes fell closed for a second as she held Ally just a moment more before releasing her with a smile. "Okay, let's do this thing called sleep."

Though Catania was a bit taller, the two women weren't that far apart in size, so she borrowed a T-shirt and pair of shorts to sleep in. She lay on her back on the left side of Ally's bed, her heart racing. She took several deep breaths, surprised—not for the first time—by how Ally was beginning to affect her. She was a beautiful woman, no doubt, but it was so much more than that. She felt protective of her, needed to be around her, almost as though her energetic spirit and vivacious smile was a balm to her soul.

"That guy reminded me of Ian," Ally said, unwittingly interrupting Catania's syrupy sweet thoughts.

She turned her head to look into the darkness that was the bedroom area of the lower floor of Ally's apartment. Ally lay in bed next to her, also on her back. She couldn't see any hint of her, could only hear her voice. "He really spooked you today, didn't he?"

"He did. That kind of intimidation, like he was doing to you, that's what Ian used to do to me. I hated it. So insecure, you know?" she said.

Catania nodded, even though she knew it wasn't seen. She could, however feel Ally's gaze on her. She turned to look in her general direction. "How long were you married to him?"

"Sixteen years."

"Wow," Catania whispered. "That's a long time. How did you get out?"

"Have you ever seen that nineties' movie with Julia Roberts, *Sleeping With the Enemy*?" Ally asked.

For a moment Catania thought maybe Ally wasn't going to answer the question and was trying to change the subject. So, she said, "Yeah. It's been a while, but I saw it a couple times back in the day."

"Well, that movie is what inspired me to leave," Ally said with conviction.

"Wait, you didn't fake your own death like the Roberts character did, right?"

"No," Ally chuckled. "No, but when I watched that scene when she's gathering all her stuff to get the hell out of there, I knew I had to do something. So, we had these good friends, Melanie and Scott. We were in Omaha at the time, and Scott was Air Force. He was going to be transferred to Nevada. We hatched a plan that I'd help them move, then return on the ten forty-five Amtrak back to Omaha. Nope."

Catania could almost feel the smile on that lovely face.

"Caught the seven thirty-three flight to Tacoma, instead."

Catania grinned. *That's my girl.* "That took some serious guts."

"Yeah, well I was done being a prisoner. Ian worked for the railroad and he was gone a lot. I thought it would be great, having actual time to myself. Yeah, right." She let out a heavy sigh. "He bought an old farmhouse on about five acres and built his mother a little bungalow. That bitch was over all the damn time when he was gone."

Catania was surprised to hear the bad language and angry tone in her voice, but from what she said, couldn't blame her. "Did you ever see either of them again?"

"Nope. I stayed in Washington state for about a year then moved around regularly, slowly making my way back here."

"Kids?"

"You know, I think the only time I've ever believed there was a God was when I had two miscarriages. Is that a horrible thing to say?"

Catania could tell Ally was looking in her direction again. "No," she said softly, reaching over under the covers to take Ally's hand in hers. She squeezed it lightly in comfort before releasing it. She was surprised when Ally's hold tightened, keeping their fingers linked. Catania's hand stayed where it was.

"Thanks for being here with me, Nia," Ally whispered just before a small yawn escaped.

Catania smiled, lightly squeezing her hand again though not letting go. "Goodnight, Ally."

Chapter Twelve

The rains have finally stopped and Central Long Island is attempting to dry out after a Thousand Year rain event hit and hit hard!" *the distant, tinny television voice exclaimed, though no television screen was in sight.* "The twenty-four-hour deluge dropped several inches of the wet stuff, including nearly ten inches between five and seven a.m.! This storm definitely puts 2014 in the history books."

The space was small and cement-gray. A single battery-powered camping-style lantern sat on top of a red toolbox on wheels that was pushed against the wall to the left. It illuminated the jail-cell-sized room, approximately eight feet by seven feet.

To the right of the image across from the toolbox was a cot with a canvas held taut between the four-sided metal frame. Lying on the army-green material was a set of metal handcuffs.

"*Okay,*" *a disembodied male voice muttered. A hand entered the frame as it tossed a second pair of handcuffs to the cot.* "*Got those…What else? Oh!*"

The top drawer was opened on the toolbox, revealing a whole host of implements including pliers, penlights, and tightly wound wire. That drawer was closed and the second was opened, containing various sizes of dildos and an attachment apparatus. Two large tubes of lube were also placed near the side of the drawer.

"*No, damn. I thought I brought it down…*"

The drawer was slid closed and the third opened to reveal different types of badges from police to sheriff to fireman. Tucked amongst the half dozen very realistic badges was a set of small silver keys.

"Bingo," the man's voice muttered, fingers reaching into the drawer to fish them out.

The drawer was closed and the hand started toward the lantern, then stopped.

"Oh, wait. Let's see."

The angle of the camera was changed slightly, the cot filling more of the frame than it had before. The shot was tilted down slightly, looking more down upon the cot than above it.

"Perfect."

The hand reached for the lantern again, which was now out of the frame and the room went black.

🐚🐚🐚🐚

"Hey, Lizzie," Catania said, making her way through the busy lunch hour at Randy's to the breakfast counter.

"Hey, Nia. Want me to put your order in?" the older waitress asked from where she was clearing a recently vacated table.

"No, I've only got a minute. Just swung by to talk to Ally for a sec."

"Oh," Lizzie said, eyebrows rose in surprise. "She's in back, there."

Catania stepped up to the counter and tapped her fingers on the Formica as she waited. Within a few moments, Ally appeared, her arms loaded down with plates of food for two men sitting at the breakfast counter. She did a double take when she spotted

Catania, her smile bright.

"Here you go, guys," she said, delivering the orders to her customers. She chatted with them briefly before hurrying over to where Catania stood at the end of the counter. "Hey!" Her smile grew when she neared her, reaching out and quickly squeezing the hand that rested on the counter. "Your usual?"

"No, I'm just on my way through and wanted to say hi." Catania returned the bright smile.

"'Scuse me, girls," Lizzie said, squeezing by the two as she headed behind the counter.

"I'm sorry I wasn't there when you woke up the other morning," Ally said. "I had to get breakfast started for the tenants."

Catania nearly burst into laughter at the wide-eyed look on Lizzie's face as she stood at the coffee machine past Ally. "It's okay, I knew you had stuff to do. But hey," she added wiggling her eyebrows. "The pastries and coffee you left for me were totally worth it."

"Well," Ally said with flirtatious sweetness in her voice. "I didn't have any doughnuts, so I figured that would have to do."

Catania chuckled. "It did the job very well and Oscar was totally jealous." She absolutely loved the mischievous look in Ally's deep blue eyes. But, she knew she had to get down to business as she didn't have long to visit. She reached into the pocket of her jacket and withdrew the small canister that had resided in there, setting it on the counter near Ally's hand. "I picked this up for you at the cop store. I don't like you walking out by yourself so much at night, but I know you don't always have a choice. So, I got you some pepper spray."

"Wow." Ally breathed sharply in, picking up the spray deterrent and looking it over. "Thank you, Nia."

"Sure. Plus," Catania said and shrugged, suddenly feeling really unsure about what she had thought earlier was a fantastic idea. "I was thinking maybe I could teach you some self-defense techniques."

"Really?" Ally asked, eyes wide.

"Yeah, absolutely." *Whew!* "Maybe you can stop by my place Wednesday. In theory, I'm off." She grinned.

"Well, Nia, I have to stop by on Wednesday."

Confused, Catania shook her head. "Okay. Why?"

"I kinda work there on Wednesdays."

"Oh. Right." Catania brought a hand up and rubbed nervously at the back of her neck. "Yeah."

Ally grinned and leaned forward, giving her a quick hug and kiss on the cheek. "I'll see you then." She grabbed the pepper spray and dropped it into her apron pocket, then hurried over to new customers that sat down at the breakfast counter and did not look thrilled at being made to wait.

Catania watched her go, still able to feel the all-too-brief touch of Ally's lips on her cheek and smell the slight fragrance of her perfume buried under the aromas of pancakes and pot roast. She was also able to feel eyes on her.

She met Lizzie's amused gaze with a shrug. *What?*

※ ※ ※ ※

"I really appreciate you coming over to help us, Nia," Karen said, leading her newly arrived guest through the kitchen into the living room. On the rug in front of the formal fireplace were several large boxes.

"Jason got them out from the attic for me before he left this morning."

Catania stared down at them, hands on hips. "Okay. And you said you have ladders and such?"

"Yes, ma'am. I really appreciate this, Nia," she said again, grabbing hold of one of Catania's hands and squeezing in affection. "Jason got everything out that he thought you'd need."

"No problem. I just have to be out of here by one, as I mentioned on the phone." Catania gave her a smile, trying to let her know she was happy to help. She glanced at the mantel where several framed pictures of the couple sat as well as a few of their dog Sadie, who had died the previous summer. A few little carved woodland animals caught her eye. Walking over to the display, she reached out and took one, a little squirrel replete with a big fluffy tail and an actual acorn held in the wooden hands. "These are adorable. Where did you get them?"

"Oh, Jason carved those," Karen said, stepping up beside her. She laughed at Catania's shocked look. "Not many people know. He's incredibly talented. Come here, I'll show you some more." Karen led the way to a curio cabinet in the large house's foyer. Opening the curved glass door, she pulled out a dog, a cat, and a frog. "Cool, huh?"

"Wow." Catania took the cat from her, turning it this way and that, lightly running her fingernails over the carved fur. She looked at Karen. "How much?"

"What? What do you mean?" Karen asked, looking from the carved cat to Catania's eyes.

"I know someone who would absolutely love this. How much? I'll pay you for it."

Karen laughed, waving Catania's offer away.

"Take it. None of these are Jason's favorites. They're only here because I couldn't bear to see him toss out such amazing work."

"Really?" Catania asked, excited. She could easily imagine Ally's face upon seeing the surprise.

"Consider it payment for putting up the Christmas lights for me."

Catania gave her a huge grin. "Thanks. And hey, for whatever reason you've volunteered to try and impress my mother with the decorations, I understand the haste."

Karen joined her in laughter as the two women headed back to the boxes of outdoor decorations.

❧❧❧❧❧

"Ally? Are you still here?" Catania called as she jogged up the stairs after using the front entrance. With only one good arm and a hand that was throbbing, the front door was easier to maneuver than the heavy metal one at the back. "God, it smells good in here," noting the scent of fresh roses in the air. "Ally?"

"Hey. I was finishing up in the bathroom," Ally said, suddenly appearing in the hallway. She was in the process of peeling off pink rubber gloves when she froze. "What happened?"

Catania gave her a crooked grin. "Yeah, about this." She brought her hand up and tapped the sling her other arm hung in, her fingers heavily bandaged. "This is what happens when someone entrusts you with a ladder, an industrial-strength staple gun, and Christmas lights."

Ally rushed over to her, tossing the rubber gloves to the butcher block island. "Are you okay? Oh my god."

"Yeah." Catania gave her a rueful chuckle. "I accidentally stapled two of my fingers and, in the process of trying to get them free, I lost my footing on the ladder."

"Oh geez, Nia." Ally took her wrapped fingers into both her hands and held them almost as though to keep them safe. "I'm so sorry."

"Eh, it's okay," Catania said with a shrug. "Got me out of doing Jason's workshop." The two shared a smile. "So, that's why I'm so late. Karen dragged me to the emergency clinic. Do we still have time to work on some moves?"

"No, Nia. No, you're injured," Ally said, shaking her head even as she held Nia's hand closer to her chest. "We can do it another time." She grinned. "Besides, my Uber driver will be here in about ten minutes."

"Right, your lunch with Linda." Catania shook her head with a small rueful smile. She tried to ignore the heat spreading through her body at the soft warmth engulfing her hand. "I'm so sorry. I didn't know I was going to get hurt. But hey, we've still got a few minutes. I can teach you a couple things. But," she said, raising a finger of the hand on her hurt arm, the motion hurting her badly sprained wrist. "I do have something for you."

"You do?" Ally asked, eyes wide with excitement.

Catania reached into the pocket of her winter coat and withdrew the small, carved cat. She smiled at Ally's gasp. "Now, I figure this little guy doesn't need to be fed, no litter box to clean, yet he's still adorable."

Ally took the wood piece in her hands, turning it this way and that like Catania had earlier in the day, lightly running her fingernails over the finely carved fur and details. "This is beautiful, Nia. Where did you get it?"

"Well, Karen gave it to me, but my brother Jason carved it."

"Wow." Ally's look of awe as she met Catania's was filled with adoration. "Thank you." She left a quick peck on Catania's cheek before she moved away and set the gift down on the island. "Okay. Teach me."

"Okay," Catania said, grateful for the distance between them. "Very simple things to know are the obvious—crotch shot with the knee or foot if you can. But, also right here," she said, indicating the hollow of her throat. "If you do this," she explained, reaching out with her one good hand and manipulating Ally's fingers so she had a fist with her first finger bent so the knuckle protruded. She brought it to her own throat. "Okay, here," she said, lightly pressing the knuckle into the tender flesh. "It hurts like a son-of-a-bitch if you really jab it. It'll choke, or at least hurt enough to startle the guy."

"Okay," Ally said, all seriousness as she pressed in a bit a few times, almost as though to get muscle memory of exactly where to push. "I can do that."

"Okay. Another area that's easy to get to is the top of the foot." Catania lightly tapped Ally's with the heel of her boot. "These are the tarsal bones of the foot, and again, it hurts like hell when they are struck, and they can be crushed with enough force." She grinned. "Definitely a showstopper. Okay, put your hands on my arms, like you're grabbing me."

When Ally did as she was told, Catania used quick movement of a hard chop downward at the bend of Ally's arms, which instantly dropped to her sides with a small cry from Ally.

"Ow! What did you do?" she asked, bringing a hand up to rub her right arm.

"Sorry. It's a move to hit the pressure point right there," Catania explained, gently rubbing her thumb over the area. "Yes, it briefly smarts, but it's more a shock to the nerve that deadens the arm. This could potentially allow you to get away. But this," she said, reaching out to place her hand on Ally's shoulder, urging her to turn her back to her. "This could save your life."

Ally's back to her, she wrapped her one working arm across Ally's upper chest, easing her back against her front. With their bodies pressed together, Catania took a deep, quiet breath, trying to focus on what she intended to show the woman she held.

"Okay," she said, getting her mind where it needed to be. "It's very likely if someone is going to attack you, they'll grab you from behind like this. I only have one arm right now, but I'm going to hold on as hard as I can, okay?"

Ally nodded. "Okay. What do you want me to do?"

"Let go."

"What?" Ally asked, trying to turn around, but Catania held her tightly against her.

"Fall."

Catania grunted as suddenly her entire upper body was forced downward as Ally let her legs go limp. The blond woman slipped out of her grip and rolled away from her, staring up at her from the floor with wide, surprised eyes.

"Whoa."

Catania grinned even as her back and arm screamed obscenities at her. "Nicely done. See, if an attacker had a gun or a knife or some other weapon, they'd be in a pickle because they're trying to hold on to you but also their weapon. Dead weight would be impossible to control."

"Wow," Ally said, getting to her feet. "I can't believe how effective that is." She walked over to Catania, her phone beginning to thunder as she reached her. Removing her cell from the back pocket of her jeans, she glanced at the screen. "My ride is here." Pocketing her phone again, she smiled at Catania. "Thank you. It makes me feel better to have at least some rudimentary knowledge of how to help myself if I need it."

"When we have more time, I'll teach you more if you want."

Ally nodded. "I want." She brought her hands up to Catania's shoulders, glancing down at the arm in the sling before carefully pulling her into a hug. "Thank you for everything," she murmured.

Catania used her good arm to hold Ally to her once more, this time in a warm embrace. Her eyes slid closed as she felt the softness of Ally's breasts against her own, their bodies moving flush. She could smell the scent of Ally's shampoo as well as that ever-enticing perfume. She felt gentle hands move from her shoulders to her back.

Ally's head left Catania's shoulder where it had rested, her breath warm on an exposed neck. She felt her heart begin to race and her own breathing hitch. As though through some sort of magnetic force, Ally's lips moved to Catania's, their softness more than she could have ever dreamed. She felt the tiniest movement of those lips against her own and responded. She heard a small sigh escape Ally's lips as a hand glided from Catania's back toward the side of her neck.

Dark eyes widen, surprise...

Catania was startled, her hand tightening a bit on Ally's waist. She relaxed as she felt fingers lightly stroke her jaw.

The grip tightened...

She curled her fingers around a grip of cotton, pushing against the warmth of Ally's side even as she pulled on her shirt.

No breath, no breath. Can't breathe, can't breathe...

Catania moaned as she pushed fully against Ally, tearing her mouth away from Ally's, gasping for breath.

The shine gone in her eyes, mahogany skin dull, a yellowish fluid puddled at the corner of slightly spread lips. Suddenly, the eyes focused, lifeless yet direct.

"You did this," she whispered. *"You did this!"*

Catania yelled out, staggering backward as she pushed Ally away from her. She didn't even feel the pain in her wrist or fingertips as she fell to one knee, quickly scurrying away from the woman standing before her.

Ally gasped, managing to keep to her feet as she was forced a step or two backward. Her hand came up to her chest, tears welling in her eyes.

"I'm sorry," she whispered, turning and fleeing from the room, pounding down the stairs and out the front door.

Chapter Thirteen

Catania sat quietly on the floor against a wall as Matteo played his video game, undaunted by her presence. She rested her head back against the cool plaster as her fingers absently traced the details on the carved wooden cat that had been left behind in Ally's haste to leave.

Ally.

The truth was, she wasn't sure what she was more unsettled and upset about: what had happened with Ally and her understandable reaction to the events, or what Catania had experienced during it. The sight of the woman's face, the personal feelings—both physical and emotional—as that woman was being harmed.

She knew she needed to find Ally, but she felt there was little point. She had no way of explaining what had happened during their kiss, as the truth was she had no idea herself. What she did know was that there was some meaning behind it. It wasn't random, it wasn't her mind wandering, nor a flashback from a previous case. This was different and deeply disturbing.

"I'm assuming you won't be joining us for dinner?"

Catania was pulled out of her deep and troubling thoughts by her brother's voice. "What?" She was startled to see him standing over her, looking down at her.

"Dinner. Food. Sustenance. You rarely eat

when you're upset by something. We eat in less than seventeen minutes."

"Oh." Catania cradled the cat in her hand as she pushed to her feet. "Sorry, I'll get out of your way so you can get your dinner." She gave him a smile of gratitude. "Thanks for letting me hang out, Matty."

He studied her for a long moment, the usually cool, reserved dark eyes filled with brief understanding. "I don't know what's wrong, Nia, but I know you'll fix it. You always do."

Touched, she took her brother in a tight hug. He responded in the way he always did with her, not exactly with his arms, but more of his body leaning into hers. "I love you, bud," she murmured before releasing him and walking over to the door where she'd left her jacket. She flipped it over her arm as she looked down at the carved animal in her hand. "Matty," she said, holding it out toward him. He walked over to her and took it, looking down at it before meeting her gaze with confusion. "Give this to Ally tonight at dinner, okay?"

He nodded. "Okay."

She turned to leave when she noticed something. "Matteo," she said, her finger touching the hook she'd told him to always hang his key on. "Where's your key?"

He looked at it, confusion on his face. He looked like a lost little boy who had been caught doing something wrong.

"Did you misplace it?" she asked gently, yet firm enough so he knew she was serious.

"No. I put it there, where you told me to."

She could tell he was telling her the truth, yet things happened. She scanned the apartment visually from where she stood.

"There it is!" Matteo rushed the few steps over to the couch and pulled out the carabiner his house key was attached to. Looking utterly relieved, he laid it in her palm like a precious artifact.

"Good job." She hung it where it belonged.

She left his apartment, closing the door behind her. In the hall she shook her jacket open before she shrugged into it as she headed down the hall toward the stairs. The farther down she went, the more she could smell dinner. *Fried chicken.*

Stopping at the bottom of the stairs, she glanced down the long hallway that led back to the kitchen. She knew Ally was there, back from her afternoon with Linda. She'd returned after their shared moment in Catania's apartment, that look of deep hurt on her face that Catania would never forget.

As Catania stood there watching, Ally suddenly appeared, a huge basket of biscuits in her hands as she scurried to the dining room just off the kitchen. Ally didn't acknowledge her, so she assumed she'd gone unnoticed, but seeing Ally was too much. Catania quickly hurried the few scant steps to the front door.

Catania made it to her Jeep when her phone rang, the ringtone for work. She hit the answer button and put the device to her ear. "Detective d'Giovanni," she said as she inserted the key into the door lock. "Okay, I'll be at the station in three minutes."

Oscar met her at their car as she pulled the Jeep into the lot. She quickly hopped from one vehicle to the other, and Oscar got them on the road. She belted herself in and pulled the spare notebook she kept in the glove box for times like this when she didn't have time to head home and get it.

Oscar's questioning glance to her injured hand

was met by a glare from her. He quickly returned his focus to the road.

"What we got?" she asked, clicking the pen she fished from her pocket into action.

"Suicide. City Park."

She grimaced as she jotted that down. "The public ones are just not cool."

Within minutes the sedan drove the winding path or roadways through the park that was placed in the middle of the town, peppered with grassy areas, tennis courts, and a man-made lake where geese hung out and wouldn't think twice about chasing an inattentive patron.

Oscar pulled to a stop next to one of the two squad cars that were parked there. There was a silver pickup truck parked at the site, a uniformed officer going through it. Catania assumed it must belong to their deceased. The responding officers had set up lights to reveal the scene as the sun had already begun to set.

"Hey, Robert, what we got?" Oscar asked the technician from the coroner's office.

"Looks like self-inflicted gunshot wound to the head," the middle-aged man said from where he knelt next to the body that rested about fifteen yards off the paved path of the park, a large tree nearby.

The apparent suicide victim was male, looked to be in his thirties, though the distortion in his features from the severe wound made that a bit tough for Catania to determine for sure. He wore blue jeans, slightly faded and worn, though specks of blood spattered the right thigh. His unzipped black leather jacket revealed a Denver Broncos T-shirt beneath. The small patch of snow beneath him had turned crimson.

"That's a Colt 38 Super," Oscar said, nudging the ground near where the pistol lay near the man's relaxed right hand.

Catania squatted on the opposite side of the tech and did a full visual scan of his head, face, and the wound. It was the side of his head with less damage, as it was the entry side. It took a moment, but when she took in his features, she gasped. "Oh my god."

"What?" Oscar turned away from debriefing one of the uniformed officers that had walked over to him. "Know him?"

"Yeah," she said absently, eyebrows drawing as she examined him closer. "Do we have any identification on him?" she called out to whomever may have the answer.

"Yes, ma'am," the officer who had been talking to Oscar said.

"Kevin Tanner, isn't it?"

"Yes, ma'am," the officer said, consulting the wallet he held in gloved hands.

"Why do I feel I should know that name?" Oscar asked, taking a slight sidestep to get a better look at the man's face.

Catania got to her feet and walked around the body to join her partner. "Officer, excuse us, please," she said to the uniform, who moved away with a nod. "This is the guy who was the father of Anastasia Luhan's unborn baby."

"Oh, shit." He met her gaze. "This changes things a bit, doesn't it?"

Catania said nothing, though she noticed CSU arriving as she studied the positioning of the body. "He was standing when he was shot," she noted, nodding toward his legs slightly spread at the thighs, but the lower legs together and crossed at the ankles.

"Dead man's fall," Oscar said, naming the common phenomenon of humans who are killed or die while standing.

"Not saying there's anything wrong with that," she said, eyeing his hands. She considered the very public place where his body lay. "I wonder why he didn't stay in the truck," she murmured. Looking over at her partner, she asked, "Wouldn't you? I mean, in a public park, the zoo isn't too far away. If you shot yourself, wouldn't you be worried a child could find your body out like this?"

"Yeah, but consider what this dude just went through," Oscar added. "From what you said, he was pretty shaken up by Anastasia's murder and that entire mess."

"He was," she agreed. "Get his hands bagged, and I want toxicology on both his blood and hair follicles, okay?" Catania said to the CSU technician who walked up to the body. Moving out of the way, she joined Oscar and together the two walked over to the truck.

"Detective!"

Both Oscar and Catania looked up at the officer who had been going through the silver pickup. He waved them over.

The bench seat of the medium-sized pickup was littered with candy wrappers, and what looked to be junk mail flyers for car insurance and home internet service. But, what had caught the officer's attention was what he held in the palm of his latex-clad hand.

Oscar's eyes grew wide as he looked from the small, white object to Catania, who was pulling on gloves before she took it to examine for herself. Though smudged with what looked to be dried blood or dirt, her name and phone number were still visible, as was the bold *18*.

"One of your matchbooks," Oscar said, eyeing her.

She nodded. "Indeed."

"Do you know who you gave that one to?"

"I think so," she said softly, filing away the number mentally to check later.

She handed the matchbook back to the officer, who slipped it into an evidence bag. She felt a twist in her stomach, both because she knew she was about to hear it—again—from Price, but also because she was concerned about the fate of the young woman who had received that matchbook from her.

"Nia," Oscar said, his voice low and troubled. It knocked her out of her reverie.

"What?"

"Look under that Sonic bag."

Catania did as she was told and, though initially confused, when she saw the light green bottle, her breath caught. Careful not to smack her hurt wrist on the frame of the truck, she reached inside to the area on the floor of the passenger side of the truck. Pushing the fast-food bag aside, she grabbed the bottle and withdrew it, both she and Oscar deathly silent as the label was revealed.

"I cannot believe that," Oscar said, shaking his head even as his eyes never left the empty beer bottle she held. "I know it's not exactly as common as Coors or something, but there's no way that can be the missing sixth."

Catania studied the Peroni label. "No idea. We'll have to see if it's part of the same series as the other five from the Luhan house."

"We never got the video from the stores around town where it could have been sold, did we?"

She shook her head, handing the bottle to the officer so it, too, could be slid into an evidence bag. "Nope. I checked on that last week. They said they needed more time, but they're afraid it may have been deleted."

"Damn. Of course."

Chewing on her bottom lip, Catania stepped back from the truck and glanced over at the body that CSU was photographing. "Something doesn't smell right there, Oscar."

"Oh, uh," Oscar said, clearing his throat as he shoved his hands into his trouser pockets. "Sorry. I had Mexican for lunch."

She glanced over at him with a raised eyebrow.

"No, I did. Sorry." As if to emphasize his point, he placed a hand on his protruding stomach as a small belch snuck out. "Sorry," he said again.

"Linda deserves a medal." Catania shook her head. "Everything seems too convenient," she said, getting back to the situation at hand. "I want to know if he was right or left-handed."

"His wife would know, no doubt. We'll have to get over there."

Catania nodded. "God, this is going to be hard. Just when, according to Kevin, they were trying to get things back on track."

"Maybe things didn't work out," Oscar offered. "Or, I mean the obvious thing here Nia is, what if he was fucking with you in that interrogation room? What if this guy was responsible for those three murders?" He nodded toward the body. "What if his conscience got to him?"

"Or," Catania murmured. "What if he thought he was on the verge of getting caught?"

"That, too."

Catania looked to one of the uniformed officers. "Hey, any witnesses?"

He shook his head.

"Then who called it in?"

"Anonymous."

Catania and Oscar exchanged a look.

❧ ❧ ❦ ❦

Catania opted to talk to Kevin Tanner's widow alone, dropping Oscar off at the station on the way over to the townhouse on the south side of town. As she pulled the Crown Victoria to the curb in front just past the mailbox, she let out a heavy sigh. Contacting next of kin was definitely her least favorite part of her job.

Glancing over at the structure made of river rock and light gray siding, she turned off the car and pulled the keys before climbing out. She let out a heavy breath as she tugged her jacket a little closer to her body. It was getting cold as night fell. It was nearly ten o'clock and only the upstairs lights were on in the side of the townhouse where her business lay.

Trotting up the few steps to the front porch, she reached out and pushed the doorbell, rocking on her heels as she waited. After a second ring, she heard movement on the other side and, as she always did in situations like this, was very cognizant of where her weapon was. When the door was finally unlocked and opened, a woman stood on the other side, dressed in baggy black sweatpants and an oversized green T-shirt.

She was barefoot, and her brown hair was pulled back into a short ponytail.

"Can I help you?" she asked, looking Catania over.

"Are you Mrs. Tanner?"

"I'm Lisa Tanner, if that's who you're looking for." The woman's brown eyes turned concerned. "Is something wrong?"

"Ma'am, I'm Detective Nia d'Giovanni. Can I come in for a minute?" Catania asked softly, showing her badge to try to put the young woman at ease.

She brought a hand up and covered her mouth, eyes wide. "He's dead, isn't he?" she whispered.

"Can I come in?" Catania asked again, voice gentle and understanding.

Allowed into the cozy home, Catania took in the teal and cream color scheme. The townhouse was small but well-furnished, if not a bit messy. But then, who was she to judge? Lisa Tanner sat on the couch, legs closed tightly together and her arms hugging her compact frame. No instruction, Catania sat in the easy chair that was perpendicular to the couch, her forearms running along her thighs.

"Mrs. Tanner, or may I call you Lisa?" At the woman's nod, Catania continued. "Lisa, your husband was found in City Park a little earlier this evening. At this time we're calling it a suicide." She waited for the initial wave of reaction to penetrate and the emotion that would follow. It was always so hard for her to not move over to the person and physically comfort them, but she had to keep her distance both physically and emotionally. She had a job to do.

"I knew it," Lisa eventually said, tears flowing freely down her cheeks and her voice thick with emotion. "I knew it."

Feeling it was the least she could do, Catania snagged a tissue from the box on the end table and handed it to the crying woman. "Why do you say that? Was he suicidal recently, Lisa?"

Lisa accepted the tissue and wiped her nose. At the question, she stared at Catania like she'd lost her mind and shook her head. "No. There's no way he did this himself, Detective. Not a chance."

"Why do you say that?"

A fresh bout of tears erupted, Lisa pulling her legs up as she seemed to be curling in upon herself.

"Lisa, we can do this later," Catania said, her heart going out to the woman. "If you can give me a good time to—"

"No!" she exclaimed, looking up from her hands, which she'd buried her face in moments before. "No. You find him, whoever he is. You find the son of a bitch who was following my husband. Kevin told me he felt afraid. He had for weeks."

Catania was stunned by this information. "Did he ever call the police?"

She shook her head, tossing the crumpled tissue aside and reaching over to grab another one. "No. He said he didn't feel like you guys could do anything. He told me he felt like he was a target."

"Did he ever tell you why? What any of this was about?"

The younger woman shook her head. "No." Fresh tears began. "He said he had something to tell me and we were going away this weekend to talk." The tears turned to sobs, again her face disappearing into the cocoon of her hands.

Oh, man. "Lisa, did you know anything about Kevin's involvement with Anastasia Luhan?"

Lisa looked up, eyes puffy and red. "What? Isn't that the woman who was murdered?" Her eyes widened as she slowly shook her head. "You're not saying he had anything to do with that—"

"No. No, I'm not, Lisa. But, according to him," she said, feeling the disclaimer was important. "He knew Anastasia Luhan and they briefly had a sexual relationship."

"What?" the woman asked, shock in her voice. "When did he talk to you? Why?"

"He came to talk to us after the murders happened. I think he wanted to try and clear his name before we found out. The only reason I'm telling you this is because I need to know if and how much you know about that. If you can add any information to this situation, Lisa. This is hard and I'm so sorry."

Lisa let out a heavy sigh as she returned her hands to hugging herself. "I just can't wrap my mind around any of this. I mean, like I said, I knew he was scared about something, about someone."

"How long was that going on?" Catania asked, reaching into her jacket to pull out her ever-present notepad. Clicking her pen into point, she jotted the date and time across the top of the first empty page she came to.

"Maybe a week or so ago. No, I want to say two weeks. But, things intensified in the last week. He was getting really awful texts, threatening texts. And, he felt he was being followed. One night he used the word stalked."

"Okay. Did he ever show you these text messages?" Catania asked quietly, pen poised to write whatever Lisa's response would be.

"No," the new widow said just as quietly. "He

just told me his life was threatened"

"Okay. And, what about these stalking claims? Did he see anyone? A face? Male, female…?"

Lisa took a cleansing breath, wiping her nose again. "He talked about seeing a figure in the shadows, like outside his job, that kind of thing. Oh, and there was a white car. He mentioned that a few times."

Catania's eyes shot up to look at her. "A white car? Did he say what kind?"

Lisa shook her head. "No. He just said an older white car."

Catania could tell the poor woman was done. She got to her feet, as did Lisa. "Listen, Lisa, again, I'm so sorry about Kevin. If you can think of anything else or if you need anything else, you give me a call, okay?" She flipped the cover of her notebook so she could grab a business card that was paper clipped to the underside.

"Okay, thank you," Lisa said numbly, taking the card.

Catania headed for the door followed by her unexpecting host. "Oh," she said, turning to meet Lisa's eyes again. "Two last questions for you. First, did Kevin own any weapons?"

Lisa pointed to an antique cavalry sword hanging on the wall over the dining room table. "He got that from his dad. Belonged to his grandfather or something."

"No guns?" When Lisa shook her head, Catania continued with her last question. "Was he right-handed or left-handed?"

"Uh," Lisa said, rubbing her eyes. "He did everything pretty much with both, but he would write with his right hand."

"Okay." Catania gave her a warm smile and brief

squeeze to her arm. "Goodnight."

≈ ≈ ≈ ≈

Emotionally exhausted, Catania made her way up the walkway to the front door of the police station, fresh from Lisa Tanner's house. She was surprised to see someone standing off in the shadows. Realizing it was Squirrel, she smiled and walked over to her.

"Hey, kid. What did you do this time?"

"Aren't you cute." The teenager reached into her windbreaker and pulled out a pack of cigarettes. Offering the pack to Catania, who turned it down, she took one of the smokes out and tucked it between her lips before the pack disappeared again. "Waiting for a friend to finish up inside," she said, nodding her head toward the building. Most of her face was hidden in the deep shadows, but as she brought out the white matchbook Catania had given her, she peeled off a match and within moments the tip of her cigarette glowed bright orange.

"Yeah? What friend?" Catania asked, hand on hip. She was trying to peer into the dimness, concerned Squirrel was trying to conceal something from her by how far back she was standing, trying to be hidden.

"What, are you the friend police?" Squirrel asked, taking a deep drag.

"No, just the regular police."

Squirrel chuckled. "Her name is Turn Right At None of Your Business Lane."

Catania chuckled as well, nodding as she waved the expelled cigarette smoke away from her. "Okay, okay. Are you okay, other than waiting for said friend? Are you hungry?"

"Nope. Just cold."

They both turned as the glass door opened and a teenage girl walked out, all leather, dog collar, and dark makeup. She glanced over at Catania before turning away with all the attitude that went with no life experience.

"Later," Squirrel said, scurrying from the shadows.

Catania watched the two teenagers vanish into the darkness of the late night. She shook her head as she headed for the door. She'd seen Oscar's car still in the parking lot and was glad, as she wanted to talk to him.

"Hey, Nene…"

Catania whipped around, looking for the owner of the voice, who had sounded like Squirrel. The girls were nowhere to be seen. "Squirrel?"

"Do your job."

She stood there, staring out into the parking lot and night beyond. Feeling slightly uncomfortable, she quickly went inside.

"Hey, Rodney," she said, waving at her colleague on her way back to her desk, Oscar sitting at his.

"We've got a problem, Big O," she said, tossing her notebook to her desk before shrugging out of her jacket and flopping down in her chair.

He glanced over at her, looking over his reading glasses which were perched precariously on his nose. "We got a problem, Nia."

She grinned. "I'll show you my big problem if you show me yours."

He chuckled. "Okay. CSU called a bit ago. There are no prints on that gun. Now, what's your big problem?"

"I forgot," she said absently, staring at him.

Shaking herself out of her reverie, she sat forward in her chair. "What, are we chasing a goddamn ghost?" She let out a heavy sigh and ran her hands through her hair. "Okay, your big problem kind of matches up with my big problem. I just visited with Lisa Tanner, Kevin's wife, and she pretty knew exactly what had happened the second I introduced myself. She believes he was murdered."

"By who?"

"By whoever was scaring the hell out of him the last two weeks of his life. We need to get his phone records and copies of his text messages. She didn't read them, but I guess he told her he was getting some seriously threatening ones. And," she said, clasping her fingers behind her head as she lightly rocked in her chair. "He was being followed. At least he believed he was," she added. "And guess by what?"

"The Casper Mobile?" Oscar asked with raised eyebrows.

Catania shook her head. "An older-model white car."

"Nia," he admonished, shaking his head

"I know, I know. It could be total coincidence. There are a thousand older white cars in this town. But," she said, holding up a single finger. "Don't you find that a little strange? I don't know, Oscar, my gut is telling me it's intriguing, if nothing else."

"Yes, I'll give you that. You know, I've been thinking about something, Nia," he said, eyebrows drawn with the seriousness of his thoughts. "As you know, per capita, Pueblo has the highest murder rate in the state, even above Denver and Colorado Springs. Lotta gang bullshit here. Even so, we had a whopping thirteen murders or so each the last couple years. Not a lot, but we've only got a hundred thousand people here, give or take."

"Right. We've covered this before, Oscar," Catania said, not following his logic.

He sat forward in his chair and clasped his hands between spread knees. "We've had five people dead in less than a month," he said, holding her gaze. "Well, granted Megan Murphy had been dead for some time, but you get my point."

She met and held his gaze, even as her thoughts began to spin. At length, she nodded. "Okay. Are you saying you think we've got a problem here?"

"I am. Potentially a big one."

Chapter Fourteen

Exhausted after an all-nighter, Catania stumbled into her apartment, doing her usual striptease as she passed through the kitchen headed to the bedroom. She stopped short, noticing for the first time the small bouquet of roses Ally had left the previous day. She'd smelled them, but she hadn't looked at them as they'd gone directly into self-defense moves and into disaster after that.

There were three roses in a glass vase, two white and a single red bundled in. She let out a sad, tired sigh. Taking the entire vase in hand, she brought the small bouquet to her nose and close her eyes as she inhaled the heavenly fragrance. So beautiful, like the woman who had left them for her.

Putting them down again, she continued toward the bedroom. Her intention was to grab a nap, a quick shower, then head back to work.

ᴥᴥᴥᴥᴥ

Catania stood at the counter in her kitchen slapping Miracle Whip on two pieces of bread. She quickly spread it, cursing under her breath when she accidentally tore one of the pieces. Finished with that, she tossed the knife into the sink and grabbed the bottle of yellow mustard, the bottle making obscene noises as she squirted the golden goop into a zigzag pattern on one bread slice.

The truth was, she wasn't thrilled about making herself a lunch to take to work. She just couldn't bring herself to go to Randy's as she and Oscar often did. The bigger truth was that she was being a coward. The events with Ally had happened two days before, and though Catania hadn't done anything wrong, she just couldn't take seeing that hurt in Ally's eyes.

Peeling a few pieces of smoked turkey from the lunch meat package, she placed them on one slice of bread and two slices of sharp cheddar on the other.

"Ta da," she muttered sarcastically, pressing the two layered pieces of bread together to make a sandwich. "Magic."

She finished packing her lunch then headed toward the hall, running her fingers through her drying hair. She glanced at the news on the TV as she passed, intending to change from her shorts and tank top into work clothes. She stopped mid-stride when she heard the loud echo of someone knocking on the metal back door.

Her stomach clenching as nervous butterfly wings began to beat at her ribcage, she padded over and unlocked it, pushing it open. To her surprise, her youngest brother stood on the other side, and he wasn't alone.

"Oh my god, Leo! What happened to your face?"

The teen entered the apartment, followed by a second young man who had also been roughed up. She closed and locked the door behind the two boys, only realizing the unknown one was a fellow student with her brother at the high school because he, too, wore a letterman of green and gold.

"What happened?" she asked again, leading the

two farther into the kitchen. "Sit down. I'll get some stuff to clean your faces."

She hurried down the hall to her bedroom and snagged her phone off the dresser before heading to the bathroom. As she gathered a few basic first aid components, she flashed off a quick text to Oscar to let him know she may be a few minutes late.

"Alright, Leo, you've got some explaining to do," she said in her "cop voice," eyeing him. She unloaded the items in her arms onto the butcher block island.

"I'm sorry to just show up on your doorstep, Nia," Leonardo said, sitting dutifully on one of the three stools that lined the backside of the island. "Three guys jumped us."

"Jesus, that's terrible," she said, eyebrows drawn. "Who? Why? And, who is this?" She indicated the other teen. Looking at the two boys, if you removed their minor injuries, they could easily be mistaken for two young men who had stepped out of the pages of a teeny bopper magazine.

"Oh, sorry. Sis, this is Ryan. He's..." The two exchanged a brief look before Leo swallowed hard and met Catania's gaze again. "He's my boyfriend."

Her eyebrows must have nearly shot off her forehead from the explosion of laughter from Leo. "I see," she finally said, glancing at the boy with Brad Pitt good looks. "Well, Ryan, it's nice to meet you." She extended her hand out and he took it.

"So, you're the gay one, right?" he asked.

"Gay one?"

"Yeah. Leo mentioned out of all his brothers and you, there was a gay one. That's you, right?"

Catania eyed her brother, who quickly looked away. Stopping the smile that wanted to spread across her lips, Catania cleared her throat and nodded, dousing a large cotton ball with peroxide. "Yes, Ryan," she said softly, lifting the saturated cotton ball to the cut above Leo's eye. He hissed and winced at the insta-burn. *Serves you right.* "I'm a lesbian."

"Why didn't you tell me?" Leonardo asked, wincing as she gently wiped away some of the blood from the minor cut he'd taken to his left cheekbone.

Stopping her ministrations, she raised an eyebrow. "Why didn't you?"

He grinned. "Touché." He met her gaze, smile gone. "Thanks, Sis."

She patted his knee. "Don't mention it. You can, however, tell me what happened to you two." She winced when her brother jumped as she moved to a particularly sensitive cut near his mouth. "Sorry."

"We decided to walk around the River Walk after we had some burgers," Ryan offered. "Minding or own business when we got jumped by three assholes under one of the bridges."

She looked past her brother to the other young man. "Did you guys say anything to them?" When Ryan looked away, blushing slightly as he rubbed the back of his neck, she let out a sad sigh. "Were you guys…"

"We kissed," Leo added softly, sounding ashamed.

"Damn. I'm sorry, boys," she said, shaking her head. "Here we are pushing 2020 and people are still insecure and ignorant."

"Sadly, I don't think that will ever end," Ryan said. "May I use your bathroom?"

"Sure. Down the hall and second door to the right." She watched him before returning her attention to her brother. She tossed aside the cotton ball she'd been using before grabbing a tube of Neosporin. "He's cute. Care to fill me in?"

"I'm sorry I didn't tell you, Nia. I planned to."

"To be honest, I thought you were going to come out to me at the diner that night."

He grinned. "I actually was, then chickened out and told you about the show instead. It's actually Ryan that got me interested in trying out. At that point we'd only been dating for a couple weeks." He shrugged. "I guess it was just too much to say it out loud."

She nodded. "I understand." She met his gaze and gave him a winning smile. "I'm proud of you, Leo. It's not easy. What are you going to do about the 'rents?"

He shrugged with a silly smile. "I don't know. Hell, even *you* haven't come out to them, yet. Although," he teased, wiggling his eyebrows. "I'm guessing with that little blond minx, you may not have a choice, huh?" He grabbed the red rose out of the vase and tucked it dramatically between his teeth.

She snagged it from him and put it back with its other two mates. "Yeah, well I fucked that one up, unfortunately." Ryan returned. Catania was relieved by the reprieve from having to talk about Ally. "Alright, lover boy," she said, patting Leo's leg to get him to move. "Your turn."

🙙🙚🙙🙚

"Let me get this straight. You're telling me we have a mother who was mutilated like she had drinks with Jack the Ripper. We have a father who was murdered," he said, his voice rising with each person. "And we have a four-year-old child who was left to hang from a fucking ceiling fan," he said, whirling his finger round in a circle above his head. "Like he's a goddamn pine tree deodorizer hanging from my fucking rearview mirror?" He slammed large hands on his desk as he loomed over it, glaring down at Catania and Oscar who sat on the opposite side.

"Yes. Sir—" Oscar began.

"And then," the sergeant continued. "You have some guy who blows his fucking head off in a public park who is connected to those aforementioned people. There is a gun next to him. There is a bottle that you tell me is part of a six-pack from the other murder scene. And yet…" He slammed his palm on the desk, startling Catania. "And yet not one goddamn fingerprint? Not one?" He looked to Catania then Oscar and settled on Catania again. "Do you know how to do your job?"

"Sir—" Oscar tried again.

Price glared at him. "I asked you a question, Detective. Do you either of you bozos know the heat the captain is putting on me over this? Not to mention the Murphy woman. You two sitting around with your thumbs up your ass?" He glared at each in turn. "Give me one good idea or one bit of good news before I throw you both back to runnin' patrols."

"Sir," Catania said, doing her best not to smack her superior. He'd always been an asshole but had been particularly difficult lately. "I think we need to do a press conference." She wilted slightly at the look that was suddenly aimed at her.

"A press conference," the large black man said, a condescending smirk on his face. "Really."

"Yes."

"Because that's exactly what we need. We need the public to see we can't do our fucking jobs so they have to do it for us!"

Biting so hard on the inside of her cheek she tasted

blood, Catania held firm. "Sir, we've hit an impasse. Whoever did this covered their tracks incredibly well. I think we need to expand this out to the public, see what they saw, what they know." She cleared her throat. "I also think we should include Megan Murphy's white Subaru with the information we're releasing."

"That went out already, *Detective*."

"Yes, sir, I know. I called the *Pueblo Chieftain* myself." Catania's tone was more biting than it should be, but she'd had it with this guy. She and Oscar had been doing everything they could, pulling out every trick in their little bag of legalities to solve these cases. "I believe the white Subaru may be involved."

Price flopped down, the old desk chair groaning under his bulk. He crossed his arms over his chest, eyes never leaving her. "Give me your reasoning."

"Kevin Tanner's wife said he'd told her in the last week of his life he was being followed, and he'd mentioned, 'An old, ugly white car,' her words. I know," she said, raising a hand to forestall his thrashing. "It's a gut feeling. I think it's related. And if not, we still need to find it for the Murphy case. Imagine your glory in killing two birds with one press conference."

※ ※ ※ ※

Standing proud and tall in his dress uniform, Sergeant Malcolm Price stood at the bank of microphones. His voice was deep and resonating as he outlined what the Pueblo Police Department was asking of the general public. Catania was also in her dress uniform as she stood behind and to the right of him, hands clasped behind her back. Oscar stood in the same position to Price's left. They exchanged a surreptitious glance.

"My detectives and I have worked tirelessly to solve one of the most heinous crimes this town has seen in more than twenty-five years," he said, looking out over a gathered group of more than a dozen newspaper and TV reporters and cameramen. "We've overturned every stone. We need your help."

Catania watched him, doing her best not to shoot invisible arrows into the back of his head. She'd lost respect for him when his ambition had overtaken what was once a fine officer. But now...

As she looked out at the press, she noticed a large crowd of onlookers standing around, listening. But what caught her eye was a young black woman who stood back from most, her long braids pulled back away from a lovely face. She wore a denim jacket bedazzled with rhinestones spelling out various words: *Queen Bitch, Black Barbie, Kiss Mine.*

Catania watched as the young woman pulled a pack of cigarettes out of the pocket of the short jacket. The young woman's dark eyes never left Catania's as she extracted one of the slender white sticks and tucked it between painted lips. She seemed to be tonguing the filter side of the smoke as the cigarette bobbed slightly.

The woman reached up with a well-manicured hand and removed the cigarette. With a small nod, she turned and began to walk away. Catania noticed more bedazzled words on the back of the jacket. She also noticed a number: *18.*

Forgetting where she was for a moment, Catania nearly stepped away from the front of the PPD building where the press conference was being held in order to follow the young woman. She seemed so familiar to her, somehow. Instead she was brought back to the here and now with Sergeant Price's booming voice.

"I thank you for listening and," he turned to Oscar, moving far enough away from the microphones to not be overheard. "Anything to add, Detective?"

Oscar looked at him, surprised. "Uh, no."

Catania prepared to step forward after her invitation, but it didn't come. Price turned back to the press.

"Thank you."

She was supremely angry, but Catania pushed it down as soon as she realized he hadn't bothered to mention the Subaru. She quickly moved herself between him and the microphones as she reached into her pocket.

"Sorry folks. I wanted to add that we're also asking for the public's help in locating this car." She held out the copy of Lara's snapshot. "We're looking for this. It's a white 1986 Subaru wagon, Arizona plates." She read off the plate number, which she knew by heart. "This car is wanted in conjunction with cases we are currently working. Thank you." She was about to step away when a reporter shouted out a request for her name and rank. She replied, spelling her name for him then stepped away, not even bothering to look at her boss as she could feel that the quiver of invisible arrows had been transferred to Malcolm Price.

෴෴෴

Sitting in her Jeep, Catania tapped the steering wheel as she stared at the building. It was only seven thirty, so she knew Ally had only been on her shift for an hour. It had been three days since...well, since. She missed her terribly and knew she had to make it right.

Cutting the engine, she climbed out of the Jeep and hurried across the parking lot and into the diner. It was busy, the couple hours of the dinner rush in full swing. She looked around, looking for the blond woman that she craved but didn't see, only other familiar faces buzzing around carrying plates of food, working on coffee refills, chatting, and generally adding to the mayhem.

"Hey, Ally, before you head out can you please grab that phone?" someone called out.

Catania followed the voice and found herself heading toward the breakfast counter. It was then that she saw a waitress she recognized as a newbie named Thelma, who was messing with the industrial coffeemaker. A moment later, Ally zoomed around the corner from the kitchen, her winter jacket tugged on over her uniform dress. She didn't even look in Catania's direction as she hurried to the ringing phone.

"Randy's, how can I help you?"

Catania waited patiently as Ally took the call, seeming to give the caller the diner's hours before hanging up. The blonde with the ever-resent ponytail turned around, freezing when she spotted Catania.

Catania was about to open her mouth to say hello when Ally turned to Thelma, who suddenly showed up at her side.

"Cheeseburger medium-well, cheddar with side of mayo, and seasoned fries. Oh, and a Coke."

Initially Thelma looked at her, confused, but then pulled out her pad from her apron pocket and scribbled down Catania's usual order.

Ally turned to Catania. "Thelma will take care of you," she said softly, then turned to hurry from behind the counter.

"Wait." Catania reached out and lightly grabbed her arm.

"Please let go of me," Ally whispered, somehow her words heard above the roar of the busy restaurant.

"Ally—"

"I'm embarrassed enough, so please don't make this harder," Ally said, gently pulling her arm away before she hugged herself. "Catania, you have been so kind to me, such a gift to me when I needed it most."

Catania wasn't sure what hurt most: the sadness in Ally's eyes, or the sound of her full name, which sounded so formal on those beautiful lips.

"I obviously read everything very wrong and I'm so deeply sorry I offended or upset you." She stared down at her shoes, looking as though she was about to cry. "I'll leave you alone." She met Catania's gaze for the briefest of moments, giving her a tiny smile before she turned and hurried down the main aisle of the diner.

"Wait, Ally!"

Catania tried to follow but was stopped as a man headed to the men's room nearly knocked her down as they crossed paths. She tried to go left, he went right, she tried to go right, he ended up going left.

"Want to dance?" he said good-naturedly.

No time to be polite, she shoved him aside and hurried out the front door just in time to see a yellow cab pull away from the curb.

Chapter Fifteen

*S*hit."

A black screen came to life to show a man looking down at the camera. He was middle-aged with thinning light brown hair streaked with gray and a round, moon face. Above his head was the ceiling, long, fluorescent lights set into it.

"How the hell do I turn this thing off?"

A fingertip appeared, looking like a giant moon as it hovered over the screen before disappearing.

"Damn it. It's still on." His hazel eye grew huge as it neared the camera lens. "Jorge, come here, man."

A Hispanic man popped into view over the man's shoulder. "Get a new phone?" he asked, the light above shining on a bald scalp. He raised a hand and waved. "Hello!"

"Stop foolin', man, I'm trying to figure this stupid thing out."

Jorge's hand became huge as it reached toward the camera, the view suddenly moving upward until there was an extreme close-up of the paisley pattern of the man's tie.

"The phones these kids use today," he said.

"Yeah, well it was my kid who gave this damn thing to me for Christmas. Messing around with it to figure it out and I can't get the camera to shut off."

"Christmas? Rodney, Christmas ain't for another week."

"Yeah, I know. The wife's family came into town early so we did Christmas last weekend. Fine by me. Now I can watch my Steelers on Christmas Eve and be left alone." The two men laughed.

"Amen, brother."

"Hey, Rodney, Jorge, Price wants to see you," an unseen third man's voice said.

"Price? As in Sergeant Price?" an unseen Rodney asked.

"Yup."

"Why?" Jorge asked, the scene moving to his tie and a small edge of black leather with the metal of a badge attached.

"Dunno."

There was silence between the two men, allowing for noises around them to come through—typing on a computer keyboard nearby, an unanswered ringing telephone, and muffled chatter.

"What the hell does he want with us?" Rodney asked, his voice lower than before and the tone confused.

"No idea with that prick," Jorge said, just as quiet.

Suddenly the frame went black again.

"Aha! I think I got it," Jorge said, his voice still heard even as the image of his tie and badge was gone. "Here."

"Thanks." The scratchy sound of fabric rubbing against a microphone cut off anything the men were saying for a moment before their voices were heard again, though a bit muffled. "Let's see what he wants"

There were more scratchy sounds for a few moments until finally there was a firm knocking on wood.

"Come in," a deep baritone called out. A moment later, "Close the door, Rodney, then sit down, gentlemen."

"What's up, Sergeant?" Jorge asked.

"Listen, no doubt you two have heard about these unsolved cases we have going. Right?" He pushed when there was no response.

"Yes, sir."

"That's not okay with me. You see, I oversee the Homicide Department, and when my people aren't getting it done...Wait, let me cut myself off." There was the creak of wood and his next words sounded closer. "I got me some goddamn eye-talian dyke and Tweedledee missing his Tweedledum working on this goddamn thing. I am not about to let these two jackoffs make me lose Lieutenant because we can't get this shit solved."

"Wait, Sergeant Price, from what I've heard d'Giovanni and Riley are doing a great—"

"You arguing with me, Slovodnik?" Price practically growled.

"No, sir."

"Sir," Jorge said "What exactly are you asking us to do? They're in Homicide, we're in Bank Robbery."

"Are you or are you not a detective, Trujillo?"

"Well, yes—"

"Then you figure it out. Dismissed, gentlemen."

The scooting of chairs and shuffling of feet and clothing dominated the audio before the solid closing of a door sounded crisply.

"What the hell are we supposed to do?" Rodney demanded.

"I got nuthin'," Jorge responded. "Damn, I wish we hadn't fixed your camera. I can't believe that just happened."

❧❧❧❧

"I should have worn better shoes," Oscar muttered as he nearly teetered over a pile discarded carburetors. "Help me here, will ya?"

Chuckling, Catania reached out from her place in the lead and offered her partner a steadying hand until he could join her in a clearer spot. "How much further, Lego?" she called out to their tour guide who had called the tip line allocated to their cases.

"Yeah?" the thirty-something junkyard owner called back, never slowing his steady pace through the piles of junk and discarded refrigerators.

"How much further?" she asked, nearly pulled off her own feet as, yet again, Oscar got caught up. She turned to see Oscar's entire foot buried in a pile of... something.

"Lego my ankle," he growled angrily.

Catania covered her mouth with a hand for fear of bursting into entirely inappropriate laughter. "Come on, big guy." She grunted, yanking on his hand.

"You comin'?" the self-named Lego asked.

"Yup. Be with you in a minute," Catania called back. She turned back to her partner. "On three..."

Eventually the trio reached the white hatchback that sat toward the back of the junkyard, cuddled up against the weathered fence.

"Here she is," Lego said, hooking his thumbs into the belt loops of his coveralls. "My family has owned this place for three generations, and I ain't seen this car here before." He nodded at his own declaration. Looking at Catania and Oscar, he shrugged. "What'cha think?"

"Uh," Oscar said, meeting Catania's gaze briefly. "Lego, those rims are so rusted, I don't think this car has been driven in more than twenty years."

❧❧❧❧

Catania and Oscar stood outside of a storage unit at a storage facility. It was cold and she shoved her hands into her coat pockets. Looking around and seeing nobody nor any cars, she glanced at Oscar, his ever-present sucker stick bobbing from between his lips.

"When was this guy supposed to show?"

"Half past twenty-five minutes ago," he said.

❧❧❧❧

"Mr. Reeves, this is a gray Volkswagen Squareback."

"It's not white?"

"No."

❧❧❧❧

"My nephew suddenly showed up one day," Marla Abrahamson said, leading the duo from the house to the expansive pasture that was her backyard. Sitting just beside the old barn at the edge of the property was indeed a white Subaru wagon.

"How long ago did he show up?" Catania asked, wondering if for the first time in three days she'd actually need to pull her notebook. This time it was looking like there may be some potential for something.

"About nine days ago," the older woman said, huddled in her housecoat.

"And we have permission to search this car?" With the older woman's nod, Catania said, "Ma'am, why don't you go back on inside," Catania said with a kind smile, briefly touching the woman's shoulder.

"We'll let you know if we find anything or need anything, okay?"

Left alone, Catania looked the car over. It definitely could be the one they were looking for.

"What do you think?" she asked, reaching into her pocket to pull out a pair of latex gloves.

"We may finally have something," Oscar said, pulling his own gloves on. "Let's check it out."

Noticing some paperwork and things piled on the front passenger seat, Catania headed over there, pulling the door open while Oscar headed to the back, opening the hatch.

"Colorado plates," he stated.

"Not our Arizona," she admitted. "But that could have been changed." She grabbed a handful of papers. All looked to be a mixture of junk mail and bills, both opened and unopened.

"There is so much shit back here," Oscar said, tossing aside jackets, clothing, trash, and even an empty box of diapers. "I don't see how Megan Murphy's body could have ever been transported in here." He studied a jack-in-the-box toy before that too got tossed aside. "Looks like a lot of this stuff has been here awhile, too." He stood from where he'd been leaning in through the open hatch. "You know what..."

Catania watched as he made his way around to the driver's side door, tugging it open. Squatting down, he began to look for something.

"You got that VIN on ya, Nia?" he asked, pulling reading glasses out of his jacket pocket.

Catania removed her phone and pulled up the note she'd made for herself days before for this very purpose. She read the number to him. "We got the right car?"

Oscar looked up at her as he pulled his glasses off, shaking his head.

"Damn it. I was so excited that maybe we'd found it," Catania said with a heavy sigh, tossing the paperwork back onto the seat. "Guess we should have looked at that first."

"Back to square-fucking-one."

Catania stepped back from the wagon so she could slam the passenger door closed. Damn it," she said again, hands on hips as her head fell.

"We've still got the Heiner house, and the guy down by the Mill—"

"Nah," she said, waving off Oscar's words. "Let's get something to eat. I need a break."

꙾ ꙾ ꙾ ꙾

Catania could feel her partner's eyes on her as she poured the salsa from the black plastic cup onto her taco salad. "Yes, Oscar?" she asked, never taking her eyes off her task.

"You know I like Mexican," he said. "But why aren't we at Randy's? Why haven't we been there this whole week and why have you been bringing your lunch? I haven't seen you do that in about two years."

She didn't respond, had no intention of responding, but what he said next stabbed her through the heart

"And, why did Ally look like she'd lost her best friend when she was over this past weekend to help decorate the Christmas tree?" He paused and Catania didn't respond. She didn't know what to say as she felt like she was about to cry. "Nia?" he said gently, pausing until she finally did look at him, managing to swallow her emotions down. "Did something happen, kid? I know you really like her. You two seemed to have gotten really close."

She let out a heavy sigh and set the salsa cup aside as she sat back in the booth. "We kissed."

Oscar's eyebrows raised. "Uh oh. Is she not into that? Is that why you're avoiding her?"

"Something weird happened to me, Oscar."

"Look, Nia, I want to hear about that, but Linda has really grown to like Ally and, well, I have, too. You're my buddy and I care about what's going on. Don't change the subject."

"I'm not. Listen. Ally kissed me. I'm...well," she said softly, about to say it out loud for the first time. "I'm crazy about her, so obviously I responded." She hesitated to continue, not sure what Oscar would think.

"But something went wrong, I take it?"

She nodded. "Yup. While we were kissing, that's when the weird things happened. I had this, this... *vision*, I guess."

"Uh, I know I've been married forever, but isn't that called a fantasy?"

"Of a woman being murdered?" She met his surprised gaze and held it. "It was crazy, Oscar," she said almost in a whisper as she brought back the images from her memory. "I saw her so clearly, could feel what she was feeling. It scared the living shit out of me."

"Jeez, no doubt. Any idea who this woman was?"

"I—" Catania cut herself off. She had an idea, yes, but decided it would be crazy to share it with him. After work, she intended to hunt down her street girls to ask around. "No."

"So, did you freak Ally out or something?"

"No, I'm the one who freaked out." She picked up her fork to mix the contents of her taco salad around in the edible bowl. "She took it as rejection of her, I think."

"Oh. Ouch." He was silent for a moment as he cut a few bites of his burrito, ready to stab and eat. "And, I'm guessing you did that wonderful communication thing you're so good at and explained it to her?"

She smirked. "Oh yeah, sure. 'Gee, honey, sorry 'bout that. Some dead woman popped into mind. You're awfully purty, though.'" She waved his idea away. "She'd think I was nuts."

"You know, Nia, I've known you a long time, worked with you a long time, and even though I've only known Ally for a month or so, something tells me she actually would understand."

She met his gaze but said nothing, his words rolling around in her mind.

"One thing I do know, however," he continued, pointing his fork at her. "You're being unfair by letting her believe something that's not true."

She used her fork to spear a hefty bite of meat, refried beans, tomatoes, lettuce, cheese, and salsa. She put it all in her mouth and chewed as her mind did cartwheels around what he'd told her. To be honest, it felt good to finally talk about it and maybe get some good advice. Finally, she swallowed and washed it all down with a drink of Coke.

"Is she really mad at me?" she asked at length.

It was Oscar's turn to take a thoughtful moment as he chewed his lunch. "I wouldn't call it mad," he said. "She just looked very sad. I mean, we had a great time with her. She came over Saturday for dinner and we did the tree stuff, but you could tell something was wrong."

"How do you know it had to do with me?"

He shrugged, using the side of his fork to cut another bite from the large burrito that was smothered with green chili, a Pueblo staple. "I know Linda had invited both of you, so she asked why you weren't there and Ally pussyfooted around her answer. I guess she hadn't asked you, especially since you hadn't mentioned it to me."

Catania felt the need to cry return at hearing that. She took a moment to gather herself with the distraction of eating before she replied. "I tried to talk to her at the diner. For some reason she was leaving early from her shift, but she literally ran from me." She couldn't look at her partner and friend as she told him that. Instead, she forced herself to continue eating.

"Well, Nia," Oscar said gently. "You said you think she thought you rejected her. She was probably seriously embarrassed. I mean, to kiss someone, that's kinda really putting yourself out there. I'd feel really humiliated."

Catania sighed, nodding as she chewed her latest bite, smaller than the previous one so she wouldn't choke on it and her emotions. "She said that to me," she said after taking a drink. "She told me she was embarrassed. She thanked me for essentially being her friend and…" She smirked ruefully. "It really sounded like she was breaking up with me. Our friendship, I mean."

"She must really dig you, Nia." He sat back against the seat, reaching out for his own soda to sip. "I mean, she doesn't seem like the vindictive type to me, so I'd say it's more along the lines of it'll be too painful for her to be around you."

She met his gaze, a knife slashing her heart. "That hadn't even occurred to me. I just thought that maybe she was too mad."

"I mean, I'm not her, I don't know, but from what I've gotten to know of Ally, she's a pretty sensitive girl. I can see her holding on to anger like that, you know? Or," he added. "Maybe holding on to that kind of hurt, like to kinda protect herself, you know?"

She nodded. "Yeah. I know."

"By the way," he asked, forkful of food halfway to his mouth. "How's the wrist? I mean, since you listened to the doctor and everything and kept that sling on," he added sarcastically.

She grinned, glancing at the Ace bandage she'd wrapped her wrist in rather than the cumbersome sling. "It's great. It's my damn fingers that hurt, though."

"You know what's crazy?" Oscar said, amusement in his eyes. "With how deep that wound was in your fingertips, how much skin those staples took and the scar tissue that will form, your prints will be altered. Maybe you should become the criminal cop."

She chuckled. "Yeah. Great idea."

✦✦✦✦

It was a rare rainstorm in late December, Christmas only a few days away. The rain was coming down harder and so was the temperature. Catania wondered when it would ultimately turn to sleet and then snow.

She and Oscar had ended their day unsuccessful with any of the tips they'd checked out. She knew Price would be angry, but they were doing what they could. She had an appointment to meet with the lab the following day to talk about some results in the Tanner case.

For now, she was looking for her girls. She had

questions about Liv, the young African-American woman she'd seen only the one time with Trish and Maria, the young woman whom she'd given matchbook number eighteen, the very matchbook that had been found in Kevin Tanner's truck. She thought she'd seen her hanging around during the press conference a few days before, but wasn't sure.

After driving around for nearly an hour and not finding anyone—everyone likely too smart to be out in the dangerously cold temperatures—she decided to call it a night. Glancing at the clock on her Jeep's dash, she saw the late hour and decided to suck it up and head to the diner. It was way too cold for Ally to walk home.

Pulling up to the building, she saw, as she expected, the lights already dimmed and shades drawn. She was, however, surprised to see a car in the parking lot. Pulling up near the back door, she killed the engine of her Jeep and didn't even bother putting her jacket on before she climbed out and ran to the door, hair already plastered to her head by time she reached it.

Knocking loudly on the door, it finally opened and the man she recognized as the new cook stood on the other side. "Hey," she called over the deluge. "Is Ally still here?"

He shook his head. "No, she left about twenty minutes ago."

Catania nodded and thanked him before running back to her Jeep. She looked out of the windshield. Well, at the glass anyway; the rain was coming down so hard she couldn't even see the building before her. Gripping the steering wheel, she tried to decide what to do. Go home, or...

Chapter Sixteen

S he raised her fist only for it to fall back to her side. Letting out a heavy breath, she raised it again, this time actually making contact with the wood, rapping lightly as it was late. She'd let herself into the main house with the key Karen had given her as a backup person should anything happen.

There was no answer. She cleared her throat, feeling nervous. She knocked lightly again, cringing at the seemingly loud boom in the quiet hallway. She raised her hand a third time then paused, ultimately deciding to let it go.

Her nervousness turned to deep disappointment and fear that she'd lost any chance of having Ally in her life. With a heavy heart, she turned away, bringing a hand up to run through the strands of her hair, still wet from the punishing rain both at the diner and then running to the Aberdeen House. At this point, all she wanted was to take a hot shower, climb into bed, and disappear.

Her morose thoughts were interrupted when she heard the sound of a door opening and her name spoken softly. Turning, she was treated to the sight of Ally, who had taken a half step out of her door, a white bath towel held in her hands. She still wore her diner uniform dress, but it was saturated in the front and her hair hung around her face in wet blond tendrils.

Catania walked back to the door and, without

a word, Ally stepped back inside and allowed her to enter. The door closed behind them, Catania noted a lamp was lit on the entertainment center giving the small living room space a soft, golden hue.

"Sorry I didn't hear you knock," Ally said quietly, the towel clutched in both hands and held to her chest. "I was downstairs and didn't hear it."

"It's okay." She studied that beautiful face that she'd missed so much. She met Ally's eyes, which were slightly shifty, often falling downward. "I'm sorry you had to walk home in this," she said at last. "I'm sorry I didn't get there in time."

Ally looked at her and gave her a small smile. "It's okay. They told me to go ahead and go a little early. It wasn't raining as hard then, but the skies opened up and dumped buckets about a block away from the diner."

Catania gave her a small smile. "Always the way it goes, isn't it?"

"Nia," Ally said softly. "It's late. What can I do for you?"

"I'm sorry," Catania said, again running a hand through her hair, this time out of nerves. "I won't keep you. I uh…" She tucked in her bottom lip to chew on before releasing it, feeling so lost, so unsure if she'd be able to make it right between them. "I wanted to apologize. I'm so sorry I hurt you, made you feel embarrassed the other day." Now she was the one who struggled to meet Ally's gaze. She swallowed. "I won't go into it now, but something very strange happened to me and it had nothing to do with you. My reaction, freaking out, it had nothing to do with you."

"I'm sorry that whatever happened upset you," Ally said, the slightest bit of bitterness in her tone.

Catania studied her face and knew it was now or never. Her heart just couldn't take it if it was never. She took a slight step forward, flirting with Ally's personal space. "I'm sorry I hurt you," she said again, her voice not much above a whisper. She shook her head. "You didn't read anything wrong."

Catania leaned in just a bit, just enough to make sure she wasn't going to get slapped before she fully bridged the distance. The second feel of Ally's soft lips was exquisite. It felt like home. She nearly cried in relief when she felt the slightest give in that softness. She brought a hand up, her fingertips just barely making contact with the soft yet chilled skin of Ally's cheek.

Ally's body began to relax as the slow, almost hesitant familiarization of lips continued. One of her hands left the shield of her towel and lightly gripped Catania's arm. Emboldened, Catania's hand on Ally's face moved, lightly cupping her jaw, using firmer pressure with her mouth. She nearly screamed out for joy inside when Ally tossed the towel away to the couch before that hand found its way into short, damp hair.

Catania placed her free hand on Ally's lower back, gently nudging her forward until their bodies were a breath apart. She could just barely feel the light shifting of Ally's body through the thick puffiness of her jacket. Any lament of wanting to feel more was wiped away when the soft, tentative touch of Ally's tongue flicking her bottom lip brought a soft sigh from Catania's mouth.

The moment their tongues brushed against each other, it was as if a switch had been hit. The dynamite that was the years' worth of pent-up passion inside Catania had absolutely been unleashed, the fuse lit the moment she'd met Ally. Apparently, the beautiful waitress felt the same as her hand wormed between them and she grasped the large zipper tag on Catania's coat, tugging down on it until the jacket fell open.

Ally slowed down and pulled away from the kiss as she reached up and pushed the heavy jacket off Catania's shoulders, gathering the garment into her hands and tossing it over to land on the towel. She met Catania's eyes and gave her the most loving smile before she left a lingering kiss on her lips, then took her into a tight hug.

Catania understood her need for that closeness, to reconnect after their horrible misunderstanding right when things were beginning to progress. She held Ally to her, their bodies flush. She tried to ignore the cold wetness of the front of Ally's dress, which was beginning to make her shiver.

"We need to get you out of these wet clothes," she said softly, not even thinking about how absurd that sounded considering where things seemed to be headed. Her tone suggested Ally should change out of the uniform and into some dry, warm fluffy pajamas. She grinned when she heard and felt Ally's chuckle.

Ally pulled out of the hug and took Catania in a quick but heated kiss before she grabbed her hand and led her toward the stairs and down. She led them over to her bed, which had not been made that morning. She gave Catania a sheepish grin.

"I ran out of time this morning and wasn't expecting company."

"Hey, you should see my place," Catania said with a grin.

Ally gave her a sexy little smile. "I have."

"Oh. Right."

Ally made it clear talking was over. She initiated

a deep, breath-stealing kiss as her hands slid down Catania's sides to her hips, bringing their bodies even closer together. Once again, that fuse was alive and burning.

Catania gently maneuvered Ally to the bed until the smaller woman fell backward onto her behind. She quickly scooted farther onto the bed until she could lay down with her head on the pillow, her hands reaching for Catania, who followed her. She quickly moved over to Ally, resuming their kiss as her body adjusted itself partially atop the petite woman, leaving her hand a whole landscape to explore.

Slowing the kiss down to maintain some level of control, Catania's hand ran down Ally's side, her thumb just barely grazing the side of her breast. She had noticed upstairs that Ally's nipples were hard and pressing against the material of her bra and uniform dress, likely from the cold rain initially. Now, her eyes so badly wanted to see those breasts bare, her mouth watering to taste them.

Leaving Ally's lips, Catania focused on her neck, licking, nipping, and kissing her way along the soft, warm flesh. Her hand moved back up, fully covering Ally's left breast, which brought a quiet sigh from her which quickly turned to a groan when Catania dragged her fingernails over the hard nipple.

Using her nose, she nudged aside the open collar of her dress, swiping her tongue over a bit of collarbone. She used her thumb and forefinger to lightly pinch the hardened nipple, which seemed to grow even more rigid under touch. Ally's hips began to move with a sensual restlessness, which pleased Catania greatly and let her know the woman beneath her wanted more.

Dragging her hand from Ally's breast to the

buttons on her uniform, she moved back to waiting
lips as she unbuttoned one button at a time, their kiss
slow and sensuous. Once all the buttons were released,
she ended the kiss and lifted her head, watching as her
bandaged hand spread the light gray material apart,
revealing Ally's gorgeous and absolutely perfect breasts
clad in dark green satin.

"Jesus, you're so beautiful," she whispered,
fingertips brushing over the soft flesh of her cleavage.
"Happy day," she exclaimed, grinning at Ally when she
noticed the bra clasp was in front.

Moments later Ally's breasts were fully revealed,
light pink nipples turned dusky rose in their excited
state. Ally let out a loud groan as Catania slowly ran her
tongue over the one closest to her, her hand finding the
other breast again. She answered with a groan of her
own as she took in as much of the firm breast into her
mouth as she could, sucking hard a few times before
releasing it to again focus on the nipple.

Ally's entire body began to squirm, and Catania
loved it. She continued with her mouth on her breast
as her hand glided its way down over a flat tummy,
fingers gathering the skirt of the uniform dress a little
bit at a time until she felt the warmth of Ally's thigh.
She trailed her fingernails up the inside of Ally's thigh
as her legs spread slightly until she reached saturated
panties.

"Oh god," Ally breathed, her legs opening a bit
wider as Catania's fingers pressed and rubbed a bit
against her hardened clit.

Catania growled, her level of excitement growing
when she felt how wet Ally was, how ready she was.
She left her breast and watched Ally's face as her
fingers made their way inside the waistband of the silky

material, the volcanic wetness within nearly singing her flesh.

Catania felt as though she'd be able to orgasm simply from the wonderful whimpers and noises Ally was making as she began to run two fingertips over that slick, hard clit. Normally she'd take her time before she got right down to it, but with Ally, she just couldn't help herself. To her surprise, within a couple minutes Ally cried out, her back arching as Catania's hand was covered by soothing warmth.

She smiled down at her as Ally began to calm. "Hey, you. Sorry, I just couldn't help myself."

"*You're* sorry?" Ally laughed, covering her face for a moment. "God, I'm sorry. I can't believe that happened so quick."

"It's magic," Catania said, wiggling her fingers, making Ally blush. She grinned and leaned down to leave an encouraging kiss on her lips, her own body feeling as though it was about to explode.

Seeming to understand that, Ally placed her palms on Catania's upper chest and pushed her to her back. She moved on top of her, straddling her hips. She reached down and, one by one, released the buttons on Catania's blouse until she could pull it open, revealing bra-clad breasts.

Catania was nervous, watching Ally's reactions to her body. It had been a long time, and she certainly hadn't been expecting this to happen. She rested her hands lightly on Ally's hips as soft hands roamed up over her stomach to cover her breasts, dark blue eyes meeting and holding her own.

"You're so beautiful, Nia," Ally murmured.

Catania caught one of her hands and brought it to her lips, kissing her palm before releasing it. "Thank you."

Ally removed her hands from Catania's body only to bring them to the open dress she wore. She shrugged out of the garment, which sagged at her waist, then tossed the unclasped bra to the floor. Rolling off Catania's body, she quickly kicked the dress completely off and removed the rest of her clothing before returning to Catania, who stared wide-eyed at the beauty she was presented with.

With very little fanfare, Ally made quick work of Catania's blouse and slacks, then nearly tore the rest of her clothing off of her. Both naked, Ally reached down and tugged the blankets up with her as she stretched out on top of Catania, using her thigh to nudge Catania's open for her to settle in between.

"It's a cold night," she purred against the warmth of Catania's neck.

Catania hummed her agreement as she ran her fingertips down Ally's back, ending with firm buttocks filling her hands. She tilted her head back as Ally explored her neck, soft sighs escaping her lips. She was loving the feel of Ally's weight on top of her, their breasts pressed together. She moaned softly when Ally pressed their hips more firmly together, Ally's exquisite wetness mingling with her own.

Ally left Catania's neck and returned to her mouth. As they kissed, slow and sensual, she rested part of her upper body weight on a forearm as she continued to move her hips. Catania opened her legs wider, both gasping as their clits made full contact. It was like lightning in a bottle, the intensity of the jolt of pleasure that shot through her.

Ally's head fell, her hair brushing against Catania's cheek as they moved together. She placed both palms against the mattress and pushed up, using the strength and power of her body to propel them both toward immense and unexpected pleasure.

Catania wrapped her hands up around Ally's shoulders, holding on for dear life as her release gripped her hard. Her eyes squeezed shut and her fingers became like talons as her body exploded, her hips thrusting up into Ally as she pressed down into her, both jolted by a second spasm.

After a long moment, Ally lowered herself, her breasts heaving with her rapid breathing and soft whimpers. Catania wrapped her arms around her, holding them together even as her legs fell open fully, exhaustion flowing over her. She turned her head and kissed the side of Ally's neck.

"Can we sleep?" she whispered, her body and mind about to give out. She smiled at the little nod she felt in response.

Ally finally lifted her head and left a quick kiss. "I'm going to go turn off the lamp upstairs and lock up. Be right back."

Catania watched her go, unable to take her eyes off an extremely shapely behind, womanly hips dipping sensually with each step. Once Ally had disappeared up the staircase, Catania slipped out of the bed and bent down to flip on the bedside lamp so she could turn off the overhead light to make it easier for Ally.

She walked over to the shelves with the snow globes on them, smiling when she saw the carved wood cat nestled between two of them. She reached up and gave the top of the cat's head a little love tap when something caught her eye. She noticed in the drywall behind the snow globes was a nail hole. A brief thought of what a strange place to put a nail or hang something was quickly interrupted by the sound of Ally returning. She hurried over to the wall and flipped the wall switch then scurried to the bed, goosebumps erupting all over her naked body as the temperatures plummeted in the early morning hours.

"Holy cow, it's cold," Ally exclaimed, appearing with Catania's jacket and the bath towel left upstairs. She hung the jacket on the mounted wall hooks next to her own and tossed the towel into the bathroom before she hopped into bed, Catania helping to tuck her in under the heavy blankets and comforter.

Catania smiled, pulling her in close. It felt absolutely amazing to feel Ally's naked skin against her own, to feel her body heat, to just see her joy in the beautiful smile she was gracing her with. They lay on their sides, facing each other, only the minimal glow of the bedside lamp bathing them in a bit of light.

"I can't believe you're here," Ally said softly, bringing up a hand to brush some dark hair out of Catania's eyes. "I thought I was just fooling myself that someone like you would ever want someone like me."

Seeing the uncertainty and wonder in Ally's eyes, Catania felt her heart break. "No, see you have that backward." She smiled at her and scooted the scant bit forward until their bodies were flush. As exhausted as she'd been from a week of long days and the emotional exhaustion of the situation with Ally, she suddenly found herself wide awake again.

Catania gently pushed Ally to her back. Deciding she needed to show her everything she felt but just wasn't in a place to verbalize yet, Catania used mouth, fingers, tongue, and teeth to explore every hill and valley. She wanted to find all the spots and places that made Ally gasp and moan.

As she made her way down Ally's beautiful body, she felt fingers in her hair, guiding her to where she was needed. The first taste of Ally's passion was incredible. The only things she was enjoying more were the sounds Ally was making, her hips moving in tandem with Catania's mouth. She brought two fingers up and slowly pushed them inside as her tongue batted ruthlessly at Ally's clit. She sucked it into her mouth and suckled it in rhythm with her fingers thrusting inside of her.

It wasn't long before Ally's back arched and her hips bucked upward as a loud cry filled the air. Her fingers held Catania's head like a vise. She pressed the flat of her tongue against the hard bundle in her mouth, fingers stilling as they were clenched by the spamming muscles of Ally's intense orgasm.

Finally, head and fingers released, Catania gently pulled out and left a soft kiss between Ally's legs before she climbed her way back up, covering them both with the comforter and pulling Ally's trembling body into her arms.

Chapter Seventeen

*T*here was no sound, just the black-and-white images of a deluge of water flowing down the windshield and windows as the rain poured beyond. A rearview mirror came into frame as did a hand, which tilted the mirror down, slightly. Revealed in the reflection was a figure wearing a black baseball cap, the bill pulled low. Just barely able to be seen was a pair of thick, black-framed glasses, the tiniest of cameras mounted to the right corner where the arm met the frame. Dark eyes could barely be made out behind the clear lenses, though the rest of the face dipped below the boundaries of the mirror.

The hand reached up again to readjust the mirror before the view became the driver's side window. The camera zoomed across to the front passenger seat, denim-covered thighs flashed in the frame until the shot paused on a bucket seat. The fabric was a light-and-dark checkered pattern with dark leather or vinyl bordering the fabric.

On the seat was a small black bag, about the size of a fanny pack. A hand grabbed it by the strap and set it on the thighs. The hand unzipped it and reached inside, pulling out a flashlight, which was set out of frame. A moment later a hunting knife was produced from the bag, the glare from a streetlight outside glinting off the blade as it, too, was set aside. Reaching inside for a third time, the hand brought out a small black box, about the size of a Zippo lighter with twice the thickness. A coiled wad of wires was attached to it. *The hand put the gadget down before it returned to the bag a final time, a moment later removing a pair of pliers and a screwdriver.*

The knife was replaced in the bag, which was then zipped and placed on the seat. The flashlight, gadget, and tools were gathered in one large hand before the sudden blinding brightness of the dome light flooded the car as the driver's side door was opened. The left hand reached down into the pocket on the inside of the door and pulled out a small, white manual: Trek Geek Gear Car Tracker. *A picture of the gadget was featured below the title.*

The view rose as the person wearing the glasses stepped out of the car. A quick glance at it as the hand pushed the door shut revealed white paint on the car before the camera quickly zoomed past the empty, rain-swept street to a tall brick building with the architectural details of a day gone by when a master mason would leave their mark.

The camera focused on a faded painted sign on the brick, Samson Bros. Textile, *before it moved back to the sidewalk. A stray cat jetted out from a recessed doorway, disappearing into the night. The shot switched down a perpendicular sidewalk as the camera wearer turned left. The scene got darker, streetlights more random, shadows deeper. The pace of the person quickened, scenery passing by faster and a bit jostled as the quick movements rocked the glasses.*

Finally, the lens spotted an open space, a small courtyard of sorts that had a single overhead light to watch over the parking spaces, likely meant for those who lived in the building.

Off to the right was a weathered chain-link fence lined with barrel trash cans. To the left was the building and a heavy-looking metal door. A small economy car and an old, beat-up pickup truck sat in the lot. A glaring space sat empty on the end, in front of the handful of steps that led to the metal door.

The view whirled around, taking in a dark, rainy night, empty streets, and saturated weeds. A booted foot lashed out, kicking one of the trashcans in an eerie, silent explosion of rage, trash flying into the air.

The camera view whirled back the way the person had come from, the harried pace obvious as the grout in the bricks ticked by in a blur. Finally, the street opened up and a white wagon came into view. The hand that held the screwdriver and pliers appeared in the frame and tugged the door handle to open the driver's side door.

Once inside and settled, the tools and GPS system were tossed onto the passenger seat on top of the black bag, followed by the black baseball cap. The hands, balled into fists, pounded on the steering wheel once before reaching up toward the camera.

The screen went blank.

≈≈≈≈

A smile spread across Catania's lips as she felt soft kisses make their way along the side of her jaw. She let out a little groan of contentment as she moved her head to the side, allowing more access. Her smile grew at the little chuckle that earned her.

"Good morning, beautiful girl," a soft voice murmured against the side of her neck.

"Mmm. Good morning." Catania frowned when

she realized Ally's warm nakedness was no longer under the covers with her own. She peeked an eye open and turned to see that a fully dressed Ally lay atop the covers next to her, her head cradled in the palm of her hand. "Why are you up and why are you dressed?"

"Had to get breakfast started," Ally said, leaving a few more kisses. "I brought you some coffee," she explained against the corner of Catania's mouth.

Catania moved her head just enough to get a full-on kiss. She smiled against Ally's lips afterward. "Why do you have to be so damned responsible? Do I have to adult today?"

Ally returned the smile and nodded. "Yes, you do. You have to go out and save the world."

"Shit, you're right," Catania said with a sigh. She absently ran her fingers through Ally's hair as she stared up at the ceiling, not seeing the white paint but her busy schedule for the day.

"Come on, baby. Sit up so I can give you your coffee," Ally said, turning away from her to reach for the bedside table and the steaming mug that sat there.

Catania did as asked, the blanket falling away from her naked breasts as she sat up. Normally the morning after was filled with awkward smiles, a few muttered words, and dressing as quickly as humanly possible. Not that she'd had many "morning afters," but the ones she'd had were certainly left back in the memory banks. With Ally, she felt surprisingly comfortable and at ease. Even with Ally sitting there in jeans and a sweater, Catania didn't feel the need to hide herself.

"Thank you," she murmured with a kiss of gratitude as she took the proffered coffee. "Guess it's a good thing you're my waitress, too," she said with a grin. "You know how I like everything."

Ally gave her a sexy little grin as she ran a single fingernail across one of Catania's nipples, sending a shudder down Catania's spine. "I'm definitely learning how you like everything."

Catania paused, mug of coffee halfway up to her mouth. She wanted so badly to forget about the coffee and spend the morning making love to Ally, but knew it wasn't possible. Instead, she initiated a deeply passionate, almost possessive kiss that left them both breathless.

"You're bad."

Ally laughed, giving her one last peck before pushing up from the bed. "I know, and I'm sorry. I have to get back upstairs. If you want to grab a shower here, feel free." She gave her a sweet little smile. "Then you can smell like me all day." With that, she was gone.

≈≈≈≈

Fifteen minutes later, Catania headed home after taking Ally's invitation to shower at her apartment. She needed to get to the office, so planned to quickly change clothes and brush her teeth, then back out she'd go.

Pulling down the side street that would take her to the back of the building, she slowed her Jeep, noting the mess that met her. It looked as though either a bear had gotten to the trash can, or a whole army of raccoons.

"Good lord."

Pulling into her spot, she was careful to not hit Mr. Horvat, who was out there with his snow shovel trying to clean up the mess.

"Good morning, Detective," he said, giving her a warm smile as he tipped his flat cap to her. "I think we had some hoodlums out here last night," he said, indicating the mess.

"Good morning, I guess," Catania said, eyeing everything as she climbed out of the Jeep. "Give me five minutes to change my clothes and I'll be back out here to help you with some trash bags," she said, literally running to then bounding up the steps to the metal door that was her back door.

Once inside, she did her usual striptease through the apartment, her hair still damp from her shower. She had, indeed, spritzed herself with some of Ally's perfume, and every time she got a whiff of it, she smiled and felt a little tingle in places she couldn't afford to tingle in with her job.

Quickly brushing her teeth and running a comb through her hair, she was off again, nearly running out the door before she remembered the trash bags she promised. Hurrying back to the kitchen, she pulled open the cabinet under the sink and yanked four from the roll, then headed out again.

෴෴෴෴

"You ever gonna wipe that grin off your face?" Oscar murmured, tugging on the latex gloves they'd been given. "You're starting to look like that guy in that commercial for Viagra."

Catania elbowed him in the gut. "I do not!" she insisted. "Now, be a big boy and put your professional face on."

"Okay, sorry about that," Gwen said, hurrying back into the room. "Been waiting for that call all morning." The deputy medical examiner pulled the sheet back, eliciting a bit of a gasp from the detectives. "I know. It's not pretty, especially with all the blood and gore washed away."

Catania took several shallow breaths as she readied herself to deal with Kevin Tanner. No matter how many times she was there in the morgue, no matter how bad or how mild it was, it never got easier.

"Now, first of all, we found very little gunpowder on his left hand," Gwen explained, lifting the dead man's left hand and twisting the wrist to present the back of the hand to them. There was a small red circle drawn in a marker that could be washed off by the funeral home. "Right here." She pointed with a latex-clad finger as she eyed the duo. "Likely once the trigger was pulled, the gunpowder was in the air, so..."

Catania listened to what she was saying, forming a picture in her mind. She wanted to hear more.

"Now, here's where it gets interesting. Come over here."

Catania did all she could to close her mind, turn off her thoughts as she moved up around Kevin's head, which was cradled in a simple rounded metal stirrup.

"This is the entrance wound," Gwen said, indicating the area that was left of his skull behind his right ear. "There was substantial skull blow off, however I do have some good news." She looked at each in turn. "The muzzle of your weapon was pressed point blank here," she explained putting her finger behind her own ear. "You feel that part of your skull that is a bit of a bump behind your ear there?" When Catania and Oscar both followed her lead and felt what she was referring to, the pathologist continued. "The good news is that's one of the thickest areas of the skull, and we were able to get striations for your lab to test against the weapon. You turned in the weapon, right?"

"Yeah, Dr. Sweeney," Oscar said, leaning in a bit to get a better look. "Uh, it was a Colt 38 Super, found at the scene."

Gwen's brows drew. "This man didn't die from a thirty-eight, Detectives."

Catania glanced at Oscar, who was already looking at her. "What?"

"He was killed by a weapon that fires a nine-millimeter bullet."

⁂

The sedan was parked in an open field. Each held their burger grabbed from a fast-food joint, the paper bag with two large cups of fries dumped in sitting between them. Oscar had suggested the diner, but Catania couldn't allow herself to get distracted by seeing Ally.

"I'm stunned, Nia," he said, staring out the windshield at the cold yet sunny day. "I did not expect Dr. Sweeney to say that."

Catania said nothing for a moment as she chewed the bite she'd just taken from her burger. She mulled over in her mind not only what her partner had just said, but what Gwen had told them and shown them a couple hours before.

"I have a thought, Big O," she said after she'd washed her food down with a sip of her drink. She wrapped her unfinished burger back in its paper and set it up on the dashboard. "Get out of the car."

"What?"

"Get out of the car. Come on."

"What?" Oscar asked again, jumping out of the car with his napkin-bib still tucked into the collar of his shirt, the end blowing in the breeze.

Catania laughed, walking over to him and snagging the napkin free, handing it to him. "Okay, now." She turned her back to Oscar and raised her hands to the back of her head, spreading her fingers, elbows sticking out to the side. "Oscar, use your finger as a gun and put it where Gwen said Kevin was shot."

Oscar moved up to her and did as she asked, the tip of his fingers resting against the spot they'd been shown. "Okay. Bang."

"Alright. So, from your point of view, would gunpowder be where we need it to be?"

"Eh, maybe. The way your hands are right now, the left hand is fairly protected by your head. I mean, could it float through the air, sure. But, your right hand is far more likely to have residue."

"Okay. Move my hands to where it would make sense," she said, willing to play Gumby.

Oscar moved her hands this way and that, muttering to himself as he did. "So, in keeping with the theme I think you're going for here, which is Kevin was forced to walk to where he died, I think this makes the most sense."

Catania's hands had been placed at the crown of her head, left crossed over right. "This is awkward as hell," she said.

"I know, but it's the only position where the left hand is exposed, but there is also enough space for whomever to get the gun where it needs to go." To prove his point, Oscar against placed his finger at the spot behind her ear. "Bang."

Catania allowed her body to go limp, trying to

see if she could land how Kevin Tanner had. It wasn't hard, not forcing her body into any position during the fall but allowing gravity to do the work. Looking up at a surprised Oscar, she nodded.

"I think we got it."

Raising a hand toward him, he grabbed it and helped her to her feet. "I agree with Lisa Tanner, Oscar," Catania said, wiping dust, weeds, and a bit of mud off the back of her coat as they headed back to the car. "And not only that, we already knew there were no prints found on the thirty-eight at the scene." She grabbed her sandwich off the dash and unwrapped it to finish it. "I mean, would it have been some crazy, weird bacteria from Mars that got on his hands which ate away his fingerprints? Sure, why not. But, could that same crazy, weird bacteria from Mars changed the bullet from a thirty-eight to a nine millimeter, too?"

"Yeah, no," Oscar said, dipping his hand into their joint bag of French fries. "Are we still headed to the lab after lunch?"

"As far as I know." As if on cue, her phone began to ring. Looking at the contact, she chuckled. "She must be psychic." Connecting the call, she put the phone to her ear. "D'Giovanni…Hey, what's going on? We still on for—… Okay, no worries. Yeah, go ahead and tell me."

Catania listened, snapping her fingers to get Oscar's attention then pantomiming like she was writing. He quickly grabbed his own notebook and clicked the pen to life before handing both to her. She jotted down a few things as she was told them.

"Wow. Okay, I definitely appreciate the information. And by the way, Oscar and I were just with Dr. Sweeney over at the morgue. That thirty-eight you've got isn't even the weapon that killed him...I'm not shitting you. A nine-millimeter slug was found in his head." She laughed. "I know, crazy. Anyway, thanks for the info Andy, and have a good meeting. See ya."

Ending the call, she tossed her phone to the dashboard where her sandwich had been and jotted down a few last things the lab tech had told her.

"What happened?" Oscar asked. "Are we not going?"

"No, there was some sort of spill earlier today so they all have to go for a safety meeting of some kind," Catania said absently, finishing up her notes. Finally, she turned to him. "So," she said, handing the pen back to her partner before she ripped the page out of the notebook, tucking it into her own to add to her report later. "Absolutely no DNA with the empty beer bottle, however, partial good news."

"Partial good news?"

"Yup. They got a partial palm print on the bottle itself."

Oscar's eyebrows shot up. "You don't say."

"I do. No hits in the system, as there isn't quite enough to really get a good readout, but it's a start. He was pretty shocked by this gun issue, but they're sending the Colt to ballistics anyway. If this is in fact a murder, our shooter had to have brought that gun since Kevin Tanner didn't own any."

"To his wife's knowledge, that is."

Catania nodded, conceding. "To her knowledge."

⚜ ⚜ ⚜ ⚜

Catania chewed her bottom lip, horribly undecided. She volleyed between the adorable orange kitten batting at a floating ball of string, and the rainbow that seemed to be pushing through the glass globe to end in a puffy cloud off to the side.

"Okay, I found this one," the sales clerk said, walking up to her with a smaller snow globe in his hands. Catania recognized him immediately as a gay man, so it made it easier to explain to him that she was looking for a gift for her "friend." "We just got this one in on Tuesday."

Catania took the piece in her hand and was immediately amused, yet felt a connection to it. It was a young maiden with flowing blond hair, her face raised to the sky with a look of wonder on her lovely face. What made it special, however, and particularly for how Catania saw Ally, was that the young maiden held a sword in one of her hands, the blade raised to the heavens, and a colorful red butterfly sitting atop the tip.

"This is it," she said, the other two options forgotten. She looked up and met his gaze. "This is it."

"Excellent." He gave her a huge smile. "Want me to wrap it up for you? Make it special?"

Catania rubbed the back of her neck and nodded. "Uh, yeah."

"Give me just a minute."

Left alone, she walked around the gift store, looking at this and that. There were beautiful music boxes, crystal figurines, the snow globes, of course, and a few other items. Standing at a locked cabinet filled with beautifully sculpted chess pieces, she suddenly had the strong need to look out the wall of windows that fronted the store.

Now that the icy rain was over, the crowds were out in full for last-minute Christmas gifts. All of that seemed to recede as she slowly walked over to the window as if in a daze. She stood next to a rack filled with porcelain animals.

On the sidewalk across the street something moved, and it wasn't a shopper. Her gaze became focused on a shimmering patch of...nothing? She couldn't wrap her mind around what she was seeing. It was a humanoid shape, perhaps the height of a woman—a small woman or a tall child. She saw a man who was talking on his cell phone carrying several bags bearing store logos hurry behind it, his image easily seen, though suddenly it looked as though he were walking underwater, the lines of his body fluid for that split second before he became solid again. The shimmering figure remained.

Catania reached her hand out absently for the door handle, just touching the metal when she started at a touch to her shoulder.

"Miss?"

Turning, she took in a calming breath at the clerk standing there. "Yeah," she said, trying to catch her breath.

He looked past her out the window before returning his eyes to her. "Uh, we're all ready," he said, a confused smile on his lips.

"Great. Yeah. Okay."

A handful of minutes later, Catania held the black paper bag with the gift store's name stamped on the side, the beautifully wrapped gift inside as she hurried out into the cold night. She'd promised Ally she'd meet her for her dinner break at Randy's. With the holiday around the corner, the diner was busting at the seams with shoppers, so Ally was working doubles. Karen had agreed to help her out and serve breakfast and dinner at the Aberdeen House, meals Ally had already prepared and just needed to be heated and served.

So, they figured a break to eat and get Ally off her feet would be good. Also, Catania was dying to spend some time with her. They'd both been so busy in the last twenty-four hours that they hadn't seen each other since Catania had left the apartment the morning after they'd made love.

She looked both ways, waiting for a small blue sport coupe to pass before she stepped off the curb and began to make her way across the street to where her Jeep was parked halfway down the block. She lightly swung the bag with the weighted gift in it back and forth, excited to see Ally's reaction to it. She hoped she liked it.

The night was suddenly alive with the sound of a roaring engine and someone screaming, "Look out!"

She turned to see a blur of white barreling for her. She had just enough time to realize she had to get out of the way. With a grunt of exertion, Catania threw herself toward the sidewalk as she felt the heat of a squealing tire pass within centimeters of her foot. She landed hard on her left shoulder, the bag she'd carried flung off toward the building.

Pain exploded through her entire body, centering in her wrist and arm, the very same wrist that she'd sprained so badly a week before. She heard the snap as her head bounced off the asphalt. It took a moment to realize she was lying directly behind a parked SUV. She blinked up at the license plate for a moment before the roar of reality hit her.

People were screaming, some yelling to get the license plate number of the car while others gathered around where Catania lay partially on her back and partially on her twisted left arm.

"Jesus! Are you okay?" a man asked, kneeling next to her. His bright blue eyes were wide and frantic.

Catania couldn't speak, shock and adrenaline making her tongue feel as though it were about three sizes too big for her mouth.

"Somebody call an ambulance," a familiar voice yelled.

Catania looked to her left, recognizing the store clerk who was up by her left shoulder. She mumbled something to him that her brain couldn't quite make out, but apparently he was able to.

"We'll get you another one, honey," he said kindly, his hand coming up to brush some bangs out of her eyes. "Don't you worry about that snow globe."

Catania heard muffled sirens in the distance. Her vision swam as much as everything sounded like it was underwater. She felt incredibly nauseous and a loud, annoying ringing began in her ears. She tried to voice these things, but nothing would make sense in her head, the words rearranging themselves at will.

As the warbling sirens got closer, she felt herself getting further and further away. Finally, her world went black.

Chapter Eighteen

"I think she may be coming to," a female voice said.

"Miss? Can you hear me?" a male asked, followed the sound of finger snapping.

Catania groaned, her head pounding and the need to vomit becoming a critical issue.

"Uh oh, I think she's going again. Let's get her turned onto her side."

She was manhandled quickly before her stomach gave in. Once finished, the pain kicked in full force and she cried out, white-hot pain slicing through her left arm and up her shoulder.

"I know, hon," the female voice said softly, a tender touch to Catania's forehead. "Hang in there. The orthopedic surgeon is on his way down to look at your arm."

"Where am I?" Catania slurred, her eyes slowly blinking open only to tightly close at the bright light that streamed in.

"You're in the emergency room. Can you tell us your name?" the male voice asked.

"Uh," Catania said, distracted for a moment as she felt her boots being removed before her feet were moved around a bit, ankles next, followed by both legs bent and straightened. "My name, uh, my name is Nia. Catania."

"And, your last name, hon?"

"Two minutes," another woman said softly.

"Okay. Thanks, Rita," the male said. "Nia, the doctor will be here in just a couple minutes to look at your arm, okay? We saw on the back of your badge?"

"Yes," she said, groaning again as a fresh wave of pain washed through her as she was jostled a bit, barely registering the sound of scissors on material and chilly air hitting her naked torso as her shirt was cut away. "Um, d'Giovanni."

"Excellent," the woman said. "Rita," she called out. "I need you to call this number. Ask for a Detective Oscar Riley."

"What happened?" Catania asked, her head pounding and the nausea still with her, though she didn't feel the need to throw up again.

"What do you remember?" the male asked, a cold liquid making her shiver as he seemed to be wiping away something on her right shoulder.

"I was in a store," she said, remembering the clerk showing her the beautiful snow globe for Ally. "Where's my snow globe?" she asked, her voice thick and thoughts still scrambled in her head.

"You were involved in an attempted hit and run," the woman said, a quick sting inflicted on her right hand. "You took quite a hit to your head, hon. Your left arm has been broken, too. In fact, here's Dr. Cubin to talk to you about that."

"Oh. Okay," she said, feeling dizzy and as if the darkness behind her closed eyelids was growing in intensity and darkness. "Hey, doc," she slurred before she succumbed.

≈≈≈≈

"Are you comfortable, Detective d'Giovanni?" the nurse asked, the bed controller in hand.

Still groggy from surgery, Catania looked up at her. "All things considered," she muttered.

The nurse smiled. "Okay." She grabbed Catania's hand that wasn't buried in a cast. "This button right here," she said, placing her thumb on it. "This will alert the nurse's station that you need something, okay? If you're in pain, get hungry, whatever. Just let us know." She left the remote with Catania and patted her on the hand. As she turned to leave the room, she stopped and returned to the bed. "Oh, you have some visitors, Detective. I can ask them to leave or send them in. What's your poison?"

Catania rolled the words she'd just heard around in her brain. *Poison?* "Send them in," she said absently. She rested her head back against the pillow, her heavily-casted arm braced on a steadying pillow. She was tired, loopy, and just confused by everything.

The hospital room door opened and a familiar face appeared, concern in his eyes. Oscar stepped in, carrying a black paper bag by the handles. He gave her a small wave and smile before moving deeper into the room. He set the bag on a table before walking over to the bed. Hands resting on the bedrails, he looked down at her.

"How you doin', kiddo?" he asked softly.

She met his gaze, able to make him out visually though he was a little fuzzy around the edges. "Okay, I guess. I think I broke my arm," she said, her head slowly flopping over to the left so she could look down at the cast. She looked back at him. "Right?"

He smiled and nodded, hands in his pockets, rattling coins. "Yeah, that you did. Pretty severe compound fracture, the nurse said."

"I don't know what happened, Oscar," she said, eyebrows drawing in her confusion. "One minute I'm looking for a gift for Ally—" She was interrupted by Oscar reaching for the bag, lifting it by the handles with a finger. A slow, dopey smile spread across her lips. "The snow globe. Where did it come from?"

He chuckled. "Is that what it is? When we were downstairs in the ER lobby, some incredibly flamboyant kid hurries in and has this with him, insisting you get it." He set the bag back down again.

"Why am I in the hospital?"

"Seems you rattled your brain around pretty good. I think they wanted to keep you under observation for the night. I haven't spoken to your doctor yet, but the nurse didn't seem to think you'd be here beyond tomorrow." He grinned. "You know, if you wanted a day off work, you could've done it in an easier way than interrupting Linda and me at dinner."

"You were at dinner?" she asked stupidly.

"Got the lobster necklace to prove it."

Oscar withdrew his hand from his pocket, pulling a large, plastic bib out with a bright red, fat cartoon lobster printed on it along with the restaurant's name.

Despite her fogginess, Catania burst into laughter, Oscar chucking along with her. "Jesus. How does Linda do it?"

"I honestly don't know," he said, bringing up a thumb to swipe at a laughter tear. His entire demeanor changing, Oscar put the bib aside and sat down, pulling the chair up to the side of the bed. "Nia," he said, voice soft but firm. "The officer at the scene talked to me in the ER lobby. Witnesses said it was a white Subaru wagon, eighties or nineties era, that, according to every single witness, seemed to be aiming directly toward you."

It took a moment for that information to soak into her pickled brain, but when it did, she met his concerned gaze. "License plate?"

"Some said they didn't catch it and others were sure there wasn't one. One guy was positive he saw temporary plates in the back window."

"Temporary plates?" she asked, baffled. "It had plates, 'member?"

"I know. But, knowing someone had identified the car, maybe he sold it," Oscar said, shrugging. "Don't know."

Catania gasped, eyes growing wide. "Oh my," she breathed slowly, her brain working out a thought. "What if he sold it to himself?"

"To himself? I don't get it."

"Think about it, Oscar," she slurred, trying to sit up in the bed only for the scream of her arm to stop her. "Okay, I'll stay here," she said with a groan. "Think about it. He didn't own the car, Megan Murphy did. What if the title and all that stuff was in the car already when he took her?"

A grin spread across Oscar's face as he nodded. "All he had to do was forge it. A sale from 'Megan Murphy.'" he said, using air quotes, "to 'Mr. Killer.'"

"Exactly. He loses the Arizona plates and it buys him some time."

"Fucking brilliant." He reached over, his hand sliding through the space between the bedrails and squeezed her good hand. "Excellent work, kid. Even higher than a kite."

"This is the channel you asked for, right?" Ally asked, looking down at Catania where she was tucked in on the blow-up mattress that Oscar and Linda had blown up for her on the living room floor after pushing the recliner back against the wall. Catania opened her mouth to speak when the almost-manic Ally continued. "We got you tons of food, already ready to go. I put it in individual microwave dishes so all you have to do is pop them in and warm them. We got you some Coke," she said, ticking the items off on her fingers. "Stuff for hot cocoa that you love so much, extra coffee creamer." She paused and grinned. "I got you the mocha fudge almond that I know you love. We got you some bananas, easy to peel. Also, I chopped up some apples and put them into a covered dish in the fridge. Just grab one and—"

"Ally—" Catania said softly.

"Okay, I'll be off work by two and Lizzie said I could—"

"Ally—"

"I'll bring you your favorite from the diner—"

"Ally!" When she had her attention, Catania smiled up at her and patted the mattress beside her with her good arm. "Come here."

Ally let out a small sigh and moved over to sit on the mattress, keeping space between them.

"Okay, no. Come *here.*" She lifted the blankets, inviting the other woman to join her. "You're not going to hurt me, come on." Once Ally had scooted over to her and laid down, Catania wrapped her up in her arm so that Ally's head rested on her shoulder.

"Am I hurting you?" Ally asked softly, her hand resting on Catania's stomach.

"Nope." She rested her cheek against a blond head. "I really appreciate you doing all this, but you know you don't have to."

"I know. I just feel so helpless. When Linda showed up at the diner to tell me what had happened, my heart stopped, Nia. I was so worried I'd lost you."

"I know." She left a kiss where her cheek had rested. "I don't really remember what happened, but from what Oscar told me, it could have been much worse. He's going to be looking at some footage today from businesses around there."

"Are you going to have to see that, too? Due to your job?"

Catania shook her head. "Nah. I wouldn't be allowed to investigate a crime committed against me."

Ally readjusted herself as she lifted her head, cradling it in an upturned palm. She looked down into Catania's bruised and swollen face where she'd landed on the street, a bit of road rash on her cheekbone where she'd skidded to a stop.

"God, I'm so sorry," she whispered, bringing up a hand and lightly tracing her fingers just under the area where the bruising began. "It already looks so much more painful than it did last night."

Catania smiled, taking the hand and bringing it to her mouth to kiss Ally's fingers. "In other words, I look even worse." She grinned at the shy look she received. "Yeah, I know. It'll look even worse tomorrow, being the third day and all. It'll be so incredibly fun to explain to my mother what happened." She let out a sigh as she placed Ally's hand on her upper chest, lightly running her fingertips over the soft skin of the back of her hand.

"I was surprised you didn't have someone call your mom," Ally said softly, cocking her head slightly as her gaze scanned Catania's face, stopping on her eyes.

Catania chuckled. "You saw how dramatic Mamma can be. This," she said, indicating her face and encased arm, "would be too much. I didn't want to bring that drama into the hospital."

"Baby?" she said, her voice soft. "Did this have to do with this major case you're working on?"

Catania studied Ally's eyes, so relieved to be somewhat clear-headed. She was still on heavy-duty painkillers, but since her return from the hospital that morning, Ally had been attached to her like glue. She'd been texting nonstop with Linda and Karen, Karen taking over her duties at Aberdeen House that morning. The three women had been working together to make Catania as comfortable as possible since she'd be home alone for a large part of the day.

This was why they'd insisted Catania be set up in the living room on the mattress. Everything, other than the bathroom, was within close proximity, and there was a TV and fireplace. She knew so much of this was because of Ally's loving and nurturing personality. She'd never had anyone be so kind to her, so absolutely solicitous.

As she looked into Ally's eyes, she knew she was falling in love with her, and that scared the hell out of her. She gave her a final squeeze, needing to be alone with her thoughts.

"I know you need to get to work. I'm sure Lizzie is already pissed as hell at me as it is."

Ally smiled and shook her head. "No, she's worried about you." She initiated a loving kiss before pulling out from underneath the covers, tucking Catania back in. "If you need anything, I put your phone right there on the mattress next to the TV remote." She stood and put her hands on her hips, looking down at her. "It was a good thing you accidentally left it in your Jeep. Probably would have been destroyed."

"Yeah, probably. You've got a ride, right?"

"Yup. Martha is picking me up." She blew Catania a kiss before hesitating for a moment, looking as though she was about to say something but stopped herself. "Um, I'll call you in a while to see how you're doing. Bye."

"Bye."

She watched Ally go, sadness in her heart as she felt terrible that their plans had been shredded. Ally had already volunteered to work at the diner—and make an elaborate Christmas meal at the Aberdeen House for those who didn't have families—long before she and Catania had gotten together and certainly the events of the previous night. And, Catania had plans with her family, so couldn't spend part of her day helping Ally.

So, they'd made plans to spend a passionate Christmas Eve night together. She glanced over at her arm and imagined the giant black and blue bruise that was the top left quarter of her face.

☙ ☙ ☙ ☙

Catania jumped, startled. Confused, she looked around, wondering why on earth she was lying on her living room floor and couldn't move. Her mind cleared enough for her to remember she was on the blow-up mattress and she'd burritoed herself in sleep. Noting the action of the movie on the TV, she looked around, wondering if that's what had awakened her.

A knock at the door sounded.

"Oh," she muttered, wincing as she moved to her back and sat up, her badly broken arm letting her know it was still there, too. "Just a minute!" she called out, surprised it was the door in the living room where someone was knocking and not the outside door by the kitchen.

With a small groan of pain, she got to her feet, her flannel pajama pants halfway pushed down her butt from moving around in sleep, and her sweatshirt halfway pushed up to just under breasts.

"Good god," she muttered, arranging her clothing as she padded to the door. Unlocking it and pulling it open, she was surprised to see Mr. Horvat standing on the other side. "Hey there," she said with a welcoming smile.

His own smile instantly fell as he took in her arm and face. He took a step closer. "Oh my goodness," he gasped, reaching up and whipping his ever-present flat cap off his head to hold in both hands in front of him. "What happened, Detective?"

"Oh, uh, there was an accident last night," she said, waving off the incident. She didn't want to worry him or explain, *Well ya see, there's this crazy motherfucker out there who likes to kill people. But, don't you worry! All's well.*

"I should say! If you want some of Mrs. Horvat's stew, you let me know and I'll bring you some."

"Aww, thanks so much," she said, giving him a huge smile. She'd had that stew before and it was truly incredible. She leaned forward all conspiracy-like. "If she happens to have some made, I won't say no."

He chuckled. "Well, I think you're in luck. I actually came down here because I saw your Jeep back there and knew you were home. We wanted to thank you for your kindness in leaving us the roll of potica," he said with an excited smile. "We enjoyed some with our coffee this morning. You're such a good girl."

She looked at him, her gut instantly screaming at her. "What roll of potica, Mr. Horvat?" she asked, her voice low, eyes meeting his with laser focus.

"The one you left on the hood of our truck," he said, the smile freezing on his lips. "With the bow on it…"

Without further comment or bothering to close her door, she squeezed past him and sprinted as best she could down the hallway and up the staircase, taking them two at a time. Her socked feet slid on the wood floor, nearly passing their door before she grabbed the doorknob and turned it, pushing into the apartment.

Mrs. Horvat, who sat on the couch knitting, screamed, holding up her partially finished creation like a shield in front of her.

"Where's the potica?" Catania called out, looking around the small, one-bedroom apartment, noting a bread box on the kitchen counter. "In there?" she asked the terrified woman, pointing at it. "Is that potica in there?"

"Fridge," the older woman said, gasping.

Her husband rushed into the apartment, out of breath and a hand to his chest.

"I need you guys to call this number and tell the guy who answers that I said to get over here ASAP." She prattled off Oscar's cell number, waiting until she saw Mrs. Horvat pick up the house phone with a trembling hand.

Going to the fridge, Catania saw the dessert bread wrapped in a clear plastic bag. Taking it out, she placed it on the kitchen table covered in a tablecloth that looked like a giant doily. Untying the knot made by the extended end of the bag, she ignored the screaming pain in her arm and shoulder as she pulled the potica out.

Bringing it to her nose, she sniffed, trying to focus to see if she smelled anything outside of the smell of the sweet bread and its filling. She was absolutely shocked when the house phone rang and Mr. Horvat explained he had to go let Oscar into the building. Moments later, the two men arrived back in the apartment.

"What's going on?" Oscar asked, walking over to Catania, who was tearing the roll apart.

"Jesus, did you fly here?" she asked, stunned he'd arrived within a minute or two.

He smirked. "Nah, I was literally around the corner. I was coming by to check on you. What's going on?" he asked again, eyeing the destroyed treat on the table.

"This was left for them outside on their truck," she explained, grabbing a napkin from the dispenser at the center of the table to wipe her hands. "They thought it came from me because I promised I would and usually get them some from Randy's, but I hadn't done that yet." She met his gaze, noting the uncertainty in his. "Isn't this a little strange, Oscar?" she asked quietly, not wanting the older couple to hear them.

Oscar let out a long breath and gave her an understanding look. "Nia, what happened last night was traumatizing and deadly, we both know that. But..." He indicated the mutilated potica on the table. "Isn't that a little convenient? The very next day? And, why would he do something to your neighbors?"

"Excuse me, Detectives?" Mr. Horvat said from

where he sat holding his wife on the couch. They both turned to look at him. "Lizbeth just told me that came from her niece." He swallowed, heavy mustache wiggling with the action. "I didn't realize."

Oscar met Catania's gaze again, a look of *See?* on his face.

Catania walked a few steps past him so she was almost at the couch. "Mrs. Horvat, she told you she brought this?" she asked gently, beginning to feel quite stupid.

"She said she would bring it by, yes," the older woman said, nodding vigorously.

Catania's eyes fell closed and she buried her face in her one good hand. "Fuck," she whispered, eyeing the mess she'd made. Turning back to the couple, she gave them an apologetic smile. "I am so sorry. I honestly thought you two were in danger. I'm sorry. I'll clean this up."

"And," Oscar added. "We'll get you a fresh roll of potica."

Lizbeth Horvat stood from the couch followed by her husband and took a few uncertain steps toward Catania. "No, no. I take care of this." She reached up a bony hand and gently rested it on the uninjured side of Catania's face. "You good girl," she said, her accent thicker than that of her husband. "I do want fresh roll, though."

Catania smiled, relieved. "You got it." She accepted the small hug from both husband and wife, then was led out by Oscar, who closed the door softly behind them.

Once they were in Catania's apartment, he turned on her.

"What the hell are you doing?" He stood and

looked at her, hands on hips as he shook his head. "I have to blame this on pain meds, because you're a better investigator than this."

"I know," she murmured, running her hand through her hair. "Fuck. I'm sorry, Oscar. I really am. I just…I don't know."

He walked over to her and placed a beefy hand on her good shoulder. "Nia, you can't let yourself get paranoid. Not now. I don't know, maybe I can talk to Price. Maybe you need a few days off—"

"No!" she practically shouted. "That fucker tried to kill me. If you think I'm backing away now, you're as crazy as he is."

Chapter Nineteen

Catania: *Now, you remember what we talked about, right?*

Matteo: *You mean your face looking like a zombie apocalypse?*

Catania: *Part of my face being very bruised, yes. You saw the picture I texted you.*

Matteo: *Yes. Looks cool.*

Catania rolled her eyes from where she sat in her Jeep outside of the Aberdeen House. She used her good hand to chicken-peck her response.

Catania: *Glad you're amused. I'm sitting outside the house. Grab your jacket and don't forget your key, your phone, and the dessert plate that Ally gave you to bring.*

Knowing he wouldn't reply but simply follow her directions item by item until he'd fulfilled the requests, she set her phone aside and waited. She didn't go in because she didn't want to frighten anyone she ran into. As predicted, her face looked worse than it probably would the entire time it healed. It and her arm felt equally bad, as well. The truth was, she had no desire to head to Jason and Karen's house. She was tired from dealing with pain all night and just wanted to be wrapped up in Ally all day.

But, that wasn't to be. Despite the fact that Karen was hosting Christmas at her house, she'd helped Ally earlier that morning, but the rest of the day at

Aberdeen House was on her little gorgeous waitress to make happen. So, Catania had kept her word that she'd spend at least part of the day with her family. She had, however, sent them an email the previous night explaining what had happened—though she outlined it as an accident—and warned them that she was pretty banged up.

She knew for them it was simply a heads-up, but Matteo would shut down if he saw her hurt, or anything so radically different than what he was expecting. By knowing and seeing it ahead of time, he could create a fantasy in his own mind, whatever it was he needed to, to deal with it emotionally and understand it in a non-empathetic way.

Like clockwork he opened the passenger door in exactly four minutes forty-four seconds, as he always did when she waited for him outside. She looked over at him to give him a chance to soak in the swelling and bruising of her face.

"Wow," he said, reaching a hand up for what she knew he was intending to be a gentle touch. The contact nearly sent her through the roof as pain exploded through her head.

Grabbing his hand, she gave it a quick squeeze before letting it go, then started the engine.

❧ ❧ ❧ ❧

After the drama of shocked looks and cries of "Holy shit," Catania sat on a stool in the kitchen as Leonardo stood next to her, helping her with the sling she'd brought with her. Her arm was hurting and the sling helped to stabilize it a bit, but she couldn't effectively put it on herself.

"How's that?" he asked softly, meeting her gaze. There was a new softness in his. Since they'd come out to each other, a closeness had grown between them that wasn't there before. It was a quiet understanding that, though they loved their family, they were alone in their secret. "Too tight?"

"No, it's not bad. Actually, pull that a tiny bit more." She watched him tighten the sling so her arm was held a bit closer to her body. "Great, thanks, Leo."

"Karen, do you have a Sharpie?" he asked his sister-in-law, who was counting out napkins out of a large package.

"Uh, you know what, Leo, look in that drawer over there by the phone. It's basically a junk drawer," she said, indicating the drawer at the end of the counter near the French doors that led out back.

Doing as he was told, he walked over to it, moving things aside until, with a cry of victory, he hipped the drawer closed and walked back to Catania. He gave her a mischievous grin. "I get to be first."

"What are you doing?" she asked, slightly irritated and slightly amused. "Oh, Leo, no. I'm a professional."

He smirked. "Yeah, well I was a middle school student when you felt the need to write the lyrics to 'The Sun Will Come Out Tomorrow' on the cast on my leg." He met her gaze through his bangs as he pulled the cap off the black Sharpie. "Remember that?"

She gave him a devilish grin. "Just be nice, okay?"

"Mamma, did you bring that photo album?" Dino asked, sauntering into the kitchen. He glanced at Leo, who was carefully writing on Catania's cast. "Oh, I'm next."

"What photo album?" Antonia asked.

"The one you said you was bringing. Melanie

wants to see it."

Catania raised an eyebrow. "You're still with Melanie?"

"Hey," he said, resting his hand on the counter next to where she sat on the stool. "It has been the happiest nine weeks of my life. In fact…" He pulled his class high school class ring out of his pocket, the large, bulky silver highlighted by a large ruby at its center. "This baby got me through four championships. Figure I'll get lucky again today."

"Wait, what are you going to do with that?" Leo asked, Sharpie frozen mid-stroke.

Catania let out a groan. "You're going to propose with your class ring, Dino?"

"What?" the handsome twenty-five-year-old asked, looking baffled. "It's just a placeholder, Nia," he said, grinning at everyone like she was making the stupidest point ever. "I'll buy her the real thing after she says yes."

"Why didn't you buy her one before?" Karen asked, glancing at him from the stove where she was transferring dinner rolls from a cookie sheet to a basket.

"Have you priced engagement rings, Karen?" he asked. "I mean, they're *expensive!*"

"Says the guy who pays no rent, no car payment, no insur—" Catania ticked off on her fingers before she was interrupted.

"Hey, I'm a man," he pronounced, a hand spread defensively on his well-developed chest. "I got material needs, ya know? Do you have any idea what it costs to look like this?" he asked, indicating his muscular body and modern haircut. "These clothes? I have an image to project, an image of the d'Giovanni family to project." He grabbed the Sharpie out of Leo's hand. "You know what," he muttered, scribbling something before throwing the marker onto the counter and storming out of the kitchen.

Those left behind all glanced at each other, surprised. Catania shook her head. "Let's hope it wasn't the happiest nine weeks of her life and she escapes." After a moment, the room burst into laughter.

⁂

Dinner had been eaten and the paper plates and plastic cups Karen had insisted on using—to Antonia d'Giovanni's horror—had been tossed or put in the recycle bin. Catania's arm was beginning to make its presence known via an increasing, dull ache. She had an appointment with her orthopedic surgeon the following morning, but at the moment, all she wanted was to go home, take a pain pill, and vanish from the world.

Needing to be alone, as her family could be entirely too much, she wandered around her oldest brother's workshop and creative area. Karen hadn't wanted a huge mess in the house—again to Catania's mother's horror—so long tables had been set up in the four-car garage portion of the building, which was heated, for the big meal. Truth was, with this bunch Catania didn't blame her one bit, especially since Paul had shown up with three of his kids, all pretty much unattended monsters. Even their grandparents weren't quite sure what to do with them.

The family was mainly being kept in the garage area as well as what Dino kept referring to as Jason's "man cave." Jason kept telling him to grow up. In that area was a large TV, a dartboard, and a pool table.

She'd been playing darts with Leo and their father for a while, but the jerking motion of throwing the darts against two very competitive men was taking its toll on the pain scale.

So now, she was wandering in the area where Jason hadn't told anyone they weren't supposed to go, but nothing had been set up for the holiday gathering in that space. It was obviously his workshop area, a corner that had a dusting of wood chips and scraps from his woodcarving. A stereotypical workbench, the envy of most hands-on kind of people, ran along an entire wall. She noticed something interesting hanging on the wall beside the pegboard that lined the wall behind the workbench.

A long, narrow iron frame was mounted to the wall, about four feet long and hung vertically. Iron rings were attached at six-inch intervals, dark brown pots set in them that perfectly resembled wooden water buckets about four inches high and six inches around, including some sort of dark blue material inside them to resemble water. There were six buckets in all.

"There you are. Your mom is looking for you."

She turned to see Jason stepping up beside her. He looked from her to the mounted art and back. "What is this?" she asked.

He gave her a boyish grin, reaching up to adjust his ever-present Denver Broncos baseball cap. "It's my bucket list."

Catania burst into laughter of the obvious irony. "That's awesome. Did you make these?" she asked, reaching out and touching the cool clay with her fingertips.

"Yeah. Just pinch pots, no biggie. And then," he said, pride in his voice as he carefully removed the top bucket from its holder and brought it down to Catania's eye level. "This," he said, poking the "water" inside. "It's a candle gel. Have you seen those gel candles?"

"Yeah, I used to have one in 1998."

He chuckled. "Yup, same thing, dyed blue."

She reached in and smiled at the cool, springy material. "So, is it your bucket list just for the fun irony, or does it truly signify your bucket list?"

"True blue bucket list. This one, for instance," he said, lifting the one he held. "It's to signify my marriage to Karen." He grinned, leaning down to whisper. "Don't tell her, but I stole one of the flowers from her bouquet and dried it. It's in here," he added, again poking the blue gel.

Catania smiled. "I won't say anything, but I bet she'd be really touched by that. Karen was a bucket list item, huh?"

He shrugged, replacing the bucket in its ring. "I love Karen a lot, but really it's more about finding stability. You know, with my mother and her issues, moving from place to place, boyfriend to boyfriend, bouncing me from family member to family member..." He leaned back against the workbench.

"How is your mom?" Catania asked softly. She couldn't remember the last time she'd seen her. Her drug and alcohol use had all but shriveled her up to a bag of bones.

He shrugged, crossing powerful arms over his chest. "I haven't seen her in about three years." He snorted. "Doubt I'll ever see her again. She wasn't in good shape." He glanced at her, studying her for a moment. "You know, Catania, you've really made good of yourself. I'm sure you parents are really proud."

"Thanks. And hey, *our* father is proud of you,

too. I do, however, think he wonders what the hell happened to the others."

Jason chuckled. "Eh," he said, shrugging again. "I think Leonardo may actually do something. I do think he should come out already."

Catania bit her bottom lip to not burst into laughter. "Yeah. But the others…" She just shook her head.

"The one that surprises me is Paul." He shook his head then glanced down at her cast. A grin spread over his face. "You look like you belong in middle school, everyone signing that thing."

"I know, tell me about it. Leo started it." She watched as he dug through a few drawers in the workbench before he produced a black magic marker. Popping the cap, he scrawled a quick word in small, neat letters: *ouch*. Catania chuckled. "Yeah, pretty much."

"Well, hey," he said, lightly tugging on her long-sleeved button-up, which she'd worn as she could roll the broken arm sleeve up and the shirt didn't have to go over her head. Her shoulder and face were still in a lot of pain, too. "Your mom is looking for you. They're looking at pictures."

Together, the two walked over to the recreation area where the matriarch, Karen, Dino and Melanie, and one of Paul's children were huddled on or around the couch as Antonia flipped through the pages of a large photo album that sat in her lap.

"This was the snowman the boys built," Antonia was saying. She glanced up when Catania entered the room. "Nia, you remember the weekends at our lake house when you were little?"

"I do." She sat down next to her mother when

Paul's eight-year-old hopped up and ran off to join those playing pool. She looked at the page of memories, smiling at some and rolling her eyes at others.

"Look, Mel," Dino said, tapping a picture of him around seven years old, shirtless and flexing his wiry, little boy muscles. "Even then I was built."

Catania gave Melanie a side glance, hiding a smile when the brunette rolled her eyes. Her attention was pulled back to the album at the sound of her name.

"Here you are about five. Look, there's Matteo!" Antonia said, the namesake in question not even lifting his eyes from the handheld video game he'd been given for Christmas.

"Who's that?" Dino asked, pointing at the third person in the picture.

The image showed a very short and very young Catania standing in the middle of the kitchen at the lake house in socked feet, the little jeans she wore high waters. She smiled, assuming she must have been in a growing spurt. Part of her Buddha belly was exposed as her T-shirt had come up a bit as she drank from an olive-green plastic cup, both hands wrapped around it. Matteo stood nearby, tiny fingers curled into the back of her T-shirt as he looked up at someone who was handing him a bright yellow sippy cup.

The person on the other end of that sippy cup wore dark blue jeans and colorful tennis shoes. She wore a striped T-shirt and had short, somewhat shaggy dark hair which hid most of her face as she was looking down at the two-year-old who just didn't look so certain.

"Oh," Antonia said at her son's question. "That is..." She stroked her chin as heavily plucked eyebrows fell in thought. "What was her name? She used to help out your Papa. Believe it or not, she wanted to be a plumber, such a young girl to want to get all messy. Such a sweetheart. Loved you kids. Papa?" she called out to Alberto, still throwing darts.

"What?" he called back.

"That little girl you teach, the 'intern,' you called her. What was her name?"

"Oh," he said, walking toward the couch, his unthrown dart twisting in his fingers. "Amy. Amy was her name."

"Amy!" Antonia slapped her palm against the glossy page of the album. She shooed him away before continuing with her story. "She helped your father with that bathroom off the kitchen. The toilet would plug up all the time."

"Did she become a plumber when she got older?" Melanie asked, leaning past Dino to look at the pictures.

Antonia shrugged. "Don't know. Her family moved away, I think."

"Show me—" Dino began.

"Catania, it is thirty-four minutes past the time I was ready to go home," Matteo said, glaring up at her from his game. "Furthermore, it's fourteen minutes past the time you were supposed to take your pain medication."

Catania knew it was absolutely time to go, that Matteo had reached his limit. She leaned over and placed a kiss on her mother's cheek. "We need to go, Mamma."

Antonia nodded, bringing up her hand to cup the side of Catania's face, only for Catania to hiss in pain. "Oh, I'm so sorry!" She rained apologetic kisses down on the non-hurt side of Catania's face.

"Okay, while we're all here," Dino said, moving

away from the couch and moving to the center of the room. "Melanie," he said, holding out a hand to her.

"Oh shit." Antonia sighed, making Catania snort in amusement.

"Now, everyone here, they all love you," he began, her hand in his. "So, I figure, why not?" He reached into his pocket, Melanie's gaze following the movement.

Catania watched closely as her brother withdrew his hand, class ring gripped between thumb and forefinger. Melanie's look of embarrassed confusion at the sudden spotlight he'd put on her melted to hope, and finally to shock and disgust.

"Melanie," Dino said, seeming to be warring with himself as he dipped into a weird almost-curtsy, finally falling to one knee. "Will you—"

"Wait, wait," she said, taking a step back, hands up and fingers waving in a pseudo-jazz-hands move. "Are you asking me to marry you, Dino?" she asked, voice hitching to a shrill pitch on the last word.

He looked from the ring he held up to her face. "Well, yeah. Yeah, I am."

"With a *class ring*?"

"Well, uh…" He looked back to the family, all of whom had gathered, with wide eyes, almost as though he were looking for guidance. Catania wished she had a bucket of popcorn.

Melanie looked to the couch. "Mamma forgive me, but…" she turned back to Dino. "You can stick that class ring up your ass!" With that, she stormed out, high heels clicking loudly on the polished cement floor.

He seemed to be too stunned to react before he jumped to his feet and hurried after her. "But, Melanie, this ring saw me through State! Twice!"

Everyone sat in silence for a long moment.

"I like her," Antonia stated simply.

Catania shook her head as she stood from the couch.

꜀꜁꜂꜃

"Yeah, you can just set those there. Oh wait, let me move this." Catania reached into the back of the Jeep and grabbed the black paper bag that held Ally's gift. "Thanks, Paul."

"Sure. Figure you're a little, uh…" He glanced at her. "Disabled at the moment." He snickered, loading leftovers packed for her and Matteo, as well as Christmas gifts, into the back.

"Yeah, not fun, that's for sure." She closed everything up once he stepped away. "I'm glad you and the kids came. Didn't know you were coming."

"Yeah, well, the kids were hungry."

She looked at her older brother, the closest in age to her. It always saddened her to see what he'd become. Years of drinking had given him a huge gut as well as the reddish discoloration of his face, particularly on his nose. It always made her think of the popular comedian of the early nineteenth century, W.C. Fields.

Ignoring his attempt at humor, she asked, "So, how are things down at the shop?"

"Eh, you know. Things have slowed down, so Papa gave me a few days off," he said, glancing away, watching a silver Mercedes drive by.

All she could do was shake her head before he returned his attention to her. She knew that meant he'd been found drunk at work again and their father, rather than fire him, was giving him a few days to get his shit together. In truth, she wished he would just can him.

"So, you gonna tell me what really happened to you?" he asked, indicting her cast and heavily bruised face, a bit of a twinkle in his eyes.

"What do you mean?" she asked, raising her chin a bit in defiance.

"Oh, come on, Nia. We all saw that lame-ass email you sent out. Really? We're supposed to buy a car accident? From you, the Golden Child?"

She sighed. "Paul—"

"No! You're gonna listen to me, Nia. We used to be close. We used to be really close," he said, voice a bit shaky, though she suspected it was far more from withdrawal than any kind of real emotion. "Remember? We did everything together growing up. It was us, you and me, who took care of the boys. And then," he added, looking her up and down with disgust. "You became a cop. Real big shit, ain't ya?"

"Paul, stop it," she said, her voice low but soft.

"Stop what? Stop saying what we all have been thinking? What, you're so fucking great because you're a cop? Because our retarded brother will *only* talk to you?"

"Never call him that again!" She stepped closer to him, enraged. He could insult her all his pickle-brained stupidity wanted to, but Matteo was off limits.

He smirked. "I bet someone tried to kill you," he said, waving a dramatic hand at her injuries. "I bet someone had enough of your shit, your judgment." He let loose a little giggle.

Catania now suspected he had alcohol on him and it was beginning to kick in. She placed a hand on his chest and shoved him away from her. "Go find a meeting, you pathetic drunk."

"Me? Me pathetic? You stupid bitch, you talking about me?"

"Paul!"

Both turned to see a red-faced Alberto, followed by Leonardo, running over to them. "What you doing?" he demanded, a hand on his chest where Catania's had been moments before. He glanced his youngest son. "Leonardo, go round up the kids and get your brother Dino. Paul needs a ride home."

Paul began to cry. "You always take her side, Papa. Always!"

"Son," Alberto said, his voice firm but not unkind. "It's time to go home now. Go home and sleep it off."

"You okay, Papa?" Dino asked, jogging across the yard with Leo.

"Yes. Take your brother home." Alberto turned from his second eldest son and walked over to Catania, who stood watching, part disgusted and part deeply sad by what had just happened. "You okay, Kitty Cat?"

She let out a heavy sigh and nodded. "Yeah. I just want to get home."

☙☙☙☙

Matteo was safely inside his apartment, leftovers put into the fridge and a huge battery supply for his new handheld dumped into a drawer for him to grab. The beautifully wrapped gift in hand, Catania used the toe of her boot to thud a few times on the door before her. It took a moment, but finally the door opened.

Catania smiled. "Merry Christmas." She handed the gift to a surprised Ally before reaching into her jacket pocket and retrieving the sprig of mistletoe that she lifted up toward the top of the doorframe. Ally let out an adorable giggle before leaning forward to give her a lingering kiss.

"Merry Christmas," she said softly against Catania's lips. "Come in."

"I'm really sorry to just barge in on you like this," Catania said, shrugging off the jacket which she hadn't even bothered to slide her good arm into. "I brought Matteo home," she added, feeling the need to explain.

"No, I'm so excited." Ally took her jacket and laid it across the arm of the couch before taking her in a very gentle hug, avoiding all the most painful places. "I didn't think I'd see you today at all," she said softly, running her fingers through Catania's hair.

Catania wrapped one arm around her, the cast-encased one tucked between their bodies, not allowing them to be flush. "I really missed you today."

"I've really missed you for the last few days," Ally said, her voice dropping an octave, sending a surge of want south for Catania, who grinned.

Their kiss was slow and sensual, both understanding nothing more could happen, so they enjoyed the kiss to the fullest. The kiss broke naturally and Catania rested her forehead against Ally's, her hand dipping down to rest on Ally's hip. "I wish I could stay," she said softly. "But I don't think it's a good idea." She smiled, the intent behind her self-warning clear. "Plus, I have to go to my doctor early."

"Well," Ally said, leaving her with one final kiss before pulling away. She picked up Catania's gift for her from where she'd set it on the couch and grabbed her hand, leading her downstairs. "I have something for you, too."

"Baby," Catania said, following her down the

stairs. "All I want for Christmas if for you to clean my apartment naked. I'm good after that."

Ally stopped her descent and turned, swiping playfully at her. "Behave so I can."

They reached the main living area and Ally placed the wrapped gift on the small kitchen table with gentle reverence before walking over to the tiny closet. She pushed the curtain that closed it off from the rest of the room aside and reached in, retrieving a bag with the Randy's logo on it, as well as a small wrapped box. She brought them both to the table where she set them down. She spared Catania a glance before pulling out a chair to sit.

"I hope you don't find this stuff cheesy" she said, her tone filled with anxiety.

Catania smiled, taking the other seat. She reached across the small table and wrapped her fingers around Ally's. "I'll love it. And besides, I feel the same way."

Ally let out a heavy breath before squeezing Catania's fingers and removing her hand. "You first." She slid the diner bag over to her.

Catania reached in until her fingers came into contact with something hard, cold, and cylindrical. Confused, she wrapped her fingers around it and brought it out: a stainless steel travel mug bearing the Randy's logo. "This is great, baby!"

Ally smiled shyly. "There's actually another one in there for Oscar. You guys can refill these with coffee for free forever." She playfully batted her eyelashes at her. "Every cop *loves* coffee."

Catania threw her head back with laughter, giddy with happiness, in awe that the amazing and beautiful woman sitting across from her actually cared about her. She placed her hand on the table to leverage herself up just enough to reach across the table and leave a lingering kiss on soft lips. "Thank you, baby. I love this and so will Oscar. Toss in a lifetime gift card for the doughnut shop, and you're in."

"This is the one I truly hope you don't find stupid or get offended by." She handed her the small wrapped box.

"Oh, Ally. Don't worry about that."

Catania took it and slowly tugged the white satin ribbon free before carefully unfolding the red wrapping paper, not wanting to rip it. She slid out the small gold cardboard box. Lifting the top, she spied a circular pendant about the size of a half dollar lying in a cloud of cotton. Carved into it was an angel with spread wings and hands upraised from the large sleeves of her flowing gown.

"Wow," Catania whispered, plucking it out of its bed, the attached chain draping over her hand. "This is beautiful, Ally."

"I'm glad you like it. So, let me explain. I met this guy who lost his son to gun violence, so now he makes jewelry out of melted-down bullets. I wanted this for you because I worry so much about you out there every day." She pursed her lips for a moment as she looked away, seeming on the verge of tears. Clearing her throat, she said, "Especially after the other night. So, I had him make this for you as a bit of a lucky charm, I guess. Maybe help protect you a little bit."

Without a word, Catania stood from her chair and pulled Ally up from hers. She pulled her into as tight a hug as she could. "Thank you," she whispered into blond hair, inhaling deeply the scent of her shampoo and the unique scent of her—the scent of home.

Chapter Twenty

T his is the coolest thing ever," Oscar said, raising his Randy's travel mug and turning it this way and that. He sipped from it before grinning. "It just needs my name on it."

"Well," Catania said with a smile. "Change your name to Randy and it will."

He glared at her over the rim of the mug as he sipped again. He said nothing as he returned to his breakfast, making her laugh.

"So, the metal plate is staying put, huh?"

They both glanced up to see Ally standing at the table, coffee carafe in hand. She leaned over slightly to reach Oscar's mug to top it off before leaning over Catania more than she needed to, her breasts just barely brushing against her shoulder.

Catania glanced up at her, eyebrow raised in accusation. The sexy little grin she got in return ignited her. She growled playfully under her breath, only loud enough for the waitress to hear.

"Down, girl," Ally said with a smile. "Soon, soon."

"But, yes," Catania said, getting the conversation back on track. "Dr. Cubin said he wasn't sure if he'd be leaving it in or not, but after seeing the x-rays from this morning, he feels at this point it's the better bet."

"How's it feeling?" Oscar asked, adding a packet of sweetener to his topped-off coffee. "Your face isn't as swollen, but man," he said, shaking his head. "Still looks painful."

"Eh," Catania said with a shrug. "Sleeping is still pretty tough, even with pain meds, but I'll live."

"Okay guys, I'll be right back to take my fifteen. Can I bring you anything?" Ally asked, moving away from the table, looking from one to the other.

"Uh, hey," Oscar said, looking over his eggs and bacon. "Can you bring me a biscuit?" he asked with a boyish grin.

"Sure," she said, turning to leave.

"With grape jelly," he called out after her.

Catania watched her go, her gaze falling to that gorgeous behind, hips gently swaying with each step. She could feel Oscar's gaze on her and turned her head to meet it. "What?"

"It's really good to see you in love." She dropped her eyes shyly as he continued. "She's a good girl, Nia. You two are really good for each other. I know Linda absolutely adores her."

"A biscuit for you," Ally said, suddenly appearing, a lavender cardigan covering the top of her uniform and nametag. She set the small plate with the single, perfectly browned biscuit on it as well as a few packets of grape jelly. "Scoot over, beautiful," she said, sliding onto the booth next to Catania. Beneath the table where they couldn't be seen, she pressed her leg against Catania's.

"Thank you, ma'am, and," he said, rising from his side of the table and leaning over to place a soft kiss on her cheek, "thank you for my awesome new travel mug. I will wave it proudly in front of my envious colleagues."

She laughed. "I couldn't do much, but I'm glad

you liked it. And, I was so glad Linda enjoyed the baking gear I got her."

He glared at her, hands resting on his rounded belly. "Yeah. Gee, thanks." He sat back down but reached into the pocket of his jacket and removed a credit-card-sized envelope that was a light pink color and smelled of perfume. "This is from us, Linda's suggestion." He nodded at Catania. "Give Dr. Doolittle some ideas."

"Hey," Catania exclaimed, watching as Ally opened the envelope to produce a gift card within from a store that sold anything from women's pajamas to bra and panty sets to lingerie and perfume.

"Merry Christmas, sweetheart," Oscar said, grabbing his mug of coffee. "I have to admit, I don't get it, though. Can't you gals go buy this stuff at Wal-Mart or whatever?"

"I wouldn't know," Ally said softly, tucking the glitzy gift card lovingly into the envelope before hugging it to her chest. "I've never had anything fancy like this before."

Catania smiled at her. In that moment she decided there was so much she wanted to do for her. She wanted to give her a kiss but knew this wasn't the place, so turned back to her breakfast. "When a woman wears a beautiful matching set of bra and panties, or even naughty lingerie under her work clothes, it makes her feel sexy, like a sexy woman, and," she continued with a little smile, "it usually translates to her partner at home that night." Dead silence greeted her as she scooped up a forkful of hash browns. She looked from Oscar to Ally and back. "What?"

Oscar reached over for the gift card. "Give me that back."

"Mine!" Ally exclaimed, moving her gift out of reach with a laugh. Returning the favor, she pushed up from the booth and leaned over to leave a kiss to Oscar's cheek. "Thank you, Oscar. I'll text Linda later."

He cleared his throat, rubbing the back of his neck as he blushed just a bit. Clearing his throat for a second time, he looked at Catania. "Price and me looked at the video this morning."

Catania raised an eyebrow, nodding her head toward Ally.

"Wait," Ally said, glaring at her. "Don't try and push me out of this discussion, Nia. I'm a big girl and I'm involved now, so I want to know what the hell is going on and who the hell tried to hurt you."

"Okay," Catania said softly, glancing past Ally to a man at another table who was looking over at them. She smiled at him before returning her attention to Ally. "I'm sorry." She gave her an apologetic smile and reached down to lightly squeeze Ally's bare knee. She looked over to Oscar. "Go ahead."

"I'm going to be real honest with you, Nia," he continued, using his fingers to split the biscuit in two before he began to butter the two halves and spread the grape jelly. "That bastard was aiming right for you."

"Was it our guy?

"It was our car," he admitted. "It was really hard to see inside. A big person, kinda like that kid said who told us about the car to begin with."

"Jackson."

"Yeah, Jackson. Big person, looked male because of the size. It looked like they were wearing a black or dark-colored baseball cap, too."

Catania let out a sigh, grabbing her travel mug to sip from it, more for something to do with a bit of nervous anxiety than because she was thirsty. "And the license plate?"

"Sure enough, temps."

"Why would this person do this?" Ally asked quietly.

Catania snorted. "We already know he's a sick son of a bitch."

"Yes, and who knows, Ally?" Oscar added. "Maybe he feels we're too close, though how the hell that would be, I do not know."

"He hates women," Catania said, setting the mug back on the table. "Maybe it really pisses him off I'm on the case."

"What about attention?" When both detectives were looking at her, Ally continued. "I saw a show once about serial killers. They're incredibly narcissistic. Maybe by going after you, he thought he'd get the attention he wanted..." she said, voice trailing off as the uncertainty in her voice grew. She gave them a shy smile. "Just an idea."

Catania met Oscar's gaze, eyebrows raised. "Not a bad one."

❧ ❧ ❧ ❧

Catania parked her Jeep around back in its usual place and after locking it up, she walked around the building to the front where the mailboxes for the building tenants were bolted to the brick in a security box that required a key for each apartment to retrieve their mail.

Standing at the mailboxes digging for her mailbox key, she glanced to her right when she heard footfalls headed her way. A woman who looked to be in her fifties and dressed for the cold day carried a large gift bag with a snowman decorating it and tufts of colorful tissue paper sticking out the top. She gave Catania a polite smile before reaching for the door handle of the front door of the building, finding it locked as Catania knew she would.

She backed up from the building before looking to Catania again. "This is fifteen hundred West Quinn, right?"

"Yes, ma'am," Catania said, opening her mailbox and pulling out a couple envelopes sitting inside. "Who are you looking for?"

"Josef and Lizbeth Horvat." She gave her a shy smile. "My aunt is probably so mad at me. I was supposed to bring her Christmas gift by the other night but ran out of time."

Catania froze, key still in the mailbox lock as she was about to lock it back up. "Wait, you're Mrs. Horvat's niece?"

"Yes," the woman said, eyeing her. "Can you let me in? I have their gift and potica."

Catania's jaw dropped with her stomach, but they were both distracted as the wail of an ambulance barreled its way down the street, lights blazing as it pulled up in front of the building. Shaking herself out of her frozen shock, she quickly unlocked the door and pulled it open as wide as she could.

"Ma'am, you're going to need to stand over here by me. Now!"

She watched as a male and female paramedic jumped out of the ambulance, quickly gathering all the equipment they felt they'd need, strapping it on a collapsible gurney before hurrying through the front door and up the stairs. She noticed there was a third paramedic who had been driving. He had climbed out from behind the wheel to the back.

"Excuse me," she said, walking over to him and pulling out her wallet, flashing her smaller badge she kept there at him. "I'm Detective Catania d'Giovanni. Can you tell me the call you received?"

"Ma'am, that's confidential information—"

"Listen, sir, I'm working on a case right now and I think this may be connected. Are you here for the occupants of apartment B?"

"Yes, Detective."

Catania nodded, doing her damndest to keep her emotions under control, doing her best to keep her work face on. "What was the call?"

"Seventy-six-year-old female, severe abdominal pain with vomiting. In and out of consciousness, non-responsive upon relation to dispatcher."

"Fuck." She ran her hand through her hair. "Alright. Listen, you guys need to be looking for poison of some kind. I have strong reason to believe she ingested poisoned potica."

"Ma'am?" he asked, eyebrows raised in surprised confusion.

"We had what we thought was a false alarm Christmas Eve." She glanced over her shoulder at the building, looking up toward the windows that she knew belonged to the Horvat apartment. "Apparently not."

❧❧❧❧

With Josef's permission before he left with his wife in the ambulance, Catania proceeded to search their kitchen. She'd snagged a pair of latex gloves from her apartment and was now going through the trash can she'd brought from the floor to the counter. She was hoping against hope that they hadn't thrown out the bag of trash from the night she'd torn through the roll of potica, and maybe the dessert bread remnants were still there.

"Oh, awesome," she breathed, recognizing the plastic bag the potica had been in, but to her horror, there were mere crumbs left of the bread. "Fuck me," she muttered. She had the feeling that, being from the "waste not, want not" Greatest Generation, Lizbeth had eaten the rest of the potica despite its potentially dubious nature.

"What are you doing in here, d'Giovanni?"

She looked up, shocked to hear the sharp, deep voice. "Sergeant Price. I was given authorization from the homeowner. I'm looking for something useful for Mrs. Horvat's doctors, as well as this attempted murder—"

"Who gave you the authority to open this case?" the large man asked, glancing around as he walked farther into the apartment to where she stood in the kitchen. "Hmm? According to my job description, I dole out the cases."

"Sir, I left you a voicemail—"

"I don't work via voicemail!" His voice boomed as he glared down at her.

She held her ground, even as she felt sweat beading between her breasts. "Sir," she said, voice low and just this side of a bit too angry to be speaking to her boss. "Due to *my* job description working in criminal investigation, it's my duty to check things out when there's been a perceived crime. Sir."

He reached out a hand, resting it with splayed fingers on the countertop, looming over her. "Don't use that tone with me, Detective, or I'll have you tossed down to filing so fast your head will spin."

All she could do was stare, not sure what to say. She knew they were alone in that apartment, and if she tried to file a report against such a threat, it would be her word against his. She swallowed her pride but stood a bit straighter, lifting her chin almost imperceptivity in defiance. "Yes, sir."

"Now," he said, both looking toward the doorway of the small apartment as two men entered. Catania recognized them as two fellow detectives, Rodney and Verne. "While these boys do their assigned job, you and I are going to your place so you can answer some questions."

"Alright."

Without another word, Catania led the way to her apartment, using her key to unlock the door and let them both in. She didn't bother closing the door after her superior officer had entered, instead leaving it open.

"Coffee?" she asked, walking over to the Keurig to make herself a cup. At his affirmative response, she made one for him, too. "What's on your mind, Sergeant?" she asked, placing a mug in front of him where he'd taken a seat at the table.

"How do you know the occupants of apartment B?" he asked, pulling out a pad of paper from the inside pocket of his suit jacket. He uncapped the pen and looked at her expectantly.

"Josef and Lizbeth Horvat have lived in this building for more than thirty years, and I've known them as my neighbors since I've lived here."

"How long is that?"

"Four years," she said, sipping from her coffee as

she watched him take notes.

"How did you know about the potica?" he asked, glancing up at her.

She wasn't entirely thrilled by the tone of his voice, a bit too accusatory for simply talking to a witness, but she ignored it...for now. "I didn't. Mr. Horvat told me about it."

"How did he do that? He just happened to think it was information you'd want?"

"Sergeant, I give him and Mrs. Horvat a roll every year. I told him back before Thanksgiving that I would get them some."

"And, so you did, this potica in question?" He was goading her, and she did not appreciate it.

"No. With the cases Oscar and I are dealing with right now, I haven't had time and forgot. And, as for how and why he told me about it, he thought it was from me, that I'd left it for them on the hood of his truck on the night of December twenty-third."

"Where were you the night of December twenty-third?"

She looked at him like he was crazy. He knew damn well where she was. "I was in the hospital, Sergeant Price. I spent the entire night there."

"Walk me through your time after your accident."

She wanted to bitch-slap him but kept her calm, wrapping her hands around the hot mug of coffee to help keep them to herself. "After I was nearly hit, I went straight to the hospital, that was around seven forty-five. Detective Riley, Linda Riley, and my gi—." She stopped herself, remembering who she was talking to and his attitudes on most things. "My friend, Ally Findley, were there to verify."

"Ally Findley?" he asked, eyeing her. He slid his

notebook across the table to her.

She knew he wanted Ally's contact information, so she jotted it down for him. "I was released from Parkview at around nine in the morning of the twenty-fourth," she said, sliding the pad and pen back over to him. "Ally remained with me here until she left for her ten o'clock shift at Randy's. After that, I was alone here and fell asleep until I was awoken by Mr. Horvat's knock to thank me for what he perceived to be my gift of potica, which again, was not."

"What time was that?" Price asked absently, feverishly scribbling down all she'd told him.

"I do not know. I was pretty out of it, on pain medication."

The sergeant tossed the pen down and shoved the pad aside as he sat back in the chair which creaked slightly under his large frame. "I find something interesting, d'Giovanni," he said.

"What's that?" she asked, sipping casually from her coffee, wanting to get across the point that she wasn't worried and had nothing to hide.

"What on earth made you think that the potica was poisoned? Right? Wasn't that what you said in your voicemail today? Which, by the way, where were you today? How did you just so *happen* to be around again when drama broke out for those folks? Will we find your fingerprints on the packaging the potica was wrapped in?"

She met his gaze and held it. "Yes, you will, and are you accusing me of something, Sergeant Price?" she asked evenly.

"Should I be?"

"This morning, I was at an appointment with my surgeon at seven-thirty. I left his office at nine, then arrived at Randy's diner at nine fifteen to meet Oscar for breakfast. I arrived here at around eleven, give or take, which is when I ran into the Horvats' niece and the ambulance arrived within seconds after that." She rested her forearm on the table and leaned somewhat forward. "And, I knew I hadn't left that potica for them and neither did their niece, which she confirmed when we met at the door. And, after knowing them and their routine and that of their loved ones, the placement of it on Josef's truck didn't feel right to me. And, it would seem the very person we're looking for in a murder case is behind trying to kill me. I don't believe in coincidences, Sergeant Price. I could be totally wrong and Mrs. Horvat may have had something totally unrelated happen today. But, I'd rather be safe than sorry."

Catania was startled when her pocket began to vibrate then ring. She reached inside and pulled out her phone, almost wanting to burst into tears when she saw it was Josef Horvat's number. But, just as quickly, deep worry washed over her.

Answering the call, she put the phone to her ear. "Hello, Mr. Horvat. How is she doing?" She listened to her neighbor and friend's emotional explanation of what had happened. "Oh no, they did, huh?" She let out a heavy sigh. "Ethylene glycol is antifreeze, Mr. Horvat," she said softly, glancing up at Price, who quickly looked away. "Oh, god I'm so relieved." She let out a soft whoop. "Yes, of course. You're most welcome. I wanted your beautiful Lizbeth to be okay, too. I'm so glad my information helped the doctors." She smiled, tears in her eyes as they filled his voice. "Yes, yes, you tell her we'll have some stew together."

"Let me talk to him," Price demanded, large hand

held out for the phone.

"Mr. Horvat—... Yes, no, I understand. Hey, listen, Sergeant Price wants to talk to you about this case. Hang on." She handed him the phone.

"Good afternoon, Mr. Horvat. I'm Sergeant Price and my men will be working this case to find out who did this to you and your wife. From now on, any questions or comments you have, you can simply talk to Detectives Slovodnik or Trujillo, alright? They'll leave a business card in your apartment... Yes, sir, I understand she's a friend. I, as her supervisor, feel she's best utilized on other cases," he said into the phone, dark eyes meeting hers. "Yes, sir. We'll talk to you soon."

She took the phone and said a quick goodbye to her friend before ending the call and setting the phone on the table. Price pushed back from the table and gathered his notepad and pen.

"Mind if I look around?" he asked, indicating the apartment with a wave of his hand.

"Go ahead."

Staying put, Catania grabbed her cup of coffee again, sipping from the cooling liquid as she could hear her boss moving things around, closet doors opening and closing. She felt nervous, though she knew she had absolutely nothing to hide. She didn't even own a jug of antifreeze. The irony was, she had been meaning to buy some, and like the potica for the Horvat's, hadn't gotten around to it yet.

She reached up and took the pendent Ally had given to her in her hand, absently playing with it as she considered everything that had happened in the last few days. *Why? Why was he going after completely innocent people?* She smirked at the stupidity of her train of thoughts. "Like Eric Gomez wasn't innocent," she muttered.

"What's that?" Price asked, stepping up to the table.

"Nothing," she said, turning in her chair to face him as she looked up at him. "Are we done?"

"Yep," he said, tucking the notebook and pen back into his pocket. "For now." With that, he turned and left the apartment, leaving the door open as he left.

❧❧❧❧

Later that night Catania lay in Ally's bed, the beautiful waitress snuggled in against her with Catania's one good arm wrapped around her. With Ally's early morning duty of preparing breakfast and not having a license or car to drive home from Catania's place, they decided it was wiser for them to stay there.

She ran her fingers absently though soft hair, reveling in the feel of Ally's warmth pressed up against her side. They were being watched by a fair maiden holding a sword, her favorite gift she'd ever received, so claimed Ally's squeal of delight when she'd opened it. Other than some kissing and light touching, they'd done nothing else. Catania wasn't up to it physically nor mentally. The events of the day had rattled her.

"I can't believe he went through your things," Ally said. "I'm so sorry."

"Yes, it sucked, but you know in a way I'm glad he did. I have absolutely nothing to hide and I'm glad that asshole saw that I didn't."

"I was thinking today," Ally said, raising her head and looking down at her. "I find it really interesting and coincidental that the Horvats got their poisoned potica the same night you were almost hit. Seems strange, doesn't it?"

Catania studied her shadowed features. "Yes. Yes, it does."

"What if," Ally proposed, trailing her fingertip along Catania's jaw. "Going after you, regardless of the outcome, was simply a distraction?"

Dark eyebrows drew. "What do you mean?"

"Well," Ally explained. "I wonder if you living or dying wasn't the point. Either way, even if you were just hurt, which thank God was the only thing that happened, you'd still likely be out of commission and not anywhere near the Horvats' place."

"As in," Catania said, getting very interested in what she was saying. "If I were there, Mr. Horvat may have come to talk to me sooner, maybe immediately when they found it."

"Bingo."

"They probably wouldn't have eaten it."

"Exactly," Ally said, a proud grin on her face.

"But, why?" Catania asked, wondering if her pain meds were pickling her brain because nothing was becoming clear.

"What happened today, baby?" Ally asked softly.

"That bastard Price all but accused me of doing it."

Ally's smile grew. "Exactly. Throw some shade on you, distract from the investigation, what's really going on. Maybe even cause some discord in the police department."

"Make us question each other," Catania added, shaking her head. "Jesus."

Chapter Twenty-one

D amn, what condition is the other guy in?"
Catania chuckled. "Keep it up, Chuck, and you'll find out." She headed to her desk, freshly filled travel mug in hand.

She was met by some folks welcoming her back, a couple stopping her to find out details as they'd managed to keep what had happened out of the media. Reaching her desk, Catania was glad to be back to work. Her arm still hurt a lot, but at least her face was getting better. The bruising was turning what she called "piss-yellow and shit-brown." It wasn't pretty. It made the gray color of her left eye stand out in stark relief.

"Hey, kid," Oscar said with a smile, standing behind his chair as he hung his overcoat on it.

"Hey, Big O." She set her travel mug down and peeled her own coat off her shoulders. Once the long coat was gone, it revealed the holster she wore around her waist.

"Oh, that's gotta be a bitch," he said, nodding toward it as he plopped down into his chair.

"I feel like Billy-the-fucking-Kid," she muttered. "Just hope I don't shoot myself in the damn foot."

Oscar chuckled. "Yeah, well you had to land on your left side, didn't you?"

"I aim to please, my friend. I aim to please."

"Apparently so do I," Oscar said with a grin, turning the framed picture of his three children that sat on his desk.

Catania rolled her eyes. "Go look for that fourth leg, Oscar. Fetch, Fido."

He chuckled, grabbing his own travel mug for a sip, the black plastic cap with sliding drink hole revealed.

"Was Linda jealous she didn't get one of those?" Catania asked, grabbing her phone when she heard "Angel" by Sarah Brightman, which was Ally's ringtone. She looked around before answering it to make sure nobody was listening. "Hey, baby. Wuz up?" Her smile quickly fell from her lips. "Wait, calm down. Ally, calm down, I can't understand you. What?" The phone still to her ear, she gathered everything she'd just set down on the desk minus the travel mug and ran out of the detective's room, nearly knocking her chair over in her haste to leave.

She sprinted across the parking lot to the sedan she and Oscar used, not even ending the call before she shoved the phone into her pocket.

"Wait!"

She didn't turn around as with single-mission focus she unlocked the car. "Get in or go away." Oscar was panting loudly as he reached the car, sweating from his unexpected run.

Oscar had barely slammed the passenger door shut when tires squealed as Catania barreled the car backward out of the spot and then forward across the lot to the street. He glanced at her, then did a brief double take before he reached into the glove compartment, grabbed the magnetic red siren, and opened his window, reaching out to attach it to the roof.

"Oh god," she murmured as she roared up to the

Aberdeen House, two squad cars already parked out front, lights flashing.

"What's going on?" Oscar asked, removing his seat belt.

"It's Matty," Catania managed to say as she flung her door open and nearly launched herself out before sprinting through the wrought iron gate and across the winter-dry grass, which crunched underneath her boots.

Reaching the double front doors, one standing open, she stepped inside. Ally was huddled against the wall on the landing up from the first two steps on the main staircase. She was still crying, as she had been on the phone, which was clutched to her chest. She stared up the long, narrow stairs.

"Hey," Catania said, reaching out to brush her fingertips over her cheek before she turned her attention to the rest of the stairs. "Call my mother, Ally."

"Get down, now. I said, *now*! Do not make me shoot you. On your belly!"

"Fuck." She ran up the stairs, taking two at a time.

Making sure her badge was visible, she pulled her weapon and slowed once she got to the top of the stairs so she wouldn't startle the officer and get herself shot. What she saw down the hall made her blood boil.

"I said get down, goddamn it," the uniformed officer shouted, the muscles in his forearms bulging as he clutched his gun in both hands tightly, his legs spread and slightly bent.

"Hands where I can see them. Now! Do it now," he screamed.

The officer was to the left of the hallway, his gun pointed directly at Matteo, who was just outside his apartment door, partially bent over, almost in a standing fetal position. He was rocking, his hands on his head, which he kept banging against the doorframe. A low keening sound could be heard. Catania noticed his tan cords were becoming discolored and she could smell the strong stench of urine and feces.

Farther down the hall past the two men was Karen, being held back by a second officer. Catania pointed her weapon at the yelling officer.

"Detective d'Giovanni!" she yelled at the top of her lungs to be heard over the officer who was attempting to arrest her brother. "Stand down, Officer. Stand down!"

"Detective, this man is under arrest and if he doesn't follow my orders, I will shoot him."

"You shoot him and I'll shoot you." That got his attention and he spared a glance at her, eyes widening when he saw her pistol. "Stand down, Officer," she said, voice softer. "This man is on the spectrum and has no idea what you're telling him to do. Now, stand down."

"Ma'am, I cannot," he said, loosening his stance a bit but kept his weapon aimed at Matteo.

"What is this man wanted for?"

"Murder, ma'am."

The air was knocked out of her lungs at the simple statement and she literally had to take a step back or fall down. Swallowing hard, she slowly walked over to the officer. Her light touch to his hand pulled his focus again to her pistol and he lowered his gun, hands shaking.

"Let me deal with him for a moment. You're about to shoot someone who is scared to death and absolutely incapable of following your commands."

She met his gaze. "I doubt you want that on your record, Officer."

"No, ma'am. You tend to him, but I'm staying here at attention." He kept his hands on his gun but had it aimed more at the floor.

"Thank you," she said, releasing a heavy sigh. Holstering her own weapon, she slowly made her way over to Matteo, who continued to rock. "Matty," she said, her voice soft. "Hey, bud. It's me." She knew it was entirely possible for him to turn to violent in the state of mind he was in, profound fear and confusion, so she knew she had to take it easy. As she got closer, she saw he had a massive bloody nose. "Oh, Jesus," she whispered. "Call an ambulance," she called over to Karen. When she saw she wasn't moving, she felt anger flare. "Call a goddamn ambulance! He's bleeding."

She immediately cursed herself. Her yelling had made him fall to the ground, his bottom in the air as he tucked his head in by his knees.

"I'm sorry, Matty," she murmured, reaching out a hand and just barely touching his shoulder to see if he'd react. When he didn't fight her, she lowered herself to sit next to him, her hand moving to his back to rub small circles. "Come back to me, Matty. Hey, I bet I can beat you at that zombie thing you like to play," she said, a smile on her lips, waiting for him to raise his head and argue with her. He did nothing but continue to rock and make that strange sound.

Remembering his bloody nose, she glanced around, relieved to see Oscar standing at the top of the stairs. She waved him over.

"Is he okay?" he asked, looking down at him.

"Oscar, please get me some rags. His nose is bleeding badly."

He hurried back toward the stairs and down, to Ally she assumed. Moments later he returned, two dish towels in his hand.

"Hey, Matty," she cooed, scooting aside as she gently pulled on one of his belt loops until he fell to his side, which only made him curl up deeper into the fetal position. Blood was smeared all over his face and had puddled onto the floor. She brought one towel to his nose, careful to make sure his mouth was clear to breathe. She put the other towel on the floor, pressing down so it would absorb the blood from the wood flooring. "Hey, big guy. Roll over for me, huh? I've only got one arm and we've got to get you into a safe position."

"The ambulance is here, Nia," Oscar said softly.

Catania bent down and left a soft kiss on his temple. "They'll take care of you, big guy," she murmured. "I love you and I'll see you soon."

She pushed to her feet and stepped back by the officer who had lowered his gun completely. They watched in silence as the EMTs arrived, tending to Matteo's bloody nose as they slowly got him up and onto the gurney, all but picking him up. A few other tenants stepped out of their apartments and watched as Matteo was taken away.

Catania watched, tears in her eyes. Once he was gone. She brought her hand up and swiped at a tear that threatened to fall.

"Detective," the officer next to her said, holstering his gun. "Are you guys taking over here? We have to go with him."

She nodded before taking a cleansing breath. "Yes. Go ahead. Detective Riley will take over now."

"Barnes," he called to the officer standing with

Karen.

"What the hell happened?"

She turned to see Oscar walking toward her and a very shaken Ally behind him.

"I have no idea. That officer said he was trying to arrest him for murder."

"What?" Ally asked, a hand going to her mouth.

Catania ignored her. She had to get focused and get her mind on the job. "Oscar, call in that we need a couple more officers. We need some folks to talk to Karen and Ally as well as the other tenants here."

Without a word, Oscar stepped aside and removed his cell phone from his pocket to do her bidding. Catania turned to Ally.

"Ally," she said quietly, "I need you to join Karen. We'll have some people come to talk to you." She reached inside her jacket pocket, rolling her eyes when she didn't feel a pair of fresh latex gloves. "Damn it." Everything had happened so fast that morning she hadn't had time to replenish the supply she always kept either in the glove compartment of the car or on her person. Suddenly, a pair of gray-blue latex gloves were dangled in front of her face. "Thanks," she muttered, snatching them from Oscar's fingers.

Catania took several deep breaths before she felt the cold steel of professionalism slide into place, grateful for it, especially today. She noted the bloody rag that was still on the floor from Matteo's bloody nose as well as some blood that had been smeared on the doorframe. Looking past that, she entered his small apartment.

One of the chairs that straddled the little eating table was knocked on its side and the couch was pushed slightly out of its normal place, about six inches cockeyed. She glanced at the TV, initially startled by the blood-covered woman who was center screen, a scream frozen on her face. It took a second for her to realize it was one of his video games, assumedly paused when he was interrupted.

For just a moment she felt a streak of pride when she saw the bedroom area was pristine, bed made to perfection, all dirty clothes stuffed into a hamper, even if a green shirt sleeve had escaped the lid and was left dangling down the side of the wicker basket.

"Nia."

The tone of Oscar's voice surprised her, deep and deadly serious. She turned toward where he stood by the cabinet they had worked together to hang for her brother a mere couple weeks before. She ducked her head toward the wall to look into the small space created between the cabinet and the wall, Oscar's flashlight beam showing the way.

In the space was a large, gallon-size plastic bag with a zipper top. It had been flattened to fit behind, but one piece of the contents was easy to make out with the beam of Oscar's flashlight. It was a driver's license and the name revealed the smiling woman to be Anastasia T. Luhan.

"No, no, no, no!" Catania exploded, feeling faint as she felt her entire world was falling out from underneath her. The tears came hot and quick as she stepped away from the cabinet and hidden bag.

"Hey," Oscar said, moving to her side. "Nia," he said gently. "Look, partner, either you've got to pull yourself together or you've got to leave. Kiddo, nobody would blame you if you needed to walk off this case—"

"No!" Turning away from him, she squeezed her eyes shut as she took in several deep breaths, trying desperately to calm herself. Finally, she met his concerned gaze. "I'm sorry. No, I have to see this through."

He studied her eyes for a long moment before nodding. "Okay."

"Detectives?"

They turned to see two fresh uniformed officers standing out in the hall just outside the apartment door. "Hey," Oscar said. "Evidence found in here from an unsolved murder. I need you two to canvas everyone in this building, especially Karen Ross, she's the owner. She's the older of the two blond women out in the hall."

"Yes, sir."

Left alone again, Catania felt her partner and friend's gaze on her again. She met it. "Let's do this."

He gave her a reassuring smile. "Let's do this."

Returning to the baggie, Oscar pointed his flashlight beam back into the space, shining it in every direction.

"Matteo isn't into bomb making or anything, is he?" he asked.

"No. Well, not to my knowledge, anyway," she added, still in shock at what was happening. Something inside her, though, was refusing to accept this, and it went beyond that it was her Matty. Something felt very wrong. Even so, she pushed it aside. They had a job to do.

"I don't see anything, wires, any sort of a device, but I just wanted to make sure," Oscar said, bending down to visually follow his flashlight beam upward along the cabinet.

"You know, we had this thing screwed in tight against the wall, Oscar," she said. "There was no way this could have been slid behind it."

"Agreed." He took a small step back to look at the cabinet as a whole. "Hell, I was worried we'd end up screwing up Matteo's deposit whenever he moves out because of damage to the wall."

"Me, too. Okay, so it's secure?" she asked.

He nodded. "I think so." He handed her his flashlight.

Reaching in, Oscar took hold of the large plastic bag and tugged, bringing up his other hand to stabilize the bottom as it slid out from its hiding place. "Jesus," he whispered.

A hand went up to Catania's mouth as instant nausea hit her. She walked with him as he set the bag on Matteo's kitchen table. They exchanged a glance before Catania grabbed her phone and sent off a quick text that the CSU team would be needed and then snapped several pictures of the Ziploc bag from different angles before setting the phone aside.

Oscar took the plastic zipper part and tugged it back slowly, the quick tick tick tick tick of the plastic teeth giving way the only noise. The smell was atrocious as he pulled the plastic bag apart, the smell of decaying blood.

Oscar's hand reached into the bag and slowly brought out blood-soaked material, though the blood was dry. Once he laid it on the table, it was easily identified as a pair of panties. Next came the license, which had been wrapped in its own smaller sandwich baggie. After that was a black plastic bag, the type with round holes cut out as handles to carry purchases from a store. No writing on it, no logo, just plain black. Oscar pulled the bag open, and Catania was surprised to see instant tears spring to his eyes.

"It's okay, partner," she whispered, trying to steel herself for whatever was in the bag.

Oscar cleared his throat and took a deep breath before he reached inside and removed a meticulously folded T-shirt, baseball style with the main part yellow and the little sleeves blue. On the yellow shirt front was a cartoon dump truck.

Catania felt her own emotions build as she knew that Oscar was seeing exactly what she was, and that was the beautiful little face of four-year-old Eric Gomez.

Taking a steadying breath, Oscar laid the T-shirt down on the bag, which lay flat on the table. "And finally," he said, releasing a long sigh as he reached in and removed a large hunting knife, dried blood on the blade and handle.

"That it?" she asked. Oscar nodded, staring down at the collection with a clenched jaw. "I know, Oscar," she murmured, laying a hand on his shoulder. "I know."

"Is he capable of this?" Oscar asked quietly, indicating the paused screen of death behind them.

Catania studied the paused video game for a long moment before turning to him, shaking her head. "I can't see it. I'm not saying that because he's my brother. I do not believe he is emotionally capable of doing this," she said, indicating the items on the table. "Let's look at everything else, see if we find more."

Catania went through every square inch of that apartment, finding nothing of interest other than a couple of cheesy romance novels hidden under the bed. She couldn't imagine her brother reading anything like that, but wanted to make sure they were in fact his and not Anastasia Luhan's.

She came out of the bedroom as Oscar was

leaving the small bathroom. "Anything?"

He shook his head. "Nothing. There isn't a single thing in this place that doesn't belong or is giving me pause." He placed his hands on his hips and sighed, looking around.

"Same here. Other than these," she said, holding the books up.

"*Come hai potuto fare questo, puttana?*"

They both turned at the sudden yelling in the hall.

"Oh shit." She almost threw the books at Oscar before she hurried from the apartment, peeling off her latex gloves as she went. She cursed under breath again when she saw her mother shove Karen, the uniformed officer trying to separate the two women. "Mamma!"

"*Puttana!*" Antonia shrieked, Karen staring at her wide-eyed as she was slammed against the wall.

"Mamma! *Smettila, basta,*" Catania yelled, grabbing her mother by the shoulders and yanking her away from a terrified Karen. "I said, stop!"

Antonia whirled around at the sound of Catania's voice and instantly burst into tears, clutching her painfully tightly. "Is no true," she wailed. "No, I will not believe my Matteo did these things!"

"It's okay, Mamma," she murmured, holding her as best she could with her one free arm. "You need to leave. Okay?"

"I'm not leaving my son," she screamed, pushing at Catania.

"Mamma, listen. Mamma!" Once she had her attention, she cupped her face with a hand. "Mamma, they took Matteo to the hospital. You and Papa go there. I'll be there later." She looked over at Ally, who was walking up to them with the officer who had interviewed her. "Officer, are you finished with this witness?" she asked softly.

"Yes, Detective."

She turned to Ally. "Ally, would you be willing to escort my mom to the hospital? She's incredibly upset."

"Yeah, of course." Her eyes were red and swollen. "Come on, Mamma," she said softly, taking Antonia by the arm. "Let's go see how he's doing, okay?"

She watched them walk down the hall toward the stairs, a small smile on her face as Ally expertly directed her past Matteo's open apartment door, her voice muffled by the distance as she talked nonstop to her, likely about food. That was about the only thing that could distract Antonia d'Giovanni long enough to get to out of the house.

Letting out a long sigh, she ran her hand through her hair before turning to Karen, who had moved away from the wall though she still looked shaken.

"Are you okay, Karen?"

"Yes. Nia, you have to know I didn't want any of this," she said, indicating the police standing around, and Oscar, who had closed Matteo's door and was putting up yellow tape to keep curious onlookers out until all the evidence had been dealt with and gathered by CSU. "I had no idea I'd find that, never in a million years did I think I would." She began to cry, a hand bringing up a crumpled tissue to her nose. "I was just doing my weekly inspection."

"When did you last do your inspection?" she asked gently. She knew likely Karen had already gone over this with the officer, but she wanted to hear it firsthand.

"Last Friday, like I do every week."

"And, nothing? That bag wasn't there?"

Karen shook her head. "No. Nothing was."

She turned to the closest officer. "I want a full list of every single person who has access to this building and to Matteo d'Giovanni's apartment for the entire time he's been here, not just today."

"Yes, ma'am," he said with a nod.

"Karen, come with me. Oscar," she said, leading the way back to Matteo's door. She moved the tape aside and opened the door, leading her sister-in-law to the cabinet. Karen's tears began anew when she saw the objects on the table. "Karen," she said, trying to get her to focus. "You see how the cabinet is now." She indicated the slight space between the piece and the wall. "Last Friday, or the last time you were in this apartment, was it like that, or..." Oscar helped her push it back to how they'd mounted it. "Like this?"

"Oh, like that," Karen said with a nod. "Absolutely. It was flush to the wall before. In fact, that's why I looked behind there today," she explained, excited. "I worried the thing was going to fall down and tear the wall up in the process. I was going to say something to him but then I saw..." She glanced at the table and turned away, soft sobs following.

"Come on, Karen," Oscar said softly, leading her out of the apartment, exchanging a glance with Catania as they passed her.

❧❧❧❧❧

Catania hurried across the street that separated the parking lot from the hospital, a tan truck slowing to a stop allowing her to pass. She waved a thank you, then hurried to the sliding glass doors that would lead to Admissions.

To the left of the doors was a grassy expanse with a few large trees. She stopped when she saw Squirrel sitting cross-legged under one of the trees. The teen glanced over at her but then returned her attention to the adorable beagle that was with her. The dog was chewing on a bone and, for just a second, she swore it looked like a human bone, an ulna bone, to be specific. Her hand absently reached up to rest on her cast, almost protective of her arm. She blinked a few times and when she focused again, she realized the dog was actually chewing on a rawhide treat.

"It's rude to stare, you know," Squirrel called out to her with a cocky grin.

Catania watched as she got to her feet, the beagle gripping the rawhide in its jaws and glancing at her before it turned away, tail wagging happily as it followed Squirrel as she began to walk away.

"Oh, Nene?" Squirrel said, stopping just long enough to look at her over her shoulder. "Go get 'em, tiger." She flashed her a winning smile as a soft breeze caught a bit of the shaggy brown bangs falling into her eyes. She tucked her hands into the pockets of her windbreaker as she and the dog casually strolled away.

Chapter Twenty-two

*A*t the bottom of the screen in all capital white letters were the words CAM 1: LIVE. The black-and-white image was set up high and showed a bed tucked against the wall straight ahead and to the left, the head of the bed missing from the shot as a bump-out wall was in the way. An open doorway in that wall revealed just the barest hint of a shower inside.

Sitting at the end of the bed was a woman with short, dark hair, her left arm in a cast. She seemed to be crying as her body convulsed with emotion. Her legs were spread enough for a woman with longer, light-colored hair to stand between. She cradled the sitting woman's head to her chest, running her fingers through the short locks.

The scene vanished only for another to pop up, a timestamp on the bottom left: CAM 1: TAPE - DEC. 21 2017. It was the same scene, except the bed was unmade, and what could be seen of the sheet and blankets looked as though they'd been hastily tossed aside. Suddenly, the same two women—the darker-haired woman sans cast—hurried into the scene, both with wet hair hanging, the one with lighter hair wearing a diner uniform that had wet patches on the material. She led the one with darker hair over to the bed by the hand. She disappeared behind the bathroom wall, only parts of the other woman visible.

Suddenly the view changed. CAM 2: TAPE – DEC.

21 2017. The view was the same room but from the side of the bed, the entire thing visible, though the standing women—kissing—were cut off at the shoulder. The view was partially distorted on the right side as a rounded glass globe was slightly in the shot.

A wide band of moving static stretched across the view as the movement of the action was sped up, the two comically kissing, touching, and moving to the bed in hyper-speed where they continued, one on top then the other, clothing disappearing.

Finally, the scene was slowed and allowed to play at regular speed as the woman with lighter-colored hair lay atop the other woman, her lower body covered by the blankets as it moved sensually.

The shot zoomed in toward her face, in profile. The shot zoomed in a bit more until her features became slightly grainy. Her head raised and head turned, inadvertently facing her unseen audience of one. Her eyes were closed and her beautiful face was frozen in ecstasy as the frame was paused.

꩜꩜꩜꩜

Catania started, slowly becoming aware of heat along the backside of her body and a gentle touch brushing her hair back from her face. Next she came to realize the voice of an angel was speaking softly in her ear.

"Baby, it's time to get up. It's almost six. You said you needed to get up and out early."

Nia babbled something unintelligible. She was exhausted, and her head hurt. The night before came back to her, hours of lying on Ally's bed talking, crying, holding each other, and crying some more. Eventually they'd fallen asleep. It had only been when she'd accidentally rolled the wrong way and her arm let her know it that she'd woken up to find them both asleep on top of the made bed. She'd roused Ally, and they'd quietly undressed and slid beneath the covers, quickly falling back to sleep.

Her jaw popped as a huge yawn took her over. She smiled at the soft kiss she felt on the side of her neck before Ally slid away from her. She rolled over to her back from her right side and stared up at ceiling as the full weight of the day before her came crashing down.

Her trip to the hospital the day before had been fruitless. Matteo had been moved to the psychiatric wing and his doctor hadn't allowed anyone to see him, including her or their mother. As of her last call just before 10:00 p.m. the previous night, he had remained unresponsive and had been sedated to try to get his mind to calm and let go of the self-imposed cage of fear he was locked in.

Sitting up, she ran her hand through her hair. Ally stepped out of the bathroom, toothbrush in hand and hair already brushed.

"I'll head upstairs and make some coffee as soon as I'm done," she said, raising her toothbrush a bit before disappearing back into the small room.

"'Kay," Catania muttered, groaning as her back yelled at her as she crawled out of bed. She went to stand, but her exhaustion pushed her back down. "Okay, I get it."

Reaching for her phone on the bedside table, she decided to be productive even as her body refused to allow her to stand just yet. She logged into her email and scanned missed messages, stopping when she saw she had something from the lab.

Scrolling through the email, she slowed her reading, reading and rereading the results of the beer bottle found in Kevin Tanner's truck.

"Holy shit," she hissed.

Green glass bottle (qty: 1) –
- DNA – Kevin S. Tanner (contributor)
- Trace amount gamma hydroxybutyric acid

"GHB," she murmured. "Fucker drugged them to get control of them."

"What, baby?"

Catania tossed her phone to the bed and made herself get up and get dressed. "I have to go," she uttered, wincing as her arm disagreed with the way she was pulling her shirt on.

"Here," Ally said, hurrying over to her. "Let me help you. You're going to get it tangled." She looked deeply into Catania's eyes as she gently pulled the loose sleeve over the cast on her arm. "What happened?" she asked.

"I believe he drugged Kevin Tanner," she said simply.

"And, that's the 'suicide'?" she asked, using air quotes.

"Yes." Catania let out a heavy sigh, buttoning her shirt once Ally got her arm situated. "Now, I'm wondering if that's how he was able to control two adults and a child, too."

Ally studied her, chewing on her bottom lip as though in deep thought. "God, that's horrible. Would it be possible to do?"

"Extremely possible." Catania hurried over to the coat hooks on the wall and grabbed her jacket, shrugging it over her shoulders. "God, I can't wait to get rid of this goddamn thing," she said, tapping the cast with her fingers. "There were beer bottles all over that triple homicide scene. It would have been easy for him to slip something in, even just enough to make our victims a little unsteady."

"Jeez," Ally whispered, hugging herself. "That's so cold."

Catania nodded, grabbing her phone and tucking it into her pocket as well as her wallet and her keys, which lay on the kitchen table. "I'm not sure if I'll be able to call you today," she said, turning to Ally who stood a few steps behind her. She gave her a small smile and raised her hand to brush her fingers down the softness of Ally's cheek. She could see the fear in her eyes and the sadness. Catania wasn't entirely sure what would happen at the house today, and she hated that she couldn't stay there with her.

She gathered Ally into a warm embrace, burying her face in her neck. Ally clung to her and, in that moment, something unsaid passed between them.

"Please be safe today," Ally whispered into her ear.

Catania nodded and left a kiss on her neck. "I will. Call me if you need me." She ran her fingers through her hair and smiled at her as she broke the hug. Leaving a final, lingering kiss on her lips, she left.

༄ ༄ ༆ ༆

"Yeah, so go ahead and test those bottles again, that'd be great," Catania said into her desk phone, nodding as she listened to the tech on the other end. "Exactly. Okay, great. I look forward to hearing back from you... Okay, thanks. Have a good day."

"Good lord. You're here early, kid," Oscar said, stepping up to his desk and setting his travel mug down, the fragrance of fresh coffee wafting her way. "How's Matteo?" he asked, setting his phone and keys down on the desk before shrugging out of his overcoat to place it on the back of his chair.

She sighed, sitting back in her own chair. "No change. Doctors won't let family in, let alone any type of police type to talk to him, find out what happened." She grabbed a pencil from her desk and twisted it between her fingers. She gave a rueful smile still studying the yellow No. 2. "I've only seen him like this one other time. I was five, but I swear I remember it. We'd all gone to the lake house for the weekend, I guess. I don't remember anything about the weekend except this moment. My dad had his camera out." She glanced over at him to see he was giving her his undivided attention. "You know, the old-school Super 8 kind." She smiled, remembering that camera he kept for years. "Matty and I were being silly, making faces, showing off for him. Hamming it up, I guess. Suddenly, out of nowhere Jason comes running by and grabs Matty. He was only two. He took off with him, Matty screaming his little head off." Her voice broke as fresh emotion stung the backs of her eyes.

Oscar rolled his chair closer to her and reached out, placing a hand on her knee. "It's okay, kiddo."

Catania smiled at him, appreciative of his enduring friendship. "Matty didn't speak for a week. He's hated Jason ever since."

"He's gonna bounce back from this, Nia," he said softly, letting his hand drop away from her. "He's got you, he's got your mom, and hey, he even seems pretty fond of Ally." He gave her an encouraging smile.

"We're going to get to the bottom of all this. You and me, 'kay?"

She met his eyes and looked deep into their kind depths for a long moment. Finally, she nodded. "Yeah. I want blood."

"So, what did you find?"

"The beer bottle found in Kevin Tanner's truck?" Catania said, reminding him of what was found.

"Yeah…"

"Date rape drug."

His mouth fell open. "You are fucking kidding me."

"I am not," she said, tossing the pencil back to her desk. "I just got off the phone with the lab to ask them to do more testing on the beer bottles left behind at the Luhan house."

"Good thinking. That would absolutely make sense how one person took control of that scene."

"Exactly."

They both looked to Oscar's cell phone when it began to ring. He picked it up and held it to his ear.

"Riley here." He listened to the caller on the other end, glancing at her. He raised his hand and gave her a thumbs-up. "Alright, great. What's the address?" His eyebrows shot up. "No kidding, City Park, huh? Okay, on our way." He ended the call and pushed up from his chair. "Somebody found a gun."

❦❦❦❦

Catania guided the car along the exact same path they had taken not long ago when Kevin's body had been found. A man fishing with his grandson saw a pistol in the shallows not far from where they were set up on the small dock over the man-made pond of the public park. It was also not more than fifty yards from where Kevin had been shot.

Up ahead she saw the uniformed officer chatting with the older man, his grandson sitting off on a park bench playing on his phone, which Catania wagered a guess is what he'd rather be doing anyway. She chuckled at her own internal thoughts before cutting the engine and climbing out of the car.

"'Mornin'," the officer greeted as they walked over to him.

"How goes it?" Oscar asked, smiling and nodding at both men. "What we got here?"

"Found this," the old man said, handing over his treasure.

Catania stood back a bit, as Oscar was definitely the gun expert between them. She knew a lot simply from her line of work, but he'd grown up with guns and his father collected them. His knowledge was impressive, if not a bit unsettling for someone like her who respected guns but certainly wasn't an enthusiast.

Catania's phone rang so she stepped aside, pulling it out of her pocket. It came across as a restricted number. Not uncommon, as a lot of her informants called her from the random pay phone or hid their numbers when they called in tips.

"Detective d'Giovanni."

"Hey, it's me."

Catania's eyebrows drew. "'Me,' who?"

"Squirrel! Come on now, don't disappoint me and tell me you've already forgotten about your favorite monkey, Nene."

Wondering if the teen was on something, she asked, "So, what's up?"

"I've heard you've been asking around about Liv."

Instantly interested, she nodded. "Yeah, I've asked a few people about her. Have you seen her?"

"Lookin' at her right now. Listen, I need you to meet us. We're way out in the boonies, but she's been in hiding. She's got some info about this creeper you're looking for."

"Oh yeah?" she asked, tucking the phone between ear and shoulder as she searched through her pockets with her one good hand. Notepad and pen located, she managed to remove the cap with her teeth and flip the notebook open. "Where am I going?" She hurried over to their sedan and set the notepad on it as she scribbled the address Squirrel was firing off at her. "Wow. You really are way the hell out there. You there now?"

"Get here as fast as you can. Ain't gonna wait around all day."

Catania opened her mouth to speak but realized the line had gone dead. "Squirrel?"

"Aren't they up there?" Oscar asked, walking over to her, a dopey grin on his face.

Catania pulled the phone away from her face, looking at it to see her lock screen. "Guess she hung up. She wants us to meet her. She said she has Liv with her and she has information for us on our guy."

"Where are they?"

"Boone."

He looked at her. "Boone? I hope they plan to be there for a bit, that's about a thirty-minute drive from here."

"Yeah, she said hurry. Here," she said, handing him the keys. "You know that area out that way better than I do." They climbed into the car, she taking shotgun. "No go?" she asked, nodding toward the policemen who was climbing back into his squad car and the old man who was heading back to fishing.

"Nah. I told Officer Stevens to go ahead and turn it in, but that thing hasn't been fired in twenty years."

"Well, there's one lost gun down, only about a million more to go," she said with a small smile. "I'm going to call in where we're going." She reached into the glove compartment and pulled out the handheld radio they kept there at all times in case they ended up in an area with bad reception or there was some other issue. She called it in to dispatch and tossed the radio onto the dashboard. "Guessing we won't have great reception out there?" she asked. "Squirrel sounded like she was a few planets away."

"Yeah, it's pretty sporadic at best. Hell, growing up in Vineland, which isn't as far, TV reception could be fun." They drove in silence for a bit. Then, "How's Karen doing? You know," he said, sparing a glance at her, "after everything that happened yesterday."

"Uh." She sighed, running her hand through her hair, leaving it sticking up in the back. "She was shaken, no doubt. My mom said Jason is going to send her to spend some time with her mom in Kansas. She's cleared with us, so…"

Oscar nodded, glancing in the rearview mirror before his side mirror as he flicked his turn signal on and switched lanes. "Can't say I blame her. I mean, I know how upset your mom was at her last night, and I do understand why, but Karen did the right thing."

"Yeah," Catania conceded. "She did."

More than half an hour of light chatter and banter later, Oscar turned off the paved street—though it was filled with cracks and ruts—onto a long, gravel lane. Off in the distance to the right was an old farm, the house a small, white single story. There were several outbuildings, including a massive barn and a massive grain silo, which cast deep shadows over the property.

"What's that address again?" he asked, looking around as they got closer. When she read it from her notes, he nodded as he glanced to his phone's GPS. "Yeah. I mean, unless reception sent us to Nebraska, this should be it." He pulled the car onto the property. "Why don't you call her and see where we're supposed to meet her."

"Can't. It was a restricted number."

"Shit."

"Wait..." Catania strained her neck as she thought she saw movement. She peered through the shadows to the barn and saw a small, human-sized door next to the massive doors that could accommodate large equipment or animals. The person-door was open a bit. She saw a flash of light blue and gray and Squirrel waving at her. "There's Squirrel. Over at the barn."

"Of course it is," Oscar exclaimed. "Creepiest place on the whole damn property."

Catania smiled, though in truth she felt nervous, her stomach buzzing with frantic butterfly wings.

"Nia," he said, pulling to a stop about twenty feet back from the barn. "Think we should call for backup?"

She took a deep breath, a part of her wondering the same thing, but she trusted Squirrel. In her heart of hearts, she knew she was trying to help them. "No. They know where we're at."

They climbed out of the car and walked toward the barn. Catania looked around, turning in a slow circle as she went, eyeing their surrounds. She couldn't help but feel there were eyes on them, like they'd just entered an old, haunted town. A cold breeze swept through the wind tunnel created by the close-set buildings, which whistled ominously.

"Here goes nothing," Oscar said softly, reaching out to grip the iron handle on the door. He pulled it open and, hand on her weapon, the holster unsnapped, Catania entered, looking in every direction, knowing Oscar had her back.

The shadows were interrupted by patches of slated light coming in from air vents near the roof of the large structure. The floor was dirt and the building was nearly empty. There were several stalls built, though they looked rickety and nowhere near ready to house anything alive. The stalls stretched out on either side of the barn, leaving a wide aisle between them. Catania wondered if perhaps this had been a dairy at one time.

"We should call in that we arrived," Oscar said, eyes wide as he took in the expanse.

"Yeah." Catania reached into her pocket for the radio, cursing softly when it wasn't there. She remembered she'd left it on the dash. "Do you have signal?" She kept an eye out as Oscar pulled his phone out.

"Nope."

"Damn. Okay. Hey, Squirrel?" she called out. "Gonna go run out for a sec. Be right back. You better have your skinny ass out here so we can do this!"

Oscar glanced at her with a raised eyebrow as if to say, *Seriously?* "Go get 'em, tiger," he drawled.

She stared at him for a second. "What made you say that?"

"What? Why?"

She shook her head and turned to leave, jogging from the barn back to the car. She scooped up the radio and jogged back toward the building when she heard

Oscar yell, "Oh my god!"

"Oscar?" Her legs pumped to get her the remaining distance, only to nearly stumble when she heard four gunshots fired in quick succession. "Oscar!"

Reaching the door, her heart was racing as she pulled her gun. She brought the radio to her mouth. "This is d'Giovanni, shots fired, shots fired!"

She stuck the radio into her pocket and didn't even feel the pain as she used her bad hand to pull open the door. She instantly hit the dirt when she heard two more shot fired.

Heart racing, she crawled her way inside far enough so the door would close and not leave her in a spotlight. Doing a partial army crawl and baby crawl on her hands and knees, she scurried into one of the stalls. Listening, she heard groaning and prayed it was Oscar because if he'd been hit, that meant he was still alive.

Slowly raising her head so she could peek over the top of the stall's half wall, she saw a shadowy figure dart out from a stall about fifty feet away and make a run for the back of the barn.

"Freeze!" she yelled at the top of her voice. The figure did not stop. "I said freeze!"

She raised her gun and fired off three shots, the figure diving for cover, dust flying up into the air to drift around in a patch of sunlight. She ran hunched down from her stall, running as far as she could before she heard another shot. It was then she saw Oscar. He lay about ten feet away from her, out in the open on his back. She could hear him wheezing, struggling to breathe.

"Stay with me, Oscar."

The figure popped up again and sprinted on the

same path to the back of the barn. She popped up and ran after the person, unable to tell if it was male or female, though it looked to be a large-framed person. She gripped her weapon with both hands and fired until her gun ran out of bullets. Still on the run, she tossed the old clip and slid a fresh one home.

Suddenly, she was blinded by a tidal wave of sunlight as, almost instantaneously, a car started and then plowed through the wall of the barn, fishtailing as it slid on building debris and gravel.

Standing wide-legged at the gaping hole, she emptied her new clip into the back of the white Subaru wagon that roared away from the barn.

"Fucker!"

Turning, she ran back toward Oscar, the barn now aglow. It was only then that she saw a body lying in one of the stalls. She stopped only long enough to realize it was Liv.

Knowing the young woman was already gone, she ran to Oscar, grabbing her radio as she slid to her knees next to him. "Officer down, officer down!" she screamed into the radio. "Don't you leave me, Oscar! Don't you fucking leave me. Send me a goddamn ambulance!" She threw the radio aside. "Oh god, no." She sobbed, looking into his face as she brought up a hand to wipe away some ancient dried hay that was stuck to the blood on his face.

He looked up at her, though his eyes weren't focused. "Hey, bud," she managed, her tears falling and mingling with his blood. His mouth moved as though he was trying to work out some words.

"Don't talk," she whispered, cradling his head. "Help is coming." She looked out over his body, evaluating his injuries. He'd been struck three times, one in the right shoulder, one in the right thigh, and the third in his chest.

She looked up when she heard the distant sound of sirens, stunning considering how far out they were.

Looking back down at him, she smiled. "Guess they'd already sent the cavalry knowing how much trouble we get into, huh?"

In response, he began to wheeze, a horrifying gurgling sound in his throat. His eyes began to close and his body grew relaxed in her arms.

"No you don't, Oscar. Goddamn it, no you don't!"

She moved back enough to lay him flat and held his nose closed with her fingers as she pressed her lips to his, beginning CPR.

"Stay with me," she murmured, breathless as she did her compressions. "Stay with me…"

Her bangs hung damp in her eyes from exertion when she stared down at him, noting how pale he was and that he wasn't breathing. The tears began anew even as she desperately tried to hold it together. She put two fingers at his carotid artery, praying like she'd never prayed before. Nothing.

"Goddamn it," she cried, desperation hitting her harder than before.

She began CPR again, the world around her disappearing as she gave everything she had to try to bring him back, keep him alive.

"Get off me!" she yelled, lashing out when she was grabbed from behind, hands underneath her armpits. She scrambled to her feet away from the firm touch only to see a paramedic staring back at her. She fell to her knees. "You save him," she whimpered.

Chapter Twenty-three

Catania's hand shielded her eyes as she watched the medevac helicopter float up into the day, the *thup, thup, thup* of the blades deafening, the dirt and debris kicked up by the wind they caused making her squint.

She had to think it was an act of God or something that there had been an ambulance call in the remote, tiny farming town of Boone, for which the paramedics hadn't had to transport the patient back into town to the hospital, so they were open to take her call. They were able to get Oscar stable enough to be medevaced to the hospital. Now, she had the most difficult part of her job to do.

Stepping closer to the building to get away from the noise, she pulled out her phone and dialed Linda's cell. She'd prefer to be there in person, but she'd by far rather tell her than Linda hear it on the news. Luck was with her and she was able to get signal.

"Hey, Linda, it's Nia… Uh, no. No, everything isn't okay. Linda, Oscar's been shot." She squeezed her eyes shut at the instant cry of *No!* she heard on the other end of the line. "Linda, Linda, I don't have a lot of time and I need you to hear me, okay? He's being medevaced to Parkview Hospital as we speak, okay?" She brought up a hand and swiped at another tear that managed to escape. "I don't know," she whispered at the all-important question of whether he was okay. She saw one of the uniformed officers that had arrived on scene after the ambulance hurrying toward her from around the back of the barn where the gunman had blasted through the wall. "I have to run, but stay in touch, okay? See you soon, bye."

"Detective, there's nobody else here, just the body."

"Nobody? Not in the other buildings?"

He shook his head. "No, ma'am. We've searched the entire property."

She let out a sigh, tapping the side of her phone against her thigh. "Okay." One look at the seasoned officer told her something was on his mind. "What?"

"The body, Detective," he said, a slight look of disgust in his expression.

"Yeah?"

"It's frozen."

Following him inside, Catania watched as officers laid small yellow plastic markers at each shell casing, both expended from her weapon as well as the gunman's. She was shocked by how many there were. In the heat of the moment, it was very easy to lose count of just how many shots were volleyed. It was, however, very difficult to see the blood left behind where Oscar had gone down.

Looking away, she was led to the body of the young black woman. She'd only met her the one time, but she was such a lovely young woman it was easy to remember that face, now relaxed in death.

The young woman's hair was in tight braids, pulled back and cinched at the nape of her neck. Her neck. Catania's gaze was drawn to it.

Dark eyes widen, surprise...

The grip tightened...

No breath, no breath. Can't breathe, can't breathe...

The shine gone in her eyes, mahogany skin dull, a yellowish fluid puddled at the corner of slightly spread lips. Suddenly, the eyes focused, lifeless yet direct.

"You did this," she whispered. "You did this!"

She gasped, falling back to her behind in the dirt. She blinked several times before she could focus on the young woman lying on the ground instead of the one who had just haunted her mind for a second time.

"You okay, Detective?"

She looked up to see the officer looking down at her from where he stood on the opposite side of Liv's body. "Uh, yeah. Sorry."

Moving away from the deeply bruised neck, Catania took in the dark purple tank top, which had a small rip near the hem. She couldn't tell if that was from whatever ordeal the woman had been put through, or if it was dryer rot—wear from too many washes.

She wore light blue jeans that looked like they'd been painted on. She was barefoot, just like Megan Murphy.

"Any I.D. on her?" she asked softly.

"Nothing. She was left literally with what she was wearing."

Curious, Catania remembered that Megan had been found with no undergarments. She could tell Liv wasn't wearing a bra. She had no latex gloves on or with her, but noticed the officer did.

"Do me a favor and unbutton her jeans. Let's see if she's wearing any panties."

He did as asked, though he struggled with the chilled material of the denim. After several moments, he pulled apart the flaps to reveal nothing.

She let out a sigh, pushing to her feet. "He's got a thing for panties, that's for sure."

"D'Giovanni."

She turned to see Detectives Slovodnik and Trujillo headed her way. "Fuck me," she muttered. "Good afternoon, guys."

"Price wants to see you," Rodney said, glancing down at the body at her feet.

"Well, he can wait. Obviously I'm busy—"

"Now, Nia," he said gently. "We're taking over."

She looked at him sunned. "What? Why?"

He sighed and shook his head, reaching up to run his hand down the length of his tie. "We're following orders."

She shook her head, anger burning hot and heavy. "Okay," she said, not about to kill the messenger. She could see by the overwhelmed, fish-out-of-water look on her colleague's face that he wasn't thrilled, either. From embezzling crimes to murder in an afternoon.

She moved to walk past him when he stopped her with a hand on her arm. She met his gaze, hers hard and determined.

"Listen, Nia," he said softly, just loud enough for her to hear. "I don't know what's going on, but I'm so sorry about Oscar. We're all pullin' for him."

She managed a small smile. "Thanks."

❧❧❧❧❧

Catania marched to her desk, ignoring the looks she got from her colleagues, some radiating solemn support for Oscar, others expressing naked surprise. She had to figure that was from the blood that was all over her blouse. Oscar's blood.

She made it to her desk and tossed the jacket she'd been carrying onto her desk, not even able to look at Oscar's chair. If she did, she knew she'd break down.

"D'Giovanni!"

She glanced up to see Price leaning out of his office, hands braced on either side of the doorframe. His dark, hard gaze was pinning her to the spot.

Don't fuck with me today, you son of a bitch, was all she could think as she turned on her heel and marched her way to him. Without a word, she squeezed past his large bulk, nearly knocking him down. From the look on his face when he turned to her in the office, he was too shocked to say anything about that.

She sat in one of the chairs, crossing one knee elegantly over the other, waiting. She didn't even react when he slammed the door shut, her eyes following him as he walked around to the business side of his desk. He did not sit, but stood, towering over her.

"Give me your weapon," he said, voice surprisingly calm.

Without a word, she thumbed open the snap on her holster and pulled out the Glock, unloaded it, and gently laid it and the clip on his desk.

"Did you fire this weapon?" he asked, indicating the pistol lying a few inches from his coffee mug.

"Yes, sir. Fired through two clips, sir."

"What happened?" he asked, again voice calm, but his towering intimidation tactics told her where his head was.

"We were ambushed."

"Ambushed?"

"Yes. I received a call from an informant that she and Liv had information regarding this case."

"Who is Liv? And, who is this informant?"

"I don't know her full name yet, but Liv is our victim. She's a young lady I met several weeks ago on the streets. Squirrel."

"What? What the hell is that supposed to mean, Squirrel?"

"My informant. Her nickname on the streets."

"She called you, you said? On your phone or Riley's?"

"Mine, sir."

He held out a large hand. Without a word, she removed her phone from her pocket and unlocked it before setting it in his palm. He tapped and scrolled as he sat down, bouncing slightly in the springy desk chair.

"Is she listed as Mamma or Ally?" he asked, looking over the device at her.

"The number came up as restricted, Sergeant," she said, her irritation rising at his condescending tone. She was, however, baffled by his drawn eyebrows as he scrolled through the call log.

"She called you today?"

"Yes. Oscar and I were at City Park checking out the report of a found gun this morning."

"Restricted, huh?" He tossed the phone across the desk. "There is no such call, Detective."

"What?" She grabbed her phone and scrolled through the morning, all the way to two days before. Not one restricted listing.

"What else you got, d'Giovanni? You said you were ambushed. Word is, Detective Riley's gun was never discharged. Yours, by your own admission, was. Two whole clips, even."

She met his gaze, stunned at what he was

insinuating. "I would never, *ever* shoot my partner," she said slowly, conviction behind every syllable.

"So you say, but what does the evidence say?" He clasped his fingers on his desk and sat forward, eyes boring into her. "Did he figure out what was up, Detective?" he asked quietly. "You're a cop, know the ropes. No fingerprints found on any of the crime scenes, not one. Not one ounce of usable DNA evidence on our killer. A cop would know how to get around that, too, wouldn't they? Not even semen found." He smirked. "Tell me, Detective, do lesbians ejaculate? Leave behind evidence?"

"How dare—"

"Were your neighbors too close, too?" he continued, talking over her as he raised his voice a bit. "Who else is in danger, d'Giovanni? Huh? Now you're lying to me about little woodland creatures calling you," he said, casually indicating her phone with a wave of his hand. "Whispering sweet nothings in your ear. And, I gotta say," he said with a smirk. "It takes a real sick fuck to use your own family. Matteo, right? Is that his name?"

"You son of a—" she whispered, tears of rage stinging behind her eyes.

"From what I heard, the raid literally scared the shit out of him."

Catania flew across the desk, grabbing him by the front of his dress shirt, her face no more than three inches from his. "Listen, you rat bastard, don't you ever talk about my brother again. You got me?" she yelled, shaking him for good measure. "I am killing myself trying to find out who is doing this, do you get that? Oscar Riley may die because of this motherfucker! You do and say what you want to me, but I will not stop until I find him and kill him if I have to. Do you understand?" She shoved him back into his chair as she released him, her rage still burning in her belly.

"Go home," he said, his voice deadly calm, but his eyes were on fire. "You come back tomorrow morning at eight in uniform and you report to Records."

She glared at him from where she'd moved back by the chair she'd vacated in her rage.

"Now," he continued. "Get. Out."

She didn't bother to say anything or even look at him as she turned and slammed out of the office.

❧❧❧❧

Now dressed in casual clothing after going home, taking a quick shower, and tossing her blouse, she sat in a chair and studied Matteo's profile. She'd been nearly brought to tears in relief and gratitude when his doctor had told her he'd been asking for her when she called to see how he was.

They sat in the visitation area of the psychiatric ward, other visitors and patients talking quietly at tables or on the couch. Matteo stared out the window, though she wasn't entirely sure how much he was actually taking in of the trees outside that were gently swaying in the growing breeze. It felt like a storm was brewing to blow in.

"I'm so happy you're doing better, bud," she said, noting a bit of growth on his chin. She wondered if it was driving him crazy. Matteo loved to be clean-shaven, hated facial hair. When her other brothers began to get growth, they had been ecstatic. Not Matteo. He'd been annoyed. "Today was a crappy day, Matty," she said with a soft sigh.

She felt so alone even as she sat next to one of the closest people to her. She needed his quiet strength. He hadn't said a single word to her, nor had he made eye contact with her during her entire visit, which had been twenty-seven of the thirty minutes she was allowed.

Needing to feel a physical bond with him, she reached out to take his hand, but he flinched, his hand moving out of reach. "Sorry," she whispered. "Too soon."

"Alright, visitors, start wrapping it up," an orderly announced from where he suddenly appeared in the arched doorway.

Catania spared a glance at him before returning her attention to her beloved brother. "I'm going to get your apartment all clean and special for you to come home, okay? Ally misses you, and so does Doug—I guess one of the other tenants you play video games with from time to time? He told Ally to tell you that he's waiting for you guys to continue your chronicle, whatever that means." She pushed up from her chair and looked down at him. "Stand up, Matty. It's time to go."

Without a word or any indication he'd heard her, he rose to his feet, dressed in a simple pair of light gray sweatpants and a white men's undershirt.

"I have to go, but can I give you a kiss goodbye, Matty? I'll be back tomorrow, but would that be okay?"

Again, no verbal response, but he bent his head down a bit, offering his cheek to her. She nearly cried. She left a soft kiss there, lingering until he pulled away and shuffled toward the archway.

Chapter Twenty-four

Catania pulled her Jeep around the back of the building and into her spot. The headlights spotlighted an angel sitting on her back stoop. She turned off the engine and just stared at the woman she craved like a drowning man craved a life raft. She returned the soft smile she was given.

Turning everything off, she allowed her unclasped seat belt to zip back into place before she climbed out. She held only her keys, wallet, and phone, her spirit and heart left in an old barn in Boone, Colorado.

Ally said nothing, she simply stood as Catania reached the stoop and opened her arms. Catania allowed herself to be enveloped in the warmth and safety that was Ally, who cupped the back of her head and urged her to rest it on a strong shoulder.

After long minutes, the cold air became too much and Catania pulled away. She looked into Ally's sweet face. "Come inside with me?"

Without a word, she let them into the apartment, locking the door behind them. She led the way through the dark house, not bothering to turn on any lights, leading Ally by the hand to the bedroom. She had no plan other than she knew she needed to have her as close as she possibly could.

Inside the bedroom, she tossed her things to the dresser top and walked over to the bedside table, switching on the lamp. Turning to look at Ally, something overtook her. She walked over to her and, without preamble, began to undress her. She could see the surprise in dark blue eyes and she certainly hoped that she wasn't scaring Ally with her aggression, but she needed her.

Moments later they were both naked—other than the infernal cast she wore—and on Catania's bed, Ally blindly shoving at the heavy comforter, blanket, and sheet. Once they were clear of the material entanglements, she pinned Catania to the bed beneath her.

Catania looked up into Ally's face; though filled with passion, there was still that gentleness that was part of everything she did. And, as her lover's hand ran up along Catania's side to cup her breast, something in her broke.

"Hey," Ally whispered from where she lay next to her. She moved her hand from the soft flesh to cup Catania's face. "Are you okay? Are you in pain?"

She shook her head before looking away, embarrassed as tears slipped from her eye and rolled down her cheek. "I'm sorry," she said, forcing a smile and trying to get herself back into the moment.

She reached up and buried her hand in Ally's hair, bringing her down for a deep and passionate kiss which was eagerly responded to, but the feel of Ally's body pressed against her side, the warmth, the beautiful perfection of the security it brought her, was too much to take.

"Baby," Ally whispered, holding Catania to her as the tears flowed freely, sobs racking Catania's body. "It's okay. I've got you."

Catania couldn't control or stop the emotion as it erupted from her. She felt like her entire world was imploding, two people she loved most were deeply and profoundly hurt—if not worse—as well as a dear neighbor who was as innocent as anyone. She felt like her entire life was being stalked and haunted by a shadow monster that she couldn't find, let alone fight. She was overwhelmed and grief-stricken.

"Come here," Ally whispered, moving away to sit up and grab the bedding before covering them both to the upper chest as she lay on her back. She reached for Catania, who carefully scooted into her arms, head resting on her shoulder. She adjusted her broken arm until it was comfortable, then settled in.

"I'm really sorry about that." She luxuriated in the feeling of Ally's fingers running aimlessly through her hair. "I've got to be the worst blue-ball girlfriend on the planet."

Ally chuckled, leaving a kiss on Catania's forehead. "Probably the absolute most inappropriate time to ask this, but are you?"

"Am I what?" Catania asked, readjusting her head a bit lower, the softness of Ally's breast under her cheek.

"My girlfriend?"

The question threw Catania for a loop for a second before she realized that so much had happened so quickly, they'd never even discussed what had happened between them a week ago in Ally's apartment, what was happening between them by the day, and what it all meant. She raised her head, loath to leave the comfort, but she knew it was important. "Is that okay? What you want?"

Ally grinned up at her and nodded. "Yeah. That's what I want...if you do..."

Catania chuckled, leaning down to leave a

lingering kiss on soft lips. "I think we're twelve, but of course I do," she murmured against them with a grin. One final kiss and she lay her head down again. "I saw Matteo today."

"You did? That's wonderful! Did he talk to you?"

"No. He did ask for me, but no, he didn't say anything to me. But god, just to be with him, see he was okay." Catania snuggled in closer. She wanted to bring up Oscar, but she just couldn't. The words would never leave her lips without breaking down again.

⁂

Catania stood before her stand-alone mirror, freshly showered and dressed. It had been such a long time since she'd had to show up for a normal day's work in the dark blue uniform. At one time she'd seen donning it as the ultimate honor, so much pride reflected back in her mirrored smile. But today, as she worked to tie the dark blue tie that signified a desk job, she saw it for the slap in the face Price meant it to be.

"You know," Ally said from where she was sitting cross-legged on the bed. "I probably shouldn't say this, but you look sexy as hell in that."

She looked at Ally's reflected image and gave her a sardonic smile. "Gee, maybe I'll wear it for you sometime."

Ally climbed off the bed and walked up behind her, wrapping her arms around her waist and resting her cheek against her upper back. "I'm sorry he's being such an asshole, baby," she murmured.

Catania let out a heavy sigh, studying herself. She looked good, her uniform perfect. "I know and I'm sorry to snap at you. My mind is somersaulting with all that I need to be out there doing to catch this bastard, and yet I'm stuck inside like a bad girl who's grounded while the other kids get to go out and play."

"I know." Ally left a kiss on the side of her neck before she moved away from her, sitting on the end of the bed to put her shoes on. "Are those other two detectives any good?"

Catania sighed, straightening her tie and finger combing her hair. "I suppose. I don't really know Jorge all that well, but I do know Rodney. He's a good guy, and dedicated." She turned to look at the real image of the woman she was talking to. "But neither has worked homicide before. Especially a case like this."

"Is there anything you can do?" Ally asked, finishing up with her second shoe before pushing to her feet. She began to make the bed, which Catania joined her in.

"God, you turn me into such an adult," she quipped, giving the woman across the bed from her a crooked grin. "And, to a point, I fully intend on continuing to hunt this son of a bitch."

✄ ✄ ✄ ✄

One thing Catania always found interesting was that when in uniform she was treated vastly different than when in street clothes. Most treated her with a bit more respect and deference, while others glared at her or seemed standoffish.

Either way, she walked the halls of Parkview Hospital with bag of breakfast in hand as she headed to the ICU waiting room. Though Ally had wanted to join her, she had to get to the Aberdeen House to start breakfast for the tenants and get ready for her shift at

Randy's. Catania had dropped her off at the large old house with a kiss and then headed to the hospital for a visit before reporting for duty in Records.

She smiled and nodded at a passing nurse before entering the L-shaped room, padded chairs and a couple love seats scattered with a TV mounted to the wall on the larger end of the L, and an area for kids in the smaller section, replete with a Lego table and a few other toys and coloring books.

The lone occupant sat across from the TV, an open novel lying facedown on the coffee table in front of the couch she sat on, a needlepoint project in her hands as she absently glanced up at the game show on the screen.

"Hey, lady," Catania said softly, sitting down next to her. She placed the McDonald's bag down on the table, knowing that Linda loved their breakfasts, if nothing else.

"Haven't seen you in this in a while," Linda said, reaching over to tug lightly at the short sleeve of Catania's uniform shirt. "I'm so sorry Price sent you to the chain gang over this." She let out a heavy sigh, accepting the small orange juice Catania had pulled from the bag. "Thank you."

"One sausage egg McMuffin for the lady," she said, doling out the food, the breakfast sandwich followed by the hash brown patty. "I know this is your favorite, and I'd wager you haven't eaten in far too many hours."

Linda smiled, unwrapping her food. "True and true."

Catania removed the top on her orange juice and sipped before finally getting to the heart of it. "How is he?"

Linda nodded as she chewed the bite she'd just taken, as though considering her response. Washing it down with O.J., she dabbed at her mouth with the napkin she was handed. "They lost him twice on the operating table yesterday," she said matter-of-factly. "He'd lost so much blood."

Catania munched numbly on her own breakfast. Finally, she glanced at her friend. "Is he going to make it?"

She took a moment, but finally Linda met her gaze. "They don't know." She looked down at the sandwich in her hand. "Either way," she continued softly. "I'm not leaving here until he does."

🪶🪶🪶🪶

Hands on hips, Catania looked around the medium-sized room, the task she'd been given seemingly insurmountable. She stood in the middle of the room that held six long aisles of metal shelving that contained a combination of cold case files, murder books from solved cases, and random files that had been tossed in there. Essentially, the job she'd been given was to organize the Pueblo Police Department's junk drawer.

She found a large, empty trashcan and began to go through everything, looking for trash and finding it, including candy wrappers and an empty pop can. Considering the sticky condition of both, she figured the same person had been having a snack and washing it down with sugary goodness in the Records room as opposed to looking for any evidence that had been stowed away until needed.

She heard a loud *flop* on the floor from a few aisles

over. Peeking out from the aisle she was working on, she saw a light blue file folder lying on the floor, some pages scattered nearby, assumedly having fluttered out during the fall.

Walking over to it, she tucked the papers back inside and set the folder back on the shelf in an area away from the edge. Heading back to where she'd been working, she heard the same sound and whirled around, startled to see the same folder on the floor.

"What the hell," she whispered, staring at it for a long moment. Like a child afraid to open the closet door for fear of the Boogie Man behind it, she felt hesitant to pick up the folder again. It was as she studied it, though, when she saw the name printed on the outside tab: *ZUCKER, AMY R.*

Though she didn't know the name, something in her told her to pick up the file and look at it. Squatting down, she gathered the loose pages and shoved them back into the folder and picked it up, carrying it over to the small desk that was pushed into the corner, the top mostly covered with more files and a box or two of evidence that hadn't been returned to the evidence room.

MISSING PERSON:
Amy Rochelle Zucker—age 16
...reported missing December 3, 1983 by her mother...
...last seen at Loaf 'N Jug at 1:13 p.m...
...employer, Alberto d'Giovanni—

Catania froze, rereading the name of a witness that was talked to at the time. How many men named Alberto d'Giovanni were there? She sat back in the creaky chair, flipping through the rest of the file, looking for a picture of the missing girl, any updates, anything.

Where the picture should have been clipped was simply a paper clip. The last update made into the case was July 3, 1984, when her mother called in from her residence in Roswell, Georgia.

Catania tapped her fingers on the file as she considered what she'd read. Suddenly, the picture she'd been shown when she and Matteo were little came to mind, the teenage girl with them. Her name had been Amy, they'd said. She'd interned with their father, they'd said.

Turning in the chair, she scanned the room until she saw the copy machine she'd thought she'd noticed when she'd entered the room five hours before. Rolling the chair away from the desk, she got to her feet and took the file with her.

༄ ༄ ༅ ༅

The sun was already well on its way going down when Catania pulled up in front of Big Daddy's Plumbing and Heating. She noted her father's truck backed into its usual space and she knew he was in there finishing up paperwork for the day. The only other car was Dino's 2017 pearl-blue Camaro.

Parking next to the sports car, she climbed out of her Jeep and glanced at the flashy set of wheels, shaking her head. "Totally wrong color," she muttered.

She pulled the smoked glass door open and stepped inside. The front of the business was as it had been for years: a main desk for the office manager to sit at and answer phones, deal with walk-ins, and ring up sales for the cleaners and such they sold on-site. Catania had sat at that desk many, many times during her high school years.

She walked past the empty desk and through the door that was only for employees which led to back offices and the warehouse where parts, supplies, and the company vans were kept.

"Hey, Dino?" she asked, ducking her head into his office. He sat behind the desk, phone to his ear. He was giggling and laughing into it like a schoolboy.

Covering the receiver with a hand, he glared up at her. "What?"

"Where's Papa? He's not in his office," she said.

Dino shrugged. "Try the vans. I know he was planning to re-supply the staples in each."

"I see," she said hand on hip. "And, you're not helping him...why?"

Dino looked at her like she'd lost her mind. "Because I'm on the phone."

Shaking her head and rolling her eyes, she pushed away from the open office door and headed down the long hall to the windowed door that led to the large and sometimes loud warehouse.

"Papa?" she called, allowing the door to ease closed behind her.

"Over here!" came his response, which could have come from anywhere as the words echoed against the cement floors and metal walls.

"You wanna be a bit more specific?"

"Van four!" he yelled, a hand waving above the top of said van.

She headed in that direction, walking past the other vans that stood like silent warriors waiting to be sent into battle. She was proud of her father. As she understood it, he'd began with a Volkswagen bus, some tools, and her mother answering phones. Now, he had eight vans with his logo proudly painted across the side, a respected name, and booming business.

"Hey, Papa," she said, coming around to the side of the van where the sliding side door was open and her father sat. To her surprise, he was playing a video game on his phone. "And I thought you were working," she teased, plopping down next to him.

He chuckled, turning off the game and setting the phone aside. "I was. But," he said with a shrug and a little grin, "I needed some space from your brother."

She laughed outright. "Gee, I don't know why."

They shared a comfortable silence for a moment before he placed a hand on her knee and squeezed. "We're praying for him," he said quietly.

She didn't even have to ask him who he meant. She could see the worry in his eyes. "Thanks, Papa," she said softly. She smiled when he leaned over and placed a kiss on her cheek before releasing her knee. "Papa, I have to ask you a question."

"Alright, Kitty Cat. I hope I have an answer for you."

"I came across something today," she said, eyeing him. "In the missing persons files."

He nodded, almost as if silently encouraging her to continue, even as his jaw muscle pulsed a few times.

"Papa, what was Amy's last name?"

"Zucker," he supplied, no hesitation. He looked up toward the ceiling. "She was sixteen the day she disappeared."

"Why did Mamma tell me her family moved away?" she asked gently.

"They did. About a year after she went missing,

they moved, though I forget where."

"Georgia."

"Yes. The uh, the uh…" He snapped his fingers as though it would help him think. "The alien place."

Catania chuckled. "Yes. Roswell, but the one in Georgia."

He smiled but then looked down at his lap, hands resting on the edge of the van on either side of them.

"They spoke to you in 1983, Papa." At his nod she asked, "Why?"

"Because she was always here," he said simply, looking at her with profoundly sad eyes. "Her home life wasn't so good, parents always fighting, blaming her for their fighting." He smiled. "She used to call me either Mr. D or Papa D. This warehouse wasn't here then, but she was always in this building. Sometimes, I swear, sometimes I still think I see her here."

"You really cared about her, didn't you?"

"She was my second daughter. Oh, and she loved you," he said, smiling that gentle smile that he seemed to save just for his Kitty Cat. "She'd carry you like a sack of potatoes on her shoulder." He chuckled. "You crawled all over her like a little monkey, or something."

She felt the blood drain from her face and her pulse race. "Papa, are there any pictures of Amy? Other than the one Mamma showed of Matty and I with her?"

He studied her for a long moment and then, to her surprise, he leaned over and reached in his back pocket, pulling out his wallet. He flipped it open and dug around until he produced a small, wallet-sized school picture. It was a bit faded and frayed, but there was a full-on smiling young woman. Her dark eyes were guarded, but her smile was beautiful. Her dark hair was short but shaggy, the bangs a little too long.

Catania took the picture in hand and her breath caught. She held that picture in a trembling hand, tears instantly springing to her eyes. "My god," she whispered, a tear falling down her cheek and plopping onto the small, glossy shot. "Squirrel."

Chapter Twenty-five

S he looked down at the box her father had set down on the butcher block island, as well as the case that the projector was in. The rolled-up screen stood on its stand, which they'd left in the living room.

"She still angry?" she asked.

Alberto nodded. "Yes, but deep down she knows none of this is your fault," he said, accepting the cup of coffee she handed him. "I mean, she's the one who gathered all of this for you," he said, indicating all that he'd brought. "I think it's her way of not having to deal with all this by not dealing with it with busywork."

She nodded, sipping from her own coffee. She wasn't entirely sure what he'd brought her, as he'd just shown up after texting to see if she was at work. One nice thing, she supposed, of being temporarily demoted was that she had a set schedule.

"When does this nonsense stop with your work?" he asked, as though reading her mind. "You are a detective, not a secretary."

She smirked. "Don't I know it. Typically, once it's clear my gun had nothing to do with the bullets found that shot Oscar. Ballistics."

"*Sbagliato!*" he exclaimed angrily.

"I know, Papa. I'm not thrilled about it, either." She shrugged. "It is what it is."

He nodded as he finished his coffee. "I'm sorry I can't stay, Kitty Cat," he said, taking his cup to the sink and placing it inside. He gave her a bear hug, which hurt her arm a bit, but she was grateful for the affection so said nothing. "I'm so proud of you, and your Mamma is, too." He left a kiss on the side of her head. "Give her time to process everything that's happening. And, the doctors talked about Matteo getting better."

"Thanks, Papa. I love you."

She walked him out then returned, lifting the lid of the decorative box, probably from a purchase in 1964. Faded flowers were printed all over it. When she lifted the lid, she saw it was filled with a menagerie of pictures and boxed reels for the projector.

"Okay, what's the point of this," she mumbled, lifting a few snapshots out and glancing at them before setting them aside. "Mom's been cleaning out the attic again."

She glanced up when she heard her phone ring. Hurrying to the bedroom where she'd left it, she saw a number she didn't recognize. Answering the call, she put the phone to her ear.

"Detective d'Giovanni?" *Fuck you, Price,* she thought. "Hey, Rodney," she said, shocked to hear Detective Slovodnik's voice. "What's up?" She listened, her shock turning to surprise, then determination. "Yes, I'm glad you called, Rodney, thank you. Text me that address and I'm on my way."

She tossed the phone to the bed and quickly changed out of casual, lazy Saturday clothes into her professional attire before she flew out the door.

≈ ≈ ≈ ≈

It took her a while to find the remote location. She sorely missed Oscar's presence as well as his unending knowledge of anything maps or directions. Alas, she'd found it with a little help from GPS and Google. A black-and-white was on scene as well as a similar nondescript sedan like the one she and Oscar used, and a tow truck.

She turned off the Jeep's engine and unbuckled her seat belt She was about to climb out of the tall vehicle when something floated down into her lap. It felt like butterfly wings as it brushed the side of her face before it settled.

Staring back up at her was Amy Zucker. Her father had lent her the picture he'd carried for so many decades after her promise that she'd find her. Taking the small portrait between thumb and forefinger, she brought the picture up closer to her eyes, looking into those of the teenager. Again, she thought of Squirrel, but knew it just had to be an uncanny resemblance. *Right?*

Again pushing it out of her mind, she put the picture back where it had been tucked under an elastic band wrapped around her sunshade. She let out a soft sigh, then turned to see Rodney standing outside her door.

Nodding an acknowledgement of him, she opened the door and climbed down from the Jeep. "Hey," she said, reaching into her pocket to remove a pair of latex gloves she'd snagged from the box at home.

"I'm really glad you came, Nia," he said, glancing toward the action. The chain had been attached and now the white Subaru was slowly being pulled out of the water with a winch. "I don't know what the hell is going on with Price," he said softly, just loud enough for her to hear. "I don't agree with his antics, but you needed to be here for this."

"You're sure this is my car?" she asked.

"Divers were able to identify the VIN." He met her gaze. "It's a match."

The car slowly eased out of the water, the back of it riddled with bullet holes, the white paint chipped away to reveal the gunmetal-gray beneath.

Together they walked over to it, the motor of the winch loud and whining. Jorge Trujillo stood with the tow truck driver, watching. Water was pouring out of every exit it could find, including the small bullet hole in the back window.

"Kinda creepy, isn't it?" Rodney said loud enough to be heard over the winch.

Catania nodded, unable to take her eyes off the car. Finally, all four wheels were on dry land, even as the pouring water created a mud puddle beneath it. The tow truck driver turned off the winch and unhooked the cabling.

She walked over to it, mesmerized as she knew in her heart this was definitely their car, in addition to Rodney's confirmation. She could feel an aura of absolute evil coming off that wagon. The windows were fogged over with condensation and a billion tiny water droplets that clung to the glass.

She stared down at the driver's side door handle and, with steeled courage and caged rage, she reached for it, surprised to find it unlocked.

"You may want to take a step back, ma'am," the tow truck driver said. "Gonna be a deluge when that opens."

She glanced at him and gave his advice its due, stepping back as she tugged the door open. A veritable waterfall rushed forth. The mud splattered up onto her pants legs and shoes, but she didn't care. All she could see was the faces of those who could not speak for themselves any longer: Anastasia, Eric, Aaron, Megan, Liv, Oscar, and…She shook her head, pushing the image out of her mind. No. That would wait.

Focusing on the task at hand, she noticed something white fall out of the car with the last of the water. It looked to be a long, thin strip of some sort. For a moment she thought it was a fish or some sort of marine life, but on closer inspection, she was surprised.

Bending down, she grabbed a nearby stick on the ground. Something about the stick caught her eye and she looked at it, marveling at the fact that it looked more like it had been carved to look like a stick than anything from nature. Pushing that thought aside, she used it to work until she was able to drag the strip over to her to see it better.

"What is that?" Detective Trujillo asked.

"I don't know," she murmured absently, squatting down. She got it wrapped over the stick enough to bring it up closer. "Looks like a piece of medical or surgical tape. She glanced over at him and could see the confusion. "You know, like if you were to tape on a gauze pad or something."

He nodded. "Yeah, got it. It does look like that."

"Here's another one," Rodney said, looking at them through the car as he stood at the open passenger door. He held one up with a gloved hand. "Oh, one more, in the back seat. Looks like it'd gotten tangled up in the seat belt."

"What the hell?" Catania stepped over the largest portion of mud to Rodney's side of the car, which wasn't as bad.

"This one has a little bit of another piece stuck to

it, see that?" he said, holding it up for Catania to see. "Looks like it was used."

"Any blood on any of it?" Jorge asked, pulling open the driver's side back door.

"Nope."

"Blanket back there, probably what he had the girl wrapped in during transport," Rodney offered.

"This car is clean other than that," Jorge said, standing back and looking the car over. "Nothing in the glove box, center console, nothing."

"Let's get the blanket and tape bagged, then let's get it loaded up and to the station to be processed," Catania said, frustrated.

࿇ ࿇ ࿇ ࿇

"Hey, baby. Sorry I haven't called you today. I ended up out with the two detectives Price assigned to take over our case. I'll explain when I see you tonight. I hope you're having a good day and...I miss you." Catania smiled at her own shyness. "Bye."

Voicemail left, she set her phone aside. Glancing at the box of pictures she'd begun to look at before Rodney had called, she decided to figure out why her mother had sent them, and moreover, why her father had brought them over. More than once when Antonia d'Giovanni got on a cleaning kick or thought that one of her children might want her entire collection of *Cosmopolitan* for some reason, she'd sent it off with her husband to deliver. And, more than once he'd either kept "on loan" items hidden at the shop for a time until he felt they'd been "borrowed" long enough by whatever child would never want them and return them dutifully to his wife, or blatantly find an out-of-the-way dumpster in which to dispose of them.

This time, however, had not been one of those times, so he obviously saw some value there. She began to make a couple piles as she went through the mass of various-sized snapshots and professional pictures, some of the boys and her in their individual school pictures throughout the years. She cringed at a few of her hairstyle choices before tossing the pictures in the pile of what amounted to "no real need revisit." That pile was essentially filled with pictures she needed to get out of the way.

Catania didn't consider herself a particularly nostalgic person, especially when it came to pictures, so it was quite a chore for her to go through the box. There were at least some minor comedic breaks when she found the random piece of trash that had been tossed in when one or the other of the kids were asked to go through the box of pictures to find this one or that one over the years. It was a hated task, one which she'd had to partake in a few times, and retaliation took many forms for such punishment, including leaving trash behind. She laughed outright when she found Paul's fourth-grade report card buried near the bottom. She remembered that year, and how she'd tried to back him up by hiding hers and saying they hadn't received them that year.

"God, we were so stupid back then." She chuckled, shaking her head.

She reached back into the box, and found a rubber bouncing ball, which she tossed out onto the hardwood floor, watching as it bounced its way across the room. She smiled, thinking of the quirked look of confusion that would be on Ally's face if she found it while cleaning Wednesday. She left it where it settled against the wall. Her attention was grabbed from the colorful ball when she hissed in pain.

"Son of a biscuit!" she exclaimed, snatching her hand back to find her fingertip bleeding. Looking down into the box, she saw a used disposable razor that had been tossed in at some point. "Jesus, that hurt."

Ordinarily she'd just stick her finger in her mouth, but the razor was used, and even though it was her family...just, no. She held her hand up and hurried over to the kitchen sink and washed it. Snagging a piece of paper towel, she dried her finger and squeezed it to try to stop the bleeding before grabbing a fresh piece and wrapping it tightly around her cut finger.

Returning to the box, she tossed the razor out then shoved some other pictures aside when she stopped cold, her hand about to shove the picture aside. Instead, she brought it out of the box and studied it.

In the snapshot, Jason and Karen stood in front of a movie theater. Behind them in huge letters on the marquis was *Harry Potter and the Prisoner of Azkaban.* He and Karen looked much younger. She was trying to think of when this picture would have been taken because she didn't remember him having such long hair. Then again, there were a few years in her early- to mid-twenties when she saw very little of her family and pretty much not any of Jason, as she had focused solely on her career. She was also hiding the relationship she was in from all of them. Karen was giving a silly smile toward the camera, a wizard's hat on her head. Jason was looking at her, his hair pulled back into a single braid.

She dropped the picture and stepped back from the island, letting out a long, slow breath. To get some distance, she walked back over to the sink and unwrapped her injured finger, noting the bright red blood spot on the white material of the paper towel. She noticed the print left behind was distorted, a strange splice of white on the fabric.

Looking at her finger, she realized it was the one that had taken the staple just before Christmas when hanging lights for Karen. The slight wound of skin ripped out had been so deep that the blood on the surface from her cut on the razor had gone around it. It was the same idea if she'd left a fingerprint after pressing her finger into an ink pad.

She brought her other hand over and covered her fingertip with blood from that was beading up from the cut. She pressed that fingertip onto the paper towel, noting the normal, fully covered blood spot.

Rewrapping the cut finger with the paper towel, she stopped, unwinding the white towel before slowly wrapping it, watching the process closely.

"Fuck me," she whispered.

Racing around the butcher block island, she grabbed her phone and quickly sent off a text message to Rodney:

Catania: *Get that medical tape tested for fingerprints in the adhesive! The fucker was using them to wrap his fingertips!*

Rodney: *Wait, what? Are you serious?*

Catania: *You've got to see if you can find the other two if not more. See if he was wrapping all ten fingers if he has them.*

Tossing her phone aside, the picture caught her eyes again. In it, the couple stood hip to hip, Jason's left arm around Karen's shoulders, left hand dangling over her upper chest. Never taking her eyes off her target, she absently reached for her phone and, glancing at the screen, tapped on the camera function and aimed until it was focused as best she could, then snapped the picture.

Bringing it up on her photos, she eased her thumbs over the screen, the image becoming larger and larger. The larger it got the more pixelized it became, but she thought she'd seen what she needed to.

She needed to know something else, though. She hurried back to her bedroom and snagged her notebook off her dresser. Plopping down at the end of the bed, she flipped through the seemingly endless pages dealing with the cases they were working on until she found what she was looking for.

Using her finger as a guide, she trailed over the lines for the period of dates. "Okay," she murmured, resting the notebook on her thigh as she grabbed her phone and used a search engine to find out when the Harry Potter movie had been released. "June of 2004," she read aloud. Her eyes closed and she brought the phone up to rest against her forehead. "No, no, no…"

She gasped when her phone rang, nearly throwing it in her surprise. Bringing it down to look at the screen, she saw Restricted. She stared at that word, the ringtone sounding again.

Swallowing, she answered the call. "D'Giovanni."

"*Hi, Nene.*"

"Hi, Squirrel," she whispered. Suddenly, the little carved squirrel she saw on Karen's mantel popped before her mind's eye. The hot sting of tears followed. "Where are you?"

"*You didn't give me anything for Christmas,*" she said, her voice soft and unusually vulnerable. "*You know what gift you can give me, Nene?*"

"No. What?" Catania asked, her voice just as

soft. She used her sleeve to wipe away the tears that had begun to fall.

"*Come get me,*" Squirrel responded, a plea in her tone. "*I wanna go home.*"

Catania sniffled, the tears coming faster. "I don't know where."

"*Sure you do.*"

"Squirrel?" Catania said after the soft click of the line going dead. "Squirrel?" She squeezed her eyes shut. "Amy?" She let the phone slide down to the bed and let herself feel. "Okay," she whispered. "Okay, I'll find you."

☙☙☙☙

Catania sent Ally a quick text before she headed out, letting her know where she was going and that she might be out of reception range at times driving through those mountain passes and valleys. She still hadn't heard from her yet that day, which was a little surprising, But, she knew that weekends could be unreasonably busy at Randy's.

She floored the gas, taking the winding roads at speeds that were dangerous, but her heart was racing and her emotions were all over the place. She let out a roar that was ear-splitting in the confines of her Jeep, but she didn't care.

"You bastard!" she yelled, slamming her fist against the steering wheel. The tears were back and they ran hot down her cheeks.

She knew she was being reckless, but didn't care. She was filled with a flurry of shock, anger, confusion, and a whole lot of praying that she was wrong. Before she knew it, she was making her way up the long driveway. She pulled up in front of the lake house and

cut the engine. Sitting behind the wheel for a long
moment, she stared up at the large cabin, wondering
where she was supposed to go. She felt too emotionally
connected to all this to listen to her gut, which had
remained silent anyway—except for the impulse to
grab her personal .38 from her gun safe before she left
the house. Maybe The Gift wasn't totally MIA.

Finally, she climbed out of the Jeep and walked
to the front door where a large statue of a frog sat with
a welcome sign around its neck. Hidden in the open
mouth was a house key. Reaching in to get it, Catania
let herself into the cabin.

It was strange to be in there alone, without her
family. She almost felt like a child lost in a store without
her mother. She walked through the main floor, again
getting that feeling of uncertainty. This time being
there, however, she couldn't help but think that Amy
had roamed these halls. As she looked to the kitchen,
though it had been remodeled since 1983, she thought
back to that picture of Amy with her and Matteo.

"Are you in this house somewhere, Amy?"
she whispered, looking around again as though she
expected the teen to waltz out of the bathroom. But
then, she thought of Squirrel. "No," she said, shaking
her head. "No. Not the same person."

She headed upstairs to the bedrooms. The one
she had shared with Matteo and Paul when they were
kids was at the end of the L-shaped hall, their bedroom
and a bathroom in that little nook. As she walked that
way, something told her to look up.

A small, wooden painted sign was mounted
above the doorframe. She remembered well how she
and Paul had giggled as they'd painted it and nailed it
in place. They'd wondered how long it would take their

parents to notice it and how much trouble they'd be in. Ironically, their mother had never noticed it and they'd gotten away with it clean. It was a smaller version of their street signs outside all over the property:

None of Your Business Ln.

She stopped and stared at that for a long moment, a very cocky young woman outside the Pueblo Police Department coming to mind. Again, she felt the sting of emotion as she entered the room. She turned to the right and saw one of the two windows in the bedroom. Walking toward that window, she saw the expanse of the side yard, opposite the lake side. There stood a massive tree, the one they all used to climb. The one they'd christened *Squirrel Hotel.*

Feeling as though she couldn't breathe, she ran her hand through her hair and sat on one of the twin beds, the old frame creaking under her weight. She couldn't take her eyes off that tree, a tree her and her brothers climbed all over like...monkeys.

"Jesus," she murmured.

Finally, she pushed up from the bed and headed out of the house to the snow-covered ground outside. The tree loomed large, its skeletal branches raised to the overcast sky as though reaching to the heavens.

She looked down at the ground, a few rocks mixed with the snow and some patches of dark earth where the snow had either melted or been blown away. She did her best to put herself in detective mode, trying to figure out why she was standing next to that tree. Why was she drawn to it?

"Did he put you here?" she whispered, lightly kicking the hard, frozen ground with the toe of her boot. There would be no way to dig there without a backhoe or some other heavy equipment. She was considering her options when something caught her eye.

Walking over to the foot of the tree, she squatted down. It was partially buried in the snow, white against the dark brown of the tree trunk. Reaching out, she gently plucked it from the ground, her breath catching.

A white matchbook, the number nineteen penned in bold, black Sharpie. She cradled the matchbook in her hands and closed her eyes, sending a silent prayer to a girl long lost.

"Hey."

Catania's head lifted, not entirely surprised to see the young woman she'd come to know as Squirrel standing there, a hand resting on the trunk of the tree. She was in her light blue and gray windbreaker, though her face was clean, free of the streets or any injuries. She looked light, free, and beautiful. She gave Catania a winning smile.

"See ya around, Nene," she said softly.

Catania's phone rang, startling her. She looked down as she reached into her jacket pocket to fish it out. When she looked back up, she was alone. Wiping her fresh tears away, she looked at the phone, noting Karen's name.

"Hello?" She pushed to her feet, listening to her sister-in-law. "Wait, no, I left her a voicemail and texted her, but I haven't heard from her. Did you say the lady on the first floor said Ally didn't make them breakfast?" She pulled the phone away to look at the clock. "Karen, it's well after lunchtime, pushing dinner... Yeah, uh absolutely." She pocketed the matchbook as she began to jog toward her Jeep. "No, I'm headed there now. Call the diner. I'll call you when I know something."

Chapter Twenty-six

C atania entered Aberdeen House, slowly
making her way down the main hallway. She
took in everything, looking for anything out of place,
listening for anything out of place. All she heard was
the muffled sounds of someone's TV behind one of the
closed apartment doors.

She walked over to Ally's door, studying it to see
if anything stood out at her. Was there any blood on
it? Was there any sign of a break-in, had the hinges or
locks been messed with? Everything looked normal, so
she reached for the knob, expecting it to be locked, but
it turned with ease.

She stepped inside, reaching down to her holster
to unsnap the strap that held her .38 in place. The living
area was quiet, no lights on, only the multi-colored hue
from the stained glass window lit the space. The throw
that was usually folded neatly on the back of the love
seat was tossed aside, partially spread across the arm
of the couch and draping to the floor. Catania figured
Ally was likely watching TV before bed, as she often
did when Catania didn't spend the night. The previous
night Catania's arm had been hurting and, as she was
trying to take less and less pain medication, they'd
decided it would be best for her to go home and not
chance her arm being hit accidentally by Ally in the
night.

That bit of information was troubling, as she

knew that Ally wouldn't have left the apartment without everything being clean and tidy. She stood at the top of the stairs for a moment, listening. The room below was also only lit by the sunlight coming in through the small windows.

"Ally?" she called. "Ally, are you down there?"

As she expected, there was no response. She slowly made her way down, glancing behind her from time to time to make sure she wasn't going to end in a trap, though nobody appeared by the time she reached the lower rooms. The bed was not only unmade, but half the bedding was puddled on the floor as though someone had been dragged from the bed. Not just someone, but Ally.

She was startled when her text message indicator alerted. Eyes still scanning every single detail of the small apartment, she reached into her pocket and retrieved her phone, glancing down at the message.

Jason: *Don't worry, she wasn't hurt. Quite affable, really.*

Catania felt her blood go cold. She swiped out of texting and went to her contacts list when another text came in.

Jason: *Don't bother calling, I won't pick up. I'm a bit busy.*

Catania: *What do you want with her?*

Catania looked around, wondering if he could see her. It was then that she noticed the carved cat she'd given Ally sitting on the small table.

Jason: *I was surprised Karen gave that to you. But then, daddy's little Kitty Cat, makes sense.*

"Where are you, you fucker." Her heart was racing as her mind exploded with the gravity of what was happening. The problem was, she didn't really know what she was dealing with, or why.

Looking up at the ceiling fan, she nearly smacked herself. She saw the wire peeking out that she'd noticed the night Ally asked her to check the apartment for her. Now, she wondered if it wasn't connected to a camera.

Catania: *Where are you?*

Jason: *Somewhere safe, warm, and private. Snug as a bug in a rug, we are.*

Suddenly, a picture came through on their thread, a selfie of Jason with his head resting next to Ally's. She appeared to be lying down. She was gagged and her eyes were squeezed shut.

"You mother fucker!" Catania roared, grabbing the carved cat and throwing it as hard as she could at the ceiling fan, two of the glass fixtures around the light bulbs exploding, raining glass down.

Jason: *Temper temper, little one. If you involve any other member of the police other than you, now that Oscar is out of service, I'll kill her.*

Catania: *Why? Why are you doing this? Why Ally?*

She texted the message before turning and running for the stairs, taking them two at a time. She ran down the hall, ignoring curious looks from a couple of the tenants who peeked out of their apartments.

Jason: *Because she's part of my bucket list. So are you...*

Catania burst out into the late afternoon day, the sun already showing signs of calling it a day. She sprinted across the front yard to the curb where her Jeep was parked. Yanking the door open after she unlocked it, she didn't even bother with her seat belt as she squealed the tires in her haste to get to Ally.

She almost ran off the road as she looked away to grab the magnet-mounted siren out of her glove compartment and tossed it to her passenger seat as she cranked the driver's side window down to she could reach out and place the siren on the roof. That accomplished, she gunned the engine, the big tires on the rugged Jeep chewing up the streets as she raced across town and into the more rural area, the houses farther apart as horse corrals and barns began to dot the landscape.

As she got closer to the house, she slowed the Jeep. There were no cars in the expansive driveway, no signs of life. She pulled in front of the house rather than possibly getting boxed in or bulldozed in the driveway. She had no idea what was waiting for her on the other side of those four closed garage doors.

Killing the engine, Catania glanced over to her empty passenger seat. "God, I wish you were here, buddy," she whispered, a small smile coming to her lips as she knew Oscar was somehow sending her strength and courage. She bent over and reached into her glove compartment, pulling out some extra ammunition as well as the pink Derringer revolver Paul had given her when she graduated from the Academy. She rarely ever brought it out, but today she decided it was worth having additional backup. She made sure it was loaded and tucked it into the waistband of her jeans.

Closing her eyes for a moment, she reached up and wrapped her hands around the angel pendant Ally had given her for Christmas. She sent a silent message to Ally, letting her know she was on the way. She kissed the pendant and tucked away beneath her button shirt.

Pistol pulled from her holster in hand, Catania ran toward the house with catlike stealth, knowing full well she was at a horrible disadvantage. She was out in the open and she was assuming Jason and Ally were even at the house. But, something in her gut told her they were. Somewhere on that property was the monster she hunted.

She made her way to the front door, instantly ducking down out of the view or target of any window or door. She reached down to her holster belt, which seconded as a utility belt, and tugged her flashlight free from the leather ring it was tucked into. Clicking the flashlight aglow, she raised herself just enough to the bottom ledge of one of the windows on either side of the door, shining her beam inside.

The house looked quiet, no movement inside, everything as it usually was. She reached her body out to grip the handle of the glass door and opened it, the door bracing against her arm as she checked the knob of the main, heavy door. It was unlocked.

Squeezing her eyes shut and trying to calm her racing heart, she silently counted to three then let herself into the house, hitting the floor behind a wingback chair. Pistol leading the way, she scanned the room. Clear.

"Jason?" she called out. She figured if he wished to communicate with her via texting, obviously he wanted her to follow the bread crumb trail he was laying for her. Now that she was in the house, she was counting on him reaching out to her again. "Jason? Ally?"

The only thing she heard was the distant rhythmic ticking of a clock. The house felt empty, no life. All her training told her to go through the entire house and make sure it was clear, but her instincts told her that was wasting precious time that Ally didn't have.

She hurried through to the dining room where the French doors led to the back part of the property.

Instantly her gaze settled on the large structure that was Jason's workshop and rec room.

It was a wide-open space between the house and the structure, not a thing to hide behind except a few saplings. All she could do was once again put the pedal to the metal and book it across the expanse until she pressed her back against the solid side of the workshop/garage. Her heart was pounding as, with all that she was, she knew she was a breath away from Jason and Ally. For just a moment it hit her what was at stake.

For months she and Oscar had been following a trail of blood, chasing the Boogie Man from murder to murder. Now, it mattered more than ever. The woman that she loved was now being held as a pawn in a real-life game of chess, and Catania wasn't entirely sure what the rules were. So many people had gotten hurt, people close to her, people she loved. She felt the weight of each moment of suffering on her shoulders.

Taking several deep breaths, she pushed all her guilt, all her fear, and all her rage away. She had to focus and let her training kick in. Jason Ross would not win. Steeling her resolve, she grabbed the angel pendant and brought it out of her shirt. She gave it another quick kiss before dropping it back into her shirt.

"I'm coming, baby," she whispered.

She made her way to the door, which was solid, no windows. Reaching for the knob, she found it unlocked like that of the house. She turned it and pushed the door open, standing back out of danger range. When nothing happened, she peeked her head in. Pitch blackness met her. She reached in to feel for a light switch, but when she found one, nothing happened.

"Bastard," she whispered. Jason was an electrician,

and a damn good one. Lord only knew what kind of fun house he had planned.

She brought her flashlight up again, sweeping her beam over her surroundings. It was amazing how creepy the most ordinary thing could look under the beam. Shadows danced and teased her, jumping from item to item. She felt like she was about to find a decapitated head in a jar in the back seat of a limo.

Everything on both sides, the rec area and the workshop area, was exactly as she remembered it from Christmas. One thing caught her attention, though. Gripping the flashlight between her arm and her side, she brought out her phone, pain searing from her fingers to her shoulder as she used her injured arm, but she did her best to ignore it. She studied the picture Jason had sent her. As much as it tore her heart out to see the fear on Ally's face again, she had to look past it, literally.

Though it was a close-up of the two of their faces, she could see a bit of the wall beyond Ally's blond hair. It looked to be gray cement. Looking around where she stood, she knew the floors were all polished cement, but from memory and what her light shone on, all the walls were either drywalled and painted, or were covered in pegboard or hung tools.

She swung her flashlight in the area of the rec room, which she knew led to the garage portion. As her beam moved in that direction, it crossed over Jason's workbench and finally the art display on the wall of his "bucket list." He'd even mentioned that to her when she was still at Ally's apartment.

Walking over to it, she studied the clay pieces. It amazed her that such a talented, creative man could be an absolute devil in disguise. Studying the top bucket, she reached out and removed it from its iron ring. Shining the flashlight down into it, the light bounced back off the blue-colored gel to nearly blind her. No time to mess with it, she allowed the clay bucket to fall, breaking into several large pieces on the cement floor. The crash was as startling as it was satisfying.

The gel split open into three Jell-O-like pieces, revealing a metal tin, like what Band-Aids used to be in. She quickly opened it, finding as promised a dried bridal rose as well as some movie stubs, including to her surprise, those to the Harry Potter movie from the picture.

"Slimy bastard," she muttered, reaching for the second bucket. "So fucking important to you, yet you were fucking around on her..."

The second bucket met the same fate, though in this one was a small tin, the size of an Altoids tin. The contents in that one stole her breath away. She reached inside and withdrew a cold, bone-shaped dog tag: *Brewster*. The second item in the tin knocked her from her squatting position to sitting down. It was a driver's license, and the face smiling up at her had become as familiar to her as her own face.

"Amy," she murmured, fingertips running over the laminated card. She set the two items back into the tin and, with renewed vigor, she grabbed the third, fourth, and fifth buckets, smashing them to the floor. "Jesus." It was a prosecution's wet dream: Anastasia Luhan's driver's license, a bright yellow child's Lego— large size for tiny hands—with a tiny spot of blood on it. There was a pair of sterling silver dangly earrings, and Megan Murphy's driver's license with a large blood smear on it. There was also a very small clear bottle with a white plastic cap. The contents were a clear, water-like liquid. There was no label, but she had a feeling she'd found his stash of GHB.

She looked at all the evidence around her, astounded, disgusted, unsettled, and deeply fearful for Ally. She reached up and grabbed the final bucket and, about to smash it, she realized it actually was made of wood. Looking inside, she saw a thin plastic covering. Though it looked similar at a quick glance to the blue candle gel, it was nothing more than a filler.

Lifting it out, she tossed it aside to see a simple brass key. Plucking out from the bottom, she looked at it in the light of her flashlight. It didn't look like a house key and wasn't large and bulky enough to be a car key, so she began to look around.

She gasped, startled as she heard a woman's voice. Getting to her feet, key still in hand and a mess at her feet, her gaze was drawn to a strange blue light coming through the holes in the pegboard that lined the wall behind the workbench. It was about a three-foot section that she realized there was no wall behind. It was impossible to see in the light of day, but now in the darkness it was clearly visible.

Walking over to the workbench, she looked around, trying to see if there was any way behind the pegboard. She looked under the bench, nothing. She pushed on the bench, no give. She glanced at a spot where a hammer was housed between two pegs and was about to look away when she noticed something peeking out behind it. Taking a closer look, she saw a keyhole.

"Bingo," she whispered.

The key she'd found was a perfect fit. Turning it, she heard something click and she felt the workbench give a bit. Setting the pistol and flashlight on the workbench, she used both hands and pulled. Feeling as though it were rolling on casters, the three-foot section of workbench and pegboard pulled free, swinging on unseen hinges to reveal a room beyond.

Reclaiming her gun and flashlight, she headed inside and looked around, making sure she was still alone. The room was no more than the size of a small walk-in closet. Along the wall to the left was a rough, thick wood slab bolted into the wall that served as a desk. On it were two large computer monitors. The tower, speakers, and other equipment was set up on wire shelving above.

Her attention was drawn to the one monitor that was aglow. She realized where the woman's voice was coming from. She slowly lowered herself to the chair that was placed before the desk, her eyes wide with shock and horror.

Megan Murphy lay handcuffed to a cot in a cement room. She was naked, hands cuffed above her head, ankles shackled spread-eagle at the foot of the cot. She was crying, begging for her life as Jason entered the scene, in one hand a large hunting knife, the other empty, simply his large, calloused hand.

"Which is it going to be, hmm?"

"Please, Jason. Please. I'm sorry! Please!"

The video quickly disappeared and a new one appeared. Catania's eyes nearly bulged out of her head as a hand went to her mouth. She was watching herself and Ally making love. It was as though someone was standing behind the shelving where Ally kept her beloved snow globes. She remembered that strangely placed nail hole.

"Oh my god," she whispered.

"Hey, Sis."

Startled again, she looked at the second monitor, which had come to life. It was obviously a live feed as she saw "LIVE" at the bottom left of the screen. Jason's face was at the center of the frame, making it nearly impossible to see anything else or where he was.

"Being the nosey bitch you are, I know you found my stash, and that's fine. That was the point. So, now you see what I've been up to for the last bit." He grinned, and in that moment Catania knew she was absolutely looking into the face of evil. *"See, if you continue watching my Greatest Hits that I made for you, you can see the beauty of true vengeance."*

Her gaze drifted to the first screen and again, her hand went to her mouth.

The scene was Anastasia Luhan's bedroom. Both she and Aaron had already been attacked, and it looked like Aaron was already dead. Anastasia lay on her back, her throat slit and she was gurgling. She hadn't been mutilated...yet.

Heavy breathing could be heard, and it was coming from behind the camera, which was being carried and getting closer to the dying woman.

"I bet you wish you hadn't decided to throw away your baby now don't you, you fucking bitch?" His laughter was dark. *"Stupid cunt. You and that piece of shit, another father who threw away his son, his own blood, thought I really wanted to adopt your brat. Stupid bitch. Yeah,"* he said, camera shifting to Aaron, the blood stain centered directly over his chest. *"You broke my heart, so weak."* The shot shifted back to Anastasia one last time. *"I'm going to fix you, fix you so you can never throw away another baby again. You can never leave your son with that piece of shit you live with. He'll never have to worry about being bent over*

his bed like I was, no. I set him free. But now..." A knife, covered in blood, entered the frame. *"Now it's time to fix you."*

"You see, Nia," Jason said on the first monitor, catching a shaken Catania's attention again. He was on the move, walking down what looked to be a cement tunnel. *"Karen never understood why I wanted to buy this place. I mean, I was dead set on it."* He stopped, a grin spreading across his lips. *"No pun intended. Anyway, the people who lived here before, I guess they had quite the wine collection. It took some time, but the wine cellar came in handy."* He stopped walking for a moment and looked directly into the camera, directly into Catania's soul. *"Do you think you can find us?"* he asked.

"Oh, god!" Catania exclaimed, watching as the camera panned over Ally's naked body, which was chained to the same cot as Megan's had been. Her face was bruised and she fought against her restraints.

"Nia!" she screamed. *"Please! Nia!"*

Catania shoved away from the desk and nearly ran headlong into the wall in her haste to get out of the computer room. She wasn't sure what was more soul-shattering: the fact that she could still hear Ally's screamed pleas in her head, or the fact that she hadn't been able to hear it outside of the speakers connected to the monitor. She was becoming more and more frightened that Jason was off the premises after all. He obviously had no issue playing games, why not one last one?

Ignoring the monitors and Jason's *Greatest Hits*, she went on the search to find a way into the area where he claimed to be. If it was in fact a wine cellar, she figured it would likely be underground. She searched every square inch of wall and floor, looking for a door, a hatch, anything to get her down below.

She found herself in the garage portion, grateful for the little bit of light coming in from the frosted glass in the large garage doors, though it was fading fast as the sun went down. She noted Jason's truck and a couple antique cars that he seemed to be in the process of restoring, as well as lots of cabinets and a riding lawnmower parked against the side wall. There was nothing more, no doors, not even a hatch for attic space above.

She opened the doors of a few cabinets, only to find typical garage items inside: bottles of oil for cars, a replacement filter of some sort, and, interestingly enough, a large jug of antifreeze.

Slamming the door in frustration, she looked around, running her hand through her hair as she felt the sweat beginning to gather under her arms and between her breasts as she felt the heat building. Finally, a cabinet tucked over by the entrance into the large garage caught her eye.

Hurrying over to it, she noted it was twice as wide as the others, and the doors, though painted roughly the same light gray color, seemed to be made out of a stronger material than the thin metal of the others.

She looked down at the double handles, long and metal like the others. Gripping each, she turned them downward at the same time and the doors gave, opening to reveal a door in the wall.

"Bingo, you son of a bitch," she whispered, a smile spreading across her lips.

Stepping inside the confines of the large cabinet, she turned the knob on the door and pushed inward, a wide set of stone stairs immediately meeting her. She was glad she hadn't just stepped in or she would likely have broken her neck in a nasty tumble.

Flashlight beam leading the way, she scurried down the staircase. Surrounded by the cement walls and stone stairs, she felt like she was heading into the bowels of a castle. The deeper she got, the danker the air got. It was chilly and decidedly uncomfortable.

The stairs curved around to a main hallway that ran straight down. Overhead, a straight line of naked light bulbs led the way, though none were lit. At the bottom of the stairs and directly to the left was a small room. The swing of the beam gave her chills when she saw a large chest-type freezer. Moving on, she saw a second door coming up a bit farther down. She went to peek her head in when suddenly a light that seemed to be as bright as the sun was shining right in her face from down the hall.

Stumbling backward against the wall, she didn't have time to think or react when there was a bang and she cried out in pain, feeling as though her left arm had exploded.

"Ouch," Jason's voice said from beyond the incessant bright light.

Before Catania could respond, before she could even breathe, there was a second bang and she felt the fire of that sun burn into her chest. She lost her footing from the pain and fell to the floor, a second cry erupting from her at the white-hot pain that lanced through her arm and shoulder like a lightning bolt. She had no time to reach for her pistol, which had flown from her hand after the first shot struck her.

A black figure appeared in front of the spotlight, turning it into a silhouette walking toward her. As she watched, gritting her teeth against the pain, she couldn't help but think of the shadowy figure from her dream. She went to reach for her .38.

"I don't think so," Jason said, kicking the pistol away with the toe of his boot. He stood over her, his 9mm pointed directly at her forehead.

"Why are you doing this, Jason?" she asked, refusing to look away from his eyes, dimly visible now with the closeness of his bulky frame blocking the spotlight. "I know why you did what you did with Anastasia, Aaron, and Eric. Why Ally? Why Liv? Why Amy—"

"That," he said forcefully. "Was an accident. I never meant to kill Amy. She should have kept her mouth shut." He squatted down in front of her so he was more on her eye level. He looked down at her left arm, the splintered cast quickly dyed crimson from the bullet wound which had surely shattered the already fragile bones of her forearm, before his gaze traveled to her chest and the blood on the material of her shirt.

"Mouth shut about what?" she managed to ask, voice nearly breathless as she was doing her best to keep control of her pain and stay conscious.

"The same thing Megan did wrong. You see," he said softly, lightly, shaking his head as if what he was about to say was obvious to all. "Even you, a woman who loves other women, I'm sure that a woman, of all people, never, *ever* questions a man about what he's capable of doing for them."

"Jason," she gasped, blinking rapidly as her blood pressure continued to plummet. "Jason, you've gotta get me a doctor, bro."

He studied her for a moment. "You don't get it, do you? None of us are leaving here tonight, Nia. You asked why Ally? Well." He smirked. "How the hell else was I going to get you to come over and play?" He pushed to his feet, his gun never wavering in its aim at her head even as he backed away from her, once again the light blinding. "It's all about the bucket list, Nia. I took care of the past. Karen is fine in the present with her family, not a clue what's happened back here." His voice was getting farther away and then stopped.

She had no idea where he'd gone, or if he was standing down the hall behind the light watching her, waiting for her to make a move. She knew reaching for her .38 wasn't an option so, with the strength she had left, she slowly slid her right hand toward her back.

She snapped to attention when she heard the rattling of metal chains and muffled cries of distress. Again, the large silhouette headed toward her, though this time he wasn't alone. "Ally." She released a breath she didn't know she was holding, so relieved.

"It's time to take care of the final bucket list," Jason said from where he held Ally back against him. From the sound of the chains, Catania assumed Ally's wrists were still bound, though it seemed her ankles were free.

"What is that, Jason?" Catania asked, wishing so badly she could see beyond the intensity of the light that cloaked the figures before her in midnight.

"I'm taking your future from you, Nia," he said. "The way my past was stolen from me."

Ally gasped as her head was forced back. The silhouette of Jason's hand appeared, a large knife in his grasp.

"Ally," Catania called, her voice weak. "Ally…" She knew Ally could see her, and she prayed she'd get it. She dropped her gaze quickly to the floor.

In the span of a heartbeat, Ally collapsed, the

unexpected move leaving Jason unprepared as she slid out of his hands as Catania reached to her lower back and grabbed her Derringer, swinging it around. *Bang, bang.* Both .22 slugs hit him in the neck, the stinging pain enough to make him stagger back and grab for his bleeding wounds, which gave Catania time to use the last of her strength to lunge over to her .38, sliding on her right shoulder as she gritted her teeth, firing off all six rounds into the black mass that was the perfect spotlighted target.

Jason's body jerked with each shot before he fell backward, the double neck wounds causing him to gurgle as blood flooded his throat.

The pain was overwhelming her and the spotlight was growing dim. Vaguely, she felt a warm touch to her face, Ally's voice a thousand miles away as it echoed through the darkness that was closing in, the beloved darkness...

Epilogue

S lowly, oh so slowly, reality began to kiss each of her senses. She felt a soft touch wrapped around her hand, smelled the fragrant scent of roses, could hear soft murmurings of two voices that sounded familiar, and she could taste the bitter, stale taste in her mouth of the thick saliva that covered her tongue and teeth.

She let out a soft sigh and lightly squeezed the fingers wrapped around hers. She heard the soft gasp that earned her.

"Look, Mamma," Ally's soft, angelic voice murmured. "She's coming to."

Opening her eyes, she saw the most amazingly beautiful sight she could imagine. She returned Ally's smile, so much love in those deep, dark blue eyes.

"Hi, baby," Ally said softly, her fingers trailing through Catania's hair.

"Hi." She closed her eyes and happily accepted the gentle kiss that was left on her lips. Opening her eyes again, she turned to see a surprised Antonia d'Giovanni watching the two. Deciding to ignore the question in her dark eyes, she smiled. "Hey, Mamma."

"Hello, sweet girl," the older woman said, leaning over and leaving her own kiss on Catania's forehead.

"How are you feeling?" Ally asked.

"Like I've been run over by a truck...twice," Catania said, trying to take stock of her body and all its parts. She saw her arm was in a fresh cast and felt the tightness of a bandage on her chest.

"Well, close," Ally said with a small smile. "You were shot in the arm. They had to put another plate in there and do bone grafts. The second shot, on the other hand…" She reached into her pocket and removed the angel pendant. It was deformed, only one side of the wings still visible. She smiled. "Guess she saved your life after all."

Catania looked at the pendant, chuckling. "That's a seriously determined angel."

"The bullet still hit you, but its path was altered when it hit this. Minor flesh wound."

"Seriously determined, and seriously lucky. I'm never taking her off when I get out of here."

"Speaking of, I'll be right back," Ally said, rising from the chair she sat in. She gave her a second kiss before leaving.

Left alone with her mother, Catania studied the older woman's concerned face. "How long have I been here?"

"Almost a week. There's been a cop here off and on wanting to talk to you," she said. "Jason is dead." Though her voice kind, it was very matter-of-fact. "Karen is distraught."

"God, I can only imagine," Catania said, grimacing at the taste in her mouth. "Mamma, can I have some water or something? I need a toothbrush."

Antonia smiled and poured a cup of water from the plastic pitcher on the bedside table. Helping her daughter sip, she studied her. "You love her, don't you?"

Catania studied her mother, confused. "Who?"

"Ally. You love each other." A statement, not a

question.

"Yes," Catania said slowly, nervous that even lying in a hospital bed, her mother would still kill her. "I do love her."

Antonia played with the cup in her hands for a moment before she nodded and met her daughter's worried gaze. "Okay."

Catania didn't have time to think about the calm response before the door to her hospital room opened and Ally pushed someone in a wheelchair into view. Instantly tears came to her eyes when she saw Oscar's smiling face. Ally wheeled him over to the bed, where, with her help, he pushed very slowly to his feet.

"Hey, kiddo," he said.

"Hey, Big O," she replied, the tears of relief coming quickly as he bent over and hugged her as best he could.

"Good job," he whispered into her ear. He left a kiss on her cheek before pulling back, so much pride shining in his tear-filled eyes. "So proud of you."

She shook her head. "No, we did this together, bud."

"Nope.

"Yep."

"Not a chance."

"Absolutely."

Breaking into laughter, they shared a second hug. He slowly stood erect again before Ally helped him sit back in the chair, the detective already looking exhausted. "Word has it someone's nominated you for a Medal of Valor," he said conversationally.

"Oh, Catania," Antonia said, clapping her hands together.

She chuckled, turning to her mother. "Mamma,

it was Oscar who did it." She turned back to look at him. "Didn't you?"

He grinned and shook his head before nodding toward the hospital room door, which was pushed open. Catania took in the tall figure in full dress uniform, hat tucked under his arm.

"Sergeant Price?"

❧❧❧❧

"A strange case to tell you about tonight," the news anchor explained. "Pueblo serial killer Jason Ross was shot and killed by his own half-sister, Pueblo Homicide Detective Catania d'Giovanni, who was unwittingly assigned to hunt down the killer.

"Ross has now been linked to the triple murder of Anastasia Luhan, her son Eric Gomez, and the four-year-old's father Aaron Gomez in November, as well as that of Kevin Tanner, a friend of the couple, the following month.

"He has also been linked to the 2015 murder of Megan Murphy, an Arizona woman said to be involved romantically with Ross more than a decade ago. Her body had lain frozen for two years before it was found dumped along Hwy 50 in late November. The discovery of teenage prostitute Olivia 'Liv' Gleason on an abandoned property in the town of Boone led to the shooting of Pueblo Homicide Detective Oscar Riley, who, along with his partner d'Giovanni, was pursuing the missing girl. The teen was another of Ross's victims.

"Ross was shot and killed by Detective d'Giovanni Saturday evening in his home while she was rescuing kidnap victim Alexandra Findley. Detective d'Giovanni was shot twice by Ross, and she is recovering in a local

hospital. Also found in Ross's home was the body of his biological mother, found frozen in a basement freezer.

"Amy Zucker is thought to be Ross's first victim, a family friend and only sixteen when she disappeared in 1983. Her remains and that of her beagle Brewster were excavated from the grave Ross buried her in on the d'Giovanni lake-front property, and finally laid to rest in the family plot on the same property when Zucker's family could not be located.

"Authorities are looking into other cases they suspect Ross is linked to."

⚜ ⚜ ⚜ ⚜

The late July sun shone high overhead, the cheerful voices of kids running around chasing each other, enjoying the last of their summer break.

"Connor, be nice to your sister!" their dad yelled out.

Catania, who sat on a glider on the porch of the lake house with Ally, glanced over at him. "I still can't get over how much weight you've lost, Paul."

He looked at her from where he sat on a lounger, a bottle of water in his hand. He smiled and shrugged a shoulder. "Well, after everything that happened last year, it made me take a long look at myself."

"I know Mamma and Papa are glad you're coming around a lot more, bringing the kids," she said, her fingers absently running over the smooth skin of Ally's shoulder where her hand rested. "I'm proud of you."

Paul gave her a sheepish grin before looking down at his own hands, which fiddled with the plastic bottle. "I'm proud of you, too, Nia," he said softly. "I know I've been a real asshole for a lot of years, and

I'm sorry. I know I never would have had the guts to do what you did with…Jason. You inspire the hell out of me." He cleared his throat. "But anyway, how's the new place? I hear Matteo is loving his apartment above the garage."

"He's doing great," she said, meeting Ally's gaze and loving smile before turning back to him. "We love it."

"I finally got my renovation project." Ally grinned.

Catania rolled her eyes. "Tell me about it."

Ally laughed, reaching over and playfully pinching Catania's side. "Oh, you love me."

Catania leaned in and placed a lingering kiss on soft lips. "With all my heart," she whispered.

"And, you still work for Karen?" Paul asked, rubbing the back of his neck at the show of affection between the two women.

"Yup. I'm managing her properties now. Still cooking, too."

"Poor woman," he muttered. "Christ, can't even imagine."

"She's a good woman," Catania said gently. "I'm glad she chose to stay in our lives, even if she did move back to be close to her family."

"Alright, come eat!" Melanie's voice boomed from the back door, her hand resting on her pregnant belly. "Oscar and Linda are here!"

"Come on, kids!" Paul called out, pushing up from his chair and heading inside.

Catania planted her feet on the patio to stop the slow movement of the glider before standing up and taking Ally's hand to help her up.

"By the way," Ally said, tugging on Catania's

hand to stop her from heading to the house. "I got something in the mail this morning."

"Oh?" Catania asked, eyebrow rose in curiosity. "Do tell."

Ally's smile was slow and beautiful. "It's over. I am officially a divorced woman."

Catania grinned, turning to her and pulling her to her by the hips. "You don't say?"

⁁⁁⁁⁁

The Super 8 film jumped and skipped in places, the teenage girl sitting on the couch at the center of the frame. She smiled shyly at the camera, her dark eyes filled with mischief even as she exhaled dramatically to blow shaggy brown bangs out of them.

"Okay," said a man's voice from behind the camera. "What's your name?"

"My name is Amy Zucker," the girl said, making a funny face. "You know that, Mr. D."

He laughed. "How old are you this year?"

"I am sixteen years old. Finally!" She brought her hand into frame, fingers cradling a laminated card, which she pushed into the face of the camera, the smiling image and lettering on the card blurred at the closeness. "Driver's license, yeah, yeah, yeah," she sang.

The man laughed again. "Yes, congratulations, Amy. What do you want to do with your life? When you grow up?"

She looked at the camera like the man operating it was nuts. "I'm just a kid!" She laughed, running a nervous hand through her hair. "Okay, okay. Well, I want to be Kristy McNichol. Well, like her best friend, anyway." She grinned. "Nah, well yeah, but I want to do something really cool, really special. I want to change the world, Mr. D. I mean," she added with a shrug, "we've only got so much time, right? Make the most of it, 'cuz you never know when it's over."

"Wise words, Amy. Very wise. Anything else?"

The teen became very serious, a look crossing her eyes that was far beyond her years. "I don't know who will end up watching this, but live life to the fullest and love with all your heart. Always be there for those who you care about." She gave a blinding smile. "I'll always be there for you. Life's a gift, so don't blow it. Bye!"

About the Author

Kim has spent her life in Colorado and can't imagine living anywhere else. She's been writing since she was 9 and stumbled into her first book being published in her mid-20s. She's worked in the film industry as a writer, director and producer, but now enjoys the quiet, happy life of a professional author. She can be reached on Facebook and on her website at, www.kimpritekel.com

Check out Kim's other books.

Zero Ward - ISBN - 978-1-943353-19-4

Danny Felts grew up in the heart of the Midwest on a dairy farm, expected to follow in her mother's footsteps and marry a farmer and become a mother. Danny had other ideas. As World War II heats up, she makes a decision that will change her life forever as she becomes a lie, serving with the Seabees in the Navy as Daniel Felts.

Kate Adams is about to graduate high school in her prestigious and elite San Diego neighborhood when she's dragged to the USO for a dance with friends and servicemen. There, she meets the person that will catch her eye and her heart, only for jealousy and vengeance to tear her apart.

Are Danny and Kate strong enough to win the battle within and fight for their love?

Connection- ISBN - 978-1-939062-24-6

Julie Wilson lives a charmed life as a beloved teacher and aunt in the small town of Woodland. Close to her brother and guardian of two adorable Yorkies, she loves her life, the only negative being ex-boyfriend, Ray who can't seem to understand the phrase, "We're done." Believing that's her only problem, Julie has no idea what hell awaits her during a normal summer afternoon.

Remmy Foster is the quirky, friendly drifter who has

never found roots after a difficult childhood, as well as the difficulties her very special gift brings into her life. Though she may call it exploring, the truth is she's running from ghosts that haunt her every step.

After a chance meeting with Julie while hitchhiking, Remmy will be thrown head first into darkness she could never have foreseen, regardless of her abilities. As the clock ticks, life and death is on her shoulders to make the right connection.

Warning - Some scenes may be too intense for some readers.

1049 Club - ISBN - 978-1-939062-97-0

Almost two hundred souls, one plane, six survivors, endless heartbreak.

When flight 1049, headed from Buffalo, NY to Italy falls from the sky, a firestorm of drama, pain, angst and sorrow ensues. Can an author, a business owner, a teenager, good ol' boy, veterinarian and ruthless lawyer survive? Better yet, can those left behind?

1049 Club is a story of survival, love, deep regret and miracles. Can the living make peace with the presumed dead? Can the presumed dead make peace with the lives and loves they thought they had before?

Blinded – ISBN – 978-1-943353-53-8

After a horrible explosion sends local television news reporter, Burton Blinde reeling both physically and emotionally, she walks away from her life and the dream job she was about to start at a major news network.

For six long years she hides out in a small mountain town, working at the local library, though is haunted by the life she had, including mysterious messages and gifts she was receiving before her life was turned upside down, a veritable bread crumb trail leading to the unknown.

Unable to resist, Burton begins to follow the clues, which will lead her into the darkest places of human nature that she may not be able to return from.

Damaged - ISBN - 978-1-939062-45-1

Family. A group of people you are related to by blood or love.

Nora Schaeffer has come home to her family after twenty years working around the world as a photographer for National Geographic. She's welcomed into the open arms of her father and siblings.

Family. A group of people who support you, lift you up when you fall.

Shannon, the youngest of the four Schaeffer siblings, has vanished, leaving her five-year-old daughter, Bella, terrified and alone. To help find Shannon, Nora has no choice but to turn to the dark-haired specter who has haunted her for twenty years. Along the way, she finds her own long-dead heart and uncovers chilling family secrets beyond imagination.

Family. A group of people who will stick together to hide the rotten soul at its core at any cost.

Who will live? Who will die? Who will be the most damaged? And who will learn to love again?

www.ingramcontent.com/pod-product-compliance
Lightning Source LLC
Chambersburg PA
CBHW020510260626
47156CB00006B/1950